Take Six Girls

To Sheila

Best wishes, hope you enjoy it.

Be good, God Bless

Angela.
x

TAKE SIX GIRLS

Angela Mather

HAMILTON & Co. Publishers
LONDON

© Copyright 1998
Angela Mather

The right of Angela Mather to be identified as author of this work has been asserted by her in accordance with Copyright, Designs, and Patents Act 1988

All rights reserved. No reproduction,
copy or transmission of this publication may be made
without written permission.
No paragraph of this publication may be reproduced,
copied or transmitted
save with the written permission or in accordance
with the provisions of the Copyright Act 1956 (as amended).
Any person who does any unauthorised act
in relation to this publication may be liable
to criminal prosecution and civil
claims for damage.

All characters in this publication are fictitious and any resemblance to real persons, living, or dead, is purely coincidental.

Paperback ISBN 1 901668 40 1

Publisher

HAMILTON & Co. Publishers
10 Stratton Street
Mayfair
London

Chapter 1

Maurice sat hunched in the third row of the stalls and yelled petty abuse at the dancers on the stage. Joan signalled to the pianist to stop playing.

'Thank you girls, don't bother waiting. Next group please get into your places and give yourselves plenty of room to move.' Fifteen pairs of legs walked quickly into their positions. Joan showed them the steps to perform. Maurice glared at them like a petulant child, when he abruptly jerked up as the light shimmered on a silver blonde mane. He snatched up the clip board from the seat next to him, his bony finger jabbed at the names on the first sheet, as his eyes scanned it for the particular one he was looking for. 'God, it had to be her, there couldn't be two with her looks and body.' Impatiently he flicked over the page. A satisfied grin demolished his frown as his finger hovered over a name half way down the page.

'Joan start them off, then come here.' His voice now vibrated with enthusiasm. Joan had her back to him and wasn't bothering to hide her smile. She knew that he would recognise Tina as soon as he saw her. She ran through the steps once more, then nodded to the pianist to begin, and left the stage. Maurice licked his lips as his eyes fastened on that shapely body. The grace with which Tina moved had a mesmerising effect on him. She was so beautiful, her legs seemed endless, and it was pure joy to watch, as she danced. She looked terrific, even under the harshness of the unfiltered white spotlights that were switched on for the audition. All the dancers went through the steps they had been shown reasonably well, but Tina stood out from the rest, she was that good. He couldn't believe his luck. The best female dancer to be exported from the USA that year, and he'd got her! Why she should want to leave the hit show she was currently in was beyond him! But he didn't care, all he knew was that she was as gorgeous as she was talented.

'When does her present contract end?' It would not have occurred to Maurice that Joan wouldn't be able to give him the information he wanted, she always came through, that's why he employed her. How she came across it, he neither knew nor cared.

'End of this month.'

'Great! You can go back stage and any one who isn't her height, get rid of them.' Maurice rubbed his hands together. Joan nodded. She'd known, as soon as she'd seen Tina, what would happen!

'Thank you girls. Tina Wentworth please come down here. I'm sorry, but the rest of you needn't wait. Next group on stage please.' Disgruntled murmurs moved off to the right, while eagerness marched in from the left. Tina went down to the stalls. By now, Joan was in front of the next group showing them the steps. Maurice wasn't looking at the stage, he was visualising Tina performing his routines. The pianist was already playing when Joan broke into his utopia. 'The red head at the end of the front row is good, should I ask her to stay?' Maurice dragged his mind back to the present and studied the other dancer carefully.

'Good mover, what's her name? Do we know anything about her?'

Joan studied her clipboard.

'No! She's just eighteen and comes from Cardiff, goes by the name of Megan Thomas.'

'Looks older than that!' Maurice shrugged his shoulders. 'Could be hard, I don't want any personality clashes on this cruise.'

'Please yourself, only she is the right height and build. Also her hair's a lovely colour and if I'm not mistaken, there's another red head back stage. They'd look good either side of Tina, or book ends in the back row.'

'If the other can dance. Okay keep this one back, but get rid of the rest. It's a shame the little blonde in the middle of the back line isn't taller, she's got style.' Joan agreed with him as she turned away.

By the end of the audition, Maurice was feeling very pleased with himself. Tina Wentworth was centre stage and on either side of her, he had a red headed girl. In the back row, he had one chestnut, next to her was jet black hair, the girl looked as if she had some eastern blood in her veins and finally, at the other end, a dancer with a mass of long mousey curls down her back, made up the six. Maurice was not impressed with the latter hair colour, but she was a good dancer. Although if she wanted this contract, she'd have to dye it to match the other chestnut, he was sure that colour came out of a bottle, they could both use the same brand and match up. Maurice loved symmetry. He waltzed on stage going directly to the long mousy curls.

'I need you to dye your hair the same colour chestnut as em?' Joan came to his rescue.

'Tracy.'

'Right! Sorry if you don't like the idea, but I need that colour hair for balance.' He thought to himself, 'if she wants in on this deal, then she'll do it.' Joan smirked, she'd already sounded the dancer out and knew that she'd have been willing to dye her hair red, white and blue to get this job. The mousy curls bobbed in acceptance.

'That's not a problem.'

'Fine. Just make sure you have enough hair stuff to last you for the twelve months. I hate roots showing and don't want stupid excuses for looking a mess.' Maurice took a couple of steps backward to include the rest. 'That goes for you all. I will not have any slobs working for me. Make certain you always look good! Like a million dollars! Your clothes off stage are just as important as your costumes are! You'll always be on show and it's my reputation that you'll be riding on. You can do what you like in your free time on board, as long as you DO NOT cause a disturbance.' He glared at them, giving them time to take in his words. 'Watch your diets and don't get sun tan lines that will be shown up by your costumes. Is that understood?' A murmur of compliance from the six girls on stage satisfied him. 'Right! Joan has the contracts ready, they're standard Equity, so if you have no objections, I'd like them signed now.' Tina Wentworth was the first to cross the stage to a small table by the piano. She leaned over and quickly scanned the pages in front of her.

'This gives you a twelve month option after the first year. I'm sorry, but I have another assignment lined up.' Maurice shrugged his shoulders and took the pen Joan was offering, then aggressively crossed the option clause out, he initialled the alteration. Tina thanked him and signed on the dotted line. Maurice relaxed, picked up her contract, scrawled his name on its counterpart, then handed that to her.

'Anybody else want the option out?' Four heads shook. Jasmine looked petrified, but managed to mutter that she was going to university next year. Maurice looked surprised but altered her's, then signed the rest of the contracts with a flourish.

'Jasmine Chinnock' The girl with dark hair filled her lungs

with air gave a quick nod to herself, then crossed and promptly endorsed her contract. Maurice watched her with mixed feelings, she was acting as if she was facing a firing squad now, yet she'd been fine during the audition. She'd have to make the grade. Time was running out, there wasn't really any left to find a replacement. 'Mary MacDonald' The mousey curls walked over to the table and eagerly wrote her name where Joan was pointing. 'Tracy O'Flynn' A giggle with a Liverpool accent was next.

'That's me!' She tripped across exuberantly.

'Megan Thomas.' Her green eyes glinted calculatingly as she moved, her signature sprawled on the page. 'Charis Gaynor' With her nose in the air, the other red head flaunted up to the table and with great aplomb, ratified her next twelve months work. A hastily stifled shriek was turned into a cough, suppressing a giggle. Four heads turned to look at Tracy, who was resolutely trying to achieve an innocent expression. Maurice chose to ignore her, he'd keenly watched each girl in turn and had a fair assumption of their characters. He had to admit to himself that there was a greater mix than he would have chosen, if he'd had more time to look. But considering this was his second audition, the first had been a total wash out. He was as ever as optimistic as always, hoping that they wouldn't feel the need to strangle each other before the cruise had actually ended.

'Rehearsals start on the seventh of November. That's only three weeks from today!' He saw the excitement bubble in only three pairs of eyes. That surprised him, but he gave himself a mental shake and carried on. 'I've booked a room at my local leisure centre. I like to keep away from the dance studios when I'm putting new shows together. We'll work from ten in the morning until about three o'clock, then you can have a break until six. That's when I want you all for the costume fittings. Those will be at my house.' His eyes flicked from one girl to the next as he was talking. 'We leave London on the second of December for Southampton, we'll all travel down together and board the ship. We sail the next day.' A delicious gurgle erupted from Tracy. Maurice grinned at her, she was his type of person, he could tell that she grabbed at life with both hands and lived every minute to its fullest. He cleared his throat and carried on. 'Those of you who live outside London, won't have time to go back home once we start, so bring everything you need with you when you come. And I will add that I don't suffer fools gladly.' He inwardly grinned, as he knew he had all their attention. 'I expect hard work from everybody, okay?' At the end of this speech, Tracy was pinching herself to make sure that she wasn't dreaming. She knew Maurice's work and was pleased, but she wouldn't have cared if all they were expected to do was the elementary two step. To cruise out to Australia and the Pacific Islands, then go to New York and sail around the Caribbean for a couple of months, as well as get paid for dancing, seemed to her to be phenomenal. She was brought back to reality by Joan's voice.

'If any of you need lodgings for the rehearsal period, there's a good bed and breakfast place about five minutes walk away from the leisure centre, it's clean and doesn't cost the earth.' A general murmur arose from the girls.

'Me mum's got a cousin who lives in Wood Green, so I'm staying with her. That's on the Piccadilly line, is the rehearsal place near a tube station?' Tracy's Liverpool accent drowned out the other voices. She flicked her glossy chestnut locks over her shoulder as she added. 'Me Mum reckons that it's no use having family if you can't ask for a bed when you want!' Mary grinned at her. Joan twitched her thin shoulders.

'Yes the centre is at Wembley Park that's on the Bakerloo line. Just make sure that you're always on time. You'll be crucified if you hold up rehearsals.'

'I won't be late!' Joan watched the cheeky smile spread and wondered if Tracy was ever serious. 'It's one of my endearing habits, punctuality!' Charis curled her mouth into a sneer and moved away. 'Don't worry luv, it's not catching!' Tina felt that she might have enjoyed this year under different circumstances, but she doubted very much that she would now! It would be so interminable long, even if that girl could keep up her quips. She didn't want to go, he was making her do this. To be away from him for so long, it was more of a jail sentence than a cruise. She'd tried every conceivable way to make him change his mind, but he was insistent that she had to leave.

'I've got a simple street map here for each of you, Maurice's house, the leisure centre, tube station and the bed and breakfast place are all marked. If any of you are going to stay there, please make your booking before you get away today, don't leave it until you come back for the rehearsals. Now, does any one want to know anything else before we go?' No one spoke and five heads slightly shook. 'Good.' Joan handed out the directions. 'Well, we'll see you all on the seventh of next mouth, ten o'clock prompt, so good bye for now.' The chorus departed except for Megan.

'I'm staying in town, do you know if that place has a vacancy now?' It was difficult to pin point her accent to South Wales, only a slight sing song lilt gave it a sort of birthplace. Her make up was expertly applied and her ice green eyes competed with her full lipid mouth for supremacy. Joan wondered fleetingly what had happened in so short a life to make her that hard, then gave herself a mental shrug, the girl was a good dancer, so as long as she behaved herself, what did it matter?

'Actually she has. I phoned this morning to make sure that she'd have rooms for us, we're sure to need them during the rehearsals, and she was saying that she'd been let down this week over a booking. The phone number and address are on that map I've given you.'

'Thanks.' Megan turned and walked off the stage. She'd unconsciously been holding her breath and now let it hiss through her teeth, hopeful that she'd found somewhere to stay, then she'd be on a ship for the next year. She'd make the money she had with her last until she got her first rehearsal pay. Things might be tight at the moment, but the important thing was to have somewhere to sleep. Once on board, there were bound to be some willing rich punters. Getting money, or expensive presents, shouldn't be any problem at all then. She'd just have to be very careful. For an instant her expression softened as she thought of her mother. But a quick flick of her head as she gritted her teeth, banished it before she went into the changing room, giving her back the hardness that she surrounded herself with.

'My home is in York, I'm delighted to say!' Charis stressed the pronoun. 'I would not wish to live any where else! I suppose you live in town, don't you?' Tina nodded, but didn't give any further information. She shoved her things hurriedly into her tote bag. They had so little time together, she didn't want to waste even a second and found herself silently praying that he'd be there when she got to her flat.

'I've got to dash. See you all at rehearsals.' Tina rushed out of the room, her long blonde hair flying out behind her as she ran.

'Well, she was in a hurry, wasn't she!' Charis sounded affronted.

'When a girls got to go, she might as well run!' The Liverpool giggle broke out; 'I bet she doesn't even have to board a plane when she fly's across the big pond! The rate she's going, she'll take off without a runway!' Ignoring Tracy totally, Charis turned to Jasmine.

'Is this your very first job?' Jasmine swallowed, but said nothing. 'And you're going aboard?' The young girl just slightly nodded her head. 'How exciting for you.' Jasmine now looked scared.

'Why the hell don't you shut up, you're as boring as shit.' Charis looked outraged at Megan's crude outburst, picked up her bag and hurried out of the dressing room. Tracy laughed infectiously, but Jasmine seemed on the verge of panic, she stood stiffly, not moving.

'Relax Jasmine, Charis thinks too much of herself.' Mary then turned to Megan. 'If looks could kill, you'd be dead.'

'That would take a hell of a lot more than that silly cow's got in her.' Mary's hazel eyes light up as she agreed. Megan packed the rest of her things away then left without saying anything more.

'What a great time I'm going to have on this boat.' Tracy beamed at the other two. 'No don't look like that. I really mean it. This is a God given opportunity to have a ball and I never let a good thing slip by. I'm going to enjoy every minute of it.' The Scouse giggle echoed in her voice as she continued. 'A ship, unless you actually go to Alaska, is about the only place where you're out numbered by men. And me, I just love that idea.' She chuckled infectiously. 'I can hardly wait!'

'Like the male gender do you?' Tracy opened her grey eyes to their widest and nodded at Mary.

'I think sex should be classed the same as tennis. Find a partner you're well matched with and have a great game.' Jasmine was white. 'Don't look so horrified luv, sex is the best! Believe me, once you've tried it, nothing else can beat it.'

'I see you've never been in love.' Mary's voice was definitely mocking, but in a friendly way.

'No! Now I've heard that that is like living in heaven and hell at the same time! Sounds too complicated for me, I'll just stick with the pure and simple game of sex!'

'Nice if you can do it!'

'I'm doing fine for now anyway!'

'How old are you?' Jasmine faced Mary but only stared at her. 'Surely my accent isn't that bad?' There was a faint laugh in Mary's voice and although Jasmine was feeling scared as well as embarrassed, she managed to answer her.

'I'm eighteen.'

'And still a virgin!' Jasmine's head swivelled back to Tracy. 'Benevolent of your family to let you go on this cruise?'

'Don't panic!' Mary reclaimed her attention. 'Not all dancers are ravers! It's not compulsory you know. My advice is don't take the plunge until you're ready.' With this motherly comment Mary smiled and left the room.

'Did I shock you luv, I didn't mean too.' Jasmine was to shy to attempt to say anything else, she just stood in the middle of the room clutching her bag. Tracy grinned at her. 'If I were you, I'd share a cabin with Mary, she's got that maternal instinct that the Scottish are so proud of! Believe me, it's written in large capitals all over her. Now I work hard, then I put everything I've got left into my playing!' Tracy tilted her chin and laughed.

'Are you two ready to go, the caretaker is waiting to lock up.' Joan stood in the open door way. Jasmine nodded at her and walked into the passage. Tracy flung the long strap of her bag over her shoulder and began humming as she left.

'Have you got the show programmes for the cruise with you?'

'They're waiting for us to go.' Maurice gave an impatient glance at his watch, then repeated his question. Joan shrugged, nodded her head, and reached for her brief case. She picked out the folder she wanted and spread the contents on the table. Ten sheets in all, each with its own heading. Maurice rubbed his hands, he was grinning again.

'I've got a great set of girls!' He was jubilant over the quality of the dancers he'd found that morning and felt sure that, for him, the seventies would surpass the glories of the sixties, which were almost at an end. 'What artists are we still short of?' Joan produced another paper. Maurice bent over it. His head was very close to hers. She straightened her shoulders.

'Have you decided over that male singer yet?' Maurice began to blow imaginary bubbles through his lips, his fingers tapped the table.

'No, not yet. Yes I know he can sing and is good looking enough for the rich old biddies on the ship to swoon over, but I don't really like him.'

'Why not?'

'How the hell do I know.' Maurice stood upright and shoved his hands into his pockets. 'All right, send him a damn contract then.' He grinned, flung his arms up and yelled. 'No wait! Let's see what we can find tonight. We have to go and see that female ventriloquist you've found. She'd better be as good as you say!' Maurice smirked at Joan's affronted look, but ignored it. 'You never know your luck, we might even find another singer.' She didn't bother answering him, she couldn't understand why he hadn't signed Ted Hunter up straight away. Then, she'd never kidded herself that she was capable of comprehending all that Maurice ever did.

Chapter 2

Bill's stare was locked onto the clock, he knew she'd be there by now. 'God, why I am making her do this?' The question was screeching it self through his brain. The answering sap, 'it's only a year! It will fly by,' did nothing to alleviate his aggravation. Now those coming twelve months seemed to offer nothing but futile loneliness. Just thinking of her being away from him, made him inwardly cringe. 'What if she met someone else, a guy who was better looking?' At that moment, he would have willingly exchanged anything for a handsome face and a few extra inches. Then he grinned in spite of his depression, his Tina wouldn't fall for just a pretty face on top of a six footer, she'd always love the man, not just the case he was in. How someone as young and beautiful as Tina had fallen in love with him, was a miracle and one that he was eternally grateful for. She gave her love to him unreservedly in every way. He shook his head, tired of arguing with himself. Another anguished look at the clock, time seemed to have raced! 'Too late now, she's bound to have landed the job. Why did I have to tell her to sign the contract straight away? God, what have I done! I've forced her to go, when all she'd wanted was to stand by me.' Bill's mental torture was not helped by the image of Tina pleading with him not to make her leave.

'What the hell are you gawping at? That clock isn't going to jump off the wall you know.' Melissa's voice grated at the silence. Bill closed his eyes. He didn't want the hunger, he knew was prevalent in his eyes, to show. 'Hell, you make me so sick! I need a drink.' The door banged noisily behind her. He couldn't willingly give Melissa any ammunition to use. She might be going to butcher him publicly, he didn't believe that she wouldn't go to the press, she'd do anything for money. Bill was indifferent for himself that Melissa would resort to that, but not for Tina, he must protect her at all cost and that was going to be expensive. But he didn't care. After holding out for so long against giving his wife more than their main residence and alimony, Bill had surprised his lawyers when he'd told them to give Melissa what ever she was asking for, in return for an immediate divorce. What did it matter now that she took the lot? As long as he had Tina, he would survive. What was of more importance to him was time. Every day that he and Tina were apart, seemed to him to be an eternity. So that his change of mind would hopefully go unquestioned by Melissa after his months of silence, Bill had manufactured an argument with her and ended it by storming out of the room, stating that he'd had enough, she could have what ever she wanted as long as she agreed to a quick divorce. He'd known that when Melissa first filed for a separation, she'd been trying to find anything to support her claim that she was the injured party and hired a private detective to follow him. Bill had found this out by sheer accident, he'd over heard her telephone conversation with the company. Melissa had lost her temper, screaming down the phone that they couldn't be doing their job right, if they hadn't found out that Bill had been wandering. In her estimation, as she wasn't having sex with him, and hadn't done so since their honeymoon, he'd be getting it elsewhere. But that was before Tina had come into Bill's existence, therefore there had been no one in his private life to be investigated. The story Melissa had concocted was that she was the neglected wife who could stand it no more.

When Bill had realized that his marriage was a failure and that there was no hope of it ever being anything else, he'd thrown himself into his work. His career as a comedian was of long standing. But his latest show was a musical and he was enjoying it immensely. That he and it were hugely successful, was the added bonus. He'd always been able to sing, but had never taken his voice seriously until this venture. Bill had first met Tina a year ago, his leading lady in the show had broken her ankle, her understudy had had laryngitis and they'd got through the show with her miming. But with the threat of a recurring throat infection, it was decided that the understudy wouldn't be able to hold down the part over a sustained period of time. The next morning, the shows' producer had walked into the hurriedly called rehearsal with Tina. She'd been singing and dancing with an American company touring in Europe, and her contract with them had ended the previous week. Before returning to her parents home in Texas, Tina attended the London auditions that the producer had been holding for his next venture. At first she'd been dubious, being faced with a part which required her to sing solo, but delighted when told that her voice had the strength and quality needed. Tina had been asked to join Bill's musical instead of becoming a member of the chorus of another show. She'd eagerly accepted the challenge and worked hard, getting on well with everyone. Bill had agreed with the producer that she was made for the part. The morning after Tina's first night, the critics in the daily papers proclaimed her a star.

During the last New Year's party, Bill had kissed her. It was a simple friendly gesture, but they'd both realised that it had ignited a spark that would not die away. Bill was in the middle of a difficult situation with Melissa and had set himself against any involvement with another female, but Tina's charm and warmth surmounted his reserve. Two weeks later, the producer threw a surprise birthday party for Tina, after the show a group of them had gone on to a nightclub. A couple of hours later the party had broken up and Bill had offered to share a taxi with Tina. The initial intention had been to continue alone in the cab, once he'd dropped her off. But her suggestion of coffee had been eagerly accepted and, that night, Bill had stopped trying to fool himself that he'd never trust another women, honest enough with himself to admit that he'd fallen in love with Tina. And now the only safe place he was able to see her on a regular basis was the theatre and there they had very little privacy. When he did go to her apartment, he took elaborate precautions to lose anyone tailing him by changing tubes and buses several times, taking a couple of hours to travel to her, when normally it would have taken twenty minutes by road. But he never used a car, he didn't want to leave a vehicle registered to him, out side her flat. So far as he knew, Bill had been successful in duping Melissa, she was still unaware of Tina. If his wife ever found out that he was in love with another woman, her vanity would have suffered and she'd have been even more vindictive. Bill never kept to a regular routine. He changed the days and times. He and Tina could never prearrange a meeting, whenever he was certain that he would not arouse any suspicion, then he'd visit her flat. Tina was always so delighted to see him, even if they could only spend a few precious moments together. Tina was generous and charming, in contrast to Melissa's pernicious avarice. Even the fact that Bill's and Tina's finances would be severely limited after his divorce, hadn't daunted Tina. They'd pool what they had and be happy.

Bill hoped that his wife's greed would blind her mind so that she wouldn't question his abrupt change of attitude. He'd been forced to accept her grasping nature for some time. But even though their marriage was non existent, except on paper, it had been a shock to him when Melissa had openly taunted him with the fact that she'd never cared at all for him. She'd stated that if he hadn't been so wealthy, or had wanted a prenuptial settlement, she wouldn't have given him a second look. But with no bars in her way, she'd found his money irresistible. Bragging to him afterwards, how easily she'd snared him into marrying her. That row had been over a year ago when he'd tried unsuccessfully to curb her extravagances, telling her that she would bankrupt them if she didn't stop. He still balked when the memory of that evening invaded his mind. Melissa was going out alone. They had been married for eight months, but their honeymoon had only lasted four weeks. After that, she'd used insomnia as her excuse to have a separate bedroom. Always refusing any sexual overtures made by her husband. Melissa's flagrant announcement on that night, that she'd always found Bill boring and was only staying in the same house, because her lawyer stated that if she could prove that she'd tried to make her marriage work and it could be seen to have lasted a couple of years, then she had a better chance of walking away with all she wanted. She'd demanded the London house that they were living in, his bungalow on the island of Martinique in the Caribbean, and both the Rolls Royce and the Ferrari, in fact, all of his assets, including his money. Bill had dug his heels in at first and refused to concur with her demands. At that time, Bill had instructed his attorney to fight her, he hadn't cared then how long his divorce took. But that was before Tina had come into his life, now time was of the essence. It had stunned Bill how simply and quickly Melissa had found it to entrap him into a marriage that had no foundations. He accepted that she was a very striking and sexually attractive woman, with a shapely figure and a basic instinct on how to use herself to her best advantage. And she'd been able to infatuate him with remarkable ease. Bill had been so flattered by her attentions, that he hadn't stopped to think or question her way of life, or even if Melissa had really loved him at the start of their relationship. With Tina it was all so different, they shared a partnership that could only prosper with time, never shrivel, because their foundations were real, not imaginary puffs of make believe.

Melissa licked her lips, she knew that she'd worn him down. Finally, Bill had agreed to a give her everything, as long as the divorce went through without any problems and no talking to the press about it. Well she was getting everything of his that was worth having and he was going to pay all the legal expenses for both sides. She smiled as she considered the probability that he'd be broke after that, but what did she care! Bill would always work. She couldn't, she'd never had a job in her life. She'd gone from school to her boyfriends flat. He'd taken her on holiday where they visited a casino. She moved in with a bouncer and stayed on. Changing her partners only when the offer came from the holder of a larger bank balance. Melissa hugged herself at the thought of Warren. She'd had a sexual relationship with him from the first night she'd met him and that was three years ago. The only time she had been away from him was during her honeymoon with Bill. Of course, she'd had concurrent boyfriends who had money, but Warren was the only man she had ever cared for. Now he wouldn't need to bury himself in the wilds of Wyoming with that middle aged American cow. Not when she was going to have all Bill's assets within the next six months and with no strings attached! So she'd agreed to Bill's demand for a quick divorce. She'd have the lot and Warren too! Just thinking of him made her randy, he was young, extremely handsome and had a great body. He oozed sexual invitations and she wanted them all. Bill's face had never made her pant to touch him and his thick set torso didn't turn her on. Of course, during their honeymoon, she'd encouraged him to have sex with her, she'd laid back, thought of his wealth and squirmed under him. But once their marriage had been well and truly consummated, she'd shrugged her shoulders and ignored her husband. She'd never actually taken any particular notice of Bill as a man. That he was dependable, caring and true to his friends, were characteristics that she did not appreciate. But she did relish Warren. It didn't matter to her that his vanity took up so much of his time. How could she own to a fault in him, that was major in her own life and one that was not recognised by her. All Melissa knew, was that when she and Warren walked into a room, everybody stared, how could they not be admiring them? That her dresses were always tight, provocatively clinging and had low-neck lines, barely covering her nipples, never entered her head. To her, she and Warren were the perfect couple, but neither of them had money of their own. And they both idolised lucre! Warren had latched onto a middle aged wealthy widow and was living very well in Knightsbridge. They still met of course and Melissa liked spending Bill's money on him, but she knew that Warren was being tempted by American Dollars. So to her, her divorce was very timely and when it was all over, she could still sell a gory and totally untrue version to the press. All she'd have to do was to be careful how she worded her story and make sure that it wasn't taped, also, that she didn't put anything personally down on paper. Then the newspaper couldn't sue her, when Bill took them to court for libel! Anyway, that was for the future, now, she had to get rid of her husband, as she was expecting Warren to arrive in half an hour. Melissa sauntered back into the kitchen.

'For God's sake, sod off and get out of here!' She smiled as he picked up his coat and left. She returned to the lounge and was pouring herself a drink when she heard the front door slam behind him.

Bill heard the turn of a key in the lock and stopped pacing the floor of Tina's flat. 'God, if only she knew how hard it has been to make her go!' The outside door shut and he braced himself before she entered the room. He watched her as she paused in the door way. The tears running down her cheeks, wrenched at his soul. Bill didn't have to ask if she'd got the job, he knew the answer was yes. He opened his arms to her and she flung herself into his embrace.

'Don't cry darling, it's not going to be for ever! If things move smartly along here and there are no hiccups, I could even fly out and visit you later on. I'll need a break, my understudy could easily go on for a couple of weeks. Honestly!'

'I just don't want to go. It seems such a long time!' Her voice was muffled against his shoulder. He stroked her hair, murmuring softly into her ear.

'Don't dwell on this year love, just concentrate on all the rest of the time we'll have together afterwards. Then you'll be screaming at me to get out from under your feet.' Tina raised her head, trying hard to blink back her tears.

'I'll never want you to do that.' Bill moved his mouth to her cheek and let the tip of his tongue catch a tear drop. From there, it was an elementary step for him, to her lips. With very little pressure, the warm tip of his tongue, outlined the shape of her mouth, his hands gripped her waist. He groaned aloud as he felt his erection begin. Her eyes questioned him. Bill smiled, nodding his head. There was no need to say anything, he wasn't going anywhere until they'd made love. He heard her breath escape in a long sigh as she undid his zip. His mind becoming acutely focused, now her hands were erotically simulating his arousal.

'God Tina, you're so gorgeous.' His voice was husky with desire. Her muttered words of love were a catalyst to his need for her. He lifted her hands to kiss her fingers, before he slowly took her clothes off, expertly handling the obstacles he came across.

By the time she was naked, they were both panting. As Bill pulled his sweater off, Tina was unhooking his trousers and letting them drop. She then knelt before him and his shorts, socks and shoes disappeared. Now she pressed her face against him, kissing his masculinity. Bill looked down at her, his eyes burning with hunger as he watched her. The rampant desire she was giving him with her mouth, was sending erotic shock waves through his body. When he put his hands under her arms and unhurriedly raised her to her feet, Bill deliberately trailed Tina's supple shape against his, revelling in the contact of their bodies. As they stood there, pressing intimately against each other, they suspended reality, only they breathed in their world. He did not want to kiss her to soon, for he knew that if he did, he'd loose what little control he had over his passions and have to enter her immediately. Bill swallowed hard as he brought his hands to cup her up tilted breasts. His blood was pounding through his veins as he sensually teased her nipples with his fingers. He knew his erection was hard against the flat of her stomach, he could feel how tense her muscles were. In his hands, the firm rounded mounds of her breasts were heaving. He heard the primitive cry of a primeval sexual need vibrate in her throat. Her nails dug into the flesh of his shoulders. He could wait no longer. Reluctantly his hands left her breasts and swept her into his arms, almost running into the bedroom. There, as he laid Tina onto the bed, his mouth covered hers hungrily. His tongue no more avidly probing than hers.

Tina wrapped her arms and legs around Bill, pushed her eager tongue into his mouth, then sucked at his. Her pulse raced with her longing to have him penetrate deeply into her. Then when he lifted his head slightly and their eyes met fleetingly, she could see his love for her in his very being. She could feel his readiness to enter her, he was hard and firm, his whole body tensed with sexual expectancy. She depressed her back into the soft mattress, then pushed her hips up and along his body. She heard his intense craving for her grate in his voice and watched him voraciously as he lifted his torso, hovering above her. When he made his mercurial thrust ardently into her, she welcomed him fully, locking her ankles firmly together at the small of his back, ardently joining with him to sate their sexual appetites. Both rejoicing in their fusion, building it into a tempestuous vortex of emotion. After reaching this, they slowly spiralled back to reality. She was still laid under Bill, possessively clinging to him.

'I love you so much.' As Tina pulled his head towards her, the moist tip of her tongue traced his mouth before their lips met. Her kiss telling him how much she adored him.

Bill held her face in his hands, returning her kiss with a hot passion of his own. Their breath fervent as their bodies pressed erotically against each other, their needs once more emanating from source. He knew that he would have to go after they'd made love again, so to put off that inevitable departure, Bill withdrew and moved his weight onto his side, so that he could contemplate her beauty. Gazing rapturously at her, captivated by her condescend aura. Tina would always be able to fascinate him. Her clear blue eyes blazed with emotion. He watched hungrily. Her curvaceous mouth was slightly parted, showing the tip of her tongue. The curve of her neck led him to sloping shoulders, which accentuated the smoothness of her skin. Bill always found Tina so tempting to touch. The lascivious shape of her breasts, crowned with their succulent nipples, now taut and enticing, held him entranced. Then his eyes travelled along her body, following the sleekness of her stomach until he was staring at the small triangular shape of hair, now moist from their love making. Forcing himself to control his urge to plunge straight into her seductive wetness, he sat up and made his eyes traverse the elegant shape of her legs. Bill moved his position slightly and bent over her, then he erotically let his lips trail up her legs until he reached his goal. He groaned in his throat, as his mouth tasted her. His tongue probed, while his thumbs found the exact place to stimulate her. He could hear Tina gasp in pure sexual pleasure. When he lifted his head, his magical fingers continued and he watched enthralled as she sidled in ecstasy. He had to use every vestige of will power to hold on to his control.

Tina dug her heels into the bed and pushed her hips up, her voice vibrated around the room.

'Bill.' She lifted her head up and reached for his arms, pulling his hands to her mouth. Sensuously sucking at his thumbs, then burying kisses into his palms, before moving his hands to her throbbing breasts. She whimpered with longing at the sensations raging through her. He was kneading her flesh, as well as erotically teasing her nipples. She knew her hunger for him was rapidly reaching its height and very soon her hands claimed his masculinity. She could wait no more for him, she needed him insatiably. She heard the urgency for fulfilment roar from his throat as she guided him into her wetness. She received his tempestuous thrusts fervidly. Tina felt Bill's strength and passion with each inwards plunge he made into her embracing body. She jerked and moved her hips in unison with him. Her nails etched into his back as their rhythm built to its crescendo. Tina moaned as she relinquished herself to her uninhibited pleasures erupting from the physical part of her love for Bill, as his love flowed from him.

Chapter 3

Megan walked along the corridor and up the stairs leading to the stage door. There she made a telephone call to the bed sitter that Joan had recommended. She replaced the receiver, relief mingled with her satisfaction that she now had somewhere to stay, that she could afford. She'd decided to pay all the rent that would be due until the embarkation date for the ship. Having very little faith in human nature, this way, she was sure that she wasn't going to find herself out on the street. Although this course would leave her short on food money, that didn't bother her. She'd managed before on bread and milk, with the odd tin of beans thrown in, but now she'd be having a cooked breakfast as well. It would be plenty until she received her first rehearsal pay, then she'd be able to increase her diet as needed. But she'd leave buying her provisions until she'd deposited her cases at the boarding house. To shop now and then carry that as well as her luggage, would have been stupid. Once outside the theatre, she lengthened her stride deliberately and quickly passed a fast food restaurant, that was a luxury she couldn't afford at the moment. She covered the distance to Paddington railway station easily enough. There she retrieved her luggage. Four charcoal grey cases, two large, one weekend size and a make up case. She'd spotted them in one of the better charity shops in Cardiff. Even at second hand prices, they had been an expansive outlay for her, but had thought it would be a good investment, as they had to contain everything that she possessed. Megan opened the small case and took out a pair of flat-heeled shoes and her luggage wheels. She snapped the lid closed after changing her stilettos. The two heavy cases and her vanity case were secured with straps, making them easier to pull along. The bag she had her rehearsal things in was over her shoulder. Megan picked up her small case and handbag, firmly griped the handle of the wheels with her free hand, and began the walk to Wembley Park.

As she headed for the exit doors, she ignored the offer, from a young man, to help her with her things. She didn't rush, she knew it was a fair distance and didn't want to tire herself out before she reached her destination, nor did she want to arrive looking as if she'd trudged all the way. She wanted to make a good first impression on the landlady, it just might prove useful in the future. It was a cold day, but as her coat was thickly lined, she was warm enough. A flicker of a smile flashed across her face as she caught a glimpse of her reflection in a shop window. It pleased her, the clothes she had on were of a good quality, a marked difference from the gear she had worn when she'd lived with her aunt and uncle. Most of Megan's wardrobe had belonged to Miss Williams, Harold had given them to Megan when she first moved in with him. He had been sympathetic and kind and found it easy to manipulate Megan into a sexual relationship. The long charcoal grey trench coat that she was wearing today over a black trouser suit looked smart. That the mack was a man's didn't bother her. When she'd asked Harold for it he'd been surprised, but she knew that she'd need a decent coat to wear during that coming winter and her money, at that time, wouldn't have stretched to buying one. She had in her own way, turned the tables on Harold, by using sex herself as a lever. At first, Megan had been nervous, maybe afraid? She'd acknowledged, she'd been so immature then, but when maturity had been shoved in her face, she'd also aged mentally, practically over night. Megan had never wasted her time, regretting that she'd had to use her body for practical and monetary gain. It had been the quickest way out of an unbearable situation, she continued, to fund the private investigators she hired, trying to find her mother. Had her aunt's attitude been different, then Megan would have been quite contented to stay there and do the cooking and house work for them between her contracts to dance. But the bitch hadn't been satisfied with an unpaid skivvy, she had wanted total control over her niece's life. A shudder ran through Megan when she remembered the attack they had made on her. There was only one faint scar left now and that was on her lower back, a curled white line in her flesh, to remind her of that day. Megan had been busy all that morning with changing the beds and cleaning through the house, she'd lived in, with them. She had been grateful, they didn't have to give her a roof over her head, as her aunt had continually stated, bastards didn't deserve anything better than an orphanage. That Megan had worked hard and received very little in return was never mentioned. For the first twelve years of her life, Megan had been in an institution. She had a reasonable brain and never felt the need to rebel as an inmate. Megan's aunt had arrived and explained to the authorities that she and her husband had been going through some old family papers and until then, did not know of their niece's existence. Of course, now that they did, they wanted to foster her. Megan couldn't believe her luck. Horse riding, a bike, ballroom lessons, she could even go to ballet classes if she had the time.

To twelve-year-old Megan, this huge smiling lady and the thin man beside her, were opening up a new and exciting world. And while the official paper work was going through, Megan's life had been full. She'd slept in a double bed in the bedroom next to her aunt and uncle's. It was all pink and white, with frilly curtains and so warm and cosy. At that time, a cleaner had been paid to come in twice a week to do the heavy work. Aunty Ethel had explained to the child that she was too ill and couldn't manage it. Megan had quickly settled in at the local high school, her life had changed from mundane to sublime. And of all the things that the young Megan had tried out, her ballet classes were at the top of her most favourite list.

This delusion had lasted three months. The paper work had been completed, just before her aunt had gone into hospital. Uncle Albert had taken early redundancy to help look after his wife and now there was no money to spend on Megan. She'd accepted this, not crying in front of them, as she hadn't wanted to upset them. Megan didn't really mind about the rest, but it had hurt that she wouldn't be able to attend ballet classes any more. She'd loved that straight from the start. It had been with tears in her eyes that she had gone to her teacher and told her of the changed circumstances. Miss Williams had looked down her long nose and folded her graceful hands in her lap. Megan hadn't been able to believe what she had heard. 'No need to pay, just come along, when you can.' Megan had flown back to tell her aunty, who hadn't been pleased at all, stating that Megan wouldn't have time to do the house work and everything else that needed to be done, for after all, she was still at school. At the time Megan hadn't understood what was behind her aunt's outburst. Later she'd realised that her aunt had wanted to control her, sanctioning no outside interests that might have interfered with that. But then the child had pleaded and promised to do all the work, if only she could carry on with learning to dance. Her uncle had said that if Megan were so determined, that it would be best to let the child have her own way. Her aunt had yelled at him, demanding why they should spoil her. Megan could always recall his grin as he'd replied. 'If the girl didn't tow the line, then the classes would stop.' That was Megan's first introduction to blackmail, the second was if she told the social worker she was unhappy with her lot, then she would return to the orphanage and again her dancing lessons would cease.

The next four years of Megan's life had fallen into a routine of hard work, most of it physical. But she always had the knowledge that it was worth while, as long as she could dance, she'd put up with the toil and verbal abuse. The physical side of her life, sculpted her body into a lithe and attractive form. Megan had excelled at ballet. Miss Williams had provided her with the special shoes and practice clothes she'd needed. Not only that, but she had talked to Megan, telling her of the great ballerinas, even on rare occasions, taking her to the flat she'd shared with her younger bother and had let Megan pour over her books on dance. Harold had been there, always complaining to his sister that his back was hurting him and that he didn't feel very well. Miss Williams had explained to Megan that she looked after him, her mother had asked her to, she considered it her duty. Megan thought privately that he was being selfish and lazy, but as she worshipped Miss Williams, whatever her idol did, was fine with her. It had been on one of those visits that Miss Williams told Megan, that when she was older, if she'd wanted to, she could join her and teach ballet. But first, Megan's teacher had advised her, to experience dancing in the theatre. Megan had been so thrilled by this show of trust that she'd made a solemn oath to herself, to be an excellent ballet teacher and so make her mentor, very proud of her. Megan had been broken hearted when Miss Williams died, she'd felt that the only true friend she'd had in the world was gone. The ballet school had had to close. At the graveside, Megan had promised to reopen it as soon as she could do so. It was that winter that Megan went to the audition for a part in the chorus, in the Pantomime at the Pavilion Theatre in Cardiff. She had been so thrilled to get it.

The sixteen and a half-year-old Megan had been so proud at getting her first job as a dancer. Maybe if she hadn't been so ecstatic, she might be been warned of future danger by her aunt and uncle's reactions to her news. But the girl had been too jubilant to see the anger and hatred in their faces. It had been hard going during rehearsals, because Megan also had all her other jobs in the house to keep up as well, but she'd managed. The memory of that first night Megan went on stage in front of an audience always gave her warmth, happiness, and satisfaction. She'd put her very soul into her performances and wrapped herself in the applause the routines had received. Megan knew that she could never give up dancing. When she became to old for the theatre, then she'd teach. She'd listened intently to the talk in her dressing room, her ears picked up when she'd heard that Maurice Hughes was holding auditions for dancers for a years' cruise. Megan had been very disappointed, when she'd learnt that to get in for the audition, you had to be eighteen or over. But she'd been determined that when she was old enough, that she'd get that job. A couple of the girls in her dressing room were going for an audition for a revue, which was going to tour the country for six months, starting that Easter. Megan had been more than eager for another dancing job and had arranged to meet them in London and go for that. When she'd told her aunt and uncle of her plans, they had been very quiet. They'd asked her the date of the audition and when she intended to go to London, that was all. Megan had known that she'd be unable to live with them during the tour and that someone else would have to do the cooking and housework, but as her uncle seemed to spend most of his days in the local pub, or betting office and it was over four years since her aunt's operation, they'd most probably be able to manage very well without her.

After Megan had finished her house work on that fateful day, she'd gone to the bathroom for a shower. That had been when her aunt and uncle had walked in on her. There had never been a lock on that door. Megan had been startled as well as shocked at the intrusion. She'd just finished rinsing her hair and had been still standing under the jets of water. Her uncle had grabbed her, pulled her out of the cubicle, and flung her into the middle of the room. The garden cane brandished by him, produced welts across Megan's shoulders and sent all thoughts, except those of self preservation out of her head. The buckle end of the belt her aunt had had, then ripped into the flesh of Megan's buttocks. Hoarse laughter had barraged with screams. Megan, after trying to cower and shield herself on the floor, had sprung up and grabbed the cane. She'd managed to jerk, then twisted it out of her uncle's hands and had wildly slashed it towards him. He'd wrenched it back, but had stumbled and fallen. Megan had seen her chance and made a dash for the door. It had been then, that again the prong of the buckle, being wheeled by her aunt, had torn open the skin on her back. Megan had sobbed with anger as well as pain when she'd reached the safety of her attic room. The flight of stairs leading to this garret were too narrow for her aunt to climb up, her bulk would never force its way between the walls. Megan had been still shaking with fear. Hurt, but not dangerously so, just enough for her to have realized that she would be unable to catch the train that tea time for London, the audition for the touring revue had been on the following morning. Megan had felt sick with frustration. When she'd heard foot steps stomping up the bare wooden stairs, she'd guessed it would be her uncle and wedged a chair under the handle of her door. And prayed that it would hold. To her surprise, he hadn't tried to force his way into her room to continue beating her, he'd contented himself with locking her in. Shouting through the door that she might as well give up any ideas about leaving them, because they were going to see to it that she never did. If she tried to in the future, she'd get another battering from them both and next time they'd make sure she couldn't run off until they'd finished with her. She might have escaped with her face that time, but she wouldn't be able to on the next.

Megan had just stood there in the middle of her small room. Stunned by what had just happened to her. The cold and the pain from her injuries made her move. She'd twisted painfully to inspect her back. The welts and abrasions had been swollen and red, blood trickled from three of the deeper cuts. Megan did the best she could to clean them and then put on a tee shirt, it had once belonged to her uncle, and its looseness was now an asset. She hadn't known what to do next. The last threat made by her uncle had frightened her very much. She'd known that she had to leave. But go where? They had taken most of her wages for her board, she had hardly any money left, just enough for her train fare and one night's lodging in town. She was too old to go back to the orphanage.

When her aunt had come out of the hospital, they had moved the twelve years old Megan into the attic room. It measured six feet by nine and had a small barred window in the roof. There had never been a carpet on the floor and the mattress on the narrow bed was thin and uncomfortable. The wardrobe held her school skirt and blouse. She'd been allowed to keep very few of the clothes that she'd brought from the orphanage, the best of those had been sold. For the next four years, Megan had been given her aunts old cast offs and told to alter them or wear them as they were. She'd learnt how to sew. She'd had to alter everything by hand and during daylight hours, as there was no electricity in the attic.

Megan's back had been bruised and very painful. She'd forced herself to concentrate on getting away. First, she had to make sure that her uncle couldn't get into her room. Desperately she looked around and decided on the wardrobe. Pushed it in front of the door, hoping that it would be more difficult for him to dislodge than the chair. The wardrobe was very old and solidly built. The furniture hadn't been disturbed since Megan had first been moved into the attic. She shoved it along the wall, then pushed it up against the door. By moving it, she'd discovered a cupboard built into the wall by the chimney breast. Its small, badly hinged door had swung open. Megan found that it had contained some old, black and white, snap shots. At first, Megan just glanced at them. Then stared hard and studied them more carefully. Some were of her Aunty Ethel, even when younger, she'd been fat, not as gross as she'd become, but still very flabby. Next Megan had taken out an exercise book. In that she'd read all the dreams and aspirations of another sixteen year old girl. The ardent love that this girl had for her boyfriend, the relationship that had developed between them, and the consummation of it. The sorrow at parting when he'd moved away for another job. Then had come the disillusionment that followed the news of the pregnancy. The beatings from the mother and sister. The incarceration in that attic by them. The hunger that had come from the deficient amount of food that had been allowed to her. Megan had cried in pity for the hardship of the previous prisoner. Then a sprig of hope had sprouted, with the knowledge that there was a spare key to the attic door. That had enabled the pregnant teenager to creep down the stairs during the night and take such food from the kitchen, as she'd thought would go undetected. There had been very little written after the birth of the baby and it was almost illegible. The sister had held the girl while the mother had taken away the two-day-old baby girl. She'd wished Ethel had killed her, not just beaten her again, as she could not live without her baby. The last entry was that she didn't believe what Ethel had told her; how could her baby daughter be dead? That had to be a lie, to try to stop her from finding her daughter again. Well, she wouldn't ever stop looking. She was going to leave that night to find her boyfriend, surely he'd help to find their daughter.

Megan had carefully laid the book down and then spread out the photographs on her bed. She'd chosen one of a happily smiling girl and had studied it carefully. When she turned it over, the name on the back matched the one on the exercise book, Jane Thomas. There was a loose floor board in the attic and over the years, Megan had stored her little treasures there, one being a small cracked piece of mirror. Looking at herself and the snap shot at the same, the likeness had been so striking that Megan had known instantly that it had been a photograph of her own mother. She'd gone back to her bed and looked again at that last entry, she knew that her mother had never reached the orphanage. Megan wanted desperately to find her mother, she must be still out there searching! The thought that Megan, was no longer alone, filled her with hope. What had actually happened that night? Her mother must have escaped, but where was she? Megan had to find her. She would do anything. There had to be a way. But she was practical enough to accept that she couldn't even try, until she was free of her aunt and uncle. Megan had known that her own safety depended on leaving that house. If there was a key to the attic door in the hidden cupboard, then she could run away that night. But where could she go. Out of nowhere, the picture of Miss Williams flashed into Megan's mind. Quickly followed by Harold, moaning at his sister's graveside, of the fact that there was nobody to take her place and look after him. Megan collected her few meagre things together. Carefully putting the old photographs in the exercise book of her mother's. On top of her things she was going to take with her, there was a key. Shifting the wardrobe from the door was painful for Megan, but she did it. Then she'd forced herself to wait, for what had seemed like hours, after she'd heard her aunt and uncles' bedroom door close, before she allowed herself to leave the house.

Chapter 4

Joan accepted the cloakroom ticket from the attendant and slipped it into her purse. Maurice was waiting for her by the double swing doors that led into the interior of the night club. Neither spoke as they made their way towards an unoccupied table on the balcony. Their view of the cabaret floor from there would be unrestricted. Behind that, the tiny stage packed with band instruments was in semi darkness.

'We're in plenty of time. What do you want to drink, the usual?' She nodded at him. Maurice strutted towards the bar, glanced at a group of men as he passed their table, but nothing attracted his wandering eyes. Joan looked around through the blue haze, which drifted upwards, before it was furiously sucked into the whirring fans that thinned out the exhaled smoke from the room.

'Like to join me for a drink?' Joan returned a negative answer without even looking up. 'Why couldn't Maurice ask me with as much interest in his voice?' But she knew the answer to that question and had done so for years. Still every now and then, the query would pop into her mind, just to be shoved back into the hidden recess of her consciousness. She was like all women who had fallen in love with the wrong bloke and not quite learnt how to fall out again! Maurice hadn't changed that much either, still tall and thin, no grey showing in his black hair, but she knew that was due to hair dye and not nature's kindliness. He hadn't thickened out, even in middle age, he was still very angular. And she still loved him. Joan could remember the first time she'd seen Maurice on stage at a west end theatre, it had been a musical and he'd had a reasonable part. Since then, one way or another, he'd been part of her life.

'Who was that talking to you?' Joan shrugged her shoulders. Maurice grinned at her. 'Trying to chat you up! Poor old sod. Why don't you take pity on him, getting laid once in a while wouldn't hurt! And you never know your luck, you could even get to like it!' Joan sipped her drink, ignored his sarcasm, and told him that the show was about to start. Maurice settled back in his chair and meditatively tasted his whiskey. 'Descent stuff! But then it should be at these prices.'

A small blonde waltzed onto the cabaret floor, her dummy was in evening dress, its face buried into her massive bosom. The cloak it was wearing hid her right hand. 'She certainly poured herself into that gold lame. She'll cause a riot if those straps don't hold!' Joan could tell by his voice that Maurice was already interested in the act. Although he was doing his usual ironical routine, the underlying thread in his tone gave him away. 'She might be short on height, but doesn't she make up for that in voluptuous curves?' The music stopped, but the dummy's head remained in its position, nose down in one of the most impressive cleavages shown to man. The gold lame sauntered up to the microphone, sexily exaggerating her oscillating hips. A snigger rippled around the audience.

'Hadn't you better be careful you don't suffocate, my good man?' She was using a Southern States drawl. The dummy's head finally lifts up, and with a fair impression of Cary Grant's voice, delivered the punch line. 'If I have to go, what a way to do it!' The dummies head dived back into the mounds of bare flesh protruding from the low cut neck line. Laughter greeted this. 'Don't be so greedy little man, nothing is rationed and there's plenty to go around!' The dolls head swivelled round to the audience. 'What does she mean by little? I might be short on height, but boy am I big where it counts!' It was the first of many such deliveries. At the end of twenty minutes, the applause was deafening. The lady bowed and the audience held its breath, but the straps did not snap and the flesh stayed miraculously within its exiguous confines.

'You said she has three different dolls?' Joan nodded. 'And you've seen all of her acts?' Her look spoke volumes. 'Okay, so you're thorough, they're as good as this?'

'They're all excellent, but I would say that this one gets my vote. The one where the doll is a vampire is very funny, but I reckon you might think that the other one is more to your taste, where she is Maid Marion. The doll is an outrageous Sheriff of Nottingham!'

'They'll split up into ten good spots?'

'Doreen said that won't be a problem at all, in fact she intends to have the dolls in different outfits for each show. At the moment, she's working on a new dummy, it's a butler and she's the lady of the house! That will be ready to stage for the cruise. I imagine that she'll give you ten hilarious five minute spots. Joan waited for him to speak. The next act on the bill was a male singer, she had heard him before, but didn't rate his voice at all. Never the less he was young and very good looking and you could never tell with Maurice! Sometimes lust governed his sense and this young man was certainly his type. Half way through the first song, Maurice told Joan that he would wait for her in the car. She raised her eyebrows, not bothering to hide her relief. Maurice grinned at her.

'Very tempting, but I'm not ballsing up my shows with his voice. This year's shows are going to get me a ten year contract with the cruise company. God, I can't stand this bloody awful racket any more, it'll have to be Ted Hunter. Tomorrow, you'd better send fancy pants a contract as well! But phone him first and tell him that any haggling between the old dears he's after and I'll screw him myself. Give this female one and try for the option on it'. Maurice pushed back his chair and made for the exit. Joan smiled at his retreating figure, then made her way to the dressing rooms to find Doreen Sumner.

'He liked my act?'

'Of course he did. Have you managed to get out of those two weeks next June?'

'Yes.' Was uttered with relief. Joan smiled and took out two folded contracts from her bag. Doreen didn't even bother reading them, just signed both and handed one back.

'There's a year's option on that you know!' Doreen nodded eagerly. 'Don't forget, you will need ten stage outfits.'

'Yes, I'm sorting that out. I've also been working on breaking my acts down into smaller pieces, changing the doll's dress for each show.'

'Any problems?'

'No!'

'Good.' Joan put the contract back into her bag and took out a small slip of paper. 'Here's a list of the show titles, that will give you an idea of what spot will fit in where.' Doreen quickly scanned the sheet.

'Bow Bells?'

'Cockney, you know the thing, pearly kings and queens.'

'Quite a variety.' Joan could tell that she was thinking of something else.

'Anything wrong?'

'No! How about me dressed as a flower seller, the doll in evening dress.' Joan grinned broadly.

'Quick thinker, aren't you? If you could manage that, it's a great idea.'

'Actually, I have lots of material written down. Most of it is to short to make up into a full length cabaret act, but I would guess that I'll be able to make ten, five minute spots without that much trouble.' Doreen jubilantly waved the piece of paper in the air.

'Just remember, now he's seen this one, he will expect that all your performances to be of this high standard.

'Don't worry, I haven't flogged myself since I started to mess up now by being lazy. I join you on the twenty first of November?'

'Yes, the dance routines and the show formates will be already set by then. From that date Maurice will be running through each show, making sure that everything is as it should be. You'll need your costumes with you, that last week will be for dress rehearsals.'

'That's fine. I'll see you then.'

'There's nothing else you want to know?' Doreen chewed her bottom lip for a second before replying.

'Not that I can think of.'

'No problems about leaving the country for a year?'

'No, my kid sister is doing a course at the local technical college, so she's going to live at home and look after everything till I get back.'

'Good, see you then.'

'Bye and thanks. 'Joan turned in the doorway.

'Don't mention it, if you weren't as good as you are, you wouldn't have got the job.' Doreen was grinning as Joan left.

'She must be in her thirties? Why haven't I seen her before?' Joan recalled her wandering mind. Besides asking her, when she'd first got in the car, whether the contracts had been exchanged, they hadn't spoken during the drive back to London, which by now, was nearly over.

'She's only been going for six months.' Joan knew that he'd want to know all the details, so she continued without waiting for him to ask any questions. 'Doreen is the eldest of seven children. Their mother died when the baby was two years old and Doreen was fourteen. That was twenty years ago and she just took over looking after them all. Her Dad died last year and as the rest have already spread their wings, she found herself with nothing to do and all the time in the world to do it! This is something she'd always wanted to do. In fact, it had been an active hobby of hers. So when the chance offered its self, she took it. She's making quite a name for herself.' Maurice didn't make any comments and Joan added. 'She should be a success on the boat.'

'Liner.' Joan pulled a face at him.

'As long as the damn thing stays afloat!' Maurice grinned as his eyes flicked momentarily towards her. 'Stop sniggering, it doesn't become you.'

'Oh yes it does.'

'Well, it shouldn't.' He laughed aloud at that, but refrained from taunting her further and left her to negotiate the London traffic.

Joan finished her cup of tea in the kitchen. She glanced at her watch as she put her mug under the tap in the sink and rinsed it clean. She had the rest of her day planned out. Ted Hunter hadn't been overly impressed at being woken up at eight in the morning by the phone, but once she'd told him that she was sending him a contract, she could tell by his voice that she had all his attention. He would have been willing to swear on a stack of bibles that his intentions were pure! Not that Maurice gave a damn what he got up too, just as long as he knew how to do it discreetly. Looking for a rich wife on a cruise liner wasn't such a bird brained idea and as Ted had smooth manners as well as a good voice, he might just pull it off! Joan put her coat on. First the Post Office, to register the contracts to him, then she had to take the under ground train out to Hornchurch. A costumier was having a closing down sale and Maurice wanted her there. He'd told her that he hoped she'd be able find a few good sets that he'd be able to utilise on the cruise. He wouldn't get back from Birmingham until tomorrow, so she was going solo to the sale. The preview time was scheduled for the morning, the stuff went under the hammer at two o'clock this afternoon. She'd have plenty of time to grab a snack for her lunch. The carriage wasn't full and Joan was able to find a seat by a window which was unoccupied. She put her brief case down besides her and opened it. For the next half an hour she studied the plans Maurice had drawn up for the ten different shows he was going to stage on the ship. They were based on different major cities, except for the space odyssey! The Paris Night Out was complete. Maurice was opening with the girls in emerald sequinned leotards, which had short net half skirts at the back, those had matching head dresses. Then Ted Hunter would sing, followed by one of Doreen's acts. The middle routine for the girls was to be a military tap dance, royal blue velvet tunics and caps, black tights and shoes. And hopefully, the act that Maurice was in Birmingham to look at, would do a spot, after which Ginger Morris, the thinking man's comedian, as he always billed himself as, would do his thing! The dancers would then perform the can can, and Maurice would end that show by singing 'Love is a many Splendid Thing'. What that song had to do with Paris was any body's guess, but it was what he wanted. During his last chorus, the entire cast would go onto the cabaret floor and join in for the finale. That was the first show.

The train had stopped at West Ham as Joan flicked through some publicity shots from last year's cruise. Why the shipping company just didn't gave Maurice the ten year contract he wanted, was beyond her. She giggled to herself as she recalled the last meeting when this year's had been signed. Maurice had upped the anti! They didn't like it, but knew that to replace him would have been almost impossible. Yes, it was a good job, but very few would go through the maize of arrangements and hurdle the complications of producing ten different shows, just to cruise. The mental aggravation was a night mare. She knew that if Maurice didn't have her, he would never do it, he'd lose interest in all the finicky little points and the paper work.

'Oh! Show business. I was in the theatre you know. Yes dearie, for thirty years!' An artificially painted face was hovering in the aisle, nodding at Joan, causing a hiccup in the flow of movement. As by this time, there seemed to be no vacant seats, Joan was forced to gather her things up and put her brief case on her knee. 'Thanks love. Gosh, isn't it crowded today?' Without waiting for an answer, the bright red lips continued to operate at a rapid pace. 'I started off in the revues, touring you know. You'd never believe the places we went too. Some of the theatres were that shabby and the dressing rooms, well I couldn't start to tell you the states that we had to change in.' Joan accepted that she wouldn't get any further work done while she had this continual vocal garbage in her ears. 'Could I just have a little peek, I love looking at glossy pictures.' Joan handed the photographs over to eager hands, then gathered up her papers, and put them back into her brief case. 'Ooh... I love sequins, don't you? They always make me feel so gorgeous.' Joan glanced at the woman sitting besides her, it was impossible to put an appropriate age to her. Joan guessed that her make up hadn't changed since her hey day, only the quantity had increased. Her hair was still dyed platinum, even if the roots were now iron grey. Joan sat back and let the flow of gossip swirl away. She knew that she wasn't excepted to make any comments, just the occasional smile in agreement would suffice. The chatter lasted until Joan got off the train. A wrinkled hand with chipped nail varnish was still waving through the window as the train pulled out of the station.

Joan had had a successful afternoon, four sets of six costumes, all in the right sizes, together with head-dresses to match. By the time she'd returned to her flat that evening, she was tired and very hungry. She sank wearily into a chair and kicked off her shoes. What she wanted was a meal and a long hot bath. Which first? Her aching limbs demanded to be eased, but her churning stomach, also voiced its need for sustenance. She compromised by putting a frozen pizza into the oven while her bath was running. A chair pushed up to the side of the tub stood in for a table and as she soaked her body, she chomped her way through her food. The half bottle of red wine, which accompanied her meal, was good. As Joan sipped her drink, she thanked the gods that dancers were in general always a size ten or twelve. She'd also bought an odd set of Tyrolienne hats, not that Maurice needed them for this cruise, but they were going cheap and in such good condition, that she knew that it would have been stupid to let them go. But what he would be thrilled with, were the feather boas she'd bought. Eight in all, everyone a different colour. All delicate shades, just what was needed for the finale of the Hollywood show. The girls were in long white slinky evening dresses and these would just add that finishing touch to their costumes. After her last bite of dough, Joan tipped her glass, drained it, then submerged more into the water, leaving just her chin and head breaking the surface. She closed her eyes, letting the scent of aromatic herbs from the salts she'd poured into the water, carry on soothing her.

'But they're not the same.' Joan had spread the boas over a table and had to clamp her mouth shut on the retort that readily sprang to her lips.

'Just different colours, other wise they are.' Maurice pouted, tapping his foot on the floor. The costumes had arrived after lunch and they'd unpacked them immediately.

'I'll have them dyed.' He turned to her, expecting her to argue. 'Well!'

'Please yourself, if you think that you have the time, then go ahead.' Maurice almost snarled at her.

'I'm going to send them to Cuthberts. They'll do them for me.' He chewed his bottom lip, then grinned. 'Cherry Red!' Joan closed her eyes for a second, took a deep breath, then nodded. 'Remember those big silk flowers, can't think where they're are, but see if they'll dye the same colour, then the girls can wear them over their left ears!' Maurice beamed at her, he was extremely pleased with himself. 'Now show me the body suits.' Joan picked up one of the silver lycra costumes by the shoulders and held it up for inspection. The material was thin, but not transparent. Maurice just stared at it.

'What's the matter now?'

'Don't you think they're a bit plain.'

'No. Space suits are not fancy, you'll just have to contain your creative craving for ornaments and settle for this.'

'No head dresses?' Maurice curled his upper lip in disgust.

'Not if you want it to look authentic.'

'Astronauts wear helmets.' Joan knew that Maurice was determined to get his own way. She wanted to shout at him, but refrained, and answered him, with as much patience as she could muster.

'Yes I know they do, but there weren't any with these costumes.'

'I wonder if Maggy could come up with something. Ask her, see what she says.' Joan didn't bother trying to dissuade him, it would have been a waste of time. 'You did order the silver boots in the sizes we need?'

'Yes.'

'Good! Everything is going just great.' He beamed at her, almost patting himself on the back. Joan didn't bother reminding him of all the work she'd put in, Maurice was his own biggest fan.

Chapter 5

Jasmine sat facing her mother, she knew that she would have to tell her that she'd signed a contract, she just didn't know how or when. 'Straight away or in a couple of weeks? No, that would be too late. Maybe in a few days! Would that give me time to think of a way? Besides, there wouldn't be any reason to mention Hong Kong. Australia and New Zealand, yes. And stress the Pacific and the Caribbean, spout off a lot of island names, then maybe she wouldn't ask. If I don't mention the place, why should she even think of it? I must make sure that the port is not on the itinerary I give her. She'd go crazy if she thought that I was going there and if she knew that I was deliberately going to look for him.' A shudder ran through Jasmine's slender body. 'But I have too. Now that I know he's alive, I need to see him. I have to find out why she's lied to me about him, telling me he was dead. Before it was okay, I could live with what she'd told me. If only she hadn't gone so white and screwed the paper up so violently, throwing it anyway before she'd finished reading it. That made me curious to see what the article was all about.' Jasmine could still see the crumpled sheet of news print in front of her, the name of Zachery Chinnock in bold capitals. The article telling of another successful take over for the C & S Group. If only her mother hadn't reacted so badly. But she had, so that was all the proof that Jasmine had needed. It had to be her father. She knew his name, it was plain enough on her birth certificate, and she'd seen their marriage lines. The name was unusual enough for her to be certain that she was right. Her father was alive and living in Hong Kong.

'Why can't I be brave enough to tell her the truth? No, that wasn't the answer, as she'd responded so badly to the newspaper piece, it would be suicide to even mention his name. And if I tell her what I'm going to do, she'd go hysterical and forbid me to go.' Jasmine couldn't bare the thought of trying to fight with her mother over this. She was just going to say nothing and look for him by herself. As she now knew the name of the firm and the paper had said he was a partner, locating him shouldn't be that difficult. What she couldn't understand, was why her mother had told her that he'd died when she was a baby. Jasmine could remember asking about him, but her mother had been so noncommittal, always giving vague answers to her young daughter. Jasmine felt that if she could talk to him, maybe he'd have some of the answers to the questions her mother was unable to cope with. At first she'd intended to write to him, explaining who she was, then she saw the audition for the cruise. This trip was a God send and she couldn't stop herself from taking it. Jasmine's mind jumped back to the present. 'Maybe put her off the scent by talking more about the Caribbean. Pretend that my interest was in the West Indies, would she buy that?'

'You've lost your appetite, you're just messing with that food. I knew taking a year off from your studies and doing nothing except dance classes was a mistake. You're bored already.'
Jasmine looked at her. 'Was this it, the opportunity to tell her? Yes.'

'You know I was thinking about getting a part time job to pay for my classes?'
Her mother looked surprised.
'You don't need to do that, I give you an allowance.'

'I know, but I wanted to.' Before her mother could interrupt her, she went on. 'Well I couldn't find one, but I did get a years' dance contract from this November.' Silence before the expected uproar, Jasmine didn't break it.

'November? You can't do that, what about university next October? Jasmine, it's your whole future you're throwing away.' Her mother's voice was threaded with confusion as well as anger.

'No I'm not Mum. Honestly! Before I went for the audition, I phoned Professor Hendrick. We get back to Southampton in October, I'll be a week late, that's all. He's sending me a list of books that I need to read and will let me enter when I get back. Remember, all the paper work is already done. I would not have signed for the cruise otherwise.'

'A cruise? You mean you're going to work on a ship?' Jasmine saw her chance and leapt at it.

'Yes, all the Caribbean Islands you can think of, isn't it great Mum, just think of it!'

'But Jasmine...' She got no further, before her daughter interrupted her.

36

'And would you believe, New York and Boston.' Her mother's mouth dropped open. 'I thought that going on this ship would make mixing with people and going on to university next year, that much easier.' Jasmine said no more. She didn't want to blurt out too much information in her nerviness. She picked up her glass and thankfully gulped at the iced water in it. But her dark eyes never left her mother's face. All kinds of emotions were evident there. Jasmine was conscious that every muscle in her own body was tensed and she forced herself to breathe more deeply and so relax a little, but not too much. She had to be very careful that she didn't mention Hong Kong.

'You'll be spending a year there?' Jasmine faltered, but only for a second.

'No, we go out to Australia and New Zealand first.' She didn't add to that statement and prayed that her mother wouldn't ask too many questions about the ports of call, the ship would be making in the Far East.

'Twelve months at sea?'

'I know it sounds a long time mum, but really, it will pass very quickly.' Jasmine's mind was racing, trying to think of a safe topic on the itinerary. 'We did the Panama Canal in Geography, it will be brilliant to see it. Well, not only that, we actually go through it.' Her mother didn't make any comment. Jasmine's hands were clammy with sweat. She needed to break the silence, but was hesitant to continue talking about the cruise, so she decided to veer to her university course instead. 'I know I choose Literature and not Geography, but you know I've always had a keen interest in the subject, so when this audition came up it seemed like a good chance to see some of the world before I go back to my studies.' She paused, trying to detect how her mother was accepting it.

'A year, if you went, you'd need to pack quite a lot of clothes.' Jasmine blinked and grinned in relief as her mother's practical mind moved into gear. 'You'd need to take those big suite cases I used when I was posted over seas, I suppose they're still in the attic.' Jasmine didn't want her mother to dwell on her army career, so she jumped in with what she hoped was a safe topic.

'I'll need evening gowns as well as cocktail dresses.'

Jasmine's heart hammered, skipping beats, she was so afraid her mother would guess that she was impelling herself to put on a brave act. And if she did, she'd insist on knowing the truth. That must never happen, Jasmine didn't want to hurt her. 'We'll have to go shopping.' The girl forced a smile to her lips, hoping that the rest of the evening would be centred on fashion.

'Pale colours always look good on you. In that sun you'll go really dark just like Za...' Her mother stuttered and swallowed the rest of the word, but rushed on. 'When you were young, you know, you loved boating on the lake in the summer mouths.' Jasmine's throat felt constricted. She knew that her mother had nearly said her father's name and panicked in case that thought brought a fresh inquiry into the reason for taking this job. So she jumped in with both feet.

'I couldn't afford to take a trip like this and as I'm trained as a dancer; well, as I've already said, it would be stupid to miss such an opportunity to travel before I go to university.'

'I never expected you to take to the ballet classes. I had to make you go when you were five. Doctor Jones thought it might help. You were so shy and mixing with other kids of your own age would be good for you. When you went to boarding school, I thought you'd give it up. Not keep it on as an extra.' Jasmine let her mother continue taking. 'I never dreamt that you would actually consider it as a career.' She paused, Jasmine could see the fresh fear in her eyes. 'You don't do you?'

'No mum, just this one job before I go to university. But dancing has helped me. Yes I know I'm still inhibited with people, especially when I first meet them, but I'm getting better, really I am.' Her mother shook her head incredulously. 'When I know a routine and I'm dancing, shyness doesn't bother me. It's as if when I put on my stage make up and my costume and step in front of the lights. I'm sure of myself. I am that well rehearsed it doesn't matter how many people are in the theatre, they're the other side of the foot lights.'

'You've only done the amateur shows with your ballet school.' Jasmine hunched her shoulders, trying very hard to look confident. 'No foot lights on a ship. There you'll have nothing between you and the audience.' Jasmine felt her stomach viciously twist and knot itself. She mustn't let her mother know how acutely afraid she was. If she guessed that, then it wouldn't take her very long to find out the truth of why this trip was so vital. Jasmine curled her nails into the palms of her hands, clenching her fists on her lap. She could do this, she had to.

'This Saturday I'm doing a solo on a cabaret floor.' Her mother leaned forward.

'At the local old aged pensioners home! There's no comparison at all.' Jasmine felt the pain in her hands and made herself stretch her fingers.

'It will be the same to me.' She could see her mother frowning and knew that she was planning something.

'If you're sick this Saturday, then we'll get Doctor Jones to get you out of this contract.'

'No.' The word shot out with far too much emotion. But her mother seemed to ignore its intensity and pressed home her own advantage.

'Why not? If you can't handle a simple amateur night with the locals, how on earth would you cope with a professional show and one that is going to last for a year?' It was an ultimatum and Jasmine knew that she would have to accept it to stop further questions into her reasons for going. Her mother wouldn't back down, she never did. Jasmine saw no other alternative open to her, she had to accept it and manage as best as she could. When she spoke, her voice was flat and low.

'It's a deal mum.'

Veronica could plainly see the tension in her daughter's expression, she guessed that Jasmine was going through a private mental hell, but didn't know why. She'd accepted that Jasmine needed a year off from her studies, the girl had worked hard and had got really good results in her exams. She'd even cut her dance classes down to only one on a Saturday morning, just to keep fit. Jasmine had put all of her energies into her school work and it had paid off. But why she was forcing herself to work on a cruise liner for twelve months, when she knew that her shyness was such that even meeting new people in her own familiar surroundings was torture for her. What was she trying to prove? That she could control her inability to cope with meeting people? Surely not. She just wasn't only terribly shy, her nerves sometimes made her physically sick. Well Saturday night would be an end to it. Fancy thinking that she'd be able to do it. Veronica leaned back in her chair.

'It's not that I don't want you to go. It's just that I can't see you being able to, that's all.' She watched the muscles quiver in her daughter's face. 'I'm very proud of you. You know I love you, you don't have to prove anything to me.'

'I know that Mum. Maybe I have to do this for myself.'

'Why?' The colour drained from the face opposite her and the eyes reflected the pain. Veronica had seen that very same expression nineteen years ago when she'd left Zachery in Hong

Kong. 'God, how like him she is. But he was never shy.' Memories of a passionate and rapturous affair clouded her mind. They had met and fallen madly and deeply in love, listening to no words of caution from anyone, they had married four weeks later. With such intensity of emotions, they had never found the time to discuss their futures and when it forced its presence on them, they had crumpled under its demands. Six months later, she'd left him there. She wouldn't stay with him, he wouldn't leave there. She'd arrived back in England, planning to carry on with her medical career in the Army. Being pregnant had never entered her head. When she'd found out, she'd already filed for a divorce. Veronica had resigned her commission but when her baby had been six months old, she'd been talented and fortunate enough to be given a position on Sir Boyd Millar's staff. Her career had never looked back. She'd never told Zachery of the birth. As he hadn't loved her enough to stay with her, she had never given him the chance to reject their daughter as well.

'Look love, let's wait until the weekend before we say any more.' Her daughter nodded her head and abruptly left the table. Veronica cleared it and put the crockery and utensil's into the dish washer. She grinned, telling herself, everything would be back to normal by next week. She didn't begrudge Jasmine anything, all she wanted was for her to be happy. Going to university wouldn't be that bad. She'd already met her professor and he had taken pains to put Jasmine at her ease. Her classes would be small, she'd be fine once she got over the initial hurdle of facing her colleagues for the first time. But trying to endure the strain of a ship for twelve months, with different passengers on every cruise, was so stupid, there could be no earthly reason why she should. 'God knows what she's thinking.' But the china duck sitting on the window sill, kept its thoughts to itself. 'It's not the money, she doesn't need to work, I keep her.'

Veronica glanced around the kitchen, but there was nothing to do, Hilda had been as efficient as usual. So she walked through into the lounge and poured herself out a good measure of brandy. She swirled the golden liquid around the glass, then smelt it, letting the aroma fill her nostrils, holding her breath for perhaps five seconds, before slowly breathing out. The curtains in the bay window were still open, the darkness outside, only broken by a couple of street lamps. One by their front gates, the other a little further up the avenue. Even in this almost non-existent illumination, the garden matched the immaculate order of the interior. Veronica tried to remember the name of the man that worked for her. She knew it was something very outlandish, she shrugged, it was no use, she couldn't think of it, anyway, why should she bother? Hilda had found him, she was the person who handed over his weekly wages out of the house keeping Veronica gave her. The glass reached her lips, she sipped her drink. 'Have I ever met him? No! But I do appreciate his inspiration.' She gazed out at the out line of shapes and forms. Not that they showed formation, that she would have found dull. They seemed to build, then ebb, drawing the eye, never jarring it. Suddenly the garden was filled with moon light, as if some mighty hand had switched on the power. Her eyes were pulled upwards, towards the brightness. The solitary cloud that had been obscuring it was steaming westwards and didn't hold her attention.

Veronica realised that the rest of the sky was clear, just pin pricked with stars. 'The ever expanding universe.' She cradled the crystal goblet in both her hands, occasionally swallowing a little of the liquid. Her voice when she spoke out loud was questioning, but there was no other person in the room to answer her. 'Time. What is it? Infinite?' Her eyes were locked, constantly staring upwards. 'Is there life out there? Does it really matter to us? Anyway, what is life? Why should we be all so different, yet all the same?' She filled her lungs with air. 'What purpose can we have in doing anything, if there is no more than this?' Her breath automatically pushed out. 'As flesh and blood wears out, or can be destroyed, where do we fit in as energy?' The silence of the room, blocked out all other noise from her. 'What a simple, but complex word energy is. But I have to believe there is more to me than this.' A faint smile reflected in the window pane. 'How egotistical of me to be so sure! But why is there so much drive and effort in people, if this meagre span is all there is?' A quick negative shake of her head. 'No. Stop thinking that way. Not today. Not ever.'

With her glass held firmly in her left hand, Veronica moved impetuously away from the window and switched on the main lights, returning more slowly to the side of the window and pulled on the heavy cord to draw the curtains; they glided across with the soft swish of velvet, shutting out the night and the questions. Then she sat down on the settee and slipped off her shoes, before lifting her feet up. Leaning back into the cushions, she still held her glass cupped in her hands. Seven operations to day, six successfully, one hopeless. She abruptly brought the edge of the glass to her nose, submerging in the heady bouquet. Even now, after all these years, Veronica still found it dauntingly hard to accept, that a patient's term of life, could end with her. She still wanted to achieve the impossible, but with the human body, Veronica was sometimes forced to accede her own fallibility as a surgeon.

Chapter 6

Archie sat there glowering at the girl in front of him and stubbornly repeated his statement.

'You're too early, the room isn't booked until nine thirty.' Jasmine was standing about two feet away from him, but she could still smell his stale breath. She nodded her head, but didn't move. She hoped eventually, that he'd give up moaning at her and let her in. 'The heating has only just been switched on, it's still too cold, you'll freeze if you went in there now.' He seemed to think that he had her at a disadvantage. She shook her head at him. 'Yes you would!'

'No.' The simplicity of her answer seemed to daunt him for a moment, but his reply was quick enough.

'Why not?' Jasmine swallowed hard. She had to get in there before the others came. If she could do so and start warming up with her exercises, then maybe she'd be to engrossed to feel that frightened.

'I need to practice. Please let me in, I can't lose this job.' Archie grunted and made a big thing out of looking at his watch again. 'I'm going now, I'm only the night watchman and I finish at eight.' Jasmine's hand went involuntary to her mouth, her eyes wide and scared. He threw her a look under his eye brows. Muttered, but reached into a deep pocket and brought out a bunch of keys.

'You can't blame me if you're cold.' Jasmine smiled weakly at him and followed him along the corridor. 'There you are!' With a shuffle of his feet, he returned to the front door of the building. Alone in the large room, Jasmine felt herself starting to relax. She changed quickly into her practice clothes and immediately started to gently stretch her muscles. An hour later, Maurice and Joan walked in. Jasmine knew that she was no longer alone, but was by now so absorbed in what she was doing that their presence did not disturb her.

Joan walked to the table at the top of the room and put the hold all, as well as her brief case, on it. Maurice stood watching the girl, then strolled up to Joan.

'I hope she warmed up properly, that's demanding stuff she's churning out. Think she's trying to impress me?' Joan glanced up and smiled at him, his ego was always upper most, so she decided to prick his bubble.

'No, why should she. She's already got the job. She's just a very conscientious dancer who likes to prepare well for rehearsals.' Maurice sniffed. Even through he wasn't sexually interested in the fairer sex, it always gave him a buzz to think that a young, good looking female was out to catch his eye, so he ignored Joan's statement altogether.

'Plug the cassette in over there, then we'll have room on this table to spread the papers out in order. Tracy bounded in and flung her bag towards the straight back chairs, lined against the side wall.

'I'm early!' Both Joan and Maurice gave spontaneous grins. Jasmine stopped dancing, then walked slowly over to her bag, which she'd put in a back corner, nowhere near any seats. She knew that she needed time before mixing with all the girls. Tracy took her duffle coat off, then her sweater. Next she shed her boots and jeans, she already had her rehearsal gear on. She wandered over to Jasmine with a friendly smile on her face. 'You're eager, aren't you?' Jasmine was bent over her bag, trying to occupy her hands, but she looked up when Tracy spoke. Doctor Jones had told her that it might be helpful to her to be frank with the other dancers, or at least a couple of them, about her shyness. So taking her courage in both her hands she stood up and rushed into her prepared speech.

'I get very nervous when I have to mix with new people.' Tracy cocked her head to one side and smiled.

'Thought so at the audition. But don't worry about me luv, I don't bite.' Her face then changed, her eyes went big and her head jerked slightly in Maurice's direction. 'He might though!' The giggle that went with the remark made it funny and in spite of herself, Jasmine faintly smiled. 'Come on, we'll impress with our work out.' Both girls moved back into the centre of the floor.

Tina was next to arrive, followed by Mary, they entered almost together and crossed to the chairs, taking up the rest of space to that corner. A little later Megan opened the door and stood for a moment, then made her way towards Tracy's things and put her own bag down on a chair half way up the room.

Catching her eye, Tracy gave Megan the thumbs up and a grin. It didn't take her long to change. All five dancers were limbering up when just before ten o'clock, Charis made her entrance. Fur coat, stilettos and wearing a full make up. Tracy halted in mid pirouette, over balanced and sank into a heap on the floor. Joan walked over to her, trying to keep her face straight.

'Have you hurt yourself?' Tracy's head came up and her eyes were watering, she grinned and waved a wagging finger in Charis's direction. Joan nodded her comprehension and returned to the table. Charis was determined to ignore Tracy and Megan, if it hadn't been a twelve month's contract that she badly wanted, she told herself that she would have been tempted to let it go. But not this job. This was her chance to escape and she wasn't going to let those two spoil her hopes in any way what so ever. She'd put up with the common elements by keeping well out of their way. Charis walked slowly up the middle of the room and then diagonally across to the top corner, where she put her small case down.

'Rehearsals start in two minutes and I expect everyone to be ready to dance.' Charis hurriedly changed and did a few expeditious plies, telling herself, that that would be enough of a warm up, as they had to learn the steps of the routines, before they could go straight through them, the work that morning should be quiet enough for her not to pull any muscles. 'Right get in line and concentrate, we've got a lot to get through.'

Two hours later, Maurice called a halt and told the girls that they had a ten-minute break. Tracy linked arms with Mary and took her over to where Jasmine was standing by herself. Tina lay flat on the floor with her eyes closed. Charis wanted to go and talk to her, but the immobility of Tina's position was an effectual bar. Megan sat by her things, watching. She'd summed up Charis at the audition, her snobbish attitude didn't matter, if she gave any hassle, Megan would be happy to chew her up and spit her out.

Maurice was studying the running schedule for the Paris show.

'How are you going to split them up?'

'Em!' He sounded disinterested.

'You heard what I said.'

'Does it matter?' Joan nodded her head. Maurice smirked, but agreed with her. 'I suppose so. Otherwise we could end up with trouble.' Maurice turned around and let his gaze wander from girl to girl, then he sauntered over to where Tina was lying. He squatted on his haunches so that he could speak to her without anyone else hearing. When he straightened up he went back to

Joan. 'She doesn't want the single cabin, she wants to share with Tracy.'

'Put Charis in it.' Maurice's mobile eye brows rose. 'And put Jasmine and Mary in the two berth, that will give the other three the biggest cabin, so they can spread themselves out.'

'Think that will work.'

'Yes.'

'Okay, you tell them, I'm too busy.' He impatiently turned back to study the paper work laid out on the table. Joan picked up a single sheet and fixed it in her clip board. They'd been luckier this year, most of the cabins they had been allotted were singles, so the acts were fine. She started to walk down the room.

'Girls, can I have your attention for a moment please.' She stopped in the middle of the room and read out their cabin numbers. She didn't wait for a discussion, but turned around as soon as she'd finished.

'There you go Jasmine, mother Mary Mac, will look after you!'

'Don't pay any attention to her. It's coming from Liverpool, she feels obligated to try and tell jokes all the time.' Both girls were grinning encouragingly at Jasmine and were rewarded when a swift smile, flitted across her face. Charis felt relieved that she wasn't sharing with Megan and/or Tracy, but wondered how Tina would cope with them. Tina got up and walked over to Megan.

'Hope you don't mind sharing?' Appraising green eyes stared for a couple of seconds, then her shoulders shrugged nonchalantly. Tracy bounded over to them.

'What shall we be known as? The Three Musketeers?' Tina laughed and in that moment Megan decided that maybe she would enjoy being part of Tracy's set and said on a lighter note.

'No! We'll have to think of something more interesting than that.'

'Well then, how about the three witches from Macbeth?' Tina gave an exaggerated shudder and said.

'That's bad luck in the theatre you know.'

'Don't worry luv, it's a ship and sea worthy. Anyway, it won't sink.' Megan looked puzzled and asked.

'Why not? Well, what I mean is, how do you know it won't?' Tracy grinned.

'I can't drown; me Mum said she'd kill me if I do!' Tina smiled, but shook her head in disbelief, Megan laughed outright.

'Right, back in line.' Maurice was in the middle of the room waiting for then.

'Gosh it's cold,' Tracy huddled herself deeper into her duffel coat. 'Let's find somewhere to get a hot drink and a butty before we go to Maurice's house.' All six girls were stood on the pavement, outside the leisure centre. Charis turned her collar up and her back on Tracy.

'Tina, there's a lovely little tea shop about ten minutes away, shall you and I go there?' Tina was not going to play piggy in the middle, not on this particular wall! She'd asked Maurice if she could share with Tracy because she liked the girl. If Charis didn't, then that was her problem, let her deal with it.

'That's too far, there's a cafe just over there, why don't you come with us.' Charis looked surprised and shook her head, then marched off in the direction she'd pointed.

'Thank God she's gone, she'd have put me off my grub.' Tracy grinned at her audience. 'No kidding people, very delicate stomach, me!'

'Come on, let's get out of this damn wind.' Tina headed across the street, Megan and Tracy ran after her. Mary looked sympathetically at Jasmine, then linked her arm through the young girl's and walked after the others.

'Don't worry. All you have to do is sit and drink a cup of coffee. Tracy will entertain us.' Jasmine took a deep breath and allowed herself to be guided across the road and into the small cafe. 'See that corner table over there.' Jasmine nodded. 'Go and sit down and I'll bring you your drink, do you want anything to eat?'

'No thanks.' Mary gave her a gentle shove in the direction of the empty table and went to the counter. Tracy was paying for her order.

'She okay?' It was asked in a quiet voice and Mary just gave a slight nod in answer. 'Nice kid.'

The five of them got to Maurice's house some minutes before six o'clock. Tina pressed the bell, they could hear it ring out a tune.

'Well, we might have known he wouldn't have just an ordinary one, wouldn't we?' They all giggled.

'Shut up you idiot, someone's coming.' Tina hissed and playfully dug Tracy in her ribs. Joan opened the door wide and they trooped passed her.

'Straight down the stairs.' Tracy led the way, Mary gave Jasmine an encouraging smile. They found themselves in a long, low room, brightly lit with strip lighting. At one end, there were maybe a dozen or more free standing rails hung with a multitude of different costumes and all covered with large dust sheets. Then before these, there were ten rails, each with a show title taped to the top of the support bar facing them. Tina was glad to see that everything looked as if it was well organised. It had been a few years since she'd worked in a cabaret, she preferred the theatre and was talented and lucky enough to get good shows. 'Which costumes do you want to start with Maurice?' Joan was now stood by a dress makers table, pushed up against the far wall, there was also a sewing machine and a female sitting in a chair in front of it. Before he could answer, the bell went again. 'That must be Charis, I'll let her in.'

'No, let Doris get it, you hand out the can can dresses and boots.'

'Okay.' Joan moved to the nearest rail by the door, the female at the machine got up and went upstairs. 'I'm hoping that the dresses will fit, they're all size ten, but have elasticised sides, the boots are in the sizes you gave me at the audition. When you have tried them on and you're satisfied they're comfortable and you're able to dance okay in them, take the dresses over to Doris and she'll name them for you. Then bring the costumes back and hang them up again. Don't panic if the dress doesn't fit, it can be altered. Right!' Tracy walked up and beamed at Joan, she loved trying on costumes and this lot looked good. Nothing cheap or tatty about them at all. She was enjoying herself. Charis walked in and pointedly looked at her watch, it was exactly six o'clock. Maurice had his back to her and all Joan said was that she should get undressed and try her costume on. The can can dresses were in a shiny purple and silver stripped material. When the skirts were lifted, the underside was completely frilled with black and silver lace. The bodices were tight, with large metal hooks down the back and the shoulder straps were also elasticised. The black satin knickers, which went with them, were frilled with lace. 'You shouldn't have any problems with the head dresses, they're just bands with the short curly feathers sewn on one side, there's elastic that goes under your chins.'

'Let them try them on and the garters as well, I want to be sure that nothing is left to chance. They've got to be named anyway.' Joan picked a bag out of the box where she'd got their boots from and handed the things out. 'Give them the opening leotards next.' Mary was stood by Doris, unhooking Jasmine's dress for her and wondered if stripping off in front of the others would bother her unduly, but she seemed to be coping alright so far.

'Stop day dreaming girls and get the next costume on, and be careful with the feather head dresses.' There was an edge to Maurice's voice. 'It's the emerald green sequin leotards, with the black net.' After that there wasn't much conversation, just the odd, 'how does it fit; feel; is that too tight; gosh that looks good on you.'

'That's the first two shows done, any problems Doris?'

'Not for me!' There were in fact only four costumes on the table besides the sewing machine and none of them needed any major alteration.

'Good.' Maurice gave them a flashy smile. 'Right girls, you can go now. We'll see you in the morning and don't be late. By the way, do any of you sew?' Tracy grinned and volunteered that she had been known to sew on the odd button! Charis informed them, in her superior voice, that she had all her clothes made by a good seamstress.

'I do.' Megan had decided that he wasn't looking for an unpaid drudge.

'Good! I've got some odd pieces of material you might be able to do something with, I'll sort them out and you can have them tomorrow.'

'Thanks.' Maurice turned back to Doris and carried on discussing the costumes.

'Could you phone for a taxi for Jasmine, please.' Joan looked up at Mary and smiled.

'As soon as possible?'

'Yes please.' Jasmine's soft voice came from behind Mary.

'Anyone else need one?' Everyone else said 'No'. Tina had pulled on her clothes and was the first to leave. Five minutes later the door bell rang.

'That'll be your cab.' Jasmine nodded. 'I'll let you out', they went upstairs. Tracy was looking at the rail marked with the title of space odyssey, she thought that the cat suits looked terrific. She grinned at Maurice as he came up to her. She wondered if he knew how excited she was, but doubted it.

'Great costumes.' He nodded approvingly at Tracy, but said.

'Don't be late tomorrow.'

'I won't be. Good night. Anyone for the underground?' Megan and Mary both chorused 'no'. Charis didn't answer, nor did she attempt to leave, when those three left the house.

'She's such a snob.' Tracy's voice showed her disgust.

'She doesn't bother me.' Megan's tone was flat.

'What does?' It wasn't a spiteful question from Mary, just a curious one. Megan shrugged

'Some people do, but not her.' Tracy cut in.

'Tina disappeared awfully fast, didn't she!'

'Most probably got a date.' Mary's practical nature was evident.

'Well talking of dates, I've got one with a plate of steak and chips!' The other two just blinked at her. 'Aunty Val thinks I need building up. See you tomorrow.' They could hear her laugh as she hurried towards the tube station.

'Hungry?'

'As long as it's cheap.' Megan thought she might as well be straight with Mary.

'Why don't we go back to that little cafe by the leisure centre, it was okay and I looked at the menu, it wasn't pricey at all.'

'Fine.'

'Let's go, I'm staving.'

The next two weeks fell into a similar pattern. They met each morning for rehearsals and during the break, before they went to Maurice's house to try on more costumes, everyone, except Charis, went into the little cafe opposite for a hot drink and a sandwich. Although Charis was staying at the same bed and breakfast that Mary and Megan were at, she never socialised with them. Jasmine still found it difficult to join in the conversations, but she was getting used to being with them, she liked Mary a lot and found Tracy amusing. She knew her mother would be shocked if she ever found out about Tracy's attitude towards sex, in fact it had surprised her, but it didn't seem to bother the others. It wasn't as if Tracy was trying to convert anyone to her way, she just enjoyed sex a lot! Didn't hide the fact that if she found a good looking male and he was willing, then she'd have sex with him. Jasmine was sitting there one day, thinking about Tracy and wondered if she had lost count of the men she'd been with. No sooner had the thought come into her head than she found herself going very red. But as the others were all listening to a tale of Liverpool bliss from Tracy, nobody noticed her and she was able to recover her composure without any questions being asked. At first Jasmine had been apprehensive of Megan's direct and abrupt ways. But gradually Jasmine had accepted that she wasn't being unfriendly, she was, in her own way just as wary of people as Jasmine was, only Megan's defence, showed in her terseness. None of them seemed to like Charis. Jasmine assumed that was because her attitude was extremely unfriendly. Tina joined in the chatter at the cafe, but never said anything about her personal life and always rushed off after the costume fitting was over. Jasmine felt that Mary was a very caring person and in a way, just like her own mother was protective towards her. Jasmine hoped that she would be able to cope with meeting the passengers on board the ship. Not that she intended to mix with them, but she knew that she wouldn't be able to hide in her cabin for the twelve months.

Chapter 7

The alarm went off and his hand groped out in search of it. Ted knocked the clock on the floor beside the bed and swore under his breath as he sat up to switch the light on. It must of taken him a minute, or just over to stop the ringing. He then leant back against his pillows, trying to wake himself up. Ten minutes later he went to the bathroom. He'd got up half an hour earlier then he needed too, as he wanted plenty of time this morning to get ready. He was determined to put his maximum effort into these rehearsals. Nothing would be allowed to go wrong. When he returned to his bedroom and looked into the two foot square mirror, at what he could see of his reflection. He was satisfied with his appearance. Not bad for a forty eight year old, who'd been on the cabaret circuit for thirty years. But contracts had started to get thin on the ground. He had no illusions about his future, he might still have a good voice, but there were dozens of younger men, with the same ability, grasping his meal tickets from under his nose. The females in the audiences wanted youth and sex appeal; charm and sophistication didn't much matter to them.

Ted wasn't bitter, he'd had a good run and enjoyed it, but now he was forced to consider his future. It was no good trying to think of something else he could do to earn his living, there just wasn't anything that he thought he could handle as well. Being an optimist, he'd always assumed that he'd be a star by now and therefore marriage wouldn't have been a necessity. But it hadn't happened and he was honest, even practical enough, to accept that now it never would. He would have preferred to go gallantly from one female to the next, as the whim took him. He always enjoyed the hunt more than the prolonged feast. At first, the novelty was always so stimulating, but that very rarely lasted for long. In two years time he'd be fifty and he knew, that although nature had so far been kind, age had a way of bringing everyone to their knees. And as Ted felt his old age was just around the corner, he needed the comfort and security of money, in fact substantial wealth, behind him. Living off his wife's generosity wouldn't bother him.

Ted walked into the rehearsal room five minutes early. Three of the dancers were staying at the same bed and breakfast place. As well as the comedian and the female ventriloquist. The place was crowded with people from the show and two more were expected that evening. Joan had been round there last night and told the acts, that Maurice wanted to go through the 'Paris' show first, with costumes. He wanted to see that the changes were okay. Ted hadn't argued, but he privately thought that that was being overly cautious. He didn't think that a dress rehearsal for the acts was necessary, but he wasn't rocking any boats by saying so. If the boss wanted costumes, then he could have them. Ted walked down the side of the room, the girls were limbering up in the centre. When he got to the far end, Joan smiled at him and pointed to a rail where he could hang his suit up. Unknown to Maurice, Joan had told Ted when to wear a black dinner jacket and when not to, so that he and Maurice would not be dressed the same for any of the shows. Joan knew how fragile Maurice's acceptance of Ted was and didn't want any superfluous clashes. Ted hadn't needed an explanation, he'd only met Maurice the once, but he was not stupid. He'd swallowed the acid comment which had sprung to his lips and smiled. He'd placate Maurice's ego. This trip was a major opportunity and one that he wasn't going to spoil. He had, so to speak, burnt his bridges behind him. To make the proper impression was fundamental to his plan's fruitful outcome; so Ted had turned what assets he'd accumulated into cash and spent the lot on his wardrobe. After all, he did not intend returning. He didn't care where he lived in the future, but if he had a choice, it would be a warmer climate than Britain could offer. He'd spent the last summer on the island of Jersey and looked there, but without success; middle aged, wealthy females, with no attachments, seemed to be a scarcity this days. Half a dozen younger women had fitted into his wealthy criteria, but none of them had even glanced at him, let alone come near him and his invitations had been blatant enough not to be misinterpreted.

The rehearsal had gone smoothly after a bumpy start. Cindy and Crystal, the female singers had been ten minutes late. They'd arrived, bag and baggage and dumped the lot just inside the main swing doors into the room. Maurice had screamed at them that it was supposed to be a dress rehearsal and without more to do, a case had been flung open, they'd stripped off and put on the tightest and shortest silver mini dresses ever seen. The shiny material enhancing the dusky lustre of their skin. Short cropped black curly hair, and pretty round faces, framed enormous dark eyes. Bodies that curved splendidly in all the right places to anchor male observation, soon put the humour back into Maurice's voice. After that minor hiccup, things had progressed, more or less very well. All concerned were pleased that the show was slick and professional, as well as very entertaining. At the end of the rehearsal, the company had split, those living in London had gone home, and the rest had crowded into the little cafe for their evening meal. Most of the girls' costumes were now fitted and only occasionally, did one of them have to go on afterwards to try something on. Maurice was extremely relieved that everything was running well, even in advance of his schedule. But that didn't stop him from keeping the pressure on them all, he'd been in show business for too many years to relax too soon. He'd insisted that everyone in the show went through the full dress rehearsals that final week. Maurice not only wanted, but demanded, perfection.

Tracy had to stride out to keep up with Tina as they headed for the tube station.

'Where's the fire!' A quick grin flashed across Tina's face, but she didn't slow down. 'Well, I hope he's worth it.' Tracy couldn't see the reaction to her second dig, as Tina was already running down the entrance steps. The platform wasn't busy, maybe half a dozen other people were there. 'We must have just missed one.' Tina nodded and shoved her hands into her coat pockets. 'What does he think of you leaving the love nest for a year then, is he crying in his beer?' She laughed at her own joke. 'Mind you, I don't blame you wanting to go! A fantastic time is going to be had by all!' Tracy's voice was friendly, but threaded with curiosity. She'd guessed that there was a man in Tina's life and wondered how important he was to her. 'Is it major, or can't you make up your mind?' Tina looked up, her eyes wide and sad.

'You've got it wrong. He's making me go. I don't want to, but he insists.' Tracy couldn't believe her ears and therefore couldn't think of anything else to say. 'Please don't ask me any questions, I can't explain. I shouldn't really have said anything to you about it, it's complicated.' The two girls just stood there, one hoping that she hadn't made a mistake by saying anything, the other wondering what sort of a mess was just under the surface. They hadn't spoken again when the train pulled into the station. The doors opened automatically and they got in. They sat by each other, the generally chatty Tracy, for once, was quiet. There were only two stops before Tina got off. As she stood up, Tracy put a friendly hand on her arm.

'If you need any help, just give me a nod. I'm sure everything will be okay. Don't look so unhappy, I hate tears, they're so fruitless.' It had been a rushed statement. Tina only had time to give a brief nod, before she got off the train.

She didn't really know why she was even hurrying to get back to her flat. Bill wouldn't be there. If he came at all, it would be after his show was over. And only then, if he felt that he could do so without it being noticed that he did not return to his house at the time he should. Last night he'd telephoned and said that he might be able to visit this evening, because his wife might be going aboard for a couple of days. But it had been a very short call and he hadn't really given any details. Tina stood impatiently on the platform, waiting for her connection to come in.

She'd showered and changed into her night-dress and dressing gown. Now sat curled up on the couch in the dim light from a small table lamp, which was the only one she'd switched on. Haydn's Season's was playing on her stereo, but she still heard him opening the front door. She didn't move, just waited for him to come to her. But her expression had changed. The crease across her forehead had disappeared and her mouth was now relaxed, her smile transforming her expression into a welcoming greeting for her lover. She didn't speak to him as he came into the room, just held her arms out to him.

Bill stood for a moment before her, his chest already heaving, from rushing to her. He slipped his overcoat off and sat down on the couch besides her. Their arms wrapped around each other as their lips met. There was nothing gentle in their kiss, it was passionate, as if they had been together for the evening and their emotions had had time to build to that peak. His hands pushed the silky coverings from Tina's shoulder's and his mouth left her lips to devour her breasts. He groaned as he felt her arch her back for him. He could feel the shape of her nipple in his mouth as his tongue caressed it. Then he sucked gently, taking more of her flesh into his mouth. Finally he moved and slipped his hands up her legs, under her nightdress, then pulled her hips along the seat. Her flimsy night wear was now gathered around her waist. He saw her laugh as she sat up and stretch her arms above her head. Bill collected the material in his hands and knelt on the couch, as he lifted it over Tina's head. Then he sat back on his heels, drinking in her beauty.

Tina was drowning in the love and admiration, so relevant in his eyes. He started to undress, but she stopped him, she wanted to do that for him. Tina swung her legs off the couch and knelt before Bill and took his shoes and socks off. When she stood up, she pulled him to his feet. Next she slowly undid the buttons of his shirt, trailing her fingers over his chest, as she slipped it from his shoulders, no interest in where it landed. The tip of her tongue peeped out between even teeth, as she began undoing his trousers. She was badly tempted to intimately touch him straight away, but she made herself wait. She knelt back down in front of Bill, then pulled his shorts and trousers over his hips, shoving them to the floor. He stepped straight out of them. Her eyes glowed, when her hands finally came into contact with his masculinity. As her fingers seductively stroked his erection, she moved her mouth closer and passionately tasted him.

Beads of sweet glistened on Bill's body. He gulped air into his lungs, holding his breath for perhaps a minute then forcing it quickly out. He didn't know how long he'd been doing this, but he did know that he couldn't do it any longer. He swooped over and picked her up. As he laid Tina on the couch, he moved on top of her. He could feel her nails bite into the flesh on his shoulders as he lunged into the erotic wetness of her body. Again and again his hard thrusts penetrated deeply. His mind only conscious of love and his demanding intensity to explode within her.

Tina's breath was coming in ever shortening gasps. A fine film of perspiration covered her skin. She curled her nails into Bill as she pushed her hips up to meet him. She was greedy for him. Her knees automatically bent and pushed wide, opening herself more. She heard her name rip through his throat. Fire raged through her and molten heat spurted. His plunge filled her inner self. Her voice filled the room and rejoiced. She'd scaled to the heights of her desires with him and now clung to his limp body, as he lay on her.

Bill thought he ought to move, but he was so comfortable in her arms, that his will did not insist. She lay still under him, curving now into his body. A smile flitted into his eyes as his memory flooded with her movements when they made love. 'God she was so beautiful.' He moved his head so that he could kiss her.

So softly now, were his lips covering her skin, that the sensation was almost illusionary, even ethereal. Tina lay motionless, not wanting to dispel the magic. But soon the kindling of her sexual need started to permeate again through her body, sending hot currents of desire rippling. Soon they'd grow into tumultuous waves, that would rampage until he sated them once more. She cupped his chin in her hands and pulled his mouth to hers.

Her kiss took Bill's breath away. Its passion and depth made his heart pound rapidly in his chest. He sucked at her tongue now probing in his mouth. He felt her hands move down his body until they reached his groin. Tina evoked in him, his carnal need for her. Tongues still entwined. Her fingers cast erotic spells on him and his latent desires flared again. He began to move rhythmically in her, slowly at first, then steadily gained force. When she moved her hands to his chest, Bill yielded to the pressure. He stopped and sat up. Tina pushed him back against the cushions. He watched as her supple body arched gracefully as she moved.

Tina straddled across Bill's lap, her legs on the outside of his. She planted a swift hard kiss on his mouth, then sat back on his knees. 'I love you.' His answering smile spread across his face, his hands were resting on her thighs.

'I'm living just for you. You're the one who makes my life worth anything.'

'Then why do I have to go?' She heard the bitterness in her own voice and crumpled onto his chest. 'Oh Bill, I'm sorry my love. I don't mean to nag, honestly I don't, but I hate the thought of leaving you for so long.' His arms wrapped possessively and held her close. Tina could feel his strength and longed to stay within it forever.

'It's for the best. In fact, it's the only way to do it.' She didn't answer, but a sob sounded in her throat. He squeezed her tightly. 'Tina my love, you going away is the hardest thing that I'll ever have to go through.' Tina could hear the agony in his voice, now she felt ashamed at her outburst and was determined not to be childish about it any more. He'd explained the reasons to her a hundred times, she didn't need to go through them again. She just didn't want to agree with him. Yet she accepted that he was right, it was just so hard for her to leave him. 'Please love, say you understand.' Tina pushed her hands on his chest and sat back up.

'Will you miss me?' A painful grimace twisted his mouth.

'So much so, that it's already hurting.' For a second, his eyes showed a bleakness that tore at her.

'No don't.' She was very near to tears. 'We'll manage. Time will just fly by.' She swallowed hard, his pain was so real that it hurt her. Tina flung herself onto his chest again. 'Our love will get us through, then we'll never have to be apart again.' Bill stroked her head. Her fine hair spilled through his fingers like silken threads. He knew that it would be so easy to keep her with him, but he'd told himself millions of times, 'no', and he must stick to it. But he'd been so tempted. He knew how close he'd been to letting her stay, that he'd had nightmares about it.

Tina pressed herself against him. She could feel his fingers running through her hair and found it soothing. Shortly she let out a tiny sigh, then sat up. She smiled as Bill's hands slipped through her hair, over her shoulders and onto her breasts. She pushed her hair back and let her tongue moisten her lips, she could see his eyes appreciatively watching her. She felt the tenderness in his fingers as he gently kneaded her flesh. Tina leaned forward, squashing his hands on her breasts as she pushed against him, then kissed him. When she sat back, his hands were still moulding her breasts; her nipples were now very prominent again. She moved her own hands to his thighs, then knelt up. She pushed his legs apart and took his masculinity in both hands, then sat back. Slowly she began to stroke him, watching avidly as she felt his erection begin to swell. Her movements became firmer, more erotically stimulating. Very soon, she felt him harden, ready for her. Tina knelt up and forward, then sank down over him, guiding him into her. She felt his hand squeeze on her tingling and throbbing breasts. She arched her back, swaying seductively on him. They kissed, passionately. Finally she moved her hands and laughed softly as Bill gripped her wrists, taking her fingers to his mouth. Tina started to move her hips, gradually from side to side, taking enjoyment from the rapturous look on Bill's face. Then her own pulse raced to a demanding speed. Tina changed her meter. She put her hands on his shoulders and started pushing forward against him, then pulling back, her tempo, quick and even.

Bill knew that he'd climax quickly, he always did when Tina mounted him and set this pace. She had the whip hand over him and that was how he wanted it. God, how he loved her. He opened his eyes to look at her. Her back was arched. He opened his fingers covering her breasts, letting the hard peaks of her nipples show through and with each thrust forward he felt her give, he sensuously squeezed her throbbing breasts. She was now galloping on him. With her head back, the veins showed blue in the long graceful column of her neck. He tensed his muscles and knew that it would be soon. The blood scorched through in his veins, his chest heaved. He felt a thousand feet tall. He heard Tina cry out as she jerked rapidly against him. Bill's control burst. White-hot liquid from him surged into her. His hands still claimed her panting breasts and pushed her flesh into firm mounds, nipples showed dark peaks between his open fingers.

Chapter 8

Maurice was pleased with himself, all the members of his show and life in general! He'd told the cast that he wanted a word with them before they went tonight and smiled as he took in the excitement running through them. Even Jasmine seemed more at ease now, of course Mary was looking after her, a real mother type was Mary, she should have a couple of kids, that would suit her. But not yet, she might be twenty six, but she didn't need to stop dancing for two or three years. Maurice frowned as he saw Tina standing by the door, she reminded him of a grey hound in the traps, as soon as he said go, she'd be off. She puzzled him, at first he'd been so thrilled to get her that her own attitude hadn't registered. But over the three weeks they had been rehearsing, Maurice had come to realise that Tina wasn't whole heartedly in this. Not that it showed in her dancing, that was professional enough, it was just the frustrated hopelessness of her manner, and her impatient dash to where ever she went at night. Still she was good on stage and that was all Maurice could ask for, but he worried about her. Maurice grinned when he heard Tracy laugh spontaneously at something Megan had said; he nodded confidently, now there was a girl who was on top of the world. Megan had bothered him at first, but she wasn't as hard as she acted, or so he now thought. She'd been delighted with the materials he'd given her. He'd guessed that she wouldn't have many cocktail or evening dresses, well she wouldn't, being brought up in an orphanage. So he'd handed over half a dozen pieces of good fabric, all he hoped was that she knew how to sew and didn't spoil the lot. His eyes moved to Charis, she was always last, Maurice mused, wondering what went on in her head, she certainly thought a lot of herself. Well, she could lord it over her single cabin. Joan had been right about that allotment and who to share with whom. But then Maurice couldn't remember when Joan had last made a mistake; funnily, that irked, more than pleased him.

'Right, as you're nearly all ready, I've got a few words to say before you go.' Charis was the only one who wasn't fully dressed with her coat on, so Maurice had decided to start. 'We have finished with the dress rehearsals.' Everybody grinned at him. 'But I'll hold any practices I think are necessary on board the ship and they will be compulsory.' He paused, but there wasn't a murmur of protest. 'Shouldn't be many, just enough to keep you all on your toes. But what I want to say is that we meet next Tuesday morning at ten o'clock, either at my house or the boarding house. And when I say ten, I mean it, I'll crucify anyone who holds the coach up. That's it, but before you go, let Joan know where you want picking up.' Tina was the first to reach Joan's side.

'At Maurice's house.' Joan nodded as she wrote that down on a sheet of paper on her clip board. 'See you all then, bye.'

'Me too.' Joan didn't bother looking up, she recognised Tracy's voice. 'Wait for me Tina, I'm coming now.' Tracy ran to catch the other girl up. When Jasmine got outside, her mother was sitting in the car waiting for her. The sound of the engine was muffled by the expensive body work, the sound of a classical symphony diffused into the air outside. Jasmine opened the front passenger door and got in, dropping her bag at her feet.

'Anyone need a lift?'

'No Mum, most of them are staying at a local boarding house.' Veronica put the car into gear and it rolled forward into the traffic.

'Nice car.' Mary watched as it disappeared, 'it's big, they must have money'. Megan nodded in agreement. 'Hungry?'

'As Tracy would say, STARVING!' They walked towards the little cafe where they usually ate. Ted Hunter caught them up before they'd reached the corner of the street. He pushed in between them and linked his arms through theirs.

'What are you two doing for entertainment this weekend?'

'Nothing strenuous, except my packing.' Pulling a face at Mary's answer, he turned his head to Megan.

'I've got some sewing to finish.'

'Very dull work, no men to say good bye to?' They both ignored him. By now they had reached the cafe and went in.

Tracy sat back and licked her lips. She felt full, she knew she shouldn't have eaten an extra piece of fruit pie, but her excuse was that her mum's cousin was such a good cook, it would have been a shame to waste it. Not that in a house of six, there was very much left after a meal, because there wasn't. She got up and asked if it was okay for her to commandeer the bathroom and have a good soak.

'Go ahead love, nobody will disturb you.' Tracy grinned and said thanks, then disappeared up stairs. She filled the bath, poured bubbles into it, then stripped off. Her hair was still tied in a knot on top of her head, the way she'd worn it for that days' rehearsal. She was just about to get into the water when there was a tap on the bathroom door. Tracy opened it a crack, so that she could see who was there.

'Can I come in, I've got to talk to you without my dad hearing.' Tracy's arm reached around the door and dragged Joanne in. Tracy shut it with a click, then sauntered over to the tub and got in.

'This is good.' Joanne was looking at her, but said nothing. 'Well, come on, spill the beans.'

'You're very thin.'

'Elegant and slender deary, I think are the terms you're looking for.'

'Oh, I didn't mean that you weren't pretty, you are, very.' Tracy didn't try to hide her self satisfied smirk. 'But I still want you to come out with me tonight.' Tracy wasn't sure if that was a back handed compliment or not. 'Please.'

'No.'

'Tracy it's important, even crucial.'

'Now I can tell you work in a library.' Joanne grunted. 'Why do you have to go out with me, go by yourself.'

'No, he won't let me.' Tracy turned her head and looked at the other girl.

'How old are you?'

'The same age as you, twenty four.'

'Then you don't need to ask permission, just go, after all this is nineteen sixty nine.'

'You've been here for three weeks, you know very well that there'd be a catastrophic row if I tried that.' Tracy nodded. 'I did have it arranged with Wendy, but she'd phoned here before I got in and said she couldn't make it. I wouldn't ask if I wasn't desperate, honestly I wouldn't.'

'Can't it wait until tomorrow.'

'No, he's got to be back on camp then.'

'A soldier?'

'No, a sailor.'

'And daddy doesn't approve of the armed forces?'

'No he doesn't, especially the Marines.'

'Wasn't he in the Navy?'

'Yes and I'm assuming that's why!' They both grinned.

'You're serious about this bloke.'

'We're planning to get married.'

'What!' Tracy shrieked and jerked up with a splash. Joanne smiled, but told her to keep her voice down.

'When it's all arranged and they can't stop it, I'll tell them, but not before. Geoff has only got a twenty four hour pass and he wants to see me tonight.'

'And you want me to play the gooseberry!'

'Oh no, he's got a mate with him, but I can't remember his name, it'll be like a double date.'

'How quaint.'

'Does that mean you'll come?'

'Yes I suppose so, what time are we meeting them.'

'Eight o'clock in a pub in town.'

'Then sod off and let me get ready.'

The girls, were of course, late! They stood in the doorway of the crowded pub for a minute, then Joanne moved forward, through to the bar.

'Hi.' A very muscular arm practically swept Joanne off her feet.

'You made it.' The owner of the arm then kissed her, making her blush.

'Not here Geoff.'

'Who cares?'

'I do.' He shrugged his massive shoulders but grinned sheepishly at her. 'This is Tracy, her mum and mine are cousins and she's staying with us until Tuesday. Where's your friend?' Geoff jerked his head. Tracy could see what Joanne saw in him, he had a great body, that's if you liked the super man type. Tracy shook hands with him and the look he gave her was pure appraisal, but it didn't last long, it was easy to see that he was wrapped up in Joanne.

'Where did you two meet.' Tracy asked out of curiosity.

'At the Royal Tournament, Geoff was in one of the gun crews.' That of course explained his physique. Tracy was wondering what his friend would be like, then he joined them. Another muscled bound hunk, she was impressed. 'Mark this is my Joanne and that's Tracy. It's your turn to buy the drinks, we'll find a table.' Three rounds later, Joanne signalled to Tracy and got up, heading for the loos.

'Do you like Mark?'

'With a body like his, he's got my vote!' A saucy grin accompanied Tracy's quip.

'Yes, a lot of the Marines look like that.' Tracy put more lip stick on and didn't bother to answer. 'Geoff wants me to go back to the hotel with him.' Tracy eyes swivelled to look at Joanne, her colour was heightened, and her eyes were sparkling.

'And you want to go?' Joanne nodded and chewed her lips before she answered.

'I'd meet you later and we'd go back together, you seem to be getting on okay with Mark, would you mind having a few more drinks with him while I go with Geoff?' Tracy turned away from the mirror and pouted.

'Doesn't Mark fancy me?' Joanne missed her meaning, totally.

'Please stop messing around, you don't mind, do you?' Tracy was about to enjoy herself at Joanne's expense, when she thought better of the idea. Joanne was a very serious minded young lady and if she was going back to the hotel with Geoff, she wouldn't appreciate any cheap innuendoes.

'I'm easy.' They returned to their table. Geoff was at the bar and Joanne went to help him carry the glasses. Tracy sat down next to Mark and gave him one of her inviting smiles before she spoke. 'The two love birds are off to bill and coo.'

'Nice for some!'

'That's just what I was thinking myself. I've been working flat out for the past three weeks and now I think I deserve some fun.'

Mark watched as Tracy flicked her hair back over her shoulder, then felt her press against his side as she edged even closer to him. Her sigh, which lifted her shoulders up, impressed him. Her tight fitted top, accentuated the pert shape of her breasts. She wriggled sexily as she crossed her legs. As she was now sitting practically on top of him, he got the full impact of her movements. Mark grinned at her and decided to have a go, after all, she might fancy a one night stand. She didn't look common, but was definitely a good time girl, anyway, she could always say no.

'You're a good looking and sexy chick, enough to drive a bloke bonkers.' She pouted at him, then blew him a kiss. Mark knew an invitation when he was given one. He swallowed the last of his beer and put his glass down, his left hand was now on her leg.

'Strong hands.' Tracy moved her legs as she spoke, so that his hand slipped in between her thighs and she held it there. 'I'm feeling very randy tonight.' Her voice oozed with sensuality. Mark didn't need to be asked a second time.

'We've got single rooms.' Tracy beamed at him.

'I thought you were my type of guy.' Mark grinned as he felt her slacken her leg muscles and he moved his hand up under the hem of her mini skirt. When she leaned across him, he kissed her, opening his lips avidly to push his tongue into her eager mouth. He could tell by the kiss that he was going to have a good time with her. She was hot.

'Getting very friendly?' Geoff's voice ended their kiss. He and Joanne were back at the table. Tracy sat up, a cheeky grin on her face as she asked.

'Where's the hotel, is it far?' Both the men said no. Joanne looked shocked and surprised. Surely Tracy wasn't going there with a man she had just met? But she was, any fool could see that. Joanne felt embarrassed. Under different circumstances she'd have told Tracy exactly what she thought about a girl throwing herself at a man and most probably having sex on a first date. Joanne had heard about love at first sight, that's the way it had been for Geoff and her, but they hadn't made love then, it wasn't for ages afterwards and besides, Tracy didn't look like she was in love, she just seemed very pleased with herself. That last round of drinks was swallowed almost at once. The other three were waiting, almost impatiently, for Joanne to finish. In the end, she left her's half drunk.

Joanne's conscience was bothering her, she felt that she should say something to Tracy, but what? She and Geoff were walking just behind the other two. Joanne could feel herself blush. She wasn't a prude, but Tracy's attitude had made this episode seem so shallow. It wasn't like that with her and Geoff, they were in love with each other. But Tracy was behaving as if she was going to a party or something. The way she giggled at Mark and egged him on. The remarks they were making to each other were sexually blatant and often, very crude. They soon reached the hotel and went into the lobby, it was small. The night porter was a disgruntled old man, but he pocketed the money Geoff handed to him and gave them their keys.

'What time do you have to be back?' Geoff had his arm around Joanne's shoulder, he couldn't understand what was wrong with her, she seemed upset about something, but he didn't know what.

'I said we'd be late so we'd get a taxi home, Dad doesn't like me using the tube after eleven.'

'Good girl.' The lift stopped with a little jerk. They all got out.

'We mustn't be too late.' Geoff looked at his wrist watch, it was just after ten.

'Two o'clock?'

'No, I'd get killed. Midnight, we have to leave then Tracy.' Geoff blinked at the tone in Joanne's voice.

'Fine, give me a knock.' She laughed at something Mark whispered in her ear. 'Bragging again!' Tracy's last remark was to Mark. Geoff opened his door and pushed Joanne gently into the room.

'What's the matter, didn't you want to come with me?' She turned and looked at him. She stood there, stiff and straight.

'That's not the point.'

'Then what is?'

'Tracy.' She said her name with disgust.

'What's the matter with her? She didn't have to come back here, she wanted to, what's she got to complain about?' Joanne spoke through gritted teeth.

'She isn't. I am.' Geoff walked up to Joanne and put his arms around her. 'Look love, you've lost me, I don't know what you're on about.' He could feel the temper in her body.

'How could she be like that, I thought she was a decent person.' He grinned as at last he understood.

'Don't jump to conclusions about Tracy, she just enjoys sex. Lots of people are like her.'

'But how?' Geoff just shook his head, smiling at Joanne's naiveté. She was stood like a ram rod in his arms.

'Don't think of her, just concentrate on me.' He hugged her, murmuring into her ear. 'You know the way I feel about you Joanne and I want to make love to you now, all you have to decide is whether you want me, do you?' She threw her arms around his neck and clung to him. When Geoff heard her sigh, he gave a little laugh, now she was beginning to relax. 'I was told yesterday that my posting will be through next week.' Her head flew up, her eyes shone. He grinned and added. 'Six weeks later I get my embarkation leave.'

'We can get married in January?' He nodded. 'Oh Geoff, I'm so excited, at last it can all be arranged. Nothing can stop us now, can it.'

'Not a thing.' Then Geoff lowered his head and started to kiss her very gently, coaxing her to respond to him. When he felt her lips move, he slipped his tongue gently into her mouth. It always took time to sexually stimulate Joanne, but once she was fully aroused, she seemed to loose her shyness of their intimacy. But so far, she was still very coy about their nakedness. She was willingly responding to him now and so he began to undress her, she still had her coat on. When at last he dropped her dress from her shoulders, Joanne was scarlet. It amused Geoff, because her underwear was large and very plain, it did well at camouflaging her body. He guessed that her mother had bought it, with the hope that if any man ever saw it, he'd give up trying to release the girl from it. And it really was ugly! He smiled at Joanne, thinking that when they were married, he'd buy her some really exotic things to wear. Joanne wasn't tall, but was very well rounded, with heavy breasts and plump hips, she had just the sort of body that turned him on. Not, that under different circumstances he couldn't have shown Tracy a good time, because he'd have been very willing, but she wasn't the type of women that he could love, Joanne was that.

'Please Geoff put the light off.' He moved and did so, but the neon light from the hotel sign was directly outside his window. He saw her look at the closed blind. 'Can't you do anything about that?' A strong orange glow filtered through it and filled the small room. He shook his head. He could tell she was about to panic at the thought of being seen naked.

'Close your eyes.'

'Me? What about you.' He walked back to her and hugged her.

'I'm not the shy type.'

'Oh.' He wrapped her in his arms and began kissing her. His hands explored her body. 'Geoff?' Her voice was muffled in his neck.

'What?'

'Do you think I'm fat?' He stepped back and held her at arm's length, then shook his head. She smiled gratefully at him. 'Shall we get into bed?'

'Not yet.' He pulled her very close. She pressed herself hard against him. He grinned, she was trying to hide herself and by doing that, was arousing him more. He started to kiss her again, now strongly urging her responses. When he heard her groan with excitement, it took him precisely three seconds to undo the six hooks at the back of her bra. And he didn't stop to let her think about it, because immediately his fingers found their way into the volumed enclosures and succeeded in capturing her nipples, seductively teasing and kneading her flesh. Geoff was very experienced sexually and had a strong hold over his own desires.

His mind soon went to his objective. He had to get rid of her knickers. He continued his onslaught with his passionate kisses. When he felt her tongue slip into his mouth, he sucked greedily at it and was confident that she was getting sexually, very excited. Her breasts heaved under his hands, she was panting. Geoff now lifted his head to watch her. Joanne stood there with her eyes closed and her mouth open, just as he'd left it and she was erotically moaning with each gasp she made. Geoff moved his hands to waist of her knickers; he was on his knees as they landed at her ankles. Straight away, he planted kisses on her lower stomach, while his fingers gently eased into her wetness. He felt her stiffen, but his words of adoration, as well as the movements of his fingers, soon effaced her shyness. Geoff didn't want Joanne to get disconcerted at the different ways they could make love. She'd been so afraid and shy the first time they had made love and he'd guessed that she didn't know an awful lot about sexual behaviour. He'd known from the start of their relationship, that he would have to take things very slowly with Joanne. But tonight he desperately wanted to taste her and hoped, that now she loved him enough to marry him, that she would let him. He knew he'd fully aroused her. Gently he coaxed her legs apart. And eased open her flesh so that he could see. To him, she was the epitome of womanhood. When his mouth claimed her, her wail of passion encouraged him and he felt relief surge through him. When he finally stood up in front of her, Joanne's eyes were open and they blazed with emotion.

'I love you so much Geoff.'

'I know that, and you know that I worship you.'

'You make me feel beautiful.'

'That's because you are.' He quickly stripped of his own clothes, then he took her face in his hands and kissed her. This time when he thrust his tongue into her mouth, he was delighted that she sucked hard at it. He knew that she was ready for him to enter her. But now that he'd tasted her, he wanted to feel her mouth claim him. He gave her one more passionate kiss, before releasing her mouth. Then with light pressure from his hands he guided her head slowly down his body. By her kisses he could tell that she was enjoying it and she had moved her hands to his erection herself. He edged his feet apart and asked her to kneel down. Joanne did so. She smiled devotedly up at him as she tentatively stroked his swollen member. He gave her time to experience this intimate contact. When her fingers began to move more seductively, Geoff brought her face into contact with his masculinity. At first she just gave him quick tiny pecks, then inevitably, her kisses became more sensual. He moved his feet slightly further apart and guided himself into her mouth. He felt her acceptance and when she started to explore with her tongue, Geoff groaned in satisfaction. At last he pulled Joanne to her feet and kissed her mouth hard to show her how urgently he wanted her. Then swept her off her feet and laid her on top of the bed. Her hands gripped the bed covers. Geoff stood over her for perhaps a minute, watching her heavy breasts heaving and her hips jerk up, as she waited for him. He grinned as she lay there panting, ready for him, and not trying to cover herself up in shyness over her nakedness. He had never seen Joanne so sexually provoking before. She was even telling him that she wanted to make love. Geoff had planed to enter her straight away, but now changed his mind and walked to the foot, where pushed her feet apart so that he could crawl up the bed. He stopped and knelt in between her legs then planted his hands each side of her elbows, to take his weight. The hard peaks of her nipples temptingly claimed his attention and his mouth watered in anticipation. Geoff hungrily devoured first one nipple, then the other. When he sat back up, her whole body was undulating with ecstasy. Now he parted the soft moist hair and opened the lips, which covered her femininity. Then let his thumbs erotically trace the exposed outline of her wet pink flesh. By now Joanne was gyrating exquisitely. She called out his name, but that wasn't all Geoff needed to hear. It wasn't enough, not tonight. His fingers continued to incite the boiling cauldron of her desires. When she raised her head and shoulders off the bed, her hands reached out to him. Her eyes implored, her voice passionately pleaded with him.

'Geoff. Oh God, my love. You know I'm burning inside for you. Please now, oh please Geoff, make love to me now, I need to feel you right in me.' Geoff lifted himself up, filled his lungs with air, then lunged straight into her. She landed flat under him, and cried out in ecstasy as he seared into her. His thrusts were fast and hard. Joanne met his frantic pace with equal passion.

Tracy laid back with a satisfied grin on her face. Mark had been good and she was now trying to recall the other Marine she'd once been with, he'd been a terrific performer too, but now she couldn't remember his name.

Chapter 9

As the coach pulled up, Maurice, who'd spent the entire journey, bustling in the aisle, walked to the front.

'You'll have to wait until I get the okay before going on board, but you can unload the luggage.' With a cheeky grin, he left with Joan.

'Doesn't it look huge?' Jasmine had been thinking the exact opposite, in fact, just welded pieces of metal, to keep them afloat in all those hundreds of square miles of ocean. She swivelled her head to gaze in panic at Tracy. 'Just think of all those delicious men swarming around in there!'

'It's not as big as I thought.' Mary stated in an off hand way. 'One of my brother's is in the Navy and he said that sixty thousand tons was a tidy size.' Jasmine had paled, only the thought of her father, stopped the girl turning tail and running.

'You'll be safer on that tub, than crossing the road.' Ginger Morris lent across Megan, determined to put his oar in. 'Statistically speaking, that is.'

'No man! No more of your superfluous information, not now.' Ted was stood in the aisle, 'and hadn't we better do as his lordship told us and get our stuff on the quay?' Where Maurice was concerned, Ted was only polite when actually facing him.

It was bitterly cold standing on the dock, but they didn't have long to wait. Rescue came in the shape of half a dozen deck hands and as Tracy bitterly pronounced, there wasn't a decent body amongst them. That remark drew general laughter from the rest of the group. In all, it didn't take them that much time to find their way around the ship. They all had deck plans and by the time they sailed the next evening, most of them knew the routes to the dining room and the main cabaret lounge. That was where the shows were being staged. Ted hadn't lost any time in getting friendly with the purser's assistant and went to bed the first night with a copy of the passenger list to study. It seemed on the surface to be loaded with possibilities, he made a mental list of four and dreamt that night of drowning in champagne!

Tina was seated in the small reading room, on the port side. Although the ship was still docked in Southampton, she felt as if she was a million miles away from Bill already. Ginger Morris was the only other person in there.

'So he's finally come to his senses and is ditching the bitch. Well I don't blame him, but I bet she takes him to the cleaners.' Bill's separation and divorce plans had made the front page of most of the daily papers. 'You were in his show, so I suppose this is no surprise eh?' Tina was aware of a pair of very shrewd eyes watching her; she'd been looking out at the dock and took her time, turning to face him.

'In fact, it is.'

'Who's he knocking off now, someone from the theatre?' Tina thought it best not to get into that discussion and just shrugged her shoulders. 'Dark horse eh?' Again, she felt as if she was being cross examined, was Ginger referring to Bill or herself? She gave a noncommittal answer and yawned. Ginger gave up and sauntered out onto the deck, going in search of Joan. He was curious why Tina, who's career would had been assured, if she'd stayed with the show, had left! But not show business, just a successful show, and that didn't make sense. He knew that Al Stein; the show's producer had wanted her to stay on for another year. What had made her leave so suddenly. Maybe she had a very personal reason for bowing out early. He thought it might be worth his while to find out a bit more about Miss Tina Wentworth. Ginger hated Melissa Croft, as she had been, when he'd known her, with a passion. He didn't like the idea of her getting rich by her dirty tricks, but if he was any judge of character and he was, that jerk she was running around with in town, wouldn't hesitate to strip her bare, if he could do it. Ginger chuckled, wouldn't that be something to see! She takes Bill for his rhino, then gets skinned herself. Ginger believed in poetic justice!

Tracy sat down to dinner in a despondent mood. She had never seen so many old people, or family groups in her life. Hardly any decent material amongst the passengers she'd seen coming aboard the liner. Then to top it all, as they set sail, Tina had burst into tears. God only knows why and never tells anyway! Megan had just stared, then abruptly left their cabin. Tracy had tried to offer some comfort, but Tina had climbed onto her bunk and turned her back. Then had come the lifeboat drill, it had been cold and miserable and brought home to every one of them, the fact that ships had been known to sink. Conversation wasn't very stimulating now either, most of it concerned sea sickness. Ginger was in his usual role of issuing a stream of facts that nobody else was interested in, even in the vaguest terms, but his voice kept droning on.

'By the way, isn't Tina at our table?' As she had been there yesterday evening and there was now an empty place next to him, it seemed like a prying question.

'She doesn't feel very hungry.' Tracy wasn't volunteering anything more.

'Getting her sea legs eh, hope she'll be all right for the Bay of Biscay, always rough.'

Jasmine, who was sat on the next table, but directly behind Ginger and so could easily hear what he was saying, was just about to put a piece of fish in her mouth. Mary laughed at the sudden change of her expression.

Charis was sitting with Mary and Jasmine at Maurice's table, there was no way she'd have sat at a table with Megan and Tracy. In fact she was disregarding all her fellow diners. She had been the first at that table and had taken a chair in the corner, so she was facing the rest of the room and therefore had an unrestricted view of all the other tables. She picked her meal carefully and ate it slowly. Her eyes constantly flicking over to the Chief Engineers table, by the starboard wall. She was peeling an orange when her glance was held riveted to the table she'd been watching. A thin, grey haired man was just sitting down. The headwaiter was holding his chair and somebody else placed his walking stick against the wall for him. Charis was sure that was him, the photograph in Tatler had been a good one. Charis hadn't taken this job with any other idea, than that of enjoying the trip, and being able afterwards, to brag that she'd cruised the Caribbean and the Far East. But then she'd read that Lord Daniel Hill, was travelling to Australia by sea, for his health's sake. He was getting over a mild heart attack. The reporter, being witty, had volunteered the news, that Lord Hill's indisposition, as he had no money problems, was solely due to the fact that he had only three daughters from his first marriage! With the sudden death of his younger brother, the title would now go to a second cousin, which the old man detested! The article had disclaimed a future marriage as, not on! Lord Hill had been a widower for the past twenty years and was too long in the tooth to be caught. The Honourable Miss Barbara Cole, knew this to her cost and had been trying to alter that situation for the past three years. Then it had ended by adding that maybe she'd have better luck now the stakes were more in her favour, (even if she was approaching her fortieth year and tended to resemble her horses). After all, his Lordship was an extremely wealthy peer. The idea of becoming the next Lady Hill and produce a male heir had popped into Charis's head, she was addicted to historical romances. The nights during the middle week of the rehearsals had been spent in pleasant day dreaming. But the more she'd thought about it, the clearer it had become. Then it became not so much a pipe dream, as a pension plan for her future. That he was sixty years old and his daughters were all older than her, didn't matter.

Tina stood at the stern of the ship and watched the English Channel disappear from her view. She wasn't crying any more, but still felt that she wanted to be by herself. The one thought that kept her sane was knowing that she could write to him. Bill had arranged for her to send her letters to his agent, addressed to Mr. Willam, they would be safe from discovery that way. The wind whipped at her, but she wasn't conscious of the cold, only her pain of loneliness. She'd known that Bill was married at the very beginning, and the relief she'd felt when she'd learnt that his marriage was over was so immense for her. Tina was honest enough to acknowledge that if he had not wished to divorce his wife, but had been happy in his marriage, she'd have found herself in a blind canyon, which ever way she chose to walk, there could have been only grief and sadness. She loved Bill and knew that whatever conditions he'd proposed, she would have accepted. She could not think of her future without him in it.

That night Tracy and Megan were sitting at a table in the Neptune bar, the place was decorated in blues and greens and the artist had let his imagination run riot in the colours of the fishes, diving in and out of the waves around the walls. Tracy had changed into a mini dress for dinner, Megan had her trouser suit on. They had been sitting there for about an hour.

'Doesn't look like there's much talent around.' Megan shrugged her shoulders, personally she thought that Tracy was a fool hopping from one man to the next for the momentarily relief of physical satisfaction. Megan knew that she would have an entirely different attitude to sex if she had a choice, but she was desperate for the money. When she'd first tried to find where her mother was, Megan had found out just how expensive private investigators were to hire. That's where most of her money went. And she disagreed with Tracy on the lack of available males, because sat at a table across from them was a middle aged couple,

Megan assumed that they were married. The wife hadn't stopped moaning since they'd come in, he was pretending to listen. At last the female got up and marched out of the bar, Megan gave him a sympathetic smile and he'd arrived at her table with the offer of drinks. After ten minutes Tracy had yawned and offered Megan a polite way out, she'd declined.

'My wife isn't a very good traveller.' Megan knew his type, flashy! He'd made his own money and wanted everybody to be impressed. Also he had a high regard for the sound his own voice and views. She just sat there and listened. She knew from experience where to nod and smile. She stayed for about half an hour then said she ought to leave. He stood up with her and they left together. Megan didn't tell him to keep his hands to himself when he opened the door for her, or when he protected her from the wind as they walked along the outside gangway to the lobby on that deck.

'I have enjoyed our little chat.' She'd paused and smiled encouragingly at him. 'We must do it again, just the two of us.' Her emphasis was on the word two. He looked straight at her and began to leer. They had reached the lift, he punched the button and it opened at once. No sooner had they stepped inside and the doors had closed, than he grabbed her, slobbering at her mouth. She let him, then pushed him back as it stopped and the doors opened. He checked to see that there was nobody within earshot.

'Is there anywhere private where we can talk tonight?' They were now on the Promenade deck and Megan suggested the reading room. He hurried her along and she heard his breath hiss through his teeth on finding it empty. Megan let him kiss her again and this time he pulled her hard against his bulk. He was fat. 'Are you in a single cabin?' She shook her head. 'Shame, that would have made it simple.' She smiled, but said nothing, she was waiting for the right opportunity to mention money. 'You're very young and pretty.' His eyes raked over her. She kept her shoulders straight as his large hands went inside her jacket, pawing at her breasts. 'That looks like an expensive outfit you've got on.' She kept her steady gaze on his face, this was it, the chance to let him know her terms.

'It is and I am.' He didn't pretend to misunderstand and grinned at her.

'Playing it straight up front, I like that. How much?' She handed him the ball, it was in his court, now it was up to him, he could either play or walk away.

Tracy lay in her bunk and briefly wondered what could be keeping Megan. Then her mind went back to last Saturday night. Mark had been very entertaining in the sack. In fact she'd had to scramble into her clothes when they'd heard the knock at the bedroom door. Tracy had flung it open, ready with a witty remark, but never uttered it. Her planned banter had disintegrated. Tracy had been so surprised at Joanne, she'd looked so different than when she'd last seen her. Joanne had stood there glowing with an inner radiance and beauty, Tracy had only been able to stare. A basic jealousy had flickered through Tracy, not that she wanted Geoff, she didn't, just the inherent longing to experience love. Or did she? What would that do to her philosophy on life?

Ted inspected his appearance critically. Tonight was the Captain's welcoming aboard party and the cast of the show were counted on to attend, as part of the crew. He had no intention of missing it, it was the ideal opportunity to evaluate the four possibilities that he'd decided on from the list he'd studied. The lounge was already crowded as he edged his way forward, then veered as he saw Maurice loom into view. That was one person who he intended to keep well clear of. Megan was standing with Tina, they looked stunning. Tina was in a full length black velvet dress which fitted beautifully, accentuating her slender curves; Megan had a short, tight emerald green sequin cocktail dress on and the sparkle in her eyes, out did the glitter.

'You two look great.' Tina's smile was perfunctory; Megan grinned, she was pleased that the stuff Maurice had given her, had made up so well. 'You remind me of somebody.' Megan stared hard at him before she answered him.

'Who?' He grinned and shrugged his shoulders nonchalantly. Megan wasn't that interested in Ted's past life to press for more information. Ted made a couple more casual remarks then drifted off. He'd caught a mention of one of the names he wanted and discreetly homed in on it. If she wasn't ninety, she appeared it, had bad breath and looked vicious. Ted swallowed and backed unobtrusively away. One down, three to go. The second on his list, banished the thought of the other two from his mind. Good figure, even if she was a little plump, but then, he told himself, he didn't like skinny women anyway. The dress she was wearing was a model and the pearls around her neck, hadn't come from Woolworth's. And she looked to be in her late forties. Just the right age! It took him five minutes to get into her conversation and within twenty, he was sure she was interested in him. Life, he considered, was brightening up very beneficially.

Ted found out that Mrs. Diana Allsop was on the second dinner, so after he'd finished his own meal, he'd gone to the Neptune bar. He'd been there for about two hours and was contemplating going in search of her, when an red painted finger nail, tapped on his shoulder.

'I thought I might find you here.' Her smile was everything he'd hoped it would be. He offered to buy her a drink, she refused, insisting that she would pay. She ordered a bottle of champagne. It was an informative evening for Ted. He learnt that her money came from Argentinian beef and she was leaving the ship at Cartagena, the port of call before the Panama Canal. That gave him just over a week, he figured that would be ample time. He managed quite resolutely to control his grin when she asked him back to her stateroom for a night cap and just smiled warmly at her as he consented. They went via the Pursers office, where she deposited her jewellery. Ted followed her like a well-trained lackey.

There were two shows and a fancy dress ball, before they docked in Cartagena. Diana asked Ted to go to the dance as Anthony, to her Celopatra, he'd accepted, she'd provide the costumes. It seemed she had her life completely organised, down to the smallest detail. Ted never actually spent the whole night in her stateroom, just the late evening, she always asked him to leave at around three in the morning. She'd told him that they would eat in her stateroom, before the fancy dress ball, it was her last night on board the ship. Ted had soaked for an hour in the bath tub, then painstakingly shaved and used the after shave she'd given him. He gloated over the cost of it. He dressed hurriedly, she really had got to him, she was so sexy and knew how to please a man as well as be satisfied herself. Thinking of her body was making him randy and he tried to ignore the erection that was beginning to build. But the more vivid his metal picture of her was, the stronger his desire became. As he walked to her cabin, he was glad his slacks were loose fitting.

Diana had told Ted to be there at six o'clock and he was prompt.

'We'll eat a little later, your costume's on my bed, come and see if it fits.' Ted closed the door behind him and turned the key. He didn't want any interruptions while he was occupied with Diana. He followed her through the archway. She leant back against the cabin wall. The silk wrap she was wearing fell open, flaunting all her naked voluptuous curves. 'Strip off and try it on, you should look good in it.' He kicked his sandals off, his shirt and slacks were dumped onto a near by chair. 'And those.' A red fingernail indicated his jockey shorts, which were stretched taught across his swollen member. He did as he was told and stood there displaying his erection. He glanced at her and was relieved to find that sensual smile she had, playing on her lips. He breathed in and shifted his feet, knowing that she was pleased with his body and thrilled by his performances in bed. 'Maybe we should leave the costume fitting until later, you can't walk round with that bulge sticking out of Anthony's skirt!' A sexy throb had sounded in her voice. Ted grinned as he swaggered over to where she was stood.

He stopped in front of her and groaned as she cupped his masculinity. His fingers went straight in between her legs and felt the wetness already there. He leant his body fully against her and kissed her mouth hard. Then he walked her over to the dressing table, not wasting time on petting with her. After another passionate kiss, Ted turned Diana around to face the mirror; then slipped her wrap from her shoulders and dropped it onto the floor. She leant forward spreading her hands flat on the surface, slopping her shoulders so that her full breasts hung heavily, like succulent melons in some tropical forest; her dark nipples, as alluring as the large petals of an exotic flower, burgeoning in the heat. Ted gaped at her reflection. He was already panting as he pushed her legs apart and gripped her hips; he pulled her back onto his full erection, drilling rapidly into her. Reflected in the mirror, Diana's breasts swung with the motion. Ted revelled at the sight, his thrusts became uncontrolled, and he climaxed before her. Her snarl of frustration brought him back to earth; but he recovered immediately. He knelt down and twisted her to face him, then buried his face in her wetness, working erotically with his mouth and tongue. Within a very few minutes, he felt her shudder as her orgasm peaked. Then he sat back on his heels, but his fingers still stroked her intimately. Ted stared at Cartagena as the ship left the port, he couldn't believe that she'd just been using him as a diversion, to enlighten a boring voyage. Diana had laughed in his face when he'd proposed marriage. She'd calmly stated that she was very satisfied being single and wasn't about to throw away her freedom of choice for any wedded bliss that he could offer! Adding that he couldn't emulate the one marriage she'd already had! She hadn't been nasty or unpleasant to him, just practical. Ted had felt that she'd patted him on the head, told him that although his services had been faultless, that they were now, no longer required. 'How,' he'd asked himself, 'could I have been taken in so easily?' He was supposed to be dealing the cards, not her. And he'd really cooked his goose for the rest of this trip! He couldn't make a play for another female now. He'd been so sure of himself, that his attentions towards Diana, had been blatant enough to broadcast his intentions to everyone else on board the liner. He fumed to himself that he'd been stupid enough to fall for her act. He'd have to wait now, until the first cruise out of Australia and hope that there was a decent prospect presented then.

From the tail of his eye, Ted caught sight of Megan, and again a distant flash of memory flickered, then faded. He walked on with a careless shrug.

Chapter 10

The liner's approach to the locks at the Caribbean end of the Panama Canal had brought most of the passengers and the cast of the show, out onto the decks. The younger generation darted from one side of the ship to the other, shouting their views in a direct challenge to the information coming over the loud speaker system being used on board and anyone unfortunate to be within hearing, had to clap their hands over their ears in self protection. Once in the lake, which formed the major part of the Canal, breakfast resumed its important roll.

'I've just been speaking to them!' The cabin door had swung open. Megan looked up and shook her head, but grinned, in spite of herself. 'Power to the people! Especially the Jones. Fab bunch!' Tracy was now doing a sort of triumphant ritual jig in the middle of their limited space. 'Great gang, it couldn't have happened to a nicer lot!' Tina was sat on the end of her bunk, with her legs curled under her. She'd read her letter a dozen times since she'd received it, but she was still very excited over it, clasping it in both her hands.

Megan was at the other end of the bed, sewing the narrowest of hems on a long skirt of black chiffon, another of Maurice's pieces. She'd gathered the length and fitted it onto a black satin waist band. That material had been bought at a remnant stall in the Portabello market with her first weeks rehearsal money. She'd been lucky enough to get three matching off cuts of the Duchess satin, which she'd been able to make into a full length straight skirt, a fitted top, with very narrow straps, the waist band for the chiffon skirt and a Dorothy bag. 'Come on you two, you've gotta be interested?'

'No' Megan didn't lift her head from her sewing. Tina carried on with her day dreams, she was absorbed in her own abstractions.

'But 'ye canno be ignoring this ere gem.' Tracy's attempt at imitating the Gordie accent was atrocious and sounded as if she was trying, and failing utterly, to speak Mongolian with a Welsh accent.

'Go away, I want to wear this tonight.' Tracy's attention veered away from her new friends, to Megan's wardrobe.

'I thought you were keeping that for Christmas Eve? We're all going to wear something special to watch to passengers strut their stuff! Of course the Jones's are going to star, Olivia is going to sing 'Rocking Around The Christmas Tree' and the twins will do the, 'Twelve Days of Christmas.' So what do you think of that?'

'Not together!' Megan had made the remark, but hadn't stopped sewing.

'Ha, bloody ha!' Megan tried to keep her face straight, but had to resort to a grimace. Tracy this time reeled off a couple of steps stolen from the horn pipe. She chanted, in a loud soprano. 'Can't fool me, can't fool me!' Then spun round. 'Unless some real hunk got on at Cartagena and I missed him.' Megan gave up and folded her sewing away.

'You win, I'll come clean, Elvis Presley is aboard and I'm out to knock him off.' For perhaps half a second, Tracy stared at her.

'You're a lying little dragon.'

'Okay, I am, but I still don't want to hear about the Jones clan.' Megan had done her own homework on them and found out, that although Bert Jones was a regular flirt, he wasn't on the look out for extra sex and his eldest son was too young.

'Well you're going to. Mind you kid, this is only a rough translation, Daddy Jones won the pools and has treated the family to this trip.'

'All of them?' Megan sounded astonished. 'Generous of him.' Tracy nodded solemnly.

'Well from what I can gather, they all live in the same house.' Megan did a quick calculation on her fingers.

'God! I'm glad I don't live with them! I can't imagine being confined with eight other people in one house, it must be bedlam.' Megan had achieved a horrifying expression, but Tracy only chuckled.

'Actually it's an old farm house, there's bound to be plenty of rooms.'

'Does he really farm it then, Mr. Jones, I mean?'

'Bert.'

'I suppose you're now on first names terms with them all?'

'Well they're a great bunch and loads of laughs, I'm going ashore with them in Acapulco, want to come?' Megan was tempted, but she had an appointment with a customer, as soon as his wife was safely off the ship.

'I've got some odd jobs to get done first, so I won't be going into the town until about two o'clock and then I must do some shopping. Sorry!'

'It's bound to be a scream.' Tracy turned to Tina and poked her shoulder. 'Want to join us?' Tina didn't trust herself to speak, she also had a special, but very private appointment, her's was with a telephone, it was all arranged for after they docked. So she just shook her head.

Charis had been studying her prey for days and now she inconspicuously watched as Lord Hill left the dinning room after his lunch. She followed him at a discreet distance. Two minutes after he'd sat down in the reading lounge, she'd entered it. 'Excuse me, but did I leave my book in here?' Her voice was pleasant and sounded educated. Charis had realised when she first left home, that she wanted to change her speaking voice. It had taken her two years of hard work, to lose her local accent. Lord Hill looked up from his newspaper and glanced around. Charis moved into the room and picked up her volume of Mein Kampf from the table, near his usual chair. 'Here it is. I'm so glad that I haven't mislaid it.' He held his hand out, his expression was hard to read, but Charis smiled at him, as she handed him her book.

'An unusual volume for a young girl.' The movement of her head acknowledged that fact, before she'd answered him.

'I think everyone should have some interest in the man who was responsible for the Second World War.' He nodded at her, sucking in his thin lips. Charis gave herself a point for quoting him and getting away with it. Her ambition was not only to make an impression that he would remember, but he must be favourably influenced by it as well. He gave her the book back, as he asked.

'Are you interested in Modern History?'

'Passionately.' His eyes lit up and he invited her to sit down. Charis led with a question on the Treaty of Versailles and when that topic had been summarily dealt with, a query on the Assassination of President Kennedy kept Lord Hill talking for another hour. Then she asked, smiling shyly at him, would he mind giving her his thoughts on why the Duke of Windsor felt he had to abdicate. That took care of the rest of that afternoon. 'Yes, I totally agree with you.' She sat back, her hands clasped around the book on her lap. 'Could I presume on your kindness again after we sail from Acapulco?' He smiled at her eagerness. 'I find you are stimulating my mind, and your views are so very well thought out.' She achieved a contented sigh, then continued. 'I'm enthralled by the way you express them.' Here she achieved a long, thankful sigh. 'There really is no substitute for a well educated and informed mind.' Another quote she'd given in the most innocent and natural manner, had made his chest swell.

'Of course my dear, I would be delighted.'

Megan was on an upper deck as the liner approached Acapulco. The breeze which lifted her hair, made it comfortable to stand there. The ship anchored in the bay. She could see her customer leant against the rail on the deck below her, he was also watching the launch approach the from the harbour. His wife, as well as Tracy and all the Jones clan, were among the first passengers to leave. Megan saw him look at his watch and then hurry off. She straightened her shoulders and went down to D deck, there she easily found the cabin she'd been told to go to. She didn't knock, just walked in and carefully closed the door behind her.

'Lock it.' She did so. 'Strip off, I want to see what I'm paying for.' Without the least show of embarrassment, Megan pulled the cotton shift dress over her head, took off her bra and panties, then stepped out of her shoes. She kept her gaze on him, looking directly into his eyes. He was already sweating and his heavy chest started to heave as he drooled over her young nubile body. 'Let's hope you're as good as you look.' She didn't speak. 'Come on and take my clothes off, I like that sort of thing.' Megan gave a faint, knowledgeable smile as she moved towards him. Tentatively, but not too slowly, she undid his shirt buttons and pushed it back from his shoulders, then went behind him, to take it off. She filled her lungs with air before she returned to her original position in front of him. 'Get a move on, I'm not paying for more than one hour and I will get my monies worth out of you, so don't think I won't.' It didn't take Megan very long to finish undressing him and finally she knelt down to take his sandals off. She flinched as he twisted his fingers roughly in her hair, then pulled her face to his groin. She told herself that it was work and to get on with it.

Albert grunted in gratification as he felt her hands and mouth start to stimulate him. He didn't mind paying her, but he was determined to get value, all he intended to do was lay back and enjoy it. She was going to do all that was necessary to satisfy him. He still had his hands gripped in her hair, and when he was ready, he yanked her up to face him. 'Now let's see how well you ride, but first give me a kiss.' He held her head and shoved his tongue straight into her mouth and grinned to himself as he felt her suck it. He was glad she was a professional and knew her job well. When he raised his head, he let go of her hair and got onto the narrow bunk. As Megan went to put her leg across him he stopped her. 'Not yet you silly little cow, we've still got plenty of time. I want some real nice and friendly attention from you first. Now get on with it.' Albert leered as she placed her nipple in his mouth, he gripped her flesh in his teeth and sucked hard. He felt her hand creating miracles on his swollen member. He was gasping for breath when he let go of her breast. 'Bitch! Mount me now! Let's hope you're a good little fucker, or you'll suffer.'

Megan wasn't afraid of his threats, but didn't bother arguing the case. She had no intention of leaving until his hour was up, so he'd have nothing to complain about. She slid into position quickly and efficiently; and it wasn't long before she felt him climax. She stayed straddled across him for a couple of minutes while he got his breath back. Then lifted herself up, off him and moved from the bed. 'And where the hell do you think you're going.' His voice was still belligerent.

'Nowhere.' She was calm. He glared at her.

'Get back here now.' Megan turned back to him. She flinched slightly as he shoved his fingers into her. She knew that she would have to keep him better occupied for the reminder of his time, otherwise he would hurt her.

'Wouldn't you prefer to kiss me instead?' He pulled his hand free.

'Half a good idea. But as it's me paying you, you're the one going to be using your mouth. It's been years since I've been on the receiving end of a good suck.' Megan didn't pretend to misunderstand him and slowly nodded her head, she accepted that this was the best she could hope for. 'Get these pillows right so I can watch.' Megan did as she was told and propped Albert against the head board. His fat legs sprawled out on the narrow bunk. Megan gingerly got into position between his knees and screwed up her eyes, forcing her mind to think of anything else, but what she was about to do.

When Albert sat up straight, the flesh of his stomach, laid on his thighs. He couldn't remember when he'd last enjoyed having sex. This had been well worth arranging and he planned to do it again. He looked at his watch, five minutes over the hour. She was already asking enough, he wasn't offering her any more. He licked his lips as he eyed her firm young breasts disappearing into her bra, and licked his lips, as she put her panties back on. He ogled her supple body as she bent over and picked her dress up, then watched avidly as she slipped it over her head and pulled it into place. 'My wife's involved in this amateur night on the twenty third. You free for an hour that afternoon?'

'Yes.'

'Right, I'll fix up a cabin, same price?' Megan nodded her head. Albert heaved himself onto his feet and crossed over to the draw where he'd put his wallet. He paid her. She folded the notes up small and clasped them in the palm of her hand. 'Just one more little kiss before you go.' She complied with this, then unlocked the door and left.

Tina walked back to the ship in a pleasant day dream. She'd spent over an hour in a small telephone booth at the main Post Office in town. Her worry that some technical hitch, would postpone or cancel it all together, never materialized and now she was very happy. Just to hear his voice had been wonderful. The line had been clear and their time had passed far too quickly. The sob in her voice as she'd said goodbye, had been echoed in Bill's. But now she had good news to help carry her through the remainder of the voyage. His lawyers had given him the date for his divorce hearing and it was only two months away. After that, it would be just six weeks for the decree absolute to come into force, then he would finally be free. Tina could hardly wait for next April to arrive.

Most of the cast were stood on the promenade deck, watching the lights from Acapulco receding into the darkness.

'It's Olivia Jones's birthday on the fifteenth and we're all invited to a knees up in the Neptune bar. There's no show, so you can all go if you want too.' Maurice's voice sounded benevolent. Ted clamped his teeth together and swallowed hard.

'Gee thanks.' Was Tracy's remark and as Maurice had his back to her, he hadn't seen the mock curtsy she'd performed.

'That's tonight, isn't it? Well, it's already after midnight!' Everyone grinned at Doreen. Ted moved closer to her as he spoke.

'Quick, aren't you?'

'Only sometimes!' The banter was friendly. Ted had swung an attentive arm around Doreen's shoulders, but unable to resist the prominence of her breast, he'd dropped his hand onto her cleavage. 'No thanks Ted!'

'Just checking to make sure they're real.' She gave him a cool look before she spoke again.

'As you see me change during the shows and there doesn't seem to be anything wrong with your eye sight, you should know by now that they're as authentic as you can get.' Her voice was light, but firm and he knew that she wasn't going to take any nonsense from him. They drifted off, it was late and everyone was tired.

'Hey Kid, it's lunch time already.' All three of them, were laying on their bunks. 'Come on Tina, just a couple of drinks! Olivia wants us all to go.' Tracy got up and stood in front of her. 'I'll nag you all afternoon, if that's what it takes.'

'O hell Tina, you'll have to come, you can't put us through that sort of torture.' Tina looked at Megan, then Tracy.

'Okay, but only for a little while.'

'Great!'

'So now you're satisfied. What are you going to wear?' Tracy turned and swung open her wardrobe door, then got out a white dress.

'Gosh, that's pretty material.' Tina was genuinely impressed with Tracy's dress.

'What there is of it.' Megan's voice was dry.

'Feel it, it's fringed silk.' Tina obediently ran her fingers over the fabric. 'It fits me like a glove.'

'You mean, were it touches.' Megan couldn't resist adding her mite to the conversation.

'And I suppose your mini skirts would pass muster at the convent?' Megan shrugged her shoulders and grinned.

Ted opened his cabin door as Tina and Megan passed him. He stepped out and joined Tracy. 'Can you actually sit down in that dress without being indecent?'

'Only if I keep my knees together.' Tracy giggled as Ted nodded his head. 'Doesn't Tina look gorgeous.' His eyes scanned the flowing chiffon moving in front of him. The folds fell freely from the high neck, to the hem that swished over the ground. 'But then, she always does.' He cast a quick look at Tracy, but there wasn't any envy in her tone, just praise for a friend.

'Maurice has excellent taste in dancers, and that's about all I can say in his favour.' Tracy's chuckle bubbled in her throat, but he carried on. 'Megan's skirt isn't that much longer than yours either.'

'She made it and that halter top she's got on.' Ted scrutinised the silver lame walking ahead of him.

'Well, she looks good too. I wish I could remember who she reminds me of. It must be an old girl friend.'

Charis stormed into her cabin and slammed the door shut behind her. Lord Hill had left the ship without telling her. It riled her that he'd not even bothered to send a message via a steward. Nothing. 'Damn him to hell and back.' She pulled the copy of Tatler out of a drawer and tore it up into pieces. Then she sat down and burst into tears. An hour later she was still fuming, she showered and changed, then gone to the Neptune bar. Charis had started on large bourbon's, on the rocks. By eleven o'clock, she was sat with a silly smile on her lips and was still drinking far too quickly

Kevin had watched her all evening. In fact he'd been trying to get to know her ever since she had come aboard the liner in Southampton. Something about her had attracted him when he'd first seen her, but she had been difficult to talk to. He'd tried and although she spoke politely when he got near to her, she'd always managed to isolate herself from him very efficiently, before he could inaugurate a conversation with her. Out of habit he looked at his watch, but as he wasn't on duty again until six in the morning, he picked up his glass and walked over to the empty chair by Charis.

'Can I get you another drink.' She blinked at him, tried to keep her focus and nodded. The action made her even more dizzy. 'Fancy some fresh air?' He helped her to stand and guided her staggering steps out into the cool night. She reeled unsteadily. 'Should I see you back to your cabin.'

'Yes.' Her reply was uttered in a slurred but audible voice. He had to totally support her with an arm around her waist. She leant gratefully against him. 'Where's your key?' Charis held out her bag. He opened her purse, found it, then unlocked the door. As he released her, her knees buckled, but Kevin was agile enough to save her from falling and carried her inside.

'I'm going to be sick.' Kevin pushed the bathroom door open with his foot and heaped her in front of the loo, then left her to it. Ten minutes later she emerged into her cabin, rather pale, but able to walk by herself. 'Thank you, you have been most kind.' Her tone was aloof, even icy.

'Don't mention it.' He got up and walked to the door. 'Good night.'

'Please, I'm sorry, I didn't mean it to come out that way. Do you have to go?' Kevin turned around to face her, she looked fragile, like a china doll. A gentle smile softened his expression and he shook his head. 'You're one of the engineering officers aren't you?'

'Yes.'

'I'm not mechanical at all.' She was still stood by the bathroom door. Her voice had thawed a fraction, but that was all. He couldn't see any point in prolonging this conversation.

'Look, you're most probably feeling tied, I think I will go.' To his amazement, tears welled in her eyes and began to fall. Two strides and he'd reached her. 'Please don't cry.' She sagged against him and began to sob on his chest. He comforted her. 'Feel better now?'

'Yes thanks.' Charis clung to him like a young animal in need of warmth. Kevin held her close against his body. 'I can feel your heart beating.' Her voice now purred like a kitten. He closed his eyes and screwed up his face, but forced himself to say.

'I really have to go.' He felt her move in his embrace, moulding herself against him. To him it was a caress. He wanted to make love to her, but to push a female into that scenario, was against his nature, he could never take advantage, in that way. 'Charis, I can't stay here with you any longer.' As she'd raised her head from his chest, he found it easy to lose himself in her tear drenched eyes.

'But I want you to be with me, honestly I do.' Kevin swallowed hard.

'You don't seem to realise what you're doing to me.'

'Of course I do, I'm not a child.' His eyes opened wide and he stared at her, his heart was pounding uncomfortably fast. Then he felt her move her hands from his back, to slide erotically over his masculinity.

'Oh God, I want you so badly, don't do that if you don't intend me to stay the night and sleep with you.'

'Is that all you want to do? Here's me thinking you had something else on your mind.' There was a gently mocking laugh in her voice. 'Don't you intend to use this hard member in me?' Her fingers had found their way into his trousers and were erotically stroking his erection.

'You mean that?'

'Of course I do.' His lips found hers and a groan of relief surged through him. This is what he wanted, to make love to her. Now maybe his future life would have more meaning after all.

Charis didn't want to think any more tonight about Lord Hill, she'd solve that difficulty tomorrow, for tonight, she'd let her senses take over and hope to enjoy the relaxation of physical reaction.

Chapter 11

'Is it really the twenty first of December already?' Tina grinned at the amazement in Tracy's voice, as she confirmed the date. They were standing at the stern of the ship. The only activity to watch, besides the vast expanse of moving water, was an electric storm, executing its grand performance on the horizon. 'Isn't nature awesome?' Tracy dragged out the last syllable.

'Very.'

'Like being in love?' Tracy didn't turn her head to look at Tina, just slanted her eyes sideways, so that she could catch Tina's reaction.

'Yes.' The simplicity of her answer did not rob it of the depth of feeling conveyed in that one word. Tracy was satisfied, the dates that Tina had turned down, now made sense. She let her attention drift back to the view and asked.

'What's the show tomorrow?'

'Rio Carnival.' Although Tina had replied, it was obvious that her mind was far away, as she let a long, wishful sigh escape.

'You miss him that much?' There wasn't a moments hesitation.

'Yes, and,' Tina continued as she read Tracy's mind, 'it's not only making love, but also the tenderness we share.' Tina hugged herself, then added. 'There's hundreds of different ways I ache. Oh, I can't explain properly, but I can tell you, I can't wait to see him again. To be with him, no matter what, that's all I want.' Tracy whistled softly, there really wasn't anything she could say.

It had been arranged with Maurice that a Christmas grotto, including elves and a fairy, would take place on the afternoon of the twenty third. He'd persuaded his pianist to act as Santa Claus, he was a big fat chap, with a jolly personality and perfect for the part. Tracy and Megan were jubilant as elves and Tina was enchanting as a fairy. The shipping company had provided the presents for the children and the photographer was kept occupied all afternoon.

The passengers amateur night was a success, everyone treated it as a special evening and dressed for the occasion. Captain Beamish was sitting at his table at the front. His florid complexion heightened by the exaggerated complements issuing from Mrs. Jones. Her clan was offering three, of the eight turns that evening. The show opened with an American giving a reasonable imitation of Frank Sinatra. That was followed by a pretentious girl of eleven, reciting Rudyard Kipling's 'Song of the Galley Slaves', which was politely, if not enthusiastically received. Next, Mrs. Jones's twins rendition of the 'Twelve Days of Christmas', with their own personal interpretation of mimes to go with the words, left the audience in hysterics. But they came back to earth when a gangly teenager, performed the Dance of the Swans, from Swan Lake. Then relief came in the shape of Granddad Jones. He hobbled into the centre of the cabaret floor, with the aid of his walking stick. Everything about him was remarkably grey. His hair was as untidy as his full shaggy beard. His watery eyes, even his skin had not been touched by the sun and his suit was also a washed out grey; his son's money hadn't had any influence on this wardrobe. The old man's face didn't change from the morose expression which was his habitual one, but after he'd finished with 'Sam, Pick Up Thy Musket', the audience was once more laughing. Olivia's song was also a hit, but the magician that followed her, was a clumsy let down. The finale act was from a little man and he easily brought the house down, with his Benny Hill jokes.

Christmas Day itself passed in a flow of cocktails and champagne. That night's dinner was excellent and the entrance of the chef, leading a massive flaming pudding, precipitated spontaneous applause from the diners. The carol service, during that evening, was well received.

'It's a good job we don't have to dance tonight, I can hardly walk!' Tracy had sprawled herself in a chair.

'I don't know how you manage to eat as much as you do and stay so slim, I couldn't.' Tracy laughed at Mary.

'It's all that extra curriculum exercise I get. That keeps me in trim!'

'I've been on a diet since I was fourteen.' There had been resignation in Mary's voice.

'Oh God, I couldn't be doing with that.'

'Tracy, I just don't have any option. If I ate like you, I'd be the size of house in a month.'

'Oh you poor kid.' Mary shrugged her shoulders.

'It's something I've had to get used to over the years.' Jasmine looked at Mary. She hadn't really thought about her own diet. At home her meals had all been planned for her, she hadn't even had to help with the cooking, or washing up, everything had been done for her.

'You must have a slow metabolism!'

'What ever you say Tina, all I know is that its worth it, I don't think I could ever be fat and happy.' Mary had ended with a grin.

'And I know that's a typical dancer's attitude.' Tracy added her bit with a smirk.

'We'd willingly starve to look good.' The rest of them agreed with her.

'Oh what a good sin, vanity is!' Tracy still mocked.

'As long as its not taken to extremes.' The mental picture of Bill's wife, had flitted across Tina's mind as she'd spoken. Mary nodded in agreement as she'd answered.

'I suppose you're right, everything in moderation.' Jasmine was finding it easier with each passing day to be in the company of Tracy and Tina. Of course, she never went anywhere without Mary.

'Don't include sex in that!' The Liverpool accent was very prominent and Tracy had sounded outraged.

'To hear you talk', Mary put her hands on her hips as she grinned at Tracy, 'you'd think that you're a sex maniac and you're not. I heard you turn down that pimply creature yesterday and that gross fat slob the day before.'

'So what! I bet you've never seen me turn down a real hunk! That's my weakness. Any male over six foot, with a good body and I'm his for the taking!' Mary grinned as she said.

'Go on then, tell us. When exactly did you last have sex?' Tracy sheepishly looked at her.

'Just because I haven't had a good romp for a week, doesn't mean that I'm thinking of becoming celibate, I'd make a bloody hopeless nun.' She assumed a preposterous expression. 'There's no need to laugh at me, I'm very serious.' Mary chuckled as she stated.

'Not at you, just with you, you dope.'

'Oh well, that's all right then. Besides, we're at Tahiti tomorrow and you never know your luck, I just might manage to find some gorgeous hunk, who'll make me so randy, I'll seduce him on the spot.'

'No you won't. You treat sex like tennis, and we all know that you need a good court to enjoy a congenially satisfying game!' Jasmine's appreciative giggle, to Mary's remark, took everybody by surprise.

'You're blossoming alright.' The Scouse sense of humour ended their conversation on a high note.

The island of Tahiti seemed mystical to the six girls. They'd asked Charis to join them and to their surprise, she hadn't refused this time.

'You can see why Gauguin was so attracted to this place.' Jasmine was standing with the others, looking inland at the richness of vegetation and colour.

'Who?' Tina was the one to answer Tracy's question.

'He's a painter, there's a museum showing some of his work in town.'

'Bound to be!' But Tracy didn't sound enthusiastic.

'Maybe we could visit that, after this trip to see the fish in the lagoon.' Charis had pointedly directed her remark to Tina.

'Trust her to want to go high brow on us.' Mary dug Tracy in her ribs. The dig had been made in a low voice and Charis hadn't caught it.

'I'd like to.' Jasmine had looked at Mary for confirmation as she'd spoken.

'Me too as well, that's if its okay with the rest of you?' Tina looked inquiringly around.

'We could always split up, if the others want to go somewhere else.' As it seemed to Tracy that she was the only one who had any objections, she kept them too herself. They filled their day totally and didn't get back to the ship until fifteen minutes before it sailed.

'I'm done in and definitely need a drink.' The other five girls agreed with Tracy and they all went to the Neptune bar. To their relief it was empty. They settled themselves around a low table at the back and ordered their drinks. 'By the way, what're you lot wearing for the New Year's Eve party.' Mary was the first to answer.

'Red taffeta, fitted bodice, puff sleeves, full skirt.'

'Long or short?' Tracy wanted all the details.

'Above the knees, but not that much of a mini length.'

'Jasmine?' She put her glass carefully on the table in front of her. Her face started to redden, Mary came to her rescue.

'Are you going to wear the strapless dress with the mother of pearl bodice and the long cream chiffon pleated skirt.'

'Yes. Do you think it will look all right?' There was a slight questioning tone to Jasmine's voice.

'Sounds great.' Tina smiled reassuringly at her. 'I'm wearing a black satin dress, long sleeves, tight fitting bodice and straight skirt, that's got a long side split in it. So now are you going to tell us what you're going to wear Tracy?'.

'Of course I will, when I make up my mind.'

'You haven't?' Mary's voice was surprised, she always liked to plan everything well in advance.

'No, not yet.'

'I haven't either and as I'm half asleep, I might as well go to bed. See you all tomorrow. It's the Arabian show next, isn't it?'

'Yes, good night Megan.' Tina lifted her hand and gave a slight wave. There was a general murmur of 'good night' from the other's. 'Have you decided what you're wearing Charis?'

'Oh yes. I had my entire wardrobe programmed for the outward trip, very soon after I had the itinerary.' That statement brought a sarcastic remark to Tracy's lips, but Tina's timely nudge, under the table with her foot, stopped it from being uttered. 'For the New Year's Eve party, I'm wearing gold lame. The bodice has a heart shaped neck line at the front, with a wide and very stiff stand up collar at the back, I always wear my hair coiled on top of my head with this particular evening gown.'

'Well you would, wouldn't you!' Tina's foot couldn't forestall Tracy that time.

A resounding cheer vibrated through the liner, as the ship's hooter sounded the passing of the old year. Everybody threw greetings to anyone within sight. Megan told herself that she was happy, but the question of where her mother was, took the edge off her enjoyment. Tina slipped away to write to Bill, she missed him so very much. Charis was cornered by Kevin. He'd been trying to speak to her privately for over a fortnight. She'd been very elusive and made it impossible for him. But now he was stood directly in front of her and there was no retreat gangway for her to use.

'We dock in Wellington in two days time, will you have lunch with me?' There was warmth in his voice and manner.

'No.' The sharp tone she used surprised him.

'But the other week, the night of Olivia's party?' Charis glared at him. She felt he was being unreasonable referring to the night they had spent together, when she didn't want to talk, or even think about it, at all. He persisted. 'Didn't it mean anything to you?' Kevin held his breath. Suddenly he felt stupid, he already knew what her answer was going to be.

'I needed company and you where there.' He flinched as if she'd struck him. Charis walked passed him with her head in the air, leaving Kevin to stare after her, into the blackness of the night.

The decks were crowded with passengers as the liner entered Wellington's harbour. The town itself seemed to be perched in the hills around the bay. The old wooden colonial houses, now gave way to the modern buildings of the modern capital city, but still looked bright in the sunlight. They weren't sailing again until midnight and everyone was determined to do as much sight seeing as possible.

Maurice and Joan returned to the ship for their dinner. It was quiet abroad and they were served at once. Afterwards they relaxed in the evening sun shine, enjoying the luxury of coffee on a spacious deck.

'I need to speak to you Maurice.'

'Certainly Captain Beamish, when would it be convenient for you?' The protruding eyes glinted as he spoke.

'Now, if you would care to come to my office.' Maurice nodded, put his cup and saucer down, then followed the strutting officer along the deck. Once again Maurice was forcibly reminded of Buster Keaton's exaggerated walk. But his smile showed only polite interest as he faced the Captain. 'I'll come straight to the point, there has to be another show.' Captain Beamish began to chew the inside of his chubby cheeks with his teeth.

'What?' Maurice sounded stunned. 'It can't be done.'

'Why not?' The Captain looked surprised. Maurice ground his teeth together and tried to control his rising temper.

'A show has to be properly prepared. Unless you want to fall flat on your face and I don't.' Captain Beamish didn't bother to hide his smile.

'But the amateur night was a success.' Maurice snarled back his answer.

'That's different.' But he was ignored.

'I thought a Cabaret type of show would be ideal. What do you think?' The response which flew to Maurice's lips was unspeakable and as he was not stupid, he realised that no matter what he said, the Captain would insist on having his own way. But he wasn't going to give in without a last effort to get out of it and did not bother to veil the sarcasm in his voice.

'And what costumes do you propose we should use?'

'Oh I'll leave all that sort of thing to you, after all, you're the professional entertainer, it's your line, not mine. It's not until the twelfth of February, so you've got plenty of time to orchestrate it. And you'll have Sydney and Melbourne to co ordinate whatever you need. I spoke to our head office to day and they entirely agree with me, we must have one more show. The first Pacific cruise is so long, we need extra entertainment. Well I won't keep you.' With an airy wave of his hand, the Captain dismissed a seething Maurice.

'You can call a rehearsal on the fifth.' Joan lent back in her lounger and looked at Maurice from under her eye lashes.

'Why wait until then?' His tone was blusterous.

'Don't you want to think about it first?' She smiled as he stuttered in temper, then he turned around and marched off. 'Besides, I want to do some sight seeing in Christchurch, and if you don't wait, I couldn't do so.' But there was only a sea gull, hovering in the warm currents of air, to hear her.

'Another show? Have you got a theme?' Doreen sounded anxious.

'No! It's going to be a straight forward cabaret night. Have you got anything you can do?' She nodded in relief.

'Actually, I've been working on a Robinson Crusoe piece. I'm a girl Friday and the doll is...' Everyone chorused the name. Maurice looked pleased, Joan made a note on her clip board. Ted smiled innocently enough at Maurice as he spoke.

'I've certainly got the sheet music to more songs. If you like, I'll drop them off and you can decide what you want me to sing. It makes no difference to me.'

'Put Ted down for two songs.' Maurice didn't even look in Ted's direction. 'And you Ginger?'

'Don't worry your head over me, I've got material coming out of my ears.'

'What dances have you got in mind for us Maurice?' Tracy looked menacingly at Charis, her fingers itched to strangle her. It was rarely that anyone got under Tracy's sang froid, but Charis had.

'I'm not planning any routines for the six of you. I don't carry spare sets of costumes around with me. If they had wanted me to do so, then they should have said so before we left England! I'm not a bloody mind reader.' Charis smiled archly.

'I have my tap shoes with me and I already know a solo number set to 'Side Saddle'. I've got my own sheet music for the piano.'

'Fine. Put Charis down for a solo.' Maurice's tone sounded obstreperous. 'We could soon knock up a fringed skirt and waistcoat, then all she'd need would be a check shirt and maybe a hat! Those would be easy enough to buy in Sydney.' Joan watched Maurice carefully as she'd spoken, she knew that he liked to think all the good ideas were his own, but she didn't have a lot of time to pander to his ego on this occasion. The shopping for this show would have to be done in Sydney and/or Melbourne.

'I'll help with the sewing.' Megan was pleased to be able to offer this, she wanted to repay Maurice for his kindness in giving her the materials to make dresses for herself.

'You will, thank you.' It was Joan who answered her. 'That's a relief, I hate sewing.'

'I know a soft shoe duet, it's to 'Me and My shadow.' But it's with top hats and canes, if that's any good to you?' Maurice nodded at Tracy, accepting her suggestion.

'Who do you want to dance with?' Tracy had shook her head as she'd answered Maurice.

'It doesn't matter.'

'Tina, if we put you in white, you'd make the perfect shadow. Tracy can wear black.'

'That's fine with me.' Tina smiled as Tracy gave her the thumbs up.

'Okay, that's another one.' Joan gave silent thanks at Maurice's reaction. 'How many's that Joan?'

'Five, six if you're going to open the show with a couple of songs.'

'Yes, I'll do that. I'll sort that out with you later.' Ted shoved his hands in his pockets, he knew what Maurice was up to; he'd pick the best songs out, then leave the rest for him to choose from. Ted turned to stare out of the window at the calm sea. 'Anyway, what did it matter', he'd asked himself, adding that 'all my songs are good.'

'We still need two more acts. Really we should have another dance routine in.' Maurice looked at the girls and raised his eyebrows in question.

'If Cindy and Crystal know, 'Sergeant Pepper's Lonely Hearts Club Band', it should be easy enough to choreograph a marching routine to it. It wouldn't have to be complicated to look good.' Tina smiled hopefully.

'We already know it and we've got the music.' The two singers were perched on a table.

'What costumes?' Joan cringed at the thought of producing tunics.

'Black leotard and tights! Well, that's modern isn't it?' Maurice sounded mulish and very stubborn. 'We'll be able to pick up black boots for the girls in Sydney. Put it down Joan.' She wasn't about to argue, and was busy writing it down as Maurice asked the twins. 'What will you two wear?' Crystal giggled.

'Well, we've got patent thigh length boots, hot pants and tops, but they're white!'

'Hot pants! That might look better. We'll have to see what we can get hold of.' Maurice was beginning to sound more enthusiastic about the show.

'That makes seven, all you really need now, is a finale.'

'How about you singing 'I could have danced all night' with a couple of girls, in evening dresses on your arm?' Ted's voice was very blasé, but Maurice still jumped at the idea.

'Are you coming to the Captain's farewell do?'

'No, I've got a headache.' Megan threw Tracy a swift glance, but she wasn't paying any particular attention to her. Tracy was still in her dressing gown, sorting out her make up. 'Where's Tina?'

'On deck I think, but she'll be down in a bit to shower and change.' Megan laid back on her bunk. She closed her eyes and let the music from Tracy's tape recorder wash over her. She didn't move as she heard the door open. 'Hi, you're going to be late.' Tina glanced at her wrist watch, then shook her head.

'Not if I hurry.' She put her writing case on her bunk, grabbed her toilet bag and towel then went into the bathroom. Megan didn't get up for half an hour after they had left the cabin, then quickly changed into a cotton skirt and loose top. He had also stated that her bra and panties must be white, and no make up what so ever. She then sat for five minutes staring at the clock. Time seemed to be deliberately dragging its feet. Now she was ready, it would have been easier for her to go immediately. But her instructions had been specific. She was to arrive exactly on time. This was the third time with this particular client. His stipulations hadn't changed. She would spend the arranged hour with him and be able to be back in her cabin, before Tina and Tracy returned from the party.

Chapter 12

As the liner entered Sydney harbour, there wasn't a single person on board who didn't inspect the new opera house. Its shape and design were so unusual, that you were either enthralled or repulsed by it. The city itself had a lot to offer the sightseer and once the formalities of docking were over, the ship was left with only a skeleton duty crew. Tracy had persuaded Megan to check out the two main beaches of Bondi and Manly, before hitting the shops. The other four had headed straight into the centre first, before splitting. Mary and Jasmine wanted to tour the sights, Charis was intent on what the shops had to offer, and Tina had a telephone call to make. They waved to each other as they parted company; planning to meet back on board. The ship only docked for the day in Melbourne, but everyone managed to get ashore. It was found to have a unique blend of old and new and had reminded Joan of Wellington, but she couldn't really say why. There were two full days at sea before Fremantle. Tracy had spent hours trying to convince Megan that she was missing a chance of a life time, not going on the arranged trip to Perth. But Megan was adamant in refusing, she had been paid in advance by a customer, who's wife was taking the trip. Megan made herself keep her plan of making enough money, to hire a good private investigator to find her mother, as soon as she landed back in Britain, at the top of her priorities. Charis had every intention of going to Perth, the knowledge that it could boast of housing millionaires by the score, was enough to make it a special trip for her, she didn't propose to waste such an opportunity. Joan's only real hobby, outside her work for Maurice, was architecture, she had planned to hire a car and drive out along the Swan River, just to see how the other half lived. They crammed everything they could into their day.

Tina's birthday on the fourteenth of January, had been celebrated quite quietly, she hadn't wanted a party. And wouldn't change her mind, even when Tracy resorted to her verbal bombardment. They'd had the Hollywood show to perform that evening, so the cast had waited until after it, then met in the Neptune bar and opened a couple of bottles of wine. Tina had received her present from Bill before she'd left London. She'd opened it while she was by herself in the cabin. It was an antique gold locket, and inside was a miniature photograph of him. She was delighted with it; his Christmas present to her had been a gold watch, which he'd given to her before they'd parted.

Everyone of them had found Bali entrancing. The mountains teeming with vegetation, looked succulent, and not yet defiled by the domination of man. The aura of peaceful tranquillity was cocooned by nature. The ship left the Java Sea behind it and headed for the port of Singapore.

There had been three rehearsals for the extra show since leaving Freemantle. Maurice was, as usual, pleased with himself. Joan was relieved that everything had gone so smoothly. She'd been lucky enough to find a large theatrical costumiers in Sydney, where most of what was needed had been purchased. Also they'd discovered a delicious boutique, which had had dozens of different styles and colours of hot pants and tops; Maurice had had a ball choosing what he'd wanted for the show. Melbourne had provided the remaining gear needed. Megan had been busy and finished what sewing had been necessary, now the costumes were ready.

She sat hunched over the toilet, fine beads of sweat covered her body. This was the third morning running that she'd vomited as she got up. When she'd finished, she stood up and turned to wash her face and hands. Pale grey eyes looked questioningly into the mirror above the basin. Her hands gripped it for support as a horrifying thought flashed into her brain and stunned her. She'd missed her monthly period. Charis shook as she showered, then dressed. Her fingers faltered as she fastened her clothes. She had to find Kevin and ask him to help her. She felt numb with shock. No doubt later, anger at her stupidity, would set in. She had to wait, he was on duty and she couldn't go into the engine room. Charis roamed around the ship, if she saw anybody she knew, then she would dodge them. She didn't want to talk of trivialities. She felt her whole life was in a turmoil and about to be wrecked and she was scared to face that alone.

'You might as well go now. Remember you're taking my place at dinner tonight.'

'Yes Sir.' Kevin flicked a careless wave to the men still working as he reached for his jacket. He was thirsty, but his first priority was to shower. Twenty minutes later he was sitting on a stool, with an elbow propped on the Neptune bar. In his other hand, was a cold glass of lager. A fifteen year old girl, experimenting with her mother's make up, tried to catch his attention. But he was too absorbed in his drink.

'I need to talk to you.' He put down his glass with a snap and turned to face Charis. She put her hand on his arm. 'Please, it's important.' Kevin looked straight at Charis and wondered what she could want. Her eyes pleaded, but what could she want from him? But he didn't want to be used by her a second time, once had been enough. 'I have to talk to you right away.' He heard the urgency in her voice. His mind told him the opposite to his heart. He didn't want to be practical, how could he be, when she looked at him this way.

'Okay.'

'Not here, it's too public. We'll use my cabin.' Without saying another word, Charis hurried out of the bar. Kevin left his lager half drunk and followed her.

Kevin dragged his fingers through his hair. He looked staggered.

'A baby! Are you Sure?' Charis wanted to scream at him that she was certain, but held her temper in check, knowing she'd gain nothing by losing it. She'd had a strong urge to hit him. Anything in fact to make him pay attention to what she had said to him. And it had also annoyed her that he hadn't immediately offered his help. She was so desperate to arrange a quick abortion.

'Yes I'm positive?'

'And I'm the father?' He grabbed her by her shoulders. 'There could be no one else?'

'It's you.' She'd answered him through gritted teeth. Kevin grinned at her and let his hands drop to his sides. He walked around in a tight circle, there wasn't any room to do anything else. He felt embarrassed over his initial reaction of wanting to boast to his ex wife that he could, after all, father a child. Then reality set in, she was long gone and now here was Charis.

'We have to get married.' His eyes shone and he looked happy, even satisfied.

'Surely you don't want this to happen.' Kevin hadn't paid a lot of attention to what Charis had actually said. From the moment she'd mentioned that she was pregnant and he was the father, his mind had raced ahead, and made plans for their future. He had always wanted to be a father. His first marriage had failed after three years and no baby. He and his wife had had some tests, and they'd discovered that Kevin's sperm count was very low. When he'd returned home, after his next trip at sea, he'd found that his wife was divorcing him. Kevin had been very hurt by this and never even thought seriously about a lasting relationship with another female. But now Charis was pregnant, he was too thrilled to think of the consequences of marrying her. Only the fact that there was a baby, dominated his mind.

'I've got a good job and the house is big.' Charis stared hard at him. He didn't behave as if he came from a wealthy family and he had a broad, south London accent. But still, you never knew were the real money was these days. Maybe she would marry him, if it was worth it. 'You could live with my parents in Clapham. They'd help you with the baby while I'm at sea.' His grin was pure triumph. His words had pricked the bubble of wealth and security she'd just begun to form. Her heart sank, for a brief moment, she'd thought that he'd had something substantial to offer her, but he didn't. Instead of organizing everything simply, he'd gone insane.

'I don't want to have a baby.' Kevin's expression fixed on her face.

'What?' Charis was about to go into specific details, when she realised that she'd be a fool to do so. It would have been a waste of her time, trying to dissuade him from what he saw as the advantages of this pregnancy. He seemed very pleased with the idea of being a father. Charis knew that she'd made a grave error in judgement, in telling Kevin about her condition.

'I have to think this out.' She watched him carefully, trying to gauge what his reactions were going to be, when he learned that she did not intend to go through with this. 'Wouldn't a baby complicate your life right now?'

'Good God no! Why should it?' His reply had sounded arrogant to Charis. She just shrugged her shoulders. What was crucial to her now, was to find a way of keeping this a secret. If Maurice found out, he'd have a fit.

'We can't tell anybody.'

'Why not?' Charis wanted to lash out at him, but instead, turned her back. Kevin moved close to her and wrapped his arms around her. 'Don't worry, everything will be alright.' She closed her eyes, the temptation to relax back on him was there. After all, she could do worse. 'You're not afraid of your Mum and Dad getting upset because you're expecting, are you?' The mention of her mother banished all cosy thoughts of married life out of her head. Her mother had thrown herself at the first man to ask her to marry him and she'd ended up in a terraced house with six children and never enough money to go around. Always scrimping and saving every penny. Her father had worked, and worked hard, but he was a labourer and his wages weren't high. Charis was adamant that she would not end up in a similar situation. She had to get herself out if this, and soon. She moved out of the circle of his arms and turned to face him.

'Promise me that you won't tell anyone?'

'Why?' Charis swallowed and took a deep breath.

'Maurice would have me thrown off at the next port.' Kevin looked unconvinced. 'He would. He told us so during rehearsals.'

'Oh! Well I suppose we can keep it to ourselves for a bit longer.'

'That's a promise?'

'I've said yes.'

'And no writing home.' She put up her hand to stop his next argument. 'I want to tell my parents myself. So you'll have to wait.' Kevin was just about to argue when he remembered his mother. He knew that she'd be unable to keep such a secret, she'd want to meet her son's future in laws, and so be on the next train to York.

'You have my word, nobody will know until you tell them. Okay?' For the first time that day, Charis saw a light at the end of this particular tunnel. She nodded her head. 'Look, I know that you weren't thinking of getting married so soon, but it will work out.' Kevin took her in his arms again and kissed her. Charis let him, she didn't want to raise any doubts in his mind of what she was going to do. She was trying to think of a way to get rid of him, she didn't want to have intercourse with him again, once had been enough. At last he raised he head. His eyes glinted and he hugged her. 'I have to go. It's a shame but I'm substituting for the Chief Engineer at dinner to night, and I've got to change into my dress uniform.' Charis was so relieved that her smile was spontaneous. Kevin planted a swift kiss on her mouth, then left on a cheerful note, telling her that he'd see her later that night. Charis nearly blurted out that he couldn't come back to her cabin, but stopped herself. No need to make him wary. When he turned up, she'd say she felt ill and needed to go straight to sleep.

Charis next had the intention of asking the ship's doctor to help her, but after a little thought, dismissed that idea as futile. Then she'd checked the itinerary. Relief had steadied her nerves. They arrived in Singapore the next day and she did not have a show until after Hong Kong, that would give her eleven days to recover. Of course, there were other ports of call and cocktail parties, in fact lots of entertainment, but she could get out of those if necessary. And if anything went wrong, then she could see another doctor, without anyone being the wiser, as next week they were docked in Hong Kong for two and a half days. The show that night was the Rio Carnival. After it was over, Charis went straight back to her cabin to study the brochures on Singapore that she'd picked up from the information desk, after Kevin had left her cabin.

'We have to visit Raffles Hotel and drink Singapore Slings.' Tracy's voice drowned out whatever Tina was saying to Jasmine. 'Lots of them!'

'Why?'

'Oh come on Mary, everyone does it, it's the in thing. Even in Liverpool, the Long Bar is famous.'

'Oh well then! Lead on.'

'Everyone ready?' Tracy was agog with excitement.

'I think so. Where's Charis, did we ask her to come along?' Tina's question was directed at no one in particular, but Megan answered her.

'Yes, Mary did, but Charis said she already had a private trip planned and those, I believe, were her exact words!' The sarcasm was plain to hear in Megan's voice.

'Thank God for that.' Tracy laughed as the others told her off. 'It's no good, I just don't like her and there's nothing I can do about it.' Tracy had ended on a smug note.

'Who's got the name of the Chinese restaurant that the Chief Engineer recommended?' Tina waved a piece of paper at Tracy.

'Me! But don't forget, first I have to make my telephone call from the main Post Office.'

'And tonight we're going to Boogie Street with Maurice. That should be a hoot! All those men in drag.' Tracy giggled as she strutted out of the cabin. The other's followed her. They were all excited about the prospect of exploring Singapore.

Kevin had been on duty from noon, on the previous day, when they'd sail out of Singapore, so he'd been unable to see Charis. But he'd been making plans. He'd found it hard to give Charis the time and space she'd asked him for. He couldn't understand what she had to think about. Surely getting married was simple. She wouldn't be able to finish the cruise working for Maurice, some of the routines were very strenuous and also, she'd never fit into the costumes in another couple of months. There wasn't any spare room at all! Kevin had made up his mind, after the Fancy Dress Ball that night, he'd tell Charis that he was going to arrange for a special licence, so that they could get married in Hong Kong. That way, he'd be able to wangle it, so that she could move into his cabin, when Maurice fired her. As his wife, he'd be able to look after her. The Captain might pull a face, when Kevin asked for permission for Charis to continue the trip with him, but the old man would come round. As long as they were legally married, everything would turn out all right.

Charis had had to get out of bed to let Kevin in. She'd tried to persuade him to go away, but he'd insisted on talking to her.

'I will arrange everything. We're in Hong Kong for two and a half days. That's enough time.' Charis knew that she couldn't put off telling him any longer.

'We don't have to get married now. I'm not pregnant any more.' There was silence, he neither moved or spoke. She backed away from the anger and hatred in his eyes. 'It was the only thing to do. Can't you understand that?' She flinched as he took a step towards her.

'You bitch. You rotten little killer.' Charis stepped away from him. She felt the cabin wall against her spine and realised that there was no more room to retreat.

'Please go. It's no good you staying here. There's nothing you can do. It was my problem and I solved it.'

'I could kill you, but then I'd be in the same league as you and I couldn't live with myself if I thought that.' To her relief, he spun round and rushed out of her cabin.

Kevin raced along the corridor and took the stairs two at a time. As he turned a blind corner, he bumped into Megan, knocking her off her feet. She yelled at him as she landed on the floor.

'Hey, watch out.' Megan picked herself up. Kevin had stopped and now made an effort to pull himself together. 'What an earth is the matter with you? You look awful.' Kevin shook his head, but didn't speak. 'Are you ill, is anything wrong?' He stared at her as if she was a stranger. 'Do you need the Doctor?'

'No.' Kevin's voice was harsh. Megan could see the visible effort he'd made as he'd steadied himself. 'But if I don't get out of here fast, I'll kill that bitch for what she's done.' He charged forward, and Megan had no opportunity to stop him. She wondered who and what he was so wound up about, but couldn't hazard a guess. She decided to ask Tracy.

Kevin reached his cabin an opened a new bottle of whiskey. It had been a present, that he was going to give his father. He used the tumbler from his bathroom as a glass. Half an hour later, the only thought in his mind was that Charis had destroyed his only chance to become a father. When he'd emptied the bottle, Kevin was so drunk, that he'd fallen flat on his back in a stupor. When he'd failed to turn up for his duty the following morning, his cabin had been checked. He was found to be dead. The Doctor had told the Captain, with the evidence of the empty whisky bottle, it had been assumed that Kevin, as a result of the quantity of drink he had consumed, had become unconscious, therefore when he was sick, he had inhaled his own vomit, and so died.

An hour after Kevin had left, Charis was still lent against her locked cabin door, hoping against hope that he would not tell anyone about her.

Chapter 13

The sea was calm, an unruffled blue, heat beat down from a cloudless sky. Tina was sitting in between Tracy and Megan on the port side of the ship.

'Is it me, or is there something going on with the crew?'

'It's you Megan! By the way, has anyone seen Charis since we left Singapore?' Tracy didn't give the other's time to answer as she continued. 'Don't tell me that she jumped ship there and is now working in a paddy field, picking rice?' Megan grinned, but shook her head and said.

'Chance would be a fine thing!' But Tracy was persistent.

'She wasn't at the Fancy Dress Ball last night, was she Tina?'

'Leave me alone, I want to read my letter.'

'But you've read it a dozen times already!' There was now an exaggerated whine in Tracy's voice.

'And I'm going to carry on for as long as I want to!' Tina pulled her knees up and bent her head over her letter.

'Maybe Charis has hibernated for the rest of the cruise.'

'Megan, you shouldn't build my little old hopes up like that, only for them to be dashed down later.'

'Don't worry girl, you don't know the meaning of fragility.'

'Yes I do!' Tracy sat up straight and looked indignant. She was just about to go into some detail, when a male hunk walked passed them. 'Where the hell did he come from?' Megan supplied her with answer.

'He got on in Singapore and isn't getting off until Port Moresby, he's something to do with oil.' Tracy did a quick mental arithmetic sum.

'That gives me a couple of weeks.'

'Shouldn't think you'd need more than the cocktail party tomorrow night!' Megan's tone had been very bland. Tracy giggled and got up.

'Just going to stretch my legs and admire the scenery!'

Charis got out of the shower and dressed, she knew that she'd have to face everyone sooner or later, so it might as well be at dinner. It was the twenty eighth of January and her twenty fifth birthday. Events weren't happening as she had pictured in her mind before she'd started the voyage. In her day dreams, her birthday had been a glorious affair, not a simple dinner, with no celebration what so ever. But, she told herself, things could only get better. As Kevin hadn't come back last night after he'd stormed out, or bothered her today, she was hoping that he wasn't going to make any trouble over her decision. Her one prayer was that he had not told anyone that she'd been pregnant. When he hadn't returned, she'd assumed that he'd calmed down and thought about it, coming to the realisation that she'd been right. She glanced at her watch, it was too early to go to the dining room just yet. She sat on her bed and fiddled with the tie belt of her chocolate brown silk evening trousers. Charis had matched them with a pale cream satin fitted top, her light weight jacket, was on the bed besides her. She was pleased with her outfit. There was no show that evening and the atmosphere that night, should be relaxed. As she must show her face to day, just to keep everyone from wondering why she hadn't been at the Fancy Dress Ball last night. If asked, she was going to plead a migraine. Not that she ever had headaches, but she could always improvise when necessary.

As Charis left her cabin, she met Ginger in the corridor. She stared at him, but there was no sarcastic comment about abortions. Charis felt a little relieved, if Kevin had spoken of it and rumours had spread around the ship, Ginger wouldn't have been able to resist a choice comment to embarrass her.

'What are you looking at. I'm not from outer space you know.' Charis didn't reply. She very rarely spoke to the other members of the cabaret, except Maurice of course, and Joan. To her own amazement, Charis had enjoyed the day she'd joined the girls in Tahiti, but would not allow herself to become friendly with Megan and Tracy. In keeping those two at arms length, Charis had excluded herself from most of the joint ventures that the others enjoyed. Charis walked slowly through the dining room and sat at her table. She was early and there were only a very few other people scattered around the room. The waiter came to her and she ordered a salad and fruit juice. Charis was half way through her meal when Doreen came in and sat down. Very soon after that, the room started to fill up. Charis began to feel uneasy, there seemed to be something in the air. Everyone was talking in low, subdued voices, something was very wrong. She wanted to know what, but was afraid to ask. She cast a speculative glance at Doreen, but she was studying the menu. Charis began to panic. What if Kevin had talked to someone about her. What if everybody knew what she'd done. She wanted to get out of that room as soon as possible, but didn't want to give anybody the conviction that she was afraid of their condemnation over what she had done. What business of theirs was it anyway? Charis flinched as she heard Kevin's name mentioned at the next table.

Megan looked astounded, she shook her head, but managed to utter.

'Dead! Are you sure?'

'Of course I am. It's all over the ship.' Tracy's voice held impatience, as well as agitation.

'But how? I only saw him last night.' Megan's hand went over her mouth.

'When?' Tracy almost shrieked at Megan, but she didn't answer her. Megan's hand dropped before she spoke again.

'Oh my God! I knew there was something wrong.'

'How?' Tina's question hung heavily in the strained atmosphere around the dining table. Megan nodded to herself.

'Last night. Kevin was tearing around the corner leading from C deck to the outside walk way. He knocked me over.' She added nothing more. The room seemed to hush. At the other table, Charis shivered as a cold fear clawed at her.

'Go on, don't stop there.' Tracy nudged her with her elbow.

'But there's not really anything else to tell.'

'Of course there is, what did he say to you?' Tracy's flat palm hit the table as she'd made her demand. Megan screwed her face up and chewed her bottom lip. 'Can't you remember?'

'Of course I can. But I couldn't get any sense out of him, but he did say that he had to get away, because if he didn't, he'd kill her.'

'Who?' Ginger had leant forward in his chair.

'I don't know. He rushed off without saying anything else.' Charis was conscious of letting her eyes travel in Megan's direction. But was afraid of staring at her, so forced herself to look back and study her dinner plate.

'Could he have been murdered?'

'Don't be stupid Crystal. You'll have to excuse my sister, she reads too many, who done its.' Cindy seemed to be the only one taking the news of Kevin's death in her stride. Not uncaring, just philosophically.

'Ted, come over here mate, I want to talk to you.' Ginger smiled as Ted obediently changed his course. 'Know anything about Kevin?' Ted's eyes momentarily flicked over to Maurice's table, then back and around the people sitting at Ginger's table. There was a smirk on Ted's face, but all he did was shrug his shoulders and shake his head, then without saying anything, walked over to the table he sat at with the band. They were all smokers and it had been Joan's idea for them to sit together. 'Well, he was a lot of good, I must say!' Ginger was disappointed at Ted's response, but not surprised. He had an idea, that the outwardly flamboyant style Ted showed to the world at large was just a cover and that he could keep things close to his chest, when he wanted to. But what could he know?

Doreen was sitting at Maurice's table, she'd been able to clearly hear the conversation at the other table. Last night she'd heard the argument between Kevin and Charis after the fancy dress ball. Being a light sleeper, she knew about the night of Olivia's party, actually, she'd seen Kevin leave Charis's cabin in the early morning. So it hadn't taken her long to sort out the facts and come to the right conclusions. But she wasn't going to add her information to that which was already flying around. What Charis did, Doreen considered was her own business and interference would only do more harm than good. Let the others puzzle themselves over why Kevin had got so drunk, that he died. Blaming Charis wouldn't bring him back, it could only hurt her. As Charis had decided against having a baby, that was her choice, it was, after all, her life; she had done what she thought best for herself. Doreen sipped at her glass of wine, as she glanced at Charis sitting besides her. The girl had gone white under her tan. Doreen could plainly see the tension in her. Charis was sitting bolt up right in her chair and not moving. Nobody else seemed to be taking much notice of her, except of course for Joan. She very rarely missed anything that was connected with the cabaret members. Doreen watched Joan steadily, wondering what she'd do. Would she start to ask awkward questions. That wouldn't solve anything, just make things worst.

Joan became aware of Doreen's eyes on her and returned the look. She received a half smile and a raised eye brow, but nothing more. Joan had summed most of them up during the rehearsal period and since then, she had only confirmed her first impressions. She knew that she had faith in Doreen's judgement, as much as she trusted her own, and as Doreen was not putting any cards on the table, Joan accepted that that would be the best way to handle this situation, whatever the circumstances turned out to be.

Charis forced herself to stay in her seat. She had to find out if Kevin had spoken to anyone else after he'd left Megan. As he hadn't said anything to her about the abortion, Charis felt a little safer. Maybe he had died straight away. She hoped that she would be safe from any gossip over his death.

'I wonder who Kevin was talking about?' Tracy looked expectantly at Megan.

'How should I know. There are hundreds of cabins on C deck. Has anyone seen him with a particular female. Well, you know what I mean, as if he was really interested in her?' Megan's green eyes flitted around the table. Everyone shook their heads. 'Tracy, ask at Maurice's table.'

'Hell no!' She hissed. 'He'd bite me! And keep your voice down.'

'No he wouldn't.' Megan hadn't altered her tone.

'Then you do it. I'd feel awful asking questions like that, when the poor bloke has only just gasped out.'

'Then it's a good job you're not a copper, ain't it?' Ginger looked snug at the startled expression which had sprung across Tracy's face. Megan's teeth clamped together, but she refrained from making any comment to him. Ginger shoved his chair out and turned sideways in it, this brought him up against the back of Joan's chair and facing Maurice. 'Well, can you throw any light on the proceedings?' Maurice didn't pretend to misunderstand him.

'Not a thing. All I know is, that the fact that Kevin had been drinking spirits, that had surprised the Captain and Chief Engineer. According to them, he only drank lager. And not a lot of that either! So when he downed a full bottle of whiskey, he wasn't used to it and it knocked him out. He was unconscious when he died. The Doctor is putting it under the heading of accident.' Joan glanced quickly at Doreen, but she was carefully studying her glass of wine. Charis, Jasmine and Mary, seemed to have lost their appetites. All the girls looked shocked. Ginger hunched his shoulders and muttered about boring diner companions, then got up and left the room. Maurice finished his coffee before he spoke again. 'I'm just glad that none of the cabaret had anything to do with him. That would have really stirred things up.' Doreen didn't let her eyes waver from Maurice's face as he continued. 'Well, the poor sod must have been screwed up about something big to get so stoned.' Joan nodded sympathetically, she could see out of the corner of her eye, that Doreen was quietly agreeing with him.

Charis decided that she was safe. Kevin couldn't have told anyone about her, if he had done so, it would have come out by now. She felt relief start to creep through her. But she was cautious. She would be careful how she reacted to this, people were always watching, ready to pounce on the worst, rather then looking for the best of what there is. She didn't want to give anyone the slightest hint, that she was in some way connected, or had anything to do, with Kevin's death. She was glad that the Doctor had decided to call it an accident, and she hopefully anticipated, that would be the end of it. She wanted it to be over. Finished with. Charis excused herself and left.

Joan sat at the dining table, taking her time over her coffee. Doreen was the only other person at their table, but Cindy and Crystal were still sat at the next one. How those two could eat as they do, and manage to stay so slim? She pondered shortly on the wonders of youth! Joan didn't want to speak until she was sure that she wasn't going to be over heard. At last, they left, she cast a quick look around, just to make sure that it was clear, then she moved to the chair next to Doreen before she spoke. 'I'm glad you stayed here, I wanted to talk to you.'

'I guessed that, that's why I did.' Joan nodded and smiled.

'Do I need to know anything?' It was a simple question, but Doreen didn't answer it straight away. She instinctively knew that she could trust Joan not to spread any rumours about, but was there any real need for her to say what had actually happened. Before she answered her, Joan spoke again. 'I'm not curious for the details, I only wish to know if it's about to explode in my face.'

'There aren't any volcanoes about to erupt, if that's what you mean.'

'That's a relief. Well, you've taken a load off my mind. Maurice has been known to stir up a hornets nest, quite needlessly, when a little thought and subtle action could have avoided the disaster very easily.' Doreen grinned at her and nodded. They got up and left the dining room together.

Ginger had spent the rest of that evening prowling around the bars and lounges, but there didn't seem to be anything new to learn. He'd found out that Kevin had been popular with his fellow officers and respected by most of the crew members under him. None of the passengers that Ginger had talked to, seemed to know anything at all about Kevin's private life. Who ever the female had been, it looked as if Ginger was not going to be able to find out her name.

Jasmine and Mary went straight back to their own cabin. Mary said she had letters she wanted to write, so that she could post them in Hong Kong. Jasmine was terribly upset. Her nerves were raw because of the forthcoming meeting she hoped to have with her father. The news of Kevin's death had chipped at the fine balance she'd managed to create. She lay on her bunk, with her back to Mary, crying silently.

Mary had covered half a sheet of paper, but had written no more. She was sitting there, but her mind was in another bedroom. She'd wanted to die herself then. At nineteen, she'd realised that she was a lesbian and had been so ashamed and shocked, that she'd wanted to go to sleep forever and never wake up. She already knew what her family thought about those people who were different in that way. She'd been brought up to think that they were sinful and wrong, and ought to know better and behave properly. How could she admit that the thought of a man touching her in an intimate way would make her feel used and so disgusted with herself. They wouldn't listen, they wouldn't want to know at all. So the younger Mary had tried to take an overdose while she was away from home, but all she'd done was to sleep for a day and a half. Now, of course, she was glad that she hadn't died, but not then; she'd spent the next year, planning how to enact a successful suicide, that would look like an accident. It had to be that way, so that nobody would know and her parents would have been able to bury her in church. They were strong Roman Catholic, and killing herself would have been a terrible blow for them. Mary hadn't been able to think of a way around it and eventually, she'd given up on the idea. But going home had been getting more and more difficult over the passing years. Each time she went home, both her mother and father plagued her to settle down and get married. They kept reminding her that she was getting older and that it was about time that she had children. They blamed her stage career for her lack of boyfriends, saying that she wasn't in one place long enough to find one. Now, Mary used whatever excuse she could not to go home. That way, she didn't have to listen to them going on at her to get married. At first she'd tried hard to please them, having boyfriends, even going as far as to have intercourse with a couple of men that she'd come to care about as good friends. But on each occasion, it had been no good. Those experiences had only left Mary feeling sick and used, and very disgusted with herself. So much so, that she'd known, that she'd never be able to sustain a genuine relationship with a man.

Tina remembered that she'd spent a very pleasant evening with Kevin, soon after they'd sailed from Southampton. He'd seemed a happy and congenial person, with easy going manners. Why should anyone who behaved as if they hadn't a care in the world, get so drunk that they passed out and so, precipitated their own death? Tina couldn't make any sense out of it. How could a person like Kevin, willingly act in a way that caused their own demise? Tina shook her head and made herself concentrate on what Tracy and Megan were saying. They'd spent the past hour in the Neptune bar, talking about Kevin's death and were still going around in circles.

'Look, this isn't getting us anywhere. We could spend the rest of this cruise guessing at reasons why he got so drunk; but, even if we did hit upon the right one, we'd never know, because he isn't here to tell us.' Tracy and Megan both looked at Tina and nodded in agreement with her. 'Please, let's change the subject.'

'But I feel so bad.' Megan slumped back in her chair.

'Why?' Tracy sounded puzzled.

'Because I didn't stop him.'

'Rot.' Was delivered in broad Liverpudlian. Tina learned forward in her chair, then said.

'How could you have known what he was going to do, you idiot, it's got nothing to do with you, it's not your fault.'

'I should have guessed he was over the top. He was so very angry and upset. Maybe I should have stayed with him.'

'Talking about Kevin?' The three of them looked up at Ted, he'd walked up to their table and behind Tina's chair.

'Yes.' Tracy answered and poked Megan as she continued. 'And this crazy kid reckons she should have looked into her crystal ball and seen what he was about to do, so she could have saved him.' Ted looked at Megan, he saw the perplexed frown on her face and something else deep in her eyes; he couldn't place it. But he knew he'd seen that particular expression, somewhere in his past.

''You know, you do remind me of someone, where did you say you came from?' Megan answered him nonchalantly, her mind was still dominated with Kevin.

'Cardiff.' Ted nodded, he'd worked there a few times. It was there that he'd got a good break. About twenty years ago, he'd been at a local night club and was seen by a London agent who was in the town on business and had signed him up. From then on,

Ted hadn't been out of work until lately. In fact, it was only in the last couple of years, that he hadn't been fully employed all the time. He leant on the back of Tracy's chair and with a grin, said.

'Well, as there is no irate female screaming that he's got her pregnant and won't marry her, you can take it from me, that wasn't the reason.' With that remark, he walked off, casually glancing at Charis who was sat with Maurice. Ted was pleased with himself, he liked to store up favours!

Chapter 14

Another night spent restlessly in her bunk, had left Jasmine looking strained. She'd been glancing at her bedside clock constantly, wanting to get up, but made herself lie there in consideration of Mary, who was still asleep. When the ship's engines cut out at seven that morning, Mary stirred and, at last, Jasmine got out of bed. Mary sat up in her bunk and look at the young girl, then asked.

'Are you sure that you don't want me to come with you?' Jasmine didn't know. Was she afraid of going to see her father by herself? Her stomach churned relentlessly. But should she ask Mary to give up her time, it might take all day! A cold sweat covered Jasmine's body. Mary was in a quandary, she didn't know whether to persevere in persuading the girl, to let her go along, or, would it be better, if Jasmine went by herself. 'You shower first. I'm just going to stay here for a bit. Isn't it funny, when we first came aboard, the sound of the engines kept most of us awake. Now we're so used to them, immediately they stop, it's like an alarm call and we wake up!' Jasmine didn't respond to this light hearted chatter, so Mary didn't attempt any more. The younger girl looked so lost and afraid; even as she moved around the cabin, she fidgeted aimlessly with her things, not really, doing anything constructive at all. Mary decided to go for it. 'I would really like to meet your father. Would you mind?'

'No.' Jasmine had surprised herself as well as Mary. She hadn't been conscious of any thought, just voiced an involuntary answer. Jasmine was glad that she would be with a dear friend, but asked. 'Are you sure that you don't mind?'

'Positive. Now go and have a shower, you'll feel much better after that.' Jasmine nodded her head. And the feeling of relief, that she wouldn't have to be alone at this major time in her life, now overwhelmed her.

Mary stared at the ceiling of their cabin, wondering what sort of a man he would turn out to be. Jasmine had only recently told Mary, her main reason for being on the ship. Mary hoped, for the girl's sake, that he would be able to accept that he had a daughter, whom he knew nothing about, even the fact that she'd been born. How did one feel, being presented with an eighteen year old girl and being told that she was your daughter? God only knew how Zachery Chinnock would react. Was it going to be a difficult day? Jasmine was still in the bathroom when Tracy hammered on the cabin door. Mary had to get out of bed, to let her in.

'We've docked.'

'Yes I know.' Tracy was already dressed for town, she was wearing a brightly coloured, sarong styled outfit, she'd bought in Singapore.

'You and Jasmine are coming with us, aren't you?' Mary turned away from Tracy's eager eyes. She had to think of a plausible reason for Jasmine and herself, not to join the other dancers this morning. Stalling for time, she said.

'We'll see you at breakfast.'

'Where's Jasmine, how long will you be?' Tracy was almost breathless in her excitement.

'Eh... I don't really know, but if you're in a hurry, go without us. We'll catch you up.' Tracy blinked at her, then shook her head.

'Where? None of us know this place, so how could you do that kid!' Mary shrugged her shoulders. She knew she'd have to get rid of Tracy right away. Jasmine had asked Mary not to tell anyone about her father, not until she'd actually met him.

'Look, Jasmine's stomach is a bit on the queasy side today. So instead of us holding the rest of you up. You go with Megan and Tina, and we'll follow on afterwards. We're bound to bump into each other.' Tracy dithered, she didn't want to seem uncaring, but she and the other two were all ready; in fact, they weren't going to have their breakfast on board, but had planned to eat ashore. 'Go on, honestly, we'll most probably see you later.' Tracy didn't need any further encouragement.

'Okay! We'll keep an eye out for you.'

'Yes, that's fine, see you later, bye.'

'Too dle oo!' Tracy disappeared quickly. Mary gave herself a clap. It was half an hour later that Jasmine came out of the shower. Mary didn't bother giving her an explanation of how she'd got out of a joint trip with the others, only that she had.

Mary had tried to get Jasmine to eat a little breakfast before they left, and although, she'd sat at the table and let Mary order for

115

her, Jasmine had eaten nothing. Mary shepherded her down the gangway and into one of the waiting taxis. The building they stopped outside was huge and very impressive. Modern, with a glass frontage, and when they went inside, their heels echoed expensively, on the patterned, tiled floor. Jasmine didn't speak, she let Mary ask to see Mr. Chinnock. The receptionist's eyebrows raised, as he asked them if they had an appointment. They were easily able to understand his English, it was excellent.

'No.' Mary's voice wasn't flustered at all, she hadn't expected to just be able to walk straight in and see him. 'I'm afraid we have only just arrived in Hong Kong and so were unable to prearrange a meeting. But it is urgent that we see Mr. Chinnock today, it concerns a private family matter.' She ended with a confident smile. The receptionist's eyes moved from Mary's face to Jasmine's. He stared punctiliously. Jasmine's colour rose in her cheeks.

'Your names please?' Jasmine's hand flew to grip Mary's arm.

'McDonald.' After a slight pause, the receptionist smiled politely and wrote down the one name. He then picked up a telephone and spoke in rapid Chinese.

'Mr. Chinnock is not in his office at this moment. We do not know when he will come in.' Jasmine's face now drained of colour. She felt sick, she turned to Mary.

'We will wait. As I have said, the significance of this meeting, is extremely important.' Again a quick conversation into the mouth piece.

'Would you kindly like to wait upstairs, it would be more comfortable.' Mary smiled and agreed. More Chinese travelled over the wire, before he slowly replaced the receiver.

'Please wait and you will be escorted up.' Mary inclined her head slightly.

They had been sitting there for over three hours and Mary cringed as her stomach voiced its disapproval. She stood up and walked over to speak to a female, who was busy typing at a desk near to an internal door.

'I'm sorry to interrupted your work, but is Mr. Chinnock expected soon?'

'I am sorry, we do not know.' Mary nodded and returned to her seat

. 'Have you brought the papers with you?' Jasmine swallowed and tried to nod her head, she managed a tentative movement. 'Well, I've been thinking, maybe you should write him a letter and leave it here for when he does arrive.' Mary could see by Jasmine's expression, that she didn't think a great deal of her idea.

'No. You can go. Really, I have to wait.' Mary wanted to hug Jasmine to console her. The girl's voice was hardly above a whisper, and had trembled as she'd spoken. Mary knew that she couldn't leave her by herself and lent back, more comfortably, in her chair. About ten minutes later the door to the corridor opened and both Jasmine and Mary's heads jerked towards it. A tray was placed on the low table in front of them.

'Please eat. And also drink.' A bow and the person, who had placed the tray in front of them, beamed before he moved away. Mary dived at the food and enjoyed her impromptu lunch of sandwiches and fruit juice. But Jasmine ate nothing at all. Mary did manage to get her to drink a little juice.

Mary wondered exactly how long Jasmine intended to stay. It was after four o'clock in the afternoon all ready and there was still no sign of her father turning up. Mary pushed her shoulders against the plush chair back, trying to ease the stiffness that was beginning to make her back ache. She couldn't remember ever sitting still for so long before. The only time they had moved that day, was after lunch, to visit a bathroom. That had been luxury, dark amber marble, and gold. She judged that the company must be financially, very sound. Mary was speculating on what sort of a day the others had had, when the doors to the main corridor swung open and a group of men walked in. The leader went straight up to the female at the desk and a low voiced conversation took place. When he turned and approached them, Jasmine and Mary, stood up.

'I am Zachery Chinnock, I believe you wish to see me?' His voice was calm and professional. His English pronunciation was impeccable, and his attitude, that of polite enquiry. Mary glanced quickly at Jasmine and thought that she was about to faint. It must have occurred to Mr. Chinnock as well, because he didn't wait for either of them to speak, but invited them both to sit down. A strangled sound from Jasmine's throat made him stare at her.

'It's very private and confidential.' It had been Mary that had spoken. A sudden frown marred Zachery Chinnock's handsome face, but he motioned the two girls, towards his private office. Although one of the other gentlemen had opened the connecting door, Zachery was the only one to pass though with Jasmine and Mary.

Jasmine felt her heart hammer wildly in her chest, and her fingers fumbled in her bag, as she took out the envelope with her birth certificate and her parents marriage lines in. She handed it to him without saying a word. She wanted to speak, but found that her brain could not put her convoluted thoughts into words.

Zachery looked puzzled at the girls in front of him, one was trying to look confident, but was very uneasy, and the dark haired one, seemed to be on the verge of collapse. Maybe he should have asked them to sit down, but he felt at a disadvantage already, and did not intend to compound that until he was in control of this situation. He took the envelope out of a shaking hand and held it. He did not like being in a blind scenario. He had risen to his present position, by always integrating, a thorough preparation. No matter who or what, was before him, Zachery would have done his research and known all that there was to find out. He did not consider himself ruthless, only extremely competent, always holding the maximum amount of information he could have. He flicked the envelope against the fingers of his other hand, his attention, now solely on the dark eyes, staring so hopefully at him. For an instant, the memory of his maternal grandmother flashed into his mind. He straightened his shoulders and looked down at the envelope in his hand. Then he opened it. He took the two folded documents out and was surprised to see his marriage lines, then he studied the other paper. His eyes flew to Jasmine's face, then back to the paper.

Whatever Mary expected Zachery to do, it was not to turn on his heels and march over to his desk. When they had entered his office, they had stopped in the centre of the floor. Now she looked with concern at Jasmine, but she was watching her father. He'd snatched up the telephone and the fact that he was speaking in a language that neither Jasmine or Mary understood didn't matter, the tone of the hasty course of Chinese crackling over the wire, left them in no doubt what he was saying. He was checking up on the evidence that had just been presented to him.

Zachery put the receiver down and slowly turned to face the two girls. His eyes searched Jasmine's face. Then he walked quickly to the connecting door and disappeared through it.

Mary's mouth dropped open and she turned to Jasmine, just in time to grab her, as she fainted. Mary was manfully struggling with Jasmine, when Zachery rushed back to them. He picked Jasmine up in his arms. He seemed to be able to carry his daughter without too much effort and walked over to a long leather couch by the nearest wall. He lay Jasmine down, then went over to a cabinet. He opened the ornate lacquered doors and poured a liberal measure of brandy, into a goblet. He surprised

Mary when he returned, as he didn't hand her the glass, but sat on the edge of the seat and lifted Jasmine's head up, so that he could make her sip a little of the liquid. Once she had recovered, he put the glass down and moved to a chair at right angles to the couch, were he sat down. Zachery indicated with his head, for Mary to sit. As she was standing beside Jasmine, she moved across her and sat down next to her on the couch.

'Why wasn't I told?' His voice was hard, and to say that he was angry, was the understatement of the decade. 'Why now and not before?'

Jasmine was sitting with her shaking hands, gripped together in her lap. The only answer she could give him, seemed like a betrayal of her mother. What could she say, to make him perceive something that she did not understand herself? If he didn't look so bitter, maybe she would feel more capable. But she had to say something now. Maybe later, she and her father would be able to discuss why her mother had cut him, so totally, out of her's and Jasmine's lives. Jasmine watched him intensely. The implacable expression on his face, frightened her. When she at last spoke, her voice trembled with each syllable.

'When I was a child, I asked her and she told me that you had died during my infancy.' He seemed almost to snarl his next question.

'And when did you find out that I was alive?' His obdurate stance, startled both the girls. Jasmine swallowed and started to speak, but her voice was too low to be understood. Mary, afraid that Jasmine would faint again, rushed into speech.

'There was an article in the Times last summer, when you were in London, taking over a merchant bank. Jasmine read it.' Mary didn't say any more about how Mrs. Chinnock had drawn attention to the article, she didn't think that those details were very relevant at the moment. 'So as her mother insisted that you were dead, Jasmine decided to come and find you herself.' Mary paused, to see how he was taking the information, it was hard to tell. She took a deep breath and carried on. 'It's been hard for her, she's very shy, and to take this initiative was a difficult thing for her to do. But she was determined to find you.'

That Jasmine was his daughter, he acknowledged, he didn't need any confirmation, it had been his business mind, that had demanded that it checked out. Why Veronica had treated him this way, denying him the chance to know his daughter, made him so enraged, but that, he would confront his ex wife with. For the present, he would waste no more precious time, his daughter was here and he wanted to reach out to her. That she was timid, was apparent and perplexing. His lips curved into a half smile, as he wondered how two such forceful people as himself and Veronica, could have produced, between them, this shy girl. Then again, the memory of his grandmother merged with his present thoughts, and his smile broadened, that was where Jasmine's shyness came from.

Mary found it hard to believe that his change of expression, could be so vicissitudinous in nature. His warmth now, was magnetic. She turned to look at Jasmine and found that she was timidly returning his smile. Relief mingled with happiness for her. Mary thought, that maybe she was now surplus to Jasmine's needs and suggested, that she should return to the ship.

'You didn't fly in?' Mary shook her head. 'When do you sail?' There was a slight aggressive tone, which had crept back into his voice again. He was certainly a man who was used to having his own way. 'Can you stay longer?' This question was solely to Jasmine. She shyly shook her head. Mary filled in the missing information.

'We work on the ship. We're dancers in the cabaret.' For the first time that day, Mary smiled at the shocked expression which crossed Zachery's face, but was instantly masked into a polite look of enquiry.

'You're a dancer?' Jasmine nodded at her father. 'I have a lot to learn about you.' His tone held humour, his eyes had regained their warmth, and Mary was confident that she could leave Jasmine with her father. She gave Jasmine a hug, then stood up and shook hands with Zachery. 'My assistant will take you down to the lobby, so that she can give your destination to the driver.'

'There's no need to bother, I can easily get a taxi.'

'It is no trouble.' It was more his tone, than anything else, that had stopped Mary from arguing. He walked in front of her to the door and opened it for her, then gave his orders. Mary thanked him, then followed his secretary out of his office suite, into the main corridor.

Zachery returned, and sat down in the chair he had left.

'I've ordered something to eat and drink to be brought up for us.' He watched as she smiled at him. There were a million important things he wanted to ask her, but all he could think of was that she was a dancer. 'You must like it very much.' A slight frown flitted into Jasmine's eyes. Zachery grinned, then added. 'Dancing I mean.'

'Oh! Well yes, I do. Originally, I went to the classes because I'm shy and my mother and our doctor, thought that it would help me to mix with children of my own age. It has, I'm not as bad as I used to be.' She smiled and lent a little forward in her seat. 'In fact, I'm looking forward to going to university.' Now it was Zachery's turn to look puzzled. Jasmine laughed and the echo of her mother ripped into his memory like a rapier. 'I took a year out, my mother and our doctor thought I should. My shyness; well, it sometimes makes me very nervous.' She paused, but he only smiled encouragingly at her, so she continued. 'This job turned up, just after I'd discovered that you were alive and where you were.' Her hands fluttered as she spoke. 'And I got it. That surprised me, but I was desperate to find you without my mother knowing.' Jasmine saw the hard lines return around her father's mouth. She stretched out her hand and gently put it on his arm. 'I don't know why she lied to me about you, I thought that maybe you would?'

Zachery had always believed that he and Veronica had been in love, maybe too passionately for reason, but none the less, they'd adored each other, or so he'd thought; but her action concerning Jasmine, was surely, one of hate. But he would deal with Veronica, at a later date. Now he wanted to find out more about his daughter.

'You mentioned university, which one?'

'Cambridge. I'm reading literature, modern and classical.' He was impressed. The refreshments arrived and he placed a delicate feast in front of Jasmine and she found that she was hungry. Zachery made a telephone call, then returned to his chair. They talked to each other for another three hours.

'It's time that I took you back to your ship. Would you spend tomorrow with me?' Jasmine nodded eagerly at him and he returned her smile, with one of equal warmth.

'I'll be there to collect you at nine o'clock, that's not too early, is it?' Jasmine was too happy to talk, she grinned at him and let out a contented sigh.

Chapter 15

Jasmine could hardly believe that so much had happened to her in the past two days. It was fantastic! She still felt breathless, even as her eyes gazed at the small temple, built high in the side of the hill, which formed the natural east boundary of the estate. Three terraces led down from the house, then to reach the temple, one used the steps of the temple gardens, which had been artistically formed to blend in with the design. The setting sun, now seemingly hovering on the horizon, shone into the open front of the temple, colouring the marble, from its soft pink, to a vibrant crimson. The designs on the interior ceiling still showed its original carved splendour, and Zachery had told Jasmine, that this affirmed, that the temple had been dedicated to Kuan Yin, the goddess of mercy and compassion. When first built, there would have been a statue of her on the central podium, but that had long since disappeared, now there was a terra cotta tub, with a bonsai magnolia in it. The magnificence of the mosaic floor, still proclaimed its right to reverence. The columns were two feet in diameter, cylindrical and straight; even a little servere, but so very classical, that there beauty was timeless and they easily held up the roof, of four equally shaped sides.

The opulence of the house had staggered Jasmine when she'd first seen it. Her father had picked her up from the ship at the arranged time and then driven her through the central part of Hong Kong, into a residential area. The architecture of each house they'd passed was oriental. Zachery had explained that this was an enclave of the older style of Chinese homes. That it was a wealthy area, was apparent and needed no clarification. The car had turned off from the road and stopped before two large wooden doors, set into a thick stone wall, which reached a foot above and over them; the hinges and handles on the gates, looked to be made of beaten brass, intricately etched. These outside barriers were immediately opened by a waiting servant. The car drove through and followed a sweeping driveway, the gradient of which gradually rose for perhaps twenty yards, then there were another set of gates, this time made of open iron work; but the design was so elaborate, that the bars crossed and recrossed themselves many times. Again the wall bridged the gates. The third set were made of bamboo, but still formed a barrier. The drive way between each gate, had led to a higher level and at the end, the car was parked in an underground area. Zachery had told her, that during the time the house had been built, security had been of paramount importance. And added ruefully, that it still was.

Jasmine and her father had left the car and entered a lift, which had deposited them at the back of the main entrance hall to the house. Jasmine had stood in the comfort of her father's arm and his encouraging smile, had helped momentarily, to subdue her panic as she had faced, Kim Su, Zachery's wife and Kwong Yuen, his son and Jasmine's half brother. The meeting had been pleasant and very polite. Jasmine's fear that she was guilty of trespassing, soon vanished and she had found, after a very short time, that she'd felt comfortable within this family unit. Kwong Yuen was an energetic child of ten. His grasp of the English language had surprised Jasmine, until it had been explained that the child's nanny had been English. Zachery had wanted his son brought up to speak both languages and so had hired her. The result being, that Kwong Yuen could chatter away, in either English or Chinese. The boy was dark and his smile, an exact copy of his father's. Jasmine thought that Kim Su was the most beautiful woman she'd ever seen, so delicate and seemingly fragile; her nature gracious and charming. Her bone structure belonged to that of the classical pulchritudinous era of womanhood, the slant of her eyes, almost an after thought, of the creator.

'Here they are, I've got them all.' Kwong Yuen bounced back onto the veranda, from which Jasmine had been studying the temple. 'See, it's quite plain, the house is built on the island that was left, when the land was scooped from the side of the hill.

'A little bit like an English castle with a moat.' Jasmine looked at him to see if he'd understood her meaning. Kwong Yuen nodded his head, then produced another photograph.

'This one was taken from an aircraft and shows the tiers of the gardens, very well.' The boy's voice held excitement, as well as pride.

'It must have taken years of hard work to excavate all this ground, to leave these steps and the knoll, for the house to be built on.' Jasmine's finger pointed to the photograph and added. 'The temple as well, I wouldn't have liked to be a member of that particular working party.'

'Nor me!' Kwong Yuen grinned, an impish smile hovered around his mouth. 'Mind you, the gardens of the temple are not squared and levelled off like the house, and its back is the actual hill. Father reckons this house was built in this position because of the water well. That's why it is in the inner court yard of the actual house, so that it could have been protected. The house and gardens were built so that the family would have been safe in the inner court yard, even during a battle.' His enthusiasm was abounding. 'You know, the enemy couldn't have poisoned the water.' Here he'd nodded solemnly, before he'd stated. 'In the olden days, poison was very popular. That's why the chop sticks were always made of ivory.' Jasmine looked puzzled at him, and he grinned as he explained. 'They change colour, if something nasty is in your food!' And ended, with a simple pride in the ingenuity of some of his ancestors. Jasmine had laughed.

Jasmine had been asked to spend that night with her father and family, so she didn't return to the liner until an hour before it was due to sail. Lee Chung carried Jasmine's things aboard. Zachery, Kim Su and Kwong Yuen had all come to wish her bon voyage.

'Lee Chung is staying aboard. He will look after you.' Jasmine stared at her father opened mouthed. 'You don't seem to realise that you are a very wealthy young lady, and so, need a body guard.' Zachery smiled fondly at her. Kim Su moved close to Jasmine and put her arm around the girl's waist.

'Your father is thinking only, of what is for your good.'

'Oh, I know that, it's just that I don't think that I could possible be in need of a body guard. I'm not that rich.'

'You are now.' There was no emotion in Zachery's voice, his tone was authoritative and business like. Jasmine looked shocked and shook her head. She tried to speak, but only managed a faint shriek. 'You are my daughter, and I have set up a trust for you, just as I did for Kwong Yuen. By the way, where is the boy?' His wife answered him.

'He is with Lee Chung, they're exploring the ship.' Kim Su squeezed Jasmine's waist. 'It is right for your father to do this for you.' Jasmine felt numb. Her happiness at finding him, was now clouded with the deluge of money. She could only shake her head. Zachery moved close to his daughter and took her trembling hands in his firm grip.

'There is nothing to trouble you. Lee Chung will take care of you.' Jasmine's dark eyes filled with tears. 'Does having money bother you?' Her voice quivered and was very low, but Jasmine managed to say.

'I didn't find you for that reason.' Zachery laughed, the concern vanished from his face.

'Of course I know that. You are my daughter and it is natural that I should do this for you.' As an after thought, he added. 'And Lee Chung stays. Now that we've found each other, I'm taking the greatest care of you.' It seemed to take an age before Jasmine was happy again and it was almost time for Zachery and his wife and son to leave the ship.

Charis had only gone ashore on the afternoon of the second day in Hong Kong. She'd fully recovered from her termination, but had no wish to tire herself unduly. She'd spent her time just wandering around. It had cost her most of her ready cash in Singapore, so she could only window shop here. She'd declined an invitation to join the others on their trips. She was becoming more and more isolated from the group. Charis did not trust anyone. She would not even allow herself to consider that Kevin's death was in anyway connected with the consequences of her abortion. To her, she had taken the only possible course open to her, and the fatal outcome, was totally unrelated to that, and had no integral association to her. He'd got himself drunk, so what had happened to him was, in her opinion, his own fault. It had nothing to do with her. As there had been no uproar, involving her after his death, Charis now felt safe from any involvement with him.

Tracy and Megan had both enjoyed their shopping sprees in Hong Kong, and were discussing their purchases in their cabin.

'Megan, that looks fantastic! What are you going to do with it?'

'Make a dress out of it!'

'Evening?'

'Of course stupid, what the hell did you think I was going to do with it?' Megan sounded a little bad tempered, but Tracy ignored that.

'What style?' Tracy chewed her bottom lip in concentration. 'I mean, it's such gorgeous material.' Megan draped the sari length on her bunk and studied it. The emerald green matched her eyes and the gold hand embroidered thread, showed exquisite craftsmanship. The pattern of petals multiplied, from a single row at one edge, to a delicate profusion at the other.

'A full gathered skirt, so that I can keep this!' Megan pointed to the deep gold embroidery, 'as the hem, and maybe a strapless top.' Tracy nodded as she delicately fingered the material.

'You've got loads, maybe you could manage a little jacket as well.'

'I'll have to see. Well now you've seen what I brought, lets have a look at your stuff.'

'Less of the stuff mate, I'll have you know that I've spent my dough very wisely.' Tracy produced a jeweller's box from her handbag and grinned at her friend as she opened it. The glint of gold caught by the light made Megan's eyes open. In the box, there was a necklace and a bracelet, in a heavy gold chain link. Megan picked both up and weighed them in her hand.

'These must have cost you a bomb.' Tracy grinned and nodded her head excitedly. 'You'll have to put them somewhere safe.' Tracy's eyebrows went up. She hadn't really considered that aspect. She kept the rest of her jewellery, rolled up in a jumper, in her bottom draw. It hadn't been cold enough since the ship had crossed the Atlantic, to wear warm clothing, and she thought it would be safe there. 'You'll have to use a safety deposit box in the Purser's office. Tracy groaned, but agreed. She'd have rather died than lose them, now she'd finally managed to afford to buy them for herself. Since the very first show of her stage career, when the female singing star had put on her glad rags for a back stage party, and had the men begging her for her favours, Tracy had wanted the exact outfit. She'd already got the black satin jump suit. It clung to her body like a second skin, until it flared out around her ankles. The strappy, black patent stiletto shoes were still in the box, wrapped in tissue paper to stop them from getting scratched. But the jewellery had taken some effort to buy. It was all gold and a lot of it! Three chains, two rings on each hand and a bracelet. It was during that first show when Tracy had been sixteen, that she'd gone from blonde to brunette, the singer had had long curly chestnut hair. The singer had enjoyably gone through all the reasonable looking men in the theatre that season, and Tracy had copied her. And now she had the complete outfit, all she had to do, was to decide when to wear it. She could hardly wait to see the men's reaction to her. Would it be the same as it had been for the singer?

Tina was in a Utopian state. During the two and a half days, that the ship had been docked in Hong Kong, she'd spent over four hours talking to Bill on the telephone. And his news had been great. He was going to be in New York when the ship docked there at the beginning of June. They would have three blissful days with each other, plus the remainder of the day they docked, as well as the hours before the liner sailed. His divorce would be over. They would be able to be together, without hiding away, as if they were criminals. Tina was standing by herself, looking out at a scene, without really seeing any of the activities that were going on. Her mind only planning for her future with her lover. She knew they'd be happy. A simple word to use now that he was going to be free to marry her.

Maurice had been taken by Alexander, a deck officer, to a country house just outside of the main town. It was in a secluded position and the perimeter fence had been patrolled with guards and dogs. It had been an expensive excursion, but he'd enjoyed himself and thought it well worth his money. The hotel was run purely for homosexuals. And the staff were professional male prostitutes. When Maurice and Alexander had arrived, they'd been shown straight to their bedrooms. Maurice had been delighted with his balcony, the view from it was deliberately exotic. From then on, it had been one long orgy. He'd been bathed, then fed. He'd behaved like a small boy, given carte blanche, in a sweet shop! He'd returned to the ship exhausted, but with a genial smile on his face. What he had enjoyed even more than the incessant sex, had been the quality of the pot he'd smoked. Maurice was very strict with himself over smoking marijuana, and only did so when he was on holiday. He'd seen too many of his friends balls up their careers, by over indulging. The problem with over use was that one became dissatisfied with it and ventured into uncharted regions; those frenzied habits inexplicably became a nightmare, from which one very rarely woke up. Now Maurice was looking forward to New York. Alexander had promised him that he knew of a place in the Big Apple, where they could experience a like form of entertainment, and in his opinion, the cannabis, would be even better!

Joan knew all about Maurice's trip. He'd bragged about it to her. Making fun of her and calling her a prude for disapproving of it. The first afternoon, she'd gone shopping and had spent far more money than she'd intended too. That evening she'd got drunk with Doreen. And had ended the night, by crying herself to sleep.

Doreen hadn't attempted to undress Joan, she'd just laid her down in her bunk, but still had the sense to see that Joan was on her side; then Doreen slouched in a chair, trying to keep her eyes in focus. She'd lost count of the number of champagne and brandy cocktails they'd drunk. After ten minutes of trying to stay awake, Doreen was satisfied that Joan would be okay and staggered out of her cabin to teeter unsteadily to her own. Once inside, she'd stripped off her clothes, let them drop in a heap on the floor, then fell on her bed. She remembered thinking that, she was glad it was warm, as she didn't have the dexterity to get under the cover!

As he'd sauntered around Hong Kong, Ted's outward appearance was carefree. A man about town, just savouring the ambiance. The females on this cruise had proved incompatible to his plans. But being the eternal optimist, he considered that he still had plenty of time to pull off a marriage to a wealthy woman. He had a great deal of egotistical superiority. Only briefly, did the idea that he would fail, ever enter into his head. When it did, he'd always banish it immediately. Never doubting in his own expertise where the female gender was concerned. He'd never been without a women. From the age of thirteen, when the next door neighbour had introduced him to sex, he'd surveyed women as relaxation. He enjoyed his sex life. His morals were easy and one of his first priorities, when he moved to a fresh gig was to find a woman who was available. He preferred them to be good looking and in general, he'd always found what he wanted. Usually it was a bar maid. Even if married, this fraternity, in the establishments that Ted worked in, could always be depended on to want a fling and know how to take the chance when it was offered. Ted's philosophy was 'no commitment, just a good romp in bed, satisfaction guaranteed!'

Ginger had haggled over the price for nearly two hours, but eventually he'd had to pay what had been asked for. The package was put into a man's shoe box and wrapped innocently in plain brown paper, before being put into a well known stores carrier. He folded the bag over and tucked it under his arm, then nodded to his guide. The walk back through the numerous alleys and back streets didn't take very long. Once Ginger was in the main shopping area, his guide had unobtrusively disappeared in the throng. Ginger had slowed his pace down, but kept his eyes peeled for any possible trouble. There had been none. When he'd arrived back on the ship, he'd gone straight to his cabin. Then nonchalantly put the package in the bottom of his wardrobe. It would be safe enough there. He wasn't stupid enough to try to sell its contents on the ship, besides, there would be a better profit for it once he got to New York. He considered users to be brain dead. He'd never tried heroine himself and didn't intend to, his one foray with L.S.D., had been enough for him. But he found the profit from selling drugs, well worth the effort.

As the liner slowly left the shelter of the harbour, all the girls were standing on the dock watching the impressive outline of Hong Kong melt away. Even Charis, although she was a little withdrawn from the main group, was there. Numerous thoughts filled each mind, but it was easy to see that Jasmine and Tina were jubilant.

Chapter 16

The news of Jasmine's parentage was common knowledge by the following day. Captain Beamish informed her that a single cabin could be arranged for her. Jasmine refused! The second person to treat her with a marked, ulterior degree of politeness, was Charis; none of the other members of the cabaret fawned her. Ted of course, was relieved that he hadn't upset the apple cart, but dismissed Jasmine as unobtainable. Tracy teased Jasmine on her recently acquired shadow, but as most of them liked Lee Chung, his presence didn't cause any major upset. Maurice took it as a personal compliment to himself, that he always knew class when he saw it.

Megan was the first one of the girls to see Patrick Connor, the replacement Engineering Officer, and she'd enthusiastically told Tina and Tracy about him before dinner that evening.

'But how tall is he?'

'Tracy, height isn't everything.'

'It is to me Megan, I never go with a bloke if he's under six foot!'

'You're a fool!' There had been a hard tone in Megan's last comment. Tina glanced up from her make up mirror, but Tracy only shrugged her shoulders and carried on getting ready for dinner. There wasn't a show until the following night, so the game plan was to meet after their meal, for drinks in the Neptune bar. That was when Tracy met Patrick. They liked each other straight away. Their common heritage being Liverpool. Although there was only two years in age difference, coming from diverse areas, they had never met before.

It was past midnight and only about twenty people were still in the bar, including Tracy and her six foot two, rough neck, the American she'd been having a sexual relationship with over the past ten days. He'd told her that, oil men, working on the rigs, were always given that title. So that is what she called him. He had mentioned his name, but she didn't remember it. They left the bar and walked along the deck, it was a beautiful night. The stars in the southern hemisphere, were effulgent in the sky. But neither Tracy, or her partner, had looked up, their preoccupation was with booze. They had stopped on the out side deck and lent against the rail, their destination was his cabin, but were now debating on whether they wanted a bottle of wine. They faced each other and his arms were around her waist, holding her very close against his body.

'Well, do you want me to go back to the bar and get a bottle?' His manner was casual, but his muscles were tense. She was good in the sack and he wanted her. He pushed himself against her and planted a swift, hard kiss on her mouth. He knew that it wouldn't take long before he became fully erect. He was relieved when she grinned and shook her head. They almost ran along the deck. He needed the relaxation of this voyage; when working on the rigs, the pressure was always so immense, that his mind was never out of top gear.

Patrick looked along the deck. He shrugged his shoulders fatalistically. She was certainly involved with the Yank. Shame, he thought, she had the looks he could have gone for that way himself!

When Tracy and her rough neck reached his cabin, he stripped her clothes off, then started to kiss her, pushing his tongue into her welcoming mouth. Five minutes later, he was on top of her. He was only partly undressed. His shirt was open, his trousers and underpants, were around his knees. But he couldn't wait, not the first time. It was always the same, he had no control over his first climax, but once he'd passed that, he'd enjoy spending the next couple of hours, satisfying his partner.

Tracy lay under him. The first time they'd had sex, she'd thought that she'd blown it and picked a dud. But then she'd changed her mind. He might jump on her straight away and come within a couple of minutes, but it didn't take him long to get his wind back; then he certainly knew some gorgeous tricks to please a gal! She waited impatiently for him to start on her.

He raised his shoulders up and took his upper body weight on his elbows. The muscles in his arms flexed as his hands covered her breasts. When he teased her nipples, a smile curved her mouth. He moved slightly sideways so that his right hand was free to peregrinate her receptive body. He watched as she squirmed in ecstasy, under his manipulation. When at last, his fingers titillated the vestibule of her sexuality, he heard with satisfaction, the groans of delight that she uttered. His fingers now delved into her throbbing wetness, probing her sensuality. Then he effectively quickened the manoeuvre. He watched as her breasts heaved, her hands gripped at the cover under her, her back arched up, thrusting her hips higher. The cry which erupted through her throat, as she reached her orgasm, brought a smile to his face. But he wasn't finished yet! He moved between Tracy's legs and bent her knees up, pushing her feet apart. As he lent forward over her, he placed his hands flat on the bed, by her shoulders, then kissed her full on the mouth. Her breath was still ragged, but she responded to him. When his lips moved slowly across her check, to her ear, Tracy gasped in sheer pleasure. From there he travelled erotically down her neck and shoulder, to her breast. Where he took her nipple and the surrounding flesh into his mouth, sucking until she groaned in pure sexual excitement; only then, did he turn his attention to her other tingling breast. After this blitz, he moved with amatorial precision down her body, until he had reached the lips of her moist slit. Then he tasted her delectable wetness.

She opened to him, like a flower blossoming in the heat, then lay there, under the tantalizing onslaught of his tongue. From the beginning, Tracy never actually touched back to earth for two hours. After she had reached her first climax from his fingers; his tongue had created, wave after wave, of electrical voltage through her. She'd felt the tip of his tongue traverse her wetness, then push into her, tasting her creamy depth. She'd accelerated from the ebb of her first orgasm, into her second.

When he knelt up straight in front of Tracy. His position was still between her legs. He laughed. He felt good with himself. He knew that she'd climaxed twice. He looked down at his member and grinned. The tip was already beginning to swell again. He concentrated on it, for perhaps a minute, but no longer, before he moved. First he pulled her legs straight between his, and then walked on his knees, along the outside of her body. He scooped her head up, shoved the pillows behind her and propped her back against them.

Tracy grinned at him, she felt good. She relaxed back into the pillows, as she cupped his masculinity in her hands. Slowly she began to stroke some firmness back. With every touch, her fingers seductively caressed. Soon, she moved her position, so that she could take his budding erection into her mouth, which coaxed a more accelerated response from him. When she knew he was ready for her again, she lifted her head up and grinned as he moved. Then she gripped her calves with her hands and pulled her legs wide apart. She groaned out loud as he plunged deeply into her, enjoying his pummelling action. They rapidly climaxed again.

They lay there, physically exhausted, but Tracy was still mentally restless. She'd been sexually satisfied and had enjoyed the romp she'd shared with her rough neck. But now it was over, she was going back to her cabin, she could never sleep contentedly after one of her revelling sex frolics. Idly, she wondered, where she'd find another bloke, when this one left the ship the following week.

It was the day after the ship had left Port Moresby. There wasn't a show that evening and it was Patrick's birthday, he was twenty seven. The Chief Engineer, who'd heard Patrick singing in the engine room, demanded a performance from him. As soon as it became general knowledge that Patrick was the birthday boy, he got no peace until he agreed to sing a couple of songs, so he went off to get his guitar. Half an hour later the whole of the Neptune bar was enthralled. Patrick had already been singing for twenty minutes, but everyone demanded more. By the time the impromptu party had finally broken up, out of the dancers, only Tracy and Megan were left. Doreen said good night to Patrick and kissed him on his cheek, wishing him a happy birthday before she left the bar. Then it had emptied, except for Tracy and Megan.

'What the hell are you doing here? You should be recording with a voice like that!' Patrick looked at Tracy, then shook his head, but she wasn't being put off the track so easily. 'Why not? You're great. And I don't give out compliments, that's praise mate.' She was in front of him, with her hands on her hips and her feet slightly apart.

'Stop acting like a fish wife.' Tracy's reaction was to thump him, but Patrick was too quick for her, and stepped back out of her range.

'Are you two going to argue all night.' Both Patrick and Tracy ignored Megan. She gave them another swift glance, then left the bar.

'But you can sing, you've got a great voice.' He looked at her and filled his lungs with air. He put his guitar into its case and closed the lid, before he turned back to face her.

'I don't want to sing professionally, so let's just leave it at that.'

'No.'

'You can please yourself what you do with your own life, but you can't make me do anything I don't want to do. So forget it kid and go to bed.'

'No.'

'You might as well, because you'll get nowhere badgering me.'

'How do you know. You don't know me.'

'No, I don't!' Patrick grinned at her. 'But I do know me, very well.' Tracy walked up close to him and smiled coaxingly at him, before she spoke again.

'But it's such a waste of talent, if you won't even give it a go.' Patrick wasn't that tall, only five foot ten inches, but his body was well developed and his muscle tone was excellent. So when Tracy stood directly in front of him, as she was wearing heeled shoes, their eyes were on a level. His were pale blue, with a darker outside ring to the iris. Quite unusual. His hair was thick, black and straight, he had it cut short, it was safer that way in the engine room. Patrick was surprised to feel the urge to kiss her. But he didn't, because he knew that she had a boyfriend. Alright, the Yank had got off the ship the day before, but that didn't mean that she was free. Following that thought, he asked her.

'When are you seeing him again? Do you have to wait until we dock again in Port Moresby in April?'

'Who?' Tracy blinked at Patrick, then grinned at him. 'Don't think that you can fob me off, I never chase red herrings.' Now it was Patrick's turn to look puzzled.

'Didn't the American you're going out with, leave the ship yesterday?' Daylight dawned on Tracy.

'Oh, him! He's not my boyfriend.' Then she inwardly cringed at the look of shock, that flashed across Patrick's face. She wasn't stupid and didn't need his explanation of why he'd assumed that she was going steady with the guy. So she decided to jump in before he could say anything else. 'What the hell has it got to do with you who I lay?' Patrick stood in front of her, but didn't say anything. Tracy ground her teeth in anger. 'You're just a chapel going bastard, who has one convenient law for you men to lay every skirt you like, but let a women have a go around and she's labelled a slut.' Tracy was speaking through gritted teeth. 'Well?' She'd almost shouted her last demand at him. Patrick didn't know what to say. He liked Tracy, but his upbringing had instilled in him, that it was all right for a man to have sex with any female he fancied, but not for the petticoat wearer's to have that same privilege. Tracy ground her teeth and then screamed at him. 'Oh you make me sick. Why don't you go to hell and stay there! You organ grinders are all the bloody same at judging people.' With that last embittered remark, Tracy left the bar.

Patrick slumped back into a handy chair, then slouched forward, putting his head in his hands. He didn't know what to think. He felt hurt that she'd blasted him. 'God, she was worse than a bottle of pop! What right had she to explode like that? After all, why should I care what she does, or doesn't do with other men?' He liked her and didn't see why he couldn't be friends with her. That thought cheered him up. He stood up and picked up his guitar case and walked back to his cabin.

Tracy was too upset to go straight to her cabin, she didn't want to be cross examined about her bad mood. Asking herself, 'why should I bother about what Patrick thinks of me? He's the idiot, not me. If I had his talent, then I'd be trying to use it, not hiding behind a day job, scared of failure. He is just chicken!' She shrugged as she silently added, 'what a waste of a great fellow!'

The cabaret on the following night after Patrick's birthday, was the Broadway show, and the opening music, from Forty Second Street, fitted the bill admirably. Patrick stood at the back of the room by the door. He only had time to watch the opening routine the girls did, because he was on duty in ten minutes. But the glitter of the gold sequined costumes looked good enough to make him wish that he could stay and see the rest of the show. The opening number was slick and professional. And as he watched the dancers, his eyes were unconsciously drawn to Tracy. He was still looking at her when the dance routine had ended. Tomorrow they were at sea, then the next day, the ship was docking at Suva, the chief port for the Fijian Islands. Patrick had tried to wangle time off, but had been unsuccessful. But as he was on duty during the day, his evening would be free. He'd talk to Tracy then. 'After all,' he'd told himself, 'I just want to be friends with her.'

On shore, the girls had split up. Charis went off by herself; Tina headed for the main post office, where she spent a frustrating day, but was rewarded for her patience, by a twenty minute call from Bill, there had been major problems with the overseas connections. Megan had personal shopping to do, then she was returning to the ship, she had a previous appointment to keep with a client and pleaded a headache as an excuse to curtail her day ashore. Mary and Jasmine went on a sight seeing tour, accompanied by Lee Chung. So that left Tracy by herself, she was restless and irritable, all she did, was wander around the main shopping area. She wasn't concentrating on the displayed goods, Patrick kept intruding into her mind and refused to be ejected. This annoyed her. She moaned to herself about anything and everything, then finally returned to the ship in the middle of the afternoon.

They sailed from Suva on the evening tide. The girls, with the exception of Charis, were stood aft, on the promenade deck. Nobody spoke, everyone seemed to be full of their own private thoughts. Once at sea, they drifted into the Neptune bar and ordered drinks. Patrick found them there later that evening.

'Hi girls, can I get anyone a refill?' He was greeted with smiles from Tina and Megan, Tracy deliberately turned to look in the opposite direction. Mary and Jasmine had gone back to their cabin a little earlier. Patrick grinned at his reception and went to the bar. He came back with a tray, he'd brought drinks for them all.

Half an hour later, Tina and Megan left. Tracy hadn't touched the drink that Patrick had bought her. 'Look, I've only come to say I'm sorry. You're right, your sex life is none of my business. I just thought that we could be like, well, be like mates.' Tracy stared hard at him for about a minute.

'Really!'

'Come on Tracy, be a sport. What do I have to do, beg?' She grinned cheekily at him and nodded her head. Patrick was not a guy to back off from a challenge and immediately went down on his knees in front of her. Tracy laughed and to cover up his audacious action, also got on her knees, pretending to be looking for something on the floor. Patrick's head was very close to her's, he looked enquiringly as he asked. 'What are we doing now?'

'Haven't you lost your contact lens'?' He grinned, shook his head and got up. 'That's it, leave me on the floor.' Patrick gripped her elbows and pulled her to a standing position. They stood momentarily very close to each other. He felt an irresistible urge to kiss her, but didn't, instead he smiled at her. Tracy looked into his eyes and became aware of a tingling sensation in her lips, her stomach flipped over and she wanted to fling her arms around his neck.

'Is this a private party or can anyone join in?' Ted's question broke into their moment and dispelled it. 'What're you two drinking, I'll get them in.' Patrick let his hands drop to his side and then turned to answer Ted.

'Tracy is on white wine, mine's a Budweiser, thanks.' Patrick and Tracy sat down and started talking about the Amateur show that was scheduled for tomorrow night. 'The Captain has told me that I'm singing.' Tracy raised her eyebrows. 'It seems that this cruise is short on volunteers!' She nodded.

'There hasn't really been another passenger show to beat the one that the Jones's starred in. They were good.' Ted joined them and the conversation became general.

On the last evening at sea before they docked in Sydney, there was a late night supper on deck. Patrick wasn't on duty, and was enjoying the relaxation of the party. By the end of the night, Tracy asked him if he was going to sing again. He shook his head.

'Well, I think that the Captain is looking for you!' Patrick grabbed her hand, then ran along the deck with her and up the steps at the far end. Pulling Tracy after him. 'What are you doing?'

'Hiding!' She giggled and let him lead her onto a small forward deck, which only led across the deck directly below the bridge and was therefore not used, except by the crew, as a thoroughfare. There was just two feet of space between the bulk head and the hand rail, which crossed from the port to the starboard side. Patrick led Tracy to the middle of this walkway. There, they were sheltered from anyone using the stairway.

'You're mad, what are we doing now?' He turned to face her.

'I've already told you, we've absconded.'

'Don't you like singing?'

'Yes, of course I do, it's just that I didn't feel like it tonight. Don't you ever have times when you want to run away?' Tracy pushed the breath out of her lungs. He'd said he was sorry for judging her, and that he wanted to be friends, it was just that she'd never had a man as a good mate before, sex had always got in the way. 'What's the matter?' Before she realised it, she'd told him what she'd been thinking. Patrick laughed at her.

'Sex on tap. My God, I'll bet you're a popular girl!' His voice had been pleasant enough, but Tracy felt that underneath, there was disapproval, well maybe not that exactly, but something. 'Don't look so puzzled. You and me are just bosom buddies.' Tracy smiled at him and nodded, then stated.

'No sex please, were from Liverpool!' They both howled with laughter. And ended up bent over the hand rail. They heard a voice shouting to someone from the stairs and automatically stepped back into the cover of the bulk head. Patrick was in dark trousers and shirt, so he stepped in front of Tracy, who was wearing a pale green mini dress. He bent his head low to whisper in her ear.

'I feel like a kid playing hooky from school.' Tracy could feel the nearness of his body and pressed herself flatter against the metal of the ship behind her. But it didn't stop her mind trying to imagine what it would be like to be kissed by him. She had her eyes closed and her lips were slightly parted, her breath was shallow and fast. Patrick became very aware of her so close to him and he didn't think about what he was doing, he just let his senses take over and kissed her full on her mouth. Within seconds, they were clinging to each other, their kiss deepening dramatically. When they finally broke apart, both of them were breathing hard.

'I told you that sex would get in the way.' Her voice was barely above a whisper. He shook his head. His mind refused to operate within its unusual confines, but he managed to say.

'No.' Tracy blinked at him.

'What the hell do you mean, no?' To tell the truth, Patrick didn't know, but what he was sure of was that he wanted to get to know Tracy as a person, not as a partner for casual sex.

'It didn't happen.' Tracy opened her eyes to their fullest extent.

'Didn't it!'

'No. Just friends, that's what we are, okay.' She nodded. She didn't know what he was up to, but she did know that she wanted him on her side, as a pal. His friendship was already inestimable to her, even though she'd only known him for a short time. And she knew after all, that sex was so easy for her to get.

Chapter 17

The second cruise had been advertised as a relaxing two week dream voyage, visiting four different and idyllic Pacific Islands, calling at Auckland, New Zealand, before returning to the home port of Sydney. And for the crew, it was certainly less traumatic then the first cruise had been.

Charis appeared for the shows and was always present at the cocktail parties, but had no other contact with the rest of the girls. She never accepted their invitations to join them on their jaunts ashore, and only spoke to them when personally addressed; then her answers were short and noncommittal. Joan and Doreen, had both individually tried to talk to Charis, but by now, she'd put up such an impregnable psychological barrier around herself, that nobody could break through it. Charis knew that she was alone, and she was afraid of loneliness; but she felt that this was the only way to protect herself from any onslaught. It did not enter her head, that perhaps, someone would be on her side.

Tina was jubilant, everything she'd hoped for since falling in love with Bill, was going to happen. She could hardly wait to take him home to meet her parents and family. Tina's childhood had been happy, she'd grown up in the Southern Texan town of Beaumont. The dancing school she'd attended, had been professional enough to nurture her own talent and enable her, at the age of eighteen, to win a scholarship, to attend the State College for the Performing Arts. She'd stayed there for two years and landed her first stage contract with an off Broadway show, when she was twenty. The following season, the show had moved onto Broadway and her career had gone from strength to strength. Tina had been picked for the European tour, and that's when she'd gone to the audition held by the producer of Bill's show. Once she'd meet Bill, she wanted to be with him. She would mix her career with his.

Megan was amassing a reasonable bank balance. When she returned to Britain, she intended to hire a reputable private detective to find her mother. Megan was extremely careful how she chose her clients, this eliminated the real threat of exposure, which would result in scandal over her activities. Discretion was all important to her. She could have doubled the number of men, but she knew that she was treading a fine line and intended not to fall into the quick sand surrounding her. If she let her guard down for a moment, then the end would be immediate. She would lose the means at her disposal, of earning the amount of money she needed to enable her to trace her mother. That was the driving force of her present life. That was the only goal she had. Nothing else mattered to Megan. She would not allow herself the indulgence of thinking beyond that point. When she'd found her mother, then together, they'd make their plans for their future.

So far Mary had managed quite successfully to decline the offer of drinks and dates from the male passengers who'd asked her. But during this cruise, there was a man who belonged to that persistent class of male who didn't understand the word 'no', when said politely. It had ended in a fight. Well, that would be over emphasising the simplicity, of the way in which Lee Chung handled the situation. Mr. Persistent had been making a nuisance of himself by following Mary for days. And as Jasmine was with her, so was Lee Chung, which had forestalled an awkward situation. On the particular night in question, Mary had left the Neptune bar with Jasmine and Lee Chung, they'd headed along the outside deck, which led to the main stair case, from which they could change decks. The Captain spotted Jasmine and stopped her to ask if she needed anything. His manner was gushing and it had taken all of five minutes to stem the Captain's flow. Mary had reached the lower deck before Jasmine and Lee Chung caught up to her. When they did, they found her struggling in the man's arms, in the confines of the narrow corridor. The top of her dress was already torn. Lee Chung stepped quickly passed Jasmine. He then forced the man to release his hold on Mary and as soon as she was free, Mr. Persistent just crumpled where he had been standing. Lee Chung turned and bowed politely to the girls and requested Jasmine to take Mary to their cabin. She did as she was asked. Half an hour later there was a knock on the cabin door and Jasmine answered it and asked Lee Chung in. He stepped just inside the doorway and asked if anything was needed. Jasmine shook her head, she'd already got help from Doreen. Mary had showered and was in bed with a large brandy, to help her sleep. She wasn't badly hurt, she was bruised, but was suffering more from shock, than physical injury. Mary thanked him. He just grinned at her and told her that she would not have any more problems from that man again, as he'd broken his arm, falling down a flight of stairs. Lee Chung once more bowed, then left. Nobody felt it necessary to state that the incident hadn't taken place near a stair well. The outcome of this episode, was that Lee Chung offered self defence classes; Jasmine, Tina, Tracy, Megan, Mary, Doreen and the twins, Crystal and Cindy all accepted. The lessons were held in the ship's gym and although they were hard work, everyone found them fun and very worth while.

When the ship called at Tongo, on the eleventh of March, Jasmine had received a letter from her mother. Zachery had flown to London and spoken to her, concerning Jasmine. The proposed plan, was for the three of them to meet during the next Christmas holidays. At that time, Zachery planned to bring his wife and son to London. That's all Veronica had said. She never reproached Jasmine for contacting her father. Nor did she communicate anything of the conversation which took place between the two of them. The rest of her mother's letter was the usual local news, which she conveyed in her normal correspondence to Jasmine. But her letter had left Jasmine nervous of what would transpire over the next Christmas vacation. How would her mother react to Zachery and how had Veronica really accepted the fact that Jasmine had found him without telling her? There were a lot of questions that Jasmine would have liked answers to, but couldn't ask her mother. It was Mary's suggestion that she could write to her father. Jasmine hadn't thought of that way, for so long, it had just been her mother and herself, that it just never occurred to her to write to her father and ask about how his meeting had gone with her mother. But it proved a difficult letter to construct and Jasmine was relieved that it became unnecessary, when Lee Chung informed her that her father would be in Sydney on the sixteenth of March, at end the end of the cruise, he wanted to speak to Jasmine on family matters. Jasmine found herself impatient for this trip to finish, she wanted to see her father again. Although Lee Chung seemed to be always with her, he never intruded into her life. She began to take him into her confidence. Her shyness still bothered her, and Jasmine never left Mary's side at the formal functions she attended on the liner; but she'd improved enormously and the members of the cast of the show, that she'd got to know, found her more relaxed at the informal gatherings that she went to.

Tracy seemed to find Patrick at her elbow whenever he wasn't on duty. Their kiss had not been discussed. It was if it hadn't actually happened. And the physical attraction that Tracy felt for Patrick, she dismissed as irrelevant. She told herself that it was a quirk of nature and if ignored, would go away. That it seemed to grow with each meeting, she never acknowledged. And when all else failed to put a damper on her impulses, she always resorted to an argument over his choice of football team. She was an ardent Liverpool supporter, but Patrick followed the Blues, and whenever he was at home, he went to every Everton match that was played. During these squabbles, reason and common sense vacated the lists, and the pair of them lost comprehension for any onlookers, when they fell into abusing each other in their local vocabulary, of Scouse! On this cruise, Tracy had been asked out by two passengers, but she'd refused both. She'd told Megan, that neither of them had turned her on, and the dates would have been a total waste of her time. All the answer she had received from Megan, was a raised and slightly quizzical eyebrow. When Tracy had demanded to know why the comical look, Megan had actually laughed in her face. Tracy had left in a huff! She just couldn't accept that Patrick didn't want to sing professionally. How could he waste all his talent? Tracy had decided to take matters into her own hands. If Patrick wouldn't do anything, because he didn't have any faith in himself, she could, she believed in him! She'd tape his next jam session in the Neptune bar, then send it to Tangerine Records, in London. Simple really! If nothing came of it, then at least she'd know she had tried.

On the fourteenth of March, the liner had been docked in Auckland all day. Patrick had been on duty until eight in the evening. Then he'd showered, changed and then gone to the Neptune bar with his guitar. Tracy had asked him to sing that night. She'd asked for 'Dock of the Bay, You'll Never Walk Alone and What A Day For A Day Dream,' and to end with a couple of up beat Elvis songs. Patrick would sing those for her, he also intended to sing 'Where Do You Go To My Lovely,' by Peter Starstedt, then, Peter and Gordon's, 'World Without Love.' He wanted to please her, make her take notice of him as a man, not a guitar player with a voice she thought was good. But all he seemed to do, besides arguing about football, was to play and sing for her, when ever she wanted. He had to keep telling himself, that having an affair with her, would complicate their relationship. And he did feel that he was getting to know her. She was full of fun and always ready to laugh, but also she was kind, generous and, if you were a friend, then she'd be there for you, no matter what. That she considered sex no more serious than a game of tennis, still troubled him. What would happen when she fell in love? Would she be able to be faithful. Would she want to be? Could she, if she did? Did she think about that? Patrick found that Tracy was taking up a lot of his private thoughts, to the exclusion of any other female.

That night, Patrick's session in the Neptune bar was good. There were very few passengers present. The ship hadn't sailed from Auckland until ten o'clock that night, and only about twenty five people were in the bar. There was a relaxed atmosphere and Patrick's voice sounded great. Nobody seemed to notice Tracy tape the proceedings. She'd sat opposite to him, against the wall and her tape was on the shelf behind her. Everything went off successfully. Tracy was thrilled with the result. Patrick had even sung a couple of Beatles hits. She'd played it once the next day, before she wrapped it up and addressed it. The ship docked in Sydney tomorrow, at eight o'clock in the morning and she intended to be at the post office as soon at it opened. She had carefully constructed a letter to enclose with the tape, inferring that she was his agent and put her name forward for any correspondence. Tracy was convinced that she was doing the right thing.

The tugs nosed the liner into position and the engines were cut. Jasmine hung over the rail, waving at her father. He was on the dock waiting for her. She was one of the first to disembark. Zachery took his daughter to have breakfast. They sat on a private balcony, facing each other, the sun shining brightly from a clear sky.

'I've been to see Veronica.' Jasmine nodded quickly.

'I know, she wrote to me.' She paused, then with a rush, asked him. 'How did she react?' Zachery leaned back in his chair, his eye lids, half covered his eyes, as he watched Jasmine. He wanted to punish Veronica for denying him his daughter, but he realised that if he crucified her mother, Jasmine would be hurt and that he would never willing do. He would have no compunction sacrificing the rest of the world, but not Jasmine or Kwong Yuen; they were his children, his to protect.

'In a nut shell, the reason that she told you I was dead, was so that I could not reject you. To her, my refusal to leave Hong Kong, was a wilful expulsion of her from my life.' Zachery stopped. He could tell that his choice of words were effecting Jasmine badly. He was being deliberately cold, that way he hoped that his daughter wouldn't have too many questions, if she thought that it was still painful for him to talk about. If the truth was known, it was, he'd loved Veronica with a passion, that he could never replicate again in his life. He spoke again, threading a little warmth into his voice. 'My reasons for not leaving Hong Kong, were family responsibilities; my mother and grandparents needed me to provide for them. They were solely dependent on me. I had a good job. However, Veronica didn't recognise the necessity for me to remain and she wouldn't stay. She had her career in the Army all planned out. Neither of us were willing to compromise, so we parted. She assumed that I was taking the easy way out to end our marriage.' Zachery held his breath, he didn't want to carry on talking about Veronica, his leaden hurt was still so barbed, that the pain was as substantial now, as it had been at its birth. Jasmine trembled as she stood up and walked to her father; she wrapped her arms around him, a tentative smile flitted across her face. They stayed there comforting each other. No words were needed. Strength came from the tenderness, compassion and love, that sometimes transpires between a parent and child.

Tracy was at the doors of the post office five minutes before it opened. In her hands was a neatly wrapped and addressed parcel. Half an hour later, she was sitting in a cafe, enjoying her breakfast. In a zipped compartment of her hand bag was a receipt for a registered parcel to Tangerine Records, London, England. Tracy giggled in anticipation of what could happen if they liked Patrick's voice. He was too good not to make it. Once the record company heard him, even on her home made tape, they'd be impressed, they had to be. She smiled mischievously as she imagined how pleased he'd be, when he became a star, and all because of her! Patrick would be famous. Then the picture of adoring female fans, flinging themselves at his head, flashed into her mind. She jerked upright. For a split second, the thought of keeping him to herself flashed into her brain, but her professionalism surfaced. Talent was a God given gift and it was a crime to smoother it. She accepted as fate, that when you were as good looking as Patrick was, and were in show business, of course, there would be admirers. That was only to be expected, so what! She shrugged, he wouldn't bother with a load of screaming girls. He could have a minder to keep them from bothering him. Tracy considered it was silly the way some fans threw themselves at their idols. There were plenty of good-looking men around for sex, she could vouch for that. Besides Patrick wasn't into casual bonking. There had been a decent blonde after him for the whole of the last cruise, he'd been given every opportunity for some bayonet practice and he hadn't even bothered. If Tracy had needed any more proof, Patrick hadn't had her either. She was honest enough to know that it was him who had ended their first kiss. If he had wanted too, he could have taken her right then. She wouldn't have stopped him. A shiver trailed down her spine, as it did, every time she thought of his lips on hers. And as always she dismissed the on line chemistry she felt for Patrick. Telling herself, that sex could spoil it for her. Patrick was a mate and she cared for him. After all, she'd never been friends with any of the men she'd been with, she couldn't even remember some of their names. Of course, the odd ones stood out, but only because they'd been terrific performers sexually. But even them, she had a vague suspicion, that she sometimes confused, one with another.

Megan strolled into Lloyds bank in Sydney and made her deposit. The teller informed her that the transaction would take a week. Megan smiled. As long as it was there when she got back to England, that was all that was important to her. She was sure, that by the time she arrived back in London, that she'd have sufficient funds to find her mother, even if it took a long time. As she walked back into the sunlight, she wrapped herself in the determination to reach her goal. She believed that she'd succeed. She had too. There was nothing else in her life. The exigency to find her mother, to tell her that she loved her, gave Megan a meaning for her existence.

After the hour long telephone conversation with Bill, Tina had spent a leisurely morning shopping. She returned to the ship at lunch time with an expensive looking package dangling from her fingers. She'd seen a tempting nightdress and matching negligee, in a deep aquamarine coloured silk, with panels of delicate lace and decided that it would be perfect for New York, Bill would love it!

Charis decided that she didn't want to traipse around the town, she stayed on board the ship and sun bathed by herself on the stern of the promenade deck. As the liner was docked on the port side, she hoped she would not be disturbed by anybody.

Chapter 18

Lee Chung's classes had swollen in the number of those taking part. Margaret from the Purser's office, Linda and Janice, the nurses on the ship, and Pauline, the hairdresser on board, had joined. They met each morning that the liner was at sea, at ten o'clock. Stretched and giggled their way into some serious exercises. Lee Chung taught them simple, but very effective measures, to fend off any unwanted situations they might be unfortunate enough to find themselves in.

This cruise had progressed uneventfully, the weather had been sunny, with very calm seas. The only mishap had been in the kitchen, the chef took a strong aversion to a relief cook's scrambled eggs, the man had only been hired for this two week cruise. The Captain was called in to referee the match and decided in favour of the chef, after all, he was there for the duration, the rights and wrongs of the case, didn't come under consideration at all! As it was a short voyage, there was no passenger's amateur night, and the Fancy Dress Ball, was fitted in on the evening that the ship departed from Santa Cruz. Before they realised it, the liner had docked once more in Sydney, to exchange one group of passengers, for more to board later that day.

Jasmine was assured by the sales assistant that the flowers would arrive on her mother's birthday. There was plenty of time, four whole days. Jasmine handed over the required money and left with Mary. They had a couple of hours shopping time, before they needed to be back on board the ship, it was due to leave Sydney at eight o'clock, that evening. They'd docked this morning, and the crew was busy getting the liner ready for its departure. This cruise was different as its route was around New Zealand, calling at six different ports, as well as at Hobart, Tasmania. It was here that seventeen year old Charity Adams and her parents boarded the liner. This was only the second time Charity had left the island, and in as many months. She'd been brought up by very strict parents, arriving in their life, during their middle age and totally unexpected, but none the less, loved. Edward Adams was fifteen years older than his wife and fifty seven years older than his daughter Charity. Last month he'd suffered a heart attack and his wife had been very ill with shingles. The first time Charity had left the island was due to an out break of chicken pox in the area, it was thought that the best thing to do, was to send Charity to her Uncle, a civil servant living in Canberra. He was the only relative that Mr. and Mrs. Adams had to look after Charity. She'd nervously packed her small case. Charity's summer wardrobe consisted of three cotton dresses, each had a round neck, with a Peter Pan collar and short puffed sleeves. The bodices were designed not to show any shape what so ever; the skirts were gathered and ended below her knees; again, these dresses were in, what seemed like faded, nondescript colours. Charity very rarely saw any strangers, so she had nothing to compare her situation with. She was not allowed to have shorts, or sun tops, nor did she have a bathing suit; such pastimes as swimming and sun bathing were censored by her parents as inessential. Charity was taken to the airport by taxi.

At home, Charity's life had been hedged in. She hadn't been out with a boy, her parents didn't consider her old enough. There was no television, they didn't approve of the programmes; they did have a radio, that was switched on if there was a good orchestra playing a piece of music her father thought appropriate! He wholeheartedly disapproved of anything modern. Charity had been educated at home by her mother, who had come to Tasmania twenty years ago, to get away from the debauchery, that she abhorred in modern society. But as she was a college professor, she'd been capable of teaching her daughter, to a standard that the authorities could not complain about. Charity had not been allowed access to the short wave radio, which was kept locked in her parents bedroom. That the house, the Adams family lived in, was in one of the more remote parts of the island, had insured that Charity had grown up without the companionship, or input, from other children; this of course had passed by unquestioned. Edward was reluctant to send Charity to the mainland, he considered all contact with the outside world as superfluous to his daughter's needs, but there was no one except James.

A very immature Charity had landed in Canberra, her Uncle had buried his wife five's years earlier, a fact that he hadn't communicated to his elder brother. James was a lot younger than Edward and they had very little knowledge of each other as adults. All Edward was aware of was that James had married well, a daughter of a Canon. This he'd approved of. He had gone to the wedding and it had been a quiet affair. Edward had been impressed. James had never been tempted to ape his elder brother's ways, his estimation of Edward was so low, that it was negligible. If the truth was known, James never wrote to him. When James's wife had died, his eldest daughter had taken over the job of sending Christmas and birthday cards to Tasmania and as she was called Maud, the same as her mother, Edward was left in blissful ignorance of the state of affairs in Canberra. Maud was the eldest of six children and lazy. Luckily James was making enough money to pay a house cleaner, and as all the children were between twelve and eighteen at the time of his wife's death, James got on with his career and left the children to Maud. None of them were, what you could call stupid, or even slow on seizing opportunities that presented themselves! They soon realized that as long as they did not actually barge into Maud's life, so that she had to take notice of what they were doing, they could get away with most things.

Amy, the youngest of James's children was, at the time of Charity's visit, eighteen years old, and so Maud, who was now married and living in her own home, had given Amy the responsibility to entertain Charity. Amy didn't think much of that! She'd taken one look at the clothes Charity had arrived in and dressed her in her own gear even before the girl had unpacked her case! Amy had then taken Charity to an all night party, and introduced her to booze and men. For her first party, Charity had worn a sleeveless mini dress in cherry red. Amy had also given her some pretty underwear, Charity's was consigned to the dust bin! Amy had unbraided Charity's long hair and cut it to just below the girl's shoulders, it improved her looks no end! The party that night had opened Charity's eyes and her brain to fun, lots and lots of excitement and no disapproving parents to glower if you laughed out loud. Amy found that her cousin had been eager to learn as well as a good sport, they became kindred spirits. Charity had thrown herself into these new adventures. She'd laughed and hadn't been frowned upon; a novel experience for her! Amy had given her a number of outfits from her over stocked wardrobe. Charity hadn't needed to be asked twice not to mention the parties to Maud, or in fact, any of the family! At the end of her stay in Canberra, Charity had been planning her escape. The only thing that made her return to her parents when requested, was the fact that the cruise had been booked, the doctor had insisted; both

Mr. and Mrs. Adams were ordered to take a vacation. A leisurely sail around the coast of New Zealand, seemed to fit the bill admirably.

Mr. and Mrs. Adams were not impressed with the ship, but Charity was enthralled. Her parents retired each night at nine o'clock, and as far as they were concerned, Charity was also in bed. What actually happened was that Charity changed her plain cotton dress, which she had worn during the day, for one of the little numbers Amy had given her, and then she'd partied!

The ship had been docked at Dunelin all day, and left before dinner was served that night. There was no show that evening as the passenger's amateur was scheduled. Tina had her head bent over her writing paper. Megan had already dressed and had left the cabin. Tracy flicked though her wardrobe, she was bored, Patrick had been on duty all day and tonight he had been told by Captain Beamish to take part in the evening's entertainment. Tracy wasn't impressed, but knew there wasn't anything she could do. Patrick loved singing, and was pleased to be asked to perform. Then a grin spread across her face. She'd wear her black satin cat suit, all her gold jewellery, then just for fun, flirt with every hunk that came within her clique.

Patrick had rushed his shower after finishing his duty shift. He wanted to have a drink with Tracy before the start of the passengers show. He was sitting ideally in the Neptune bar, unconsciously staring at the door, waiting for Tracy to come in. When she did, he was just swallowing and choked.

'Hi.' Tracy beamed at Patrick as she sauntered over to him.

'What the hell do you think you've got on?' Tracy blinked. Patrick didn't sound very pleased. She couldn't understand why. She thought she looked sexy. 'You're acting like a cheap slut, just asking to be groped.' Tracy's smile vanished. Her lips curled into a thin line. He'd spoilt everything with his stuffy old fashioned notions. When she spoke her voice was low, but easily conveyed all the anger she felt.

'Since when, did what I wear, have anything to do with you?' Patrick was too mad to think how he was handling the situation. He stood before her, his eyes blazed. He wanted to grab her and shake some sense into her crazy mind. In stead he shoved both hands into his pockets and snarled at her.

'Are you going to change that get up?'

'No. Sod off and preach to someone who wants a sermon.' Tracy hunched a shoulder, turned, stormed off to the bar and ordered a double gin and tonic. She didn't turn her head as Patrick marched out. She was on her third drink when Charity and her two escorts wandered in.

Within five minutes, Tracy had joined Charity and the two Australians. After twenty minutes they left the bar, and headed for the men's cabin. Both brothers were carrying a bottle of champagne and two glasses! Tracy dismissed any thought of Patrick, if he didn't appreciate her, there were others that certainly did do so! Charity had been introduced to group sex by Amy; Tracy, for all her experience, hadn't. This was her first session. Johny and Peter couldn't believe their luck. Two good looking dolls, who wanted to rave! Charity was the ring leader, as soon as the cabin door had been locked, with a cheeky grin, she said.

'Last one with any clothes left on, has to pay a forfeit.' Charity was already stripping, Johny and Peter, once their initial surprise had vanished, were quick to follow. Tracy was still in the middle of the cabin fully dressed. 'You're last!' That seemed to Tracy to be the understatement of the year. The three of them paraded and strutted around the small cabin. 'You lose! I get to pick who I want to have first.' Charity wiggled up to Johny and kissed him. His hands were all over her naked flesh. Then she left him with his tongue hanging out and concentrated her efforts on Peter. Tracy felt bemused. She was all for freedom of sex, but this seemed to be over the top a bit. Charity was enjoying herself, next, she provocatively handled each man's member in turn. Both had the start of erections. Charity grinned as she saw that Johny was nearly ready. As she was, she chose him.

Peter strolled over to Tracy and offered her a glass of champagne. He wasn't embarrassed over his nakedness, in fact, he seemed pleased. They sat on the spare single bed and watched Charity and Johny hump on the other. To Tracy it wasn't even sensual. There was nothing romantic in their actions, they looked like two animals rutting in the straw! Tracy felt a disdainful shudder run through her. She sipped at her drink, unsure of what she wanted to do.

Charity was just getting into her rhythm when Johny sagged on her. She clenched her fist and thumped him. But he was out cold. She pushed him off her body and helped him onto the floor with her foot. Peter just laughed and explained.

'He's drunk too much. You won't get anything else out of him tonight.' Charity looked sulky. She was in the mood for sex and the one she'd chosen, had been a wash out.

'Well, don't let me stop you two.' Charity's voice sounded childish and petulant.

'Don't blow a fuse doll, I'm good for a couple of bangs.' Peter stood up, his erection now solid. Charity licked her lips and Tracy sniffed.

'He's yours first, fairs, fair!' Charity sat squirming on the bunk.

'Hadn't we better see if Johny's okay.' Tracy stood up as she spoke and moved around to where Johny was. He'd landed on his chest and his arms were sprawled out, his head on one side, he was breathing through his open mouth. 'Better cover him with something.' Charity got up from the bunk and pushed her breasts up at Peter, she wasn't interested in Johny's fate, now he was no use to her. Tracy pulled a light blanket off the bunk and shook it out so that as it landed, it covered Johny's body.

'Right, now you've played Nurse Nightingale, I'm ready to lay you; then I'll show Charity what it's like to be fucked by me!' Peter was standing with his feet slightly apart, he was over six feet in height, had blonde hair and was good looking enough, but Tracy wasn't in the mood for him. Charity could have him all to herself. Tracy smiled, waved good bye, curtsied and left.

When Tracy left Charity and Peter to their fun, she walked out onto the deck, then went forward to the narrow deck, where Patrick had kissed her. She lent on the rail, the light breeze, blew softly on her face. Tears filled her eyes, then fell. She didn't know why she crying, only that she couldn't stop. She ached with loneliness. For the first time in her life, Tracy felt vulnerable.

Patrick joined some passengers for drinks after the show. He was in a restless mood and wanted to see Tracy to apologise to her. He had no right to argue with her over what she chose to wear. But seeing her in that tight black satin, had made him want to tear it off her and take her. And he knew Tracy and liked her, so what would some man do, if all he could see was a sensual female oozing with sexual potential. Patrick groaned inwardly, more and more, he wanted Tracy, with a hunger that only grew. He was a man in love. But what he didn't know, was what Tracy wanted, lust or love? At the bar, Patrick asked the bar tender where she was. The answer robbed him of his thirst. He took his guitar back to his cabin. The room measured ten feet by twelve, and was reasonably fitted out, but tonight, it gave him an unexpected dose of claustrophobia. He left and wandered aimlessly around the open decks. He heard a female crying and took the stairs up to the next deck, two at a time. As he reached the upper deck, Patrick was shocked to see Tracy, and instinctively wrapped her in his arms, to comfort her.

'Don't cry.'

'Oh Patrick!'

'Yes.' She snuggled against him, hiccupping as she tried to stop sobbing. He gave her a couple of minutes, then asked. 'Is there something very wrong? Have you been hurt?' In some respects Patrick was an old fashioned darling, she didn't pretend to misunderstand his meaning. He was afraid she'd been sexually assaulted. She lifted her head and smiled through her tears.

'Nothing has happened to me.' She didn't add, that if it had, she'd have only had herself to blame for putting herself in such a sordid situation. Patrick felt his heart start to hammer in his chest. He gulped more air into his lungs.

'Benny said you've left the bar with some passengers.'

'I did, but I wasn't interested in them, I didn't stay with them. I'm just sad.'

'Don't be, I'm sorry, you look beautiful.' Patrick lifted her off her feet and hugged her. She smiled at him, blinking her eyes free of tears.

'No, don't cry any more.' Patrick watched as her lips trembled and his mind stopped nagging about common sense, he lowered his head and kissed her full on her mouth.

Tracy saw his lips descending and sighed, a warmth of joy spread through her as she returned his passion with one of equal intensity. She had a vague idea that this wasn't supposed to happen. But as the night breeze drifted past, her reticence capitulated under the now growing storm of hot waves of desire surging through her.

They stood on that very narrow deck, swaying with the intensity of their emotions. When Patrick raised his head, his chest was heaving. Tracy knew that if he released his hold on her, she'd fall. She felt so heady, the pluses in her body, ravaged at what was left of her balance. All she wanted was him, the way he'd kissed her had vanquished all other memories from her consciousness. She was willingly letting herself drown in him.

Patrick stared at Tracy as if he'd never seen her before. He asked himself what he was doing? Should he push her from him, but he couldn't, the nearness of her body, dominated his mind. He wanted to make love to her. To lay her down on the floor beneath them, and bury himself in the exotic essence of her being. He kissed her again, pushing an exploring tongue into her mouth, wanting to taste more and more of her.

Tracy had lost whatever reason she possessed. She pulled at his shirt, she was insane with desire for him. At last her hands were able to touch his skin. But she wanted more. She groaned at Patrick, asking him to take her now. She didn't care where they were. Her hands now went to his manhood. The material of his trousers taught across his hips, but she could still feel his member, it was swollen and distended. She wanted him. She uttered his name as her world spun widely around her.

'No!' Tracy didn't hear Patrick, her mind was encapsulated in a fog of desire, her fingers trying to achieve their destination inside his clothing. 'No. Tracy we can't do this.'

Patrick shook her roughly, his fingers dug into the flesh on her shoulders. Tracy didn't know what was the matter, she didn't care, all she wanted was Patrick. Just as her hands achieved their goal, she felt Patrick grip her wrists and wrench her arms up. They were both breathing rapidly.

She looked at him, his clothes were dishevelled, his chest was bare, his trousers almost completely undone. The nearness of him, suffocated the awareness of the pain from her wrists. She arched her back, pushing her body towards him

'Stop it. How much of this do you think I can take. What the hell do you think I am?' Tracy sucked air into her lungs. His voice was bitter, was he also disgusted? Why? What was he saying? Didn't he want her? 'For God's sake woman, don't do this to me. I can't take much more of this and stay sane.' Tracy momentarily stopped breathing, a deluge of ice cold fear overwhelmed her. She tore free of him and ran.

Patrick dived after her and caught her by the top of the steps. She'd flung herself at them, but he managed to drag her back into the shelter of the bulk head. She shook as if she was sobbing, but this time there were no tears.

With her eyes staring at the deck, Tracy stood there. She was hardly breathing. So afraid that she'd lost him before she'd really found him. All she'd had was a tentative glimpse of a Utopia, that was now being snatched out of her reach, but not out of her life. How could Patrick only want just friendship; when she'd have very willingly have drowned in her love for him. Why, of all the men she'd known, why did it have to be Patrick that didn't want her. She didn't have the personal strength to be just friends. Whoever said half a loaf was better than none, had never been in love with a person, who didn't love them back.

'We've got to talk.' Tracy looked up at him and shook her head, tonight she was incapable of coherent thought. 'Look Tracy.'

'No. Not now. Please I have to go.' Her eyes pleaded with him to let her go. Hesitantly, he moved aside. She left.

Tracy ran instinctively back to her cabin. She arrived, out of breath.

'He doesn't want me.' Megan and Tina both stared at her, then looked at each, shrugging their shoulders.

'Who?' They'd chorused their question.

'Patrick.' Megan nodded and Tina smiled.

'What am I going to do?'

'About what?'

'I've just said, Patrick?'

'You might be talking, but you're not making much sense.' Megan's tone did hold some sympathy.

'Oh, I see!' Tracy's voice vibrated with frustration and hurt. 'Well, he was kissing me, then he pushed me away. He doesn't want me.'

'Did he tell you that?' Tracy shook her head at Tina. 'Then how do you know?'

'Because he stopped!'

'Where were you?' Tracy frowned at Megan's question, but answered her.

'On the narrow deck, just forward of the bridge.'

'Has it occurred to you that he might prefer somewhere a little more private?' Tracy looked blankly at Megan.

'But it didn't matter, we were alone!' Megan snorted and Tina shook her head.

'Think about it! Maybe the bloke wants to make love to you and not have a quick lay on an open deck.' Tracy stared at Tina. 'Are you in love with him?' Tina's question hit Tracy with the accuracy of hail storm. 'Before you talk to him make up your mind.'

'But I don't have to. I am in love with him, I realised that tonight!' Both of them stared open mouthed at Tracy, it was Megan who spoke.

'Have you told him?'

'No.'

'Then maybe you should!'

Chapter 19

Captain Beamish sat in his office with something like a contented grin on his face. This was his last voyage, when the liner docked back in Southampton, he'd retire with all the glory of self satisfaction that he felt. The end of his life at sea, which had started as a lad of fourteen would culminate with suitable honours. He'd been a merchant seaman during the Second World War, ships had sunk with prosaic repetition, and with them thousands of lives, but not Joseph Beamish, he'd been one of the lucky ones. By the end of that conflict, which had indiscriminately tortured and slaughtered people, dispatching millions of lives into oblivion, Joseph had risen from a deck hand to a junior bridge officer and decided then to stay at sea, he liked the life that peace time sailing offered. From then on, his sole ambition, was to have his own ship, and he had accomplished his dream.

The Chief Engineer, suspended the Captain's propitious meditations, the smile became pinned on his face. But there was no way he was going to be persuaded to delay sailing. They were going on this evening's high tide, and that was final. The Chief Engineer kept a firm hold on his frustration.

'But Sir, if it fails, we can't fix it and a replacement is the only option.'

'I accept that. But it could last, this next cruise is only a two week voyage.' Beamish looked at his Chief Engineer impatiently, wishing the man would stick to his engines and leave the management of the ship alone. 'Do you realise what it would cost the company if our departure was delayed for twenty four hours? And who's to say that it will arrive tomorrow, we could be sat here for days. Besides you can make arrangements with the port authorities here, when the valve finally does arrive, to have it sent up to Cairns, we dock there in five days. That's plenty of time, there's no need for all this fuss, what could possible go wrong?' The Captain continued without waiting for the other man to speak.

'I have to think of the cost of any delay that occurs and whether it is really essential to incur such a price tag. You can't possibly know the amount in question. Too much, far too much. After all we do carry a spare, don't we?'

'Yes Sir, but it's not a new one. In fact it's the original valve that I had taken out in Southampton.' The Captain played his masterstroke.

'And it has been overhauled and is in working order.' The Chief Engineer shook his head. He knew as well as the Captain did, that the spare valve was one of those inexplicable entities, in the world of machinery, that nobody could explain; the valve looked okay but when fitted into the compressor, it started to falter, and was therefore unreliable. The Chief Engineer, would have liked to dump the damn valve overboard, but he knew the company accountants would have had convulsions at the very thought. He gave up the argument. He couldn't change the Captain's mind, so he left the office and returned to the engine room. Now he had to decide whether to leave the old valve in place or change it for one he didn't trust. He looked at his wrist watch. It was too late to do anything major now, there were only two hours before they sailed.

Patrick had volunteered to cover for another officer, who wanted to go ashore. He threw himself into his work, hoping that it would take his mind off Tracy, but it didn't. She filled his being. He wanted her, like he'd never needed any other female. She even pervaded his dreams, and he woke up hungry for her. The memory of her kisses made him moan inwardly. How could she do this to him, and why? He'd asked himself a million times and still didn't know the answer. He didn't want to be in love with her. How could he forget about the other men littered in her past life! How many were there? Would it be so relevant if it was just a couple of blokes she'd been with? Patrick didn't know. But the gnawing question was, had there been too many for him to ignore? Did it matter, what she'd done before he'd met her? If he loved her, surely, that was all that should count. After all, he wasn't a virgin, in fact, he couldn't remember off hand, how many women he'd laid! So why should it be a different set of rules for Tracy, than for himself? Could he shrug his shoulders and just concentrate on their life together? Would she be honest and up front with him in the future? He thought so, but even if that happened, would her past creep in and decay their love? He didn't know. But until he'd made up his mind, he wasn't going to talk to Tracy. He had to be honest with her, she deserved that much.

The old valve lasted for another six days. Its replacement had arrived in Cairns twelve hours after the departure of the ship. The Chief Engineer had informed the Captain that the replacement valve was on its way, but Beamish insisted on keeping to the arranged schedule, and the ship sailed with the tide. The liner was sailing in a northerly direction, from the main land of Australia, towards Papua, New Guinea. It would take them two days to reach Port Moresby. It was just after midnight on the twenty second of April, that the compressor valve broke down. The engines were silent, and the ship drifted for the three and half hours, while the engineering crew worked replacing the valve. Very few of the passengers were aware that anything had happened, most slept through it. The substitute valve behaved and the ship was only ninety minutes late arriving at Port Moresby. The Captain allowed an extra hour in port, so instead of departing at six o'clock that evening, they left an hour later. Dinner was served straight away, and the amateur night show began at nine that evening.

Between New Guinea and Noumea, New Caledonia, two crucial setbacks occurred. The first wasn't a surprise to the Chief Engineer, the temperamental compressor valve started its contretemps, and kept all the engineering crew busy. The second plague was for the medical staff, a thirty six hour stomach virus hopped, without inequity, through the ship. The Captain was in a foul mood. Patrick found himself, with the Chief Engineer, as one of the only two engineering officers on their feet. They had no more than half their crew at any given time, no sooner than one man came back for duty, than another fell ill. Tempers were running high. Everyone had too much work.

Maurice, who had never had a days illness in his life, and didn't intend to spoil his record now, treated everyone as if they had leprosy. He kept to the show schedule as best he could. Doreen did her cabaret spot, between bouts of sickness, but as the audience was feeling very sorry for themselves, nobody really complained on the gaps in the chorus. Ted and Ginger seemed to be immune from the virus, as they were from every day life.

Tracy went everywhere, hoping to catch the bug, she thought that if she was ill, then Patrick would take pity on her and visit her. The need to tell him that she was in love with him, monopolized her thoughts. She was aware that there were mechanical problems in the engine room, and put his reticent behaviour down to that, not the fact that he would not want to see her. Charis was very sick for the duration she had the virus.

Jasmine, like Tracy wasn't affected by the bug, but Mary did succumb and it was Jasmine's turn to be mother. Jasmine was very annoyed that Lee Chung hadn't let her know that he'd been ill. Her attitude surprised him, but it also impressed him.

Megan brushed the illness off, but found the atmosphere generally oppressive, under currents and uneasy tensions were rife through out the ship. The crew lost its accustomed geniality. Those who weren't sick, found their duties extended and the demands on their time became increased by fractious passengers, most of them weren't actually ill, but recovering, and the rest were just worried about catching the virus.

The second week of the cruise seemed to drag for the harassed crew and the ailing passengers. The last evening at sea was honoured as usual with the Captain's Farewell Cocktail Party. Tracy wore her white, fringed silk, mini dress, she was sure that Patrick would approve! And no doubt he would have, had he been there. Captain Beamish had a fixed smile pinned to his face and with every second breath, assured the passengers that the kitchens on the ship were in an immaculate state of cleanliness. Stating in his high pitched voice, that the virus had been brought aboard by those passengers who, against his advice, had eaten local food on an unorganized trip ashore. He added magnanimously, that no doubt the islanders themselves, would not be harmed by consuming this local delicacy, but the passengers should have been more circumspect! His manner was that he felt that the behaviour of those particular people, selfish in the extreme.

Even though the end of this trip was in sight, tempers were still running high in the engine room. The stokers were exhausted with over work. The inevitable scuffle broke out and soon escalated into a full blown fight. Patrick was on duty and immediately intervened. But by the time the Chief Engineer and three of the bridge Officers had finally stopped the brawl, Patrick had collapsed. He was found to have been stabbed. A deep cut of about four inches, ran from the middle of his left shoulder, just under the bone, diagonally down. His blood saturated even the overalls he wore while working. As soon as the Chief Engineer realised that Patrick was seriously injured he sent for the Doctor.

Norman Parsons was sipping his usual large brandy. This was his fourth. In all his time on the liners, this last week was the worst he'd ever experienced. He was in his late fifties, he'd taken early retirement, in order to avoid a probe into his lack of care of a number of his elderly patients. He could only ever be described as a mediocre physician. There was no doubt the he was clever, but he very rarely put himself out, even for his patients. When one of the stokers tracked him down, he staggered as he stood up. He first went to the medical centre to collect his bag, then went to find Linda, she was the staff nurse, and Norman had every confidence in her ability to cope, even if he was unsure of his own. When the Doctor and nurse arrived in the engine room, Patrick was unconscious. Linda looked hard at the Doctor, sent a message to Janice, informing her of the emergency, then suggested that it would be better to get Patrick out of the heat of the engine room, besides she couldn't strip her patient there. Four men, including the Chief Engineer, carried Patrick to the medical centre and laid him in the examination room. Janice was already there. Norman left the two nurses to divest Patrick of all his clothing, Linda then covered the lower half of the patient with a sterile sheet. Able to see what they were doing, she and Janice cleaned the wound, it was still sluggishly bleeding. Norman rubbed his eyes, then screwed up his face as he stared at the round clock on the wall of the room. It was already past midnight. The ship was due to dock in Sydney at eight o'clock that morning. He decided to wait and send Patrick to a hospital in Sydney. He couldn't operate, even if he wanted to, he'd drunk to much brandy.

'Pack the wound tight and try to stop the bleeding that way. We'll be in port soon, I'll arrange for a ambulance to be there when we dock, he'll have to go to hospital.' Linda was about to argue when she deliberately bit her tongue, and the insulting remark, remained unspoken. On second thoughts, she'd decided that Patrick would be better off without Norman, fumbling an attempt to stop the bleeding. The cut was deep, but too high in the chest to cause any irreparable damage to Patrick.

Linda and Janice worked relentlessly on Patrick, and managed between them, to stop him bleeding to death. The Doctor did go and wake the Captain up. The port authority in Sydney were warned of the emergency. The Chief Engineer had returned to the engine room and surprised the men on duty there by ordering full steam ahead. Previously he'd been handling the temperamental valve with kid gloves. The ship arrived one hour before scheduled. Patrick was immediately delivered into the expert hands of the paramedics who were waiting for him. Two hours later, the patient was in a recovery ward, it was confirmed that there would be no permanent damage, but he would be unable to sail with the ship. He'd lost a lot of blood and had to be given a transfusion. Patrick would have to stay in hospital for three weeks and then he'd need recuperation, the doctors from the Sydney hospital wanted to keep their patient under observation during this period as well. Captain Beamish had spent the morning on the radio telephone to the company's head office. It was finally arranged that Patrick would be given an air ticket from Sydney to New York, for the beginning of June. The liner was due in New York on the third, staying docked for the fourth, fifth and sixth, starting their first cruise on the evening of the seventh.

Captain Beamish behaved as if the whole episode had been orchestrated purely to aggravate him. His last cruise in the Pacific hadn't been the monumental success he'd dreamt of, but he had congratulated himself on the way he'd personally handled the awkward inconveniences of the compressor valve and the stomach virus; then, when the end of the cruise was almost reached, an impetuous young officer had been stupid enough to get himself stabbed and that didn't really look very good in a report. Really, he felt that was enough to irritate anyone!

This was the first cruise that Megan had no large deposit of money to take to the bank when they docked in Sydney. She accepted it as one of those eventualities that life throws up on the unsuspecting. She more than appreciated the convenience of choice of her clientele from the passengers on the ship. It was six months since the liner had left Southampton and her bank balance had never been so healthy. Megan had learned the hard way about the integrity of some private detectives that she had hired from the provincial towns were she'd worked, since she'd left Harold's flat. This time, when she returned to London, she'd be able to hire a reputable firm to help her, in her search for her mother.

Tracy didn't get up until lunch time, she'd spent a restless night and her dreams had been nightmares. When she finally did drag herself from her bunk, she was already late. She showered then went ashore, she had some last minute shopping to buy before they sailed that evening. The liner was heading for America, leaving the Pacific behind them. The next group of cruises, would be based from the home port of New York, and concentrate on the Caribbean. One of those voyages, included the River Orinoco, also there was a single trip that went north and visited New England. By the time Tracy returned to the ship, the passengers, for the voyage from Australia to America, were boarding. She didn't fancy making a slow crawl through the crowded decks, so she went forward and stood in her favourite place, on the narrow deck. No passengers would bother her there, and she hoped that maybe Patrick just might pass, and walk along there. Tracy had always had an idea in the recess of her mind, that love could be painful. If you gave your heart to another person, then you gave them the means to hurt you. Why couldn't Patrick love her? Was she so awful? She wrapped her arms around herself, trying for a little comfort, but found none. The noises from the ship bustled from the lower deck, but hadn't the power to penetrate her thoughts. They were entirely centred on Patrick. She loved him with her whole being. There were no restrictions, no ifs or buts on her feelings, they were his. He could trample her in the dirt, or raise her to the Elysium fields, where those people, who'd attained their dreams, trod in joy.

'Oh Bill, I can hardly believe it!'

'Well, it's true.'

'Really over?' Tina could hear the relief in his voice as he answered her.

'Yes! I'm divorced.'

'Happy?'

'Of course I am. Broke, but ecstatic.'

'The money isn't important, we can both work.' She heard his laugh over the wire and smiled. She loved him so much, it was hard to put her feelings into words, she was laughing as she told him.

'I'll always love you'.

'Have I told you lately that I adore you?'

'Yes, but please tell me again Bill.'

'I do and will for eternity.'

'Life is going to be marvellous. I can't wait to see you again. You don't know how hard its been for me.' Even now, there was the echo of hurt in her voice.

'It's only thirty five days.' His voice throbbed with intensity and emotion. 'I'll be on that dock in New York when your ship gets in.' Then he laughed. 'Maybe I should just send a car. It wouldn't be appropriate to make love on the pier. I'll have to wear hand cuffs and take a large dose of bromide before I see you!'

'Don't bother, there's always my cabin!'

'Don't you share?'

'Yes, but I'll throw the girls overboard, it will be an emergency.'

'You've better believe it. I want to make love Tina.'

'Me too, I want you so much, I ache for you.' She heard him groan.

'Oh God Tina, I need you.' She blinked back her tears and nodded, then said aloud.

'Yes.'

'I'll be there, I promise.'

'I want you to swear that you'll never make me go anywhere without you again.'

'You know that.'

'Bill, I don't think I could go through a separation again. I'm not really alive without you.'

'You will never have to in the future.' The operator interrupted them. Their time was over.

'I love you Bill, I'm crossing off the days.'

'I'm counting the minutes!'

'Bye my darling.' The sudden crackle on the line, forced her to put the receiver back in its cradle. Tina wandered back to the liner in a state of honeyed anticipation.

Chapter 20

'What?' Tracy yelled. 'Oh God, I have to get off this ship!'

'Don't be stupid, you know you can't do that.' Megan looked sympathetically at Tracy as she spoke. 'There's no need to panic, he's going to be all right. I've already told you what I over heard the Chief Engineer telling the Captain.' Tracy just stood there in the middle of their cabin and burst into tears. She was still weeping when Tina walked in.

'What's the matter?'

'Patrick's in hospital in Sydney and won't be rejoining the ship until we reach New York.' Tina nodded, then asked in a quiet voice.

'Serious?' Tracy jerked her head up and cried dramatically.

'Stabbed.'

'He's going to be fine. He just needs to stay in the hospital for a couple of weeks then rest to get his strength back. He lost a lot of blood and had to have a transfusion. But honestly, the Chief Engineer told the Captain that he'd been to see him this afternoon and Patrick was already in the general ward. He's doing okay.' Tina nodded, then spoke to Tracy.

'I know it's no use us telling you not to worry, because you can't help yourself, but New York isn't that far away.' Tina couldn't help smiling when she thought of how close she was to seeing Bill again.

'But I can't get off this damn ship, and I wanted to talk to him before then. O hell, I hate waiting!'

'Don't tell me how impatient you are! Just think of how long I've had to be resigned about being alone. We'll count the days together!' Megan raised an eyebrow. Tina laughed. 'Well, as it's going to be public knowledge when we meet in New York, I'll tell you two now, but promise me that neither of you will mention anything to the others, or anybody else before then.' Megan nodded, then dug Tracy in the ribs.

163

'Okay! But who the hell would I tell anyway!' Tracy's voice was irritable. Tina wasn't going to allow her friend's understandable bad mood to spoil any happiness.

'Bill Ryder and I are getting married.'

'Mr. Show Business himself?' Tina couldn't help grinning broadly at Megan's statement.

'His divorce has just come through. That's the only reason I'm on this ship, Bill insisted that I was away while the legal work went through. But now everything is over, we're meeting in New York, and I can't wait.' Megan smiled at Tina, she hadn't seen the other girl so happy! Tina was glowing.

At the Captain's Welcome Aboard Cocktail party, Tracy, more or less, bulldozed her way to the Chief Engineer and questioned him about Patrick. She continued to do so, until the bemused man was rescued by a junior bridge officer. Megan wandered around and saw a couple of likely clients, but she was cautious, she'd wait until a more suitable occasion presented itself to her, before she'd give out a definite proposition. But she did smile invitingly at the two men in question, before she drifted away. Megan sipped her champagne as she idly listened to a conversation between two elderly male passengers

'So you think that the Second World War, did come to a reasonable conclusion?'

'Of course.' Came the blustery reply. The quiet voice spoke again.

'I wonder if the Polish people think that? Anyway, I'm very sure that Churchill didn't, how could he? He only took Britain into the war to protect Poland from a Dictator, and ended up giving the country to another one.' The blusters became more indignant, but the quietly spoken gentleman, smiled and moved away. Megan couldn't help herself from grinning. She'd been impressed how this present conflict had been drawn up and won. She thought, the old man must be very intelligent.

The first destination was the port of Vila, Vanuatu; they reached there, six days after the liner had left Australia. During this time, the cast performed shows one and three; Maurice was saving the second show, 'Hollywood,' until the liner reached Los Angeles, on 18 May. The town of Vila was set above a pristine lagoon of diaphanous water, and backed by succulent vegetation. The island was everybody's idea of a what a South Seas paradise, should look like. The day at sea, between, Vila and Lautoka, on the island of Fiji, was when Megan gave her terms to Eddy Gunnell. He'd joked with her, as he'd agreed to them. Today was the Fancy Dress Ball. The arrangement was made for nine o'clock the following evening, the liner was due to leave Lautoka an hour earlier. Megan was looking forward to the next day. When it arrived she spent it with the other girls, needless to say, Charis had curtly refused their invitation to join them for an afternoon of white water rafting! It had taken all Tina's influence to persuade Tracy not to miss out on the fun. She was mercurial and also irritable, still very worried about Patrick. But in the end, Tracy agreed to go with them. This trip had been arranged in secret, because if Maurice had realised what his dancers were up to! Wellington's siege of Badajos, would have been cast into the shade by this particular General's actions, to stop his girls from such a hazardous escapade! The five girls returned to the ship, wet and exhausted, but none of them would have missed the experience, they enjoyed every thrilling second!

The hour from nine until ten that evening was more of a nightmare for Megan. Eddy Gunnell had proved sadistic. Nor had he given her any money; he'd stated, she could collect that, when next he wanted her services. For the first time, Megan felt a trepidation. But she was a business woman, and determined to collect what he owed her. Swallowing her fear, she stood her ground. Eddy had tossed off his drink and bluntly told her to get lost, unless she was asking to get laid again before she went. Megan felt a desperate need to run from him, but she didn't want to let him know how scared she was. When he walked towards her, she backed away from him. She found the closed door barring her exit. Eddy came very close to her and pressed himself against her. She wanted to scream, but no noise sounded. She stiffened as she felt his hands pulling at her dress. It was too late, he had her pinned against the door, she thought that he was going to rape her. She froze. The aeon of time that he held her captive, ended abruptly. He moved away from her inert form and told her to come to his cabin on the afternoon of the Mid Cruise Cocktail Party, at two. She just fled from his cabin.

The next port of call was Apia, in Western Samoa, here, history seems to march along side the present day life. The Samoans could trace their roots back to a culture which predated the European's, by thousands of years, and the people of the islands were still ruled by heredity Chieftains. When the liner left Apia, there were five days at sea before they reached Honolulu. Shows, four and five, were scheduled before the cocktail party, they were Bow Bells and China Town; a Space Odyssey and fashion show, were to follow the party.

Megan had made a plan to get the money Eddy owed her and then leave straight away, her determination to hide her nervousness, gave off an obdurate attitude.

'Want a drink?' Megan shook her head, but gave a half hearted smile, when he glared at her. She could tell that Eddy wasn't going to be easy to handle, she told herself to take things slowly and concentrate on not letting the situation get out of hand. She wouldn't have anything more to do with him. Eddy poured out two straight whiskeys and handed her one. 'Take it.' She was afraid to refuse, but asked for ice and soda. He shrugged, grumbling that she was ruining a decent malt. Eddy put her glass down on the cabinet, lifted his own to his lips, poured the content down his throat and refilled his glass. He made no move to add anything to her drink, it just stood there. Megan felt a grip of alarm, knot itself in her stomach and rushed into her prepared speech.

'I'm sorry, but I can't stay, I have to go to a rehearsal.' She watched as he turned to face her. His mouth curled malevolently as he snarled at her.

'You get paid for the other night, but only after I fuck you today. We have a deal.' Megan had deliberately worn jeans and a long sleeved top. She had no intention of allowing him to touch her again. Once had been enough. The look now on his face made her reluctant to even stay and collect what he owed her.

'Forget the money, I have to go.' She was surprised as he lunged at her and too slow to protect herself from the blow to the side of her head. She staggered under its force.

'You're a bitch on heat, and my prick is ready to ram.' He laughed as he smelt her fear. Megan made a run for the door, but was dragged back. She struggled to get free, but Eddy had her clamped to him with one arm and with his free hand, coarsely groped her breasts. She was still trying to wrench herself free from of his hold when his free hand pulled open the neck of her top, then he cruelly gripped and twisted her nipple, pulling the flesh of her breast until she cried in pain. The cabin door opened and closed, neither Megan or Eddy heard it. 'I'm going to fuck you and the more you struggle, the better I like it.' Megan's brain at last over rode her panic and then she automatically used the appropriate, protective manoeuvre that Lee Chung had taught her. Eddy's hold on her was broken. Being drunk and with the movement of the ship, he lost his balance and fell heavily. The corner of the wooden cabinet struck Eddy just below the base of his skull and broke his neck.

'Are you alright?' She heard the question but was unable to speak. With an expression of stark dread, her eyes were wide with horror. Fright had drained her of any colour. Aaron felt his memory leap back to nineteen forty one. The girl's look, was a reflection of his own nephew's, when the boy had escaped from Germany with his mother and younger sister, the body of his elder sister, had lain crumpled in the bottom of their small rowing boat. Matthias had never been able to forgive himself, but what could a seven year old boy have done, to protect his elder sister? Aaron felt all his old misery at being unable to help Matthias bear the barbaric era he had lived through. But now was a different time, and another young person was surely in need of his help. Aaron had heard and seen enough to know that the girl had acted in self defence. He decided that no good could come of stating that she had only been defending herself. Aaron knew enough about Eddy's connections with the Mafia to believe that she would be in danger of retaliation from that quarter over his death. What he had to do now was to get her out of this cabin, before the accident was discovered. His legal brain registered the facts. Without considering his own position, he poured out a third drink, then tipped it down his throat. He picked up the glass that was already there and took it over to the girl and gently made her drink it. Then he put her glass, besides his own, back on the cabinet. One more thorough look around, then he shepherded the trembling figure out into the corridor, firmly shutting the door behind them. Without speaking, he led her along the gangway to his own cabin. Once inside, he sat her in a chair, then poured out two glasses of brandy.

'Please try and drink this.' He placed a glass in her hands. She seemed unable to help herself. Aaron guided it to her lips, she sipped at the liquid. He didn't speak again until her glass was empty. 'Do you feel any better?' The stark eyes raised themselves to his face.

'I killed him.' Aaron shook his head.

'No, he fell. It was an accident.' His calm voice penetrated into her discombobulated mind. 'All you did was protect yourself, he was going to rape you.' She began to shake again. Aaron poured her another drink. 'Here.' This time, she drank it by herself. He waited patiently for her to finish. 'His death has nothing what soever to do with us. We were in his cabin this afternoon, but Eddy Gunnell was still drinking heavily when we left, which we did together. Do you understand?' She looked up at him, her green eyes dark with anguish.

'But as it was an accident, why do we have to say that?' Her question was made in a low, unnerved tone.

'Because he has strong business links with the Mafia, he's almost one of the family. You do understand why you should not be connected with him in any way?' Megan slightly shook her head. Aaron lent over her and took both her shaking hands in his firm grip. 'Reprisals!' He let that word linger in the air before he added. 'Believe me, it will be more practical for us both, this way.' Megan didn't move, then slowly she nodded her head. Aaron gave her an encouraging smile. 'I am a lawyer. And I can assure you that those people deal in wholesale retribution, whether deserved or not.' Aaron stood up and refilled their glasses. They sat in silence and drank. It was an hour later before he spoke again. 'Is there anything else that I can do for you?' His voice was still methodical and quiet. 'Will you tell me your name?'

'Megan.' He smiled encouragingly at her. He now remembered where he'd seen her. 'Are you expected at this party tonight.' She swallowed hard and jerked her head as she answered him.

'Yes, but I don't want to go, not now.' He smiled reassuringly at her.

'We could show our faces.' He paused then added, 'after all, there is no reason for us not to, is there.'

'But he's dead.' Her voice still hadn't risen above the low frightened pitch.

'We don't know that.' Her eyes flickered, he held up a warning hand. 'Eddy was still drinking when you and I left his cabin. You came with me to see my Faberge egg. I will show it to you. It is beautiful' Aaron pulled his suitcase from against the wall and put it down in the centre of the cabin. He unlocked it, and took out a smaller case, he turned this on end and opened a compartment that was hidden in its side. Out of this he took a small, square leather box, another key was used. Then solemnly he lifted the ornate, oval shaped, rarity out. Aaron placed it in Megan's hands. It was exquisite. Her eyes travelled minutely over it before she lifted her hands carefully, and gave it back to him. Aaron replaced it. 'I offered to show you my Faberge egg, as Eddy would not let you see his. Eddy Gunnell is a well known antique dealer, he and I had previously discussed the Faberge eggs he is carrying. I wanted to buy one from him. When I arrived at his cabin this afternoon, he postponed the appointment. You and I left him to his whiskey. Do you understand?' Megan looked straight into his eyes. His composed attitude at last diffused her consternation, her voice had now gathered a little strength.

'I understand. Eddy, being drunk, would not show me and you would.' Aaron smiled at her, and nodded as he said.

'Good.' Megan felt relief and anguish at the same time. Her tortured mind found some solace in tears. Aaron, once again went to her, this time he hugged her, letting her weep on his chest.

Aaron walked Megan to her cabin door, they had arranged to meet later in the Neptune bar, from there they would go to the cocktail party together. Megan showered and changed. She wasn't conscious of any rational thought, she just started her routine of getting ready for a party and let herself, with mechanical detail, continue until she was ready. Then she went to meet Aaron, he stayed by her side. He protected her, always turning, with polite deftness, any comments or questions directed towards Megan, to himself. The next day's show was the Space Odyssey. After it, not only Tina, but also Joan and Doreen had asked her if she was feeling ill. Megan had answered in a low voice that she thought it could be a migraine. Aaron again at her side, gave the girl, all the comfort she was capable of receiving.

News of Eddy Gunnell's death had spread rapidly around the ship. Roy Brent, the steward for the six first class cabins along that corridor had found him. Roy was a slow thinking man of little intelligence, but knew his job and got on with it, but he didn't like Mr. Gunnell. Not only had Eddy thrown objects at him in temper, but he'd also thumped Roy on more than one occasion. Roy had gone into Eddy's cabin as usual, to refill the ice bucket, and seen him lying on the floor by the cabinet. The steward had thought that Eddy was so drunk, that he couldn't get up; so he'd collective the used glasses, gleefully stepped over the body and left. When Roy reappeared later that night to turn the bed covers back, he had realised that something was wrong. He'd quickly called for the Doctor. Norman Parsons was beginning to think that life at sea, for a Doctor, was too problematic for his taste. Now he had to write a death certificate. And it was hard to say how long Gunnell had been dead, maybe three or four hours. The Captains's report stated that Mr. Edward Gunnell, had fallen heavily, the corner of the wooden cabinet had struck the base of his skull and so broken his neck. Roy had been afraid that if he admitted, he had left Eddy lying on the floor for hours, then he'd lose his job; so when asked, the steward stated that Eddy was alive that afternoon, when he'd brought more ice cubes to the cabin; but added, remembering the glasses, that he was drunk. The Captain and the Doctor came to the conclusion that it was simply, an accidental death.

Chapter 21

As dawn broke on the fifteenth of May, the island of Oahu shimmered in the morning light. The ship was heading for the port of Honolulu. The islands lay on the northern rim of the tropic of Cancer. When the liner reached Hawaii, it would have crossed two thirds of the Pacific Ocean, going from Australia to the American West Coast.

Aaron was on the forward deck looking at the fast approaching land, but he turned as Megan stepped beside him.

'Good Morning.' She smiled at his greeting. They both lent on the hand rail as he spoke again. 'We should dock at about ten o'clock this morning. Shall we go ashore?' Megan kept her eyes straight ahead, but nodded. 'I'll take you to the Iolani Palace, it's the only royal residence in the United States!' Megan glanced up at him, a flicker of warmth visible in her face.

'I'd like that.'

'There you are, I missed you at breakfast.' With the arrival of that blustery voice, Megan turned back to look at the horizon. Aaron greeted the interloper cooly, but it did not stop the man from adding. 'I only made this trip by sea so that I could visit Pearl Harbour again. I haven't been back since the war. Nasty business that. God awful it was. I was there you know. Hell of a day. Some of the men, who were based here when it happened, still have nightmares. Only thing to do, is confront it.' All eyes were locked onto the outline of the land ahead. The noise of the ship and the sea seemed loud in their silence. Then suddenly he spoke again. 'How do you do, my name's Joe Longton.' Megan was forced to turn and shake hands, but she didn't join in the conversation. Joe didn't seem to expect her to, as he continued. 'It was a bitch of a way to get into the war. Americans will always remember that day. It was murder.'

'All war can be so described. Japan certainly misread the American will.' Joe beamed, taking the compliment as personal.

'We lost a lot of men. But we showed them.'

'I would have thought that dropping two Atom bombs four years later, certainly did that.'

'That ended the war!' Aaron looked at Joe Longton for perhaps a minute before he spoke again.

'I know, but I have never understood why America didn't use the bombs before the conference at Yalta.'

'What for?'

'Don't you think that maybe Stalin could have been politely persuaded to go back to the existing Russian boarders that were theirs at the time, instead of occupying Eastern Europe.' Aaron smiled faintly! 'Then, not only would the war in Asia have ended, but also the Russian rape of Eastern Europe, could have been avoided.' Joe growled his answer.

'You don't know that would have happened.'

'Of course not, and I know what else you're thinking, and you are right, on paper the deal that Britain and America had with the Russians, seemed favourable. There was just one thing wrong. Stalin!' Aaron turned to look ahead. Joe muttered under his breath, something about ungrateful Europeans and stomped off.

'Where do you come from.' Megan looked up at Aaron as she spoke.

'I was born in Germany, but I left in nineteen twenty. Now I live and work, in New York and Zurich.'

'So you are German.'

'Yes, and Jewish.'

'Are you!'

'You seem surprised.' He gave Megan a philosophical look, then added. 'Remember the Allied Forces, not only stopped a mad dictator, they also liberated the ordinary German people, and I don't mean just the Jews. We, as a race, have been persecuted by more than Hitler.'

'My knowledge of world history is negligible.' He smiled at her as she nodded to herself. 'But I know that six million Jews were killed in the concentration camps.'

'Yes, it's a sobering thought, but did you know that twenty million Chinese were killed.'

'Oh! No.'

'As I've said, war is barbaric, the Japanese slaughtered people wholesale. Do you know something Megan, no matter how long I live, I'll always be astounded by man's inhumanity to man. But I'm wandering from the point! Hitler had to be stopped, a world where he was allowed to reign would have been.' Here Aaron stopped and looked up at the sky over Megan's head. 'Do you know, I can't think of any word to explain what that thought conjures in my mind.'

'Don't think about it, it didn't happen.'

'No, and I shall always remember, and be grateful, to those who fought for liberty.' She smiled as the pain shifted from his eyes.

'Can I ask you something?' Megan wanted to tell him the reason for her presence in Eddy's cabin, but she dreaded what the consequence could be, if she lost his friendship. She had come to rely on him so much, he had stepped into the role of a parent and she needed him. But she also knew that she respected Aaron so much, that she had to be honest with him.

'Of course you can, go ahead.' He smiled down at her.

'Why did you help me?' Aaron took her hand is his.

'In the first instance, I realised that you reminded me of my nephew, Matthias, and then because you needed protection.'

'Does he live with you?' She watched Aaron fill his lungs with air before he answered her.

'No, he's dead.'

'Oh, I'm so sorry.' Megan lifted her other hand to his arm.

'His father, my younger bother, didn't believe that Hitler would try to exterminate the Jews living in Germany; after all, we were Germans, we'd even fought in the First World War. Nothing I said to him, made him change his mind. When he finally did, it was too late. He was shot. His family then tried to escape. I was in hospital with a burst appendix, and couldn't go myself. Matthias, his mother and two sisters lived near Friedrichshafen, very close to Lake Constance, it was only a short trip across the lake to Switzerland and safety. I'd arranged for a boat to pick them up. But before they could get away, a car had driven up. Katrin, the eldest girl, was the only one not in the boat, when the two soldiers fired at them and shouted for them to halt, she unhooked the rope, and pushed the boat away from the shore. It was dark and the current was strong enough to carry it along. Katrin was raped, and then murdered. Matthias and his mother and younger sister, heard everything, they were desperately trying to turn the craft around. The man I'd paid, must have lost his nerve, he'd moored it for them, but he hadn't waited to help them to safety. They were unused to handling even such a small boat. By the time they got back to where Katrin was, the soldiers had left. They lifted her body into the boat and finally did escape. Gabriela, the youngest girl, was a child of three and doesn't remember anything. But

Matthias never forgave himself. Don't ask me what he thought he could have done to save her, he was only seven years of age at the time.' Megan lent her head on Aaron's shoulder to hide her tears. 'After the war, as soon as he was old enough, he went to Israel and joined the hunt for war criminals. He died ten years ago in Argentina.' Aaron's face contorted with the painful memories. 'Such a waste of a life.' He'd ended with so much sadness in his voice, that Megan stayed with her head bent. She couldn't tell him now about herself, that would have to wait. But not too long, she must speak soon. Aaron and Megan stood there, nothing else was said as they shared each other's sorrow.

'It's Los Angeles tomorrow, and only sixteen days until we dock in New York, and it's Bill's birthday on the fifth of June.' Excitement threaded through Tina's voice. 'The City of Angels.'

'Well, let's just hope that God's on our side and doesn't shake things up with an earthquake.' Tracy was still in a fretful mood. No matter how many times she told herself that she'd be able to work things out with Patrick, once he came back to the ship; the haunting memory of their last kiss and his subsequent action of pushing her away, rose like a spectre and doused her expectancy.

'Oh come on Tracy, everything will turn out for the best, just look at me.' Tracy chewed her lips as she gazed at Tina, feeling a tinge of jealousy for the other's optimism, and asked herself for the millionth time, why Patrick hadn't fallen in love with her, the way she'd tumbled for him? Tina continued in a jubilant spirit. 'We have to do everything, we might not come back again. Yes I know I'm American, but I've never been to Los Angeles before!' Megan walked in, Tina greeted her buoyantly. 'Any plans for tomorrow?' She nodded at Tina's question.

'Aaron has invited us out. He's hired a chauffeur driven car for the day. It's one of those organised things, where you're taken everywhere. Look at the shops on Rodeo Drive, lunch at Venice Beach, an afternoon dip in the sea, sight seeing and a great restaurant for dinner, but I can't remember that name. Want to come?'

'Yes please, that will be great!' Tina beamed at Megan. 'How are you feeling, any better?'

'Yes thanks.'

'Those headaches must be awful, you've been off colour for a week.' Megan just shrugged and turned away. 'What are you going to wear Tracy?' The bait failed, Tracy just screwed her face up and sighed.

Aaron had given the girls an unforgettable time in Los Angeles, even Tracy had come out of her doom and gloom for part of the day. They arrived back on board the liner just before it sailed at midnight. Tina and Tracy headed to their cabin, Megan asked if she could speak privately to Aaron. They walked aft along the deck, then around to the far side of the ship, where they wouldn't be disturbed by anyone.

'What is it child?' Megan didn't want to look into his eyes, because she was scared of seeing the kindness turn to rejection, but she made herself and took a deep breath to give herself courage, then began.

'You have never asked me why I was in Eddy's cabin.'

'Your reasons are unimportant to me.'

'But not to me, I have to tell you.' She gulped more air into her lungs, then blurted out. 'I was there as a prostitute.' Aaron put his arm comfortingly around her shoulders.

'We all do what we think is right for us, I'm not judging you.' Tears of relief filled her eyes and then fell. She gladly accepted the solace from the strength from his arm, still protectively around her. Megan, with her head resting on his chest, slowly began to tell him about her life. She started with her earliest memories, skimming over the abuse doled out by her aunt and uncle. Only stressing the fact that she needed to find her mother. Even treating Harold's demand for sexual favours, in return for a roof over her head, as an everyday occurrence. And his pal Bert, who'd been the first to offer her money. She didn't moan that that had been her only way to save, so that she could move out of Harold's flat and not end up on the streets. She stated in a quiet, unemotional voice, that it had taken her just over six mouths to gather enough money together to go to London and audition for another dance contract. She'd known, that once she left Harold, he would not have her back. Not making excuses for her actions, just conveying, why prostitution was the way she had earned enough to hire private detectives to search for her mother. Aaron let her talk, when she'd finished, he gently hugged her and asked. 'Will you let me help?' Megan raised her head, a questioning look in her face. 'I have access to international organisations, who can find missing people.' She blinked, not knowing what she could say to fully express how relieved she felt, that he was going to find her mother and so alleviate her need for prostitution. The burden she'd been carrying with her since she'd learnt her mother's name, lifted from her shoulders. At last there was someone to confide in, to share the emptiness of not knowing.

'Thank you.' He patted her shoulder.

'Give me all the details and I'll start the investigation as soon as we reach New York.' They stood there together, finding compensation and comfort in each other.

Maurice had scheduled the Hollywood show for the next day, and it proved very popular with the passengers. Then Puerto Vallarta was visited on the day following that. Since Elizabeth Taylor and Richard Burton had filmed 'The Night of the Iguana', this once sleepy fishing village on the Mexican coast, had became a favourite place of the jet set. Charis went ashore by herself, she wandered slowly around the place, decided that she didn't really see what all the excitement was about, then returned to the ship. Tina gleefully ticked off the days on a large calendar she had taped onto her wardrobe door. On the twenty third, the ship once again sailed through the Panama Canal.

Ted did go ashore in Cartagena this time. He was trying hard to attach himself to a very wealthy oil tycoon's widow, but wasn't getting very much encouragement from the lady, and he hadn't been able to get into bed with her as yet, but he was living in hope. It perturbed him somewhat, that she wasn't too generous with her money, in fact, she'd only bought him a tie from the gift shop on the liner, when he'd told her it was his birthday. He had them regularly, one each cruise!

On the twenty sixth of May, the ship had arrived at Montego Bay, Tracy tried to phone the hospital that Patrick was in, but was unable to get though. That left her fretful and more despondent. Megan went ashore and had lunch with Aaron. Their relationship was growing with each passing day. He treated her as his daughter, she loved him as a father. Charis viewed the land from the security of the ship. Tina, Jasmine and Mary, spent most of the day just browsing around the shops, and they teased Lee Chung on his choice of shorts! There were two full days at sea, between Jamaica and the Bahamas. Princess Cays was found to be pretty and unspoilt.

The next day the ship docked in Fort Lauderdale. Tracy began to panic. Charis went ashore, but returned within the hour. Tina raced ashore for the prearranged telephone call with Bill, it would be their last, before they saw each other again. Megan spent the day with Aaron, he showed her around the area, and she enjoyed his company. He was intelligent and witty. To their relief, Joe Longton now gave them a wide berth! Jasmine and Mary spent a leisurely time meandering around shepherded by Lee Chung, all enjoying the easterly off shore breeze, wafting cool air around the town.

Ginger Morris strolled along the main road, then made a right, every now and then he'd glance at the piece of paper in his hand, then at his watch. If anyone had been watching him, it would have seemed that his sense of direction was somewhat aimless. He'd walked up one side of the street and down the other four times, before he, after another look at his watch, went into a telephone booth. He stood there drumming his fingers against the glass panels. When the phone rang, he grabbed at it and bent over, hunching his shoulders. It was a short telephone conversation, but when he replaced the receiver, his smile indicated that he was pleased with the outcome. Then he stepped out into the sunshine and jauntily walked down the street. He stopped by a cafe and decided that he was hungry and would eat. Now his arrangements for New York were made, the rest of the day was his.

Tracy, Megan and Charis were the only three members of the show, who didn't attend the midnight barbecue held on deck, the night following the ship's departure from Fort Lauderdale. The others sat around eating and drinking, well into the early hours of the morning. That night's show was the Finale. The ungodly of the group, mainly Ted and Ginger, voiced the opinion that Maurice had put whatever he couldn't fit into his theme shows, into this last one. Thus being free to give it, an umbrella title! Nevertheless, the pace was smart and as entertainment went, this show scored remarkably high.

The next day, Charis sat alone in the reading room on the promenade deck. Her eyes stared unbelievingly at the headlines on the newspaper in front of her. Both American and English papers had been brought abroad at Fort Lauderdale. The article transfixing her attention, concerned the marriage of Lord Hill to the Honourable Barbara Cole. The ceremony had taken place in London, had been a quiet affair and then the correspondent had inferred, that there was a happy reason for the bride's choice of a loose dress! Adding in bold print, that the new Lady Hill certainly looked blooming! 'Damn him, damn him, damn him.' Charis screwed the paper up, crunching it between her hands. Since Kevin's death, she had kept an iron control over herself, not allowing anyone to come near her, she was so afraid of saying something that would give away her secret. She still felt no regrets about her abortion. If she had to do it over again, then she would. There was no way on earth that she was going to saddle herself with a baby and be poor. Pinching and scraping an existence, not knowing how the next bill would be paid. No! She'd lived through that with her parents, she wasn't going to walk blindly into the same trap. She would marry money. Her one aim in life, since she had left home, had been to leave behind the poverty, that she had come from. To Charis, she felt that being poor had a stigma attached to it. She had legally changed her name, and acquired a new birth certificate, her passport was in her new name. Charis went from one dance contract to the next, and only went back to her parents home, when forced to by circumstances. She had nothing to associate her to her past. Except her own memories and those she'd buried deep.

Chapter 22

On the morning of the third of June, the liner eased through the bay at the mouth of the Hudson river; she was running an hour behind her time table, but as the ship would be docked until the evening of the seventh of that month, Captain Beamish wasn't unduly worried. The body of Edward Gunnell was laid in repose in the deep freeze and he wouldn't be sorry to have finished with that incident, as soon as he could, he'd hand over the responsibility to the port authorities. He smoothed the sleeve of his uniform, his first officer was on the bridge and directing operations. The Captain stepped forward as they approached Manhattan Island. From this view, the skyscrapers dominated the outline. New York was one of the busiest ports, the southern rim of the island being surrounded by docks. This sight always had a mesmerising effect on Beamish. The first officer asked permission to stop the engines, this brought the Captain back from his contemplation of the dimensions of modern buildings. Just over an hour later, the tugs nosed the ship into her berth.

The last three hours for Tina had been spent in frenzied preparation. Megan had also packed a weekend case, Aaron had invited her to spend the time that the ship was docked in New York, with him. Tracy was on tenterhooks. At last she'd be able to see Patrick again, but now the time was almost upon her, she was even more afraid of what he was going to do and say. She'd asked herself countless times, if she should tell him that she loved him, and still hadn't given herself an answer. Tracy was sitting cross legged on her bunk and was startled when Megan spoke. 'I'm going up on deck.'

'Wait for me Megan, I'm ready.' Tina picked up her weekend bag. 'Are you coming Tracy?'

'Yes.' The three of them left the cabin, Tracy was last out and locked the door behind her.

They found Jasmine already on deck with Lee Chung, Mary was there too. Zachery was only able to stay in New York for two days, and Jasmine and Mary had planned to explore the sights together afterwards. Jasmine was excited about seeing her father again. A sigh of disappointment engulfed her as she accepted that her parents could not forget their past and begin a new friendship. They had loved each other so very much that even now the pain of their parting could not be forgotten. Jasmine knew that all she could hope for now was that they could see each other as acquaintances. Lee Chung nudged her and indicated where her father was waiting. She nodded and waved.

'Bill is there, I can see him. Look.' All eyes obediently followed Tina's pointing finger. There were more than half a dozen limousines parked at the dock side. Bill was standing in front of one of them. 'Come on people, let me off.' Everyone grinned at the eagerness in Tina's voice. Tracy had scanned the figures on the dock, but she hadn't seen Patrick yet. She chewed at the inside of her cheeks in her nervousness. As soon as she was allowed, Tina flew down the gang plank, straight into Bill's arms. Megan and Aaron had followed her, there was a car also waiting for them, they left while Tina was still locked in Bill's embrace. Mary stayed on the deck and waved to Jasmine as she got into the back of her father's car, Lee Chung got in the front with the driver. Tracy picked Tina's bag up and followed, dragging her feet as she went. She put the weekend bag on the floor besides the car, then retraced her steps slowly back up the gangway to the deck. She propped herself there and waited. Mary was going ashore with Doreen and Joan, they intended to visit the Empire State Building, as well as the Statue of Liberty, tomorrow they had put aside for shopping! Maurice had made arrangements with Alexander, he still grinned to himself when he thought about his trip with the young deck officer in Hong Kong and he was hoping that this place would have even more entertainment to offer; they planned to leave by cab during the morning and wouldn't be returning until the day the ship sailed. Ginger Morris sat in his cabin, his appointment wasn't until nine o'clock that evening, and he wasn't going anywhere until he'd delivered the goods and got his money. Ted found himself alone, the rich widow he'd been trying to fix himself with, had continued to keep him at arms length and disembarked with her millions still intact.

'I think we'd better get into the car, while I can still stand.' Tina laughed and cried at the same time. She was so happy her voice sounded jubilant.

'I love you.' Bill's grin spread even wider across his face.

'And I adore you darling, but for God's sake get into the car.' The driver was standing by the open door. Tina's case was already in the trunk. Once inside the interior of the saloon, they kissed again. The driver eased the car into the traffic and wondered if the couple in the back could wait until they got to the hotel, if they did, it would be, only just!

Bill had booked into the Plaza, on Fifth Avenue. The hotel was one of New York's best, an enclave to the tradition of European elegance. The car glided to a halt at the main entrance, the sound of water from the fountain, contrasted with the hum of the New York traffic. Their room was tastefully decorated in the French Provincial style, and the adjoining bathroom was the cream on the cake! As soon as the bedroom door had closed behind the departing porter, they were in each other's arms. Their clothes disappeared at a frantic rate, and, not waiting to waste time moving to the bed, Bill laid Tina beneath him. The thick pile of the carpet, cushioned her back as they made love. All the pain and loneliness from their separation that had built up in their emotions, found a heavenly release as they passionately kissed. Hands explored as if for the first time, touches sent erotic shocks to explode in their senses. Unwilling to stem the heat of their passions, together they careered into a rapturous climax. Afterwards they clung to each other, neither wanted to move.

But soon the reality of holding her ravishing naked body in Bill's arms, started his blood pounding through his veins once more. He shifted his position slightly and eased his manhood from her, but even so, his groin throbbed and his member began to stiffen again. He raised his head and found her lips waiting to be kissed. As he lowered his mouth to her's, his mind thought fleetingly of the bed, but the demands of his body banished that abstraction.

The pressure and movement of his lips on her's, rekindled in Tina an urgency to make love again. His name whispered in her throat, as a heat built within her very centre, which sent a fire of desire racing through her body; and as his tongue traced its way into the warmth of her mouth, her hands went to his forming erection. Her fingers wound around, moving erotically to stimulate him more. She wanted him again, with all the passion and hunger she'd felt when they had first met. Never would she become inured towards him. Just to be near him, made her pulse gallop. The heat burning in her, spread with mercurial swiftness. Now the feel of his swollen and hard member in her hands, dominated her mind. She caressed the tip with her thumbs, delighting in his groans of pleasure.

'Oh God Tina, you can't know just how much in love with you, I am.' Bill sucked air into his lungs as he pulled her hands to his mouth, to lavish kisses into her palms. He felt her wrap her legs around his body, gripping him. 'And I always will.' He let go of her hands as he drove deeply into the welcoming wetness of her womanhood.

She met his thrusts with an ardent cadence of her own. Their abandoned rhythm, soon extended their shared passions, until the highs of their desires were fully ascended, and then, they cascaded back to a blissful ember of calm.

'Do you think we should move?' His voice was soft in her ear. Tina smiled and snuggled the tip of her tongue and lips against his neck. 'If you carry on doing that, we'll never reach the bed!'

'Does it matter?'

'Not really, but maybe we should eat something. Have you had breakfast yet?'

'No.' A happy giggle ran through her voice. 'This morning I could only think of you, food just didn't come into the picture.'

'Right, we'll move.'

'Must we?'

'Yes.' He grinned as he added, 'after all, the ship doesn't leave until Saturday.' Bill stood up and held his hands out to her. Tina gripped his fingers and let him pull her up. They stood there, naked, facing each other, smiling, their eyes brilliant! 'You're so beautiful Tina, love.' She moved into the circle of his arms and kissed him tenderly. When their lips finally parted, the ripples of their smouldering desires, had begun to surge through their bodies again. 'No, we must eat first.'

'Here.' It hadn't been a question, and not really a demand, just a statement.

'Yes, I'll phone for room service to bring up a trolley. Do you fancy a cooked breakfast.'

'Yes'. She patted her stomach playfully. 'I'm starving!' Tina then walked gracefully to where her weekend bag was, opened it, took out a towelling robe and put it on, her eyes enhanced by its deep sapphire blue colour. She collected their discarded clothes and dumped them in their bathroom. Then wandered around their room inspecting it, before she settled herself in a large chair by the window. 'I brought some cash with me, it's in my bag, use it.' Bill grinned, he put the receiver back and picked up his bath robe from the bed, slipped it on, then walked over to Tina.

'I've ordered the lot. It'll be here in about ten minutes.' He sat at her feet, looking up at her. 'I've got some good news to tell you.'

'What?'

'It could wait until we've eaten.' Tina gripped a handful of his hair and gently shook his head.

'No I can't, tell me now.'

'Okay!' Bill laughed at the expression of eagerness on Tina's face.

'Before I flew here yesterday, I signed a new contract.'

'That's great! Tell me more.'

'It's worth a million!'

'What?'

'Three years, television!'

'Darling that's great.'

'I know.' He nodded, 'and it's all ours. I was worried over the money and stuff that Melissa got.'

'It didn't matter to me, all I've ever wanted was you.'

'I know that my love, but I've been broke; I didn't like it then and I'm as sure as hell is hot, that I wouldn't be over the moon about it again. Most people treat you like a leper.'

'We'd have managed.'

'I know that, but now we don't have to!' She dragged him to his knees, they hugged each other, laughing until their lips met. Their kiss quickly deepened. The knock of the door, forced them to release each other. Bill stood up and went to unlock it. The waiter wheeled in a trolley, from which the succulent aroma of good food, wafted into the air. 'Thanks.' Bill handed the man a five dollar note as he left. A small table was arranged in front of an open window and they sat down to enjoy their breakfast.

The drive through town to the apartment block where Aaron lived took twenty minutes. Megan had never seen so much traffic. London's narrower streets didn't personify, the din and movement of these broad New York boulevards. The limousine drew up at the kerb. The canopy from the building stretched out overhead. The chauffeur got out of the front and quickly opened the near side door. Aaron stepped out, then turned to help Megan alight from the car. She had never been in contact with luxury before, her only experience being the ship, and although her cabin was adequate, it could claim to be, no more than staff quarters. The bed and breakfast places she'd stayed at in the past, had at best boasted of a separate toilet and bathroom. But Aaron was now leading her past a saluting door man and into a lobby, which to

Megan looked as if it could have been the entrance to an expensive hotel. She didn't speak as the lift silently soared higher.

'If I have to live in an apartment block, than I have to have a view. There are only two penthouse apartments here.' Aaron made this statement as they stepped out of the elevator and walked along the hallway. 'This is my door, that', he pointed to the other end of the corridor, 'belongs to a writer. I don't think I would recognise him if I saw him, he must spend all his time working. But I have read some of his books, they're good, but then I like the type of crime/drama novels he produces.' Aaron opened the door and indicated to Megan, that she should go in before him. She smiled faintly at him and stepped into another world. The entrance hall to Aaron's apartment was a large square area, the walls were tiled with a pale grey marble, the floor carpeted in sage green, and a small crystal chandelier, hung in a central position. A brass coat stand, a cheval mirror and four, delicate, spindle legged chairs, graced the interior. 'This way.' He led her through an archway and stopped half way along it. 'Your bedroom.' Aaron opened the door and ushered Megan in. The room was of an immense size to her. A dark wood, four poster bed, hung with white silk drapes stood at one side, the rest of the furniture matched it. The carpet at her feet was in azure, the embossed satin curtains at the windows, in the same shade of blue. By one of the windows, there were two large comfortable easy chairs in white leather, with a low table between them; by the other window, stood a writing desk and upright chair, there polished mahogany, complemented a variance, with the ebony bedroom furniture. A jardiniere, full of bright summer blooms, drew Megan's attention. She could smell the heady fragrance from where she was. 'Your bathroom is through here.' Aaron walked to the wall, opposite to the windows and opened a door. Megan went through it and then stood transfixed. She had never imagined such a bathroom. It was completely tiled in a light sand colour and on each wall, there was a mosaic, representing a scene from a desert oasis. 'If you want anything, just ask.' Megan couldn't speak, but she faintly managed to nod her head. Aaron smiled warmly at her. 'Breakfast will be ready very soon, as it's a splendid morning we'll eat on the balcony. Then we'll plan what to do while you're here.' Megan just blinked at him. 'Your case is in your bedroom, if you need help unpacking, then Jean will be glad to assist you. She and her brother Louis, look after me here. They are French, but have been over here with me for twenty years.' He left her to wander around. Megan found her case on a stand, placed near the wardrobe. It didn't take her very long to unpack. About five minutes later a tap on her door brought her away from her bedroom window.

'Ello, I'm Jean.' Megan smiled as she shook hands and returned the greeting.

'Hello.'

'Breakfast is ready, if you are?' Megan nodded her head. 'Good, I'll show you the way.' Jean's accent was still very French, but Megan had no trouble understanding her. She followed her back to the main entrance hall and then turned left, the double doors, opposite the front door, were now open and Megan walked behind Jean through them. It was a beautiful room, very spacious. The furnishings were luxury, spelt in capital letters, as far as Megan was concerned! Facing her were three pairs of glassed walk through windows, which gave access to the balcony, the room itself, spread out before her with a block, polished wood floor; a dais, raised by one step, at the right hand side, where a grand piano sedately reigned. At the other end of the room, an open fire place dominated that wall. Before this, two long, tan leather couches, with four matching armchairs, were tastefully arranged around, what looked like, a large Chinese rug. A couple of occasional tables, maybe half a dozen monthly glossy magazines, and an arrangement of amber carnations and gypsophila, caught Megan's eye as she followed Jean across the room.

'Hungry Megan?' Aaron asked, as a man held a chair for her at a small white wrought iron table, set under a large sun umbrella. The cushions on the chair, matched the table cloth. She sat down, feeling shy as she was waited on. She had never used silver cutlery before, it felt large and a little unwieldy at first. The porcelain was so delicate that she thought she could almost see through it. Aaron was his normal calm and pleasant self and before she realised it, Megan had eaten a substantial breakfast. 'Jean is going to show you around Bloomingdale's and Macy's today. Also Altman, and the Lord and Taylor department stores are both on Fifth Avenue, and between the Thirty fourth and Fifty ninth, is the golden mile!' He smiled encouragingly at her. 'Try to relax and enjoy yourself now I'm handling the search for your mother. We'll meet for dinner this evening and then catch a show at Radio City, Music Hall, I thought you might like to see the Rockettes.' Aaron's eye brows rose slightly in question, Megan just nodded her head. From the moment she had met Aaron, everything in her life had begun to change for the better. She didn't know why he was being so kind and generous to her, only that he was and she was very grateful to him.

'Thank you.' Her voice was still low with emotion, but filled now with hope for what the future could hold.

The time dragged for Tracy, she missed lunch and dinner altogether. She did dash off from her position, but only occasionally to get a cool soft drink from the bar, or visit the bathroom. It wasn't until after ten o'clock that night, that she finally gave up and went to bed. But that she told herself the next morning, had been a waste of time, she'd spent the night, tossing and turning. And when she had managed to drop into an uneasy sleep, her dreams had turned into nightmares of the tragedy of loneliness.

Chapter 23

Tracy dragged her hair brush through the tangles, then pulled on a cotton top and a pair of shorts, before slipping her feet into her sandals and leaving the cabin. It was early, but she wanted to find the Chief Engineer to see if he knew when Patrick would be returning to the ship. Last night Mary had asked her to join the spending spree planned for today, but she'd declined the offer. She was far to nervous to even contemplate the idea of a shopping expedition. Tracy pinned her objective down as he was leaving the dining room. She didn't waste her time on polite conversation and practically demanded the information she wanted.

'When is Patrick Connor due back on board?' The Chief Engineer looked a little surprised at her, but smiled as he checked his wrist watch.

'His plane is due to touch down in fifteen minutes, so I suppose, a couple of hours and he should be back.' With that, he gave her a jaunty salute and walked away. Tracy found that she was hugging herself, just two tiny hours from now and Patrick would be back, then everything would be as it should. He'd be here and she would be able to see him everyday. The doors to the dinning room were open and the smell of food, momentarily decoyed her senses. She walked in, the room was empty. She crossed to her table and sat down. Half an hour later she was back in her cabin, this time, she took care with brushing her hair. She was perched on her bunk, her eye lids itched with tiredness, it had been sometime since she had really slept well, so she thought that she'd lay down for half an hour before she went on deck to wait for him.

Patrick stretched, then eased his right shoulder in slow circles while he waited for his luggage to appear on the conveyer belt. He was glad to be rejoining the ship. He'd felt edgy of late, his usual calm manner, now tended to be somewhat elusive to him. He put his restive moods down to being injured. He'd been thinking a lot about Tracy, and over the six weeks he'd been away from her, had gradually demanded of himself, that he should keep their relationship as platonic as he had originally planned. That his heart was uncertain of the practicality of this measure, he conveniently disregarded, with a male ego that believed it could rule! He caught the bus into New York City centre, then got a cab to take him to the docks.

As Patrick walked up the main gangway onto the ship, the Captain and Chief Engineer were standing by the entrance on the deck.

'How's the shoulder?' Patrick grinned at his boss.

'Fine Sir.'

'No problems?'

'None Captain Beamish.'

'Good.' The Captain's voice had been rather chilly, he looked as if he was about to say something else, but seemed to think better of it, turned on his heels and left.

'Wow!'

'Don't fret about him, he can sometimes build mountains out of nothing!' Patrick nodded. 'By the way, I bumped into a bloke in a very trendy suit wandering around the ship looking for you. So to keep him out of the Captain's way, I put him in the reading room on the promenade deck.' Patrick's eye brows rose questioningly. 'Don't ask me, the man wasn't parting with any information.'

'Right Sir, I'll just drop my gear off in my cabin, then go and find out what he wants.'

'And also this morning,' the Chief Engineer smiled knowingly at the young man in front of him, 'there was a very attractive dancer, with long curly chestnut hair, impatiently enquiring when you would be back on board. You're a lucky young dog!' Patrick guessed that he was referring to Tracy, and fleetingly wondered why she hadn't gone ashore. He looked puzzled as he walked along the deck. It didn't take Patrick long to dump his bag in his room and then to go and find out the answer to one question; he headed for the reading room first and introduced himself.

'My name is Patrick Connor, I believe you're looking for me.'

'Hi! I'm Grant McAvoy. Your agent has contacted our company and I'm very happy to tell you that we are interested in you; I'm here to offer you a contract with Tangerine Records.'

'What!' Patrick was stunned. 'I haven't got an agent.' He also sounded annoyed.

'Look Patrick, I can call you Patrick, can't I?'

'Yes. But you've got me mixed up with someone else. I'm not interested in a record deal. I'm one of the engineering officers on this ship and this life suits me fine.' Grant was staggered by Patrick's attitude. In the general run of things, no matter what job they were in, singers were always very eager, even begging him for a contract. It was unheard of for any of them to shrug their shoulders and state that they weren't interested. Maybe the guy was right, and it wasn't his voice on the tape recording, shame about that, because this male had the right looks and body to make girls rave after him. But as he worked on this ship, if he listened to the tape, he'd recognise the voice and be able to put the right name forward.

'Sorry pal for the mistake, but maybe you could help me. I've got a tape here!' Grant opened his brief case and took out a neat battery operated machine. 'Just give an ear to this and put a name to it, then I'll be off!' Patrick shrugged his shoulders and agreed. 'This voice will earn millions of dollars if handled right. And we at Tangerine Records are the people to make that happen!' While he'd been speaking, Grant had put the cassette into the machine and switched it on. Patrick's ears picked out the sound of his guitar almost immediately, but thought that he'd made a mistake. But when his voice sang the first line of lyrics, he knew he hadn't. He shouted over the tape.

'Who sent you that?'

'Do you know the voice?' Grant flicked the machine off.

'Who?' Grant snapped his brief case shut and locked it. He didn't know what this guy was up to, but he wasn't taking any chances on losing this tape and the deal.

'Now let's be polite about this. You know the owner of that voice, and all I want is a name. If he's a friend of yours, then you'll be doing him a favour, not a disservice. Record deals don't get offered every day of the month!' Patrick shoved his hands into his pockets to stop him clenching his fists, but when he spoke, it was through gritted teeth.

'That is a recording of my voice, and I want to know who sent it to you. Have I made myself clear?' Grant opened his eyes and pulled the corners of his mouth down. Instinctively he knew this was going to be difficult to handle, but he'd never come across a situation that had proved impossible.

'You've got a great voice. Do you understand exactly what Tangerine are offering you?' Patrick didn't answer, he wasn't interested; all he wanted to know, was who had taped his voice and designated themselves as his agent; and been deceitful enough, not to mention the fact to him.

Grant watched the man in front of him avidly, hoping that persuasion would overcome his reluctance. Grant's voice purred when he spoke. 'Just think about what this proposal means. First you go into the recording studio and in a couple of months, the single is released! Wham! You've got a hit! By Christmas, you could have an album out, and if that reaches platinum; we're then talking big, big money! You could buy any damn thing you've ever wanted.' Grant paused for effect. Then continued, 'I don't know what you're getting paid now, but believe me pal, it will be peanuts to what will roll in from the record sales. And for your personal appearances, well, you can almost name your own price!' Grant ended his little speech, nodding his head. Patrick still had his hands in his pockets, but his tone dispelled any false ideas Grant might have had about his temper.

'Who sent you that tape?' Grant had never been in a situation where he had been forced to give up! He'd got where he was by hustling and sheer determination to succeed. His one aim in life was to make quick bucks, the faster the better. There was no way he'd have contemplated a career where he could not make money, as well as a name for himself, he was no shrinking violet! And his ability to unload a 'has been', before they actually dropped, had made him very profitable to employ. When he'd opened Tracy's package, after quickly scanning the letter, he'd chucked the tape into the out tray on his desk and screwed the letter up and binned it. He never bothered with amateurs! He assumed that the people in London were idiots and so short of something to do that they wasted time with every hopeful who wanted to cut a disc! Because his time was money, the artist had to be good even to get his attention. Grant had been called out of his office and as he'd gone, told his secretary to clean up his desk. She'd taken her waste paper basket with her, but as she always did, she'd tried the half dozen tapes, before she threw them out. And five out of the six had been chucked away, but she'd been impressed with Patrick's voice, and had been listening to the tape Tracy had sent, when Grant returned to his office. Luckily Tracy had put Patrick's name on the cassette, so Grant's secretary only had to go through the letters in the waste paper basket to find the one that corresponded to the tape. And so Grant was now here, he'd travelled from Nashville, but it looked like it was going to be a wasted journey. The London office wouldn't be pleased that he hadn't been able to land this fish. They had wanted Patrick signed up before he got back to England, to eliminate any competition from the other record companies. In her letter, Tracy hadn't said how many copies had been sent out. Grant tried again. 'Think about it son. There's a hell of a lot hanging on this deal. It could make you rich. The record buying public out there are just waiting for a new idol. And that could be you.' Patrick shook his head then finally took his hands out of his pockets as he lent forward and slammed a fist on the table in front of him. 'Give it back to me and go. But before you do, you can tell me who sent it?' Grant stepped abruptly out of what he considered was the other man's range, he wasn't going to get his face rearranged for anything.

'Okay, okay!' He opened his brief case and reluctantly gave Patrick the cassette, adding, 'the letter came from a Tracy O'Flynn.' Grant was going to add that she'd sent it to London and that they had sent it on to him, but he didn't get that out. Patrick had snarled, snatched up the recording then stormed out of the room. Grant grabbed his brief case and followed.

Patrick was on the main deck before he'd thought about what he was going to do. He wanted to find her quickly, so he decided to try her cabin first. He rushed along the decks and corridors and was out of breath by the time he reached her cabin. The door wasn't locked and he flung it open.

'Why?' That one word, held not only a question but the hurt he felt as well.

She had been asleep, laying on top of her bunk; her hair spread out across the pillow, the sun top and shorts she was wearing, showing to advantage, her shapely body. Tracy opened her eyes and seeing Patrick, a sleepy smile curled her mouth. Her mind still drowsy, only his actual presence registered with her. She was still smiling at him as she sat up, but his voice abruptly changed her expression.

'How could you have done this to me?' He chucked the tape on the bed, it landed besides her right hand. 'I trusted you. I really thought that we were friends.' Patrick raked his fingers through his hair. His eyes burning with the anger he felt, but her beauty taunted him. He reacted by wanting to punish her. 'You think that you can twist any man around your little finger just by batting your eye lashes and pouting at him. Well not me Tracy. I'm different. I never wanted a quick tumble from you. You got that all wrong. So this idea of yours to manipulate me is way off key.' He stopped and shook his head, as if he was trying to clear his brain. 'You're nothing but a cheap tart, who thinks men will come jumping to heel any time you want! Well, not me! You can please yourself whose life you screw up, have a ball, go through the entire crew, but leave me out of your party tricks. I've never been with a prostitute and I don't intend to start with you.' Patrick turned so quickly that he bumped into Grant who was stood just behind him. Grant landed against the door! Patrick disappeared along the corridor, he was too angry to ask himself why he'd reacted so badly to the fact that it was Tracy who had abused his friendship and trust.

Grant whistled softly, asking himself, 'are these two involved with each other? The electricity from them sure was strong enough to light up a town! But the lady seemed to have over stepped herself and put Patrick in a hell of a mood. No apparent reason why, unless the guy didn't like being led! The gal should have known better! Still she was a looker, so they'll make it up! And if I sweet talk her now, when that happens she'll be on my side!' He let his gaze wander over Tracy, taking in her long shapely legs, slender hips, attractive face, but he ended up staring at her breasts. He was definitely a 'tit man' himself. He shifted his position, edging nearer to her, muttering what he thought were soothing words. The idea of trying to lay her, flashed into his mind. But he was no fool. Even if the girl had been a reincarnation of Marilyn Monroe herself, he'd have passed. Grant had never let his hormones dictate to him and he was too old now to start. But he conceded to himself, that she sure was tempting. Still, he had other things on his mind. First he had to get her on side. He carefully shut the cabin door.

'You must be Tracy O'Flynn.' He paused and smiled, 'I'm Grant McAvoy from Tangerine Records.'

'Oh my God!' Tracy curled her legs up and hugged her knees.

'London sent me the tape and letter. You did actually state that you were his agent, has he got one?' Tracy shook her head, then stated.

'Patrick's not interested in singing professionally, but I think he's too good not to.'

'You and me both kid.' Grant began to relax, he could relate to this girl, he figured that if anyone could persuade Patrick to sign a contract, it would be her. After all, he mused, if she put her mind to it, she could certainly make him chirp sweetly enough for an afternoon! He sucked in his cheeks and brought his mind back to more pressing details. 'So let me just check that I have the facts straight. He isn't signed to any record company, hasn't got an agent, and isn't looking for a deal.' Tracy just nodded her head. 'Well girl, that's okay, all it means is that you and I have our work cut out.' Tracy sat up and stared at Grant. He laughed. 'All we have to do is persuade him to change his mind. And darlin', as you are on this ship with him, that's gonna be your job.' Tracy looked startled and opened her mouth to speak, but Grant held up a hand. 'Don't fret yourself over anything. Patrick will bless you for it, once we pull it off.'

'But he doesn't want to.'

'That's not important, you're going to change his mind for him.'

'How?'

'By being real nice and sweet to him!' Tracy snorted and shook her head.

'Didn't you just hear what he said to me?' Grant grinned and nodded his head.

'He was mad because you didn't tell him what you've done. But don't give that a thought. If you didn't matter to him, he wouldn't have blown up like that! He'll come around.' Grant paused and grinned at Tracy, then continued. 'If you put your mind to it, you're pretty enough to have him pecking seeds from between your beautiful lips before this fall comes around.' Maybe she believed him because she wanted to, or maybe his southern charm had a little to do with her ready acceptance.

'Okay.'

'You deliver him to me, ready to sign a contract and you honey, get a real handsome cheque as a present from yours truly.' Tracy wasn't concentrating fully on what exactly Grant was saying to her, the mention of Patrick and lips, had fogged her ability to distinguish between manipulation and sincerity. Telling herself that she would be only doing what was best for Patrick. To give her credit, she hadn't been listening when Grant had mentioned money!

Patrick's grip on the railings had made his knuckles white. His head was bent low and his breath came in short pants. But the more he thought about what he'd said to her, the more he cringed. He now acknowledged that he'd lost his temper and had no right to speak to her in that way. He didn't know how long he'd been staring at the dark water gently lapping at the side of the ship, but he did realise that he should apologise to her straight away. He pulled himself upright and walked back to her cabin. As he went to knock the door, it opened. Grant looked him full in the face, smiled and walked passed him. Patrick was left facing Tracy. She was stood there with an unusual expression on her face. Her eyes glowed, her lips slightly pouting. She flicked a strand of hair back over her shoulder and the movement made him focus on the shape of her breasts, concentrating on the slightly darker mounds of her nipples, easily visible through the thinness of the cotton top she had on. He swallowed and dropped his head, then breathed in fast at the sight of her legs, they seemed to go on for ever! He knew he couldn't even speak, let alone apologise; he felt ashamed that all his attention was captivated by her body. He groaned silently as he tried to excuse the fact that he was so easily stimulated by her and shifted his position, trying to ignore the start of his erection.

Tracy didn't know what to do. Why had he come back? He didn't look angry now, maybe he'd forgiven her for interfering. Should she invite him in? She wanted to. He looked gorgeous. His hair was untidy and his short sleeve shirt, practically open to his waist. And the tight jeans he was wearing showed every contour! Just looking at him made her want to make love. Being this close had the effect, of making her stomach flip and her breath quicken. Unconsciously she moved her body, arching her back, her femininity sending unmistakable invitations to the male in front of her.

Patrick tensed every muscle in his body, all his mental efforts tried to hang onto reality, but his desire to lay her under him and explore her intimately before burying himself in her, vanquished all other thoughts. In that given moment, he could only imagine the ecstasy of her.

Tracy gasped in dismay as Patrick abruptly turned away from her and rushed along the corridor.

Chapter 24

Bill and Tina did leave their room once, on his birthday, they celebrated by dining in the famous Oak Room restaurant. Jasmine briefly returned to the ship on the fifth of June, after seeing her father off at the airport; not only had he left the limousine at her disposal for the remainder of her stay in New York, but also the suite of rooms they had occupied at the Mayfair Regent, on Park Avenue. He'd told her before he went through the departure gates at the airport, to invite her friends to stay at the Regent with her, and not to even think about the bill, it was his treat and he expected them all to eat well and thoroughly enjoy themselves! So that evening, Jasmine, Mary and Lee Chung had planned how they would spend the rest of their stay in the city. Joan and Doreen had gladly accepted the invitation to join them. Tracy refused! Lee Chung's knowledge of New York was found to be excellent, and they all enjoyed the next two days chaperoned by him. Jasmine intended to spend the first day at sea, writing to her father, telling him all about their excursions.

When Patrick had stormed off earlier, he'd spent the day walking around Central Park, arguing with himself. Firstly trying to persuade himself that he wasn't that disappointed in Tracy over her actions in taping his voice and sending it off without asking him. And acknowledging that he hadn't any excuse for yelling at her the way he had done. He would apologise when he saw her again. Secondly that he didn't want anything more from their relationship other than a platonic friendship. After all, friends should be open with each other, and if Tracy was sneaking around behind his back, what chance had they of becoming closer? Patrick would not accept that their friendship was in jeopardy. But he couldn't explain, with any clarity, his acutely physical reactions to her. He told himself a dozen or more times, that she wasn't the only beautiful woman he'd ever known, so why did she have this hold over him? He wasn't even looking for an enduring relationship, he wasn't sure that he wanted to get married, he'd never actually contemplated giving up his single life. Patrick had been happy with his past liaisons, and he didn't crave a permanent partner. And between his affairs, there had been some very enjoyable one night stands. So far that life had suited him. Tracy was the only female that had made him think of marriage, and her attitude towards sex, had blotted out the thought of marrying her, how could he forget the other men in her life. He was no nearer an answer to his questions when he returned to the ship in time for dinner, but Tracy hadn't shown up in the dining room for that meal. She was sat huddled on the narrow forward deck and although the night air was still warm, she was shivering.

After dinner Patrick tried Tracy's cabin, but also drew a blank there, then intuition had stepped in, he went to the forward deck that led to the ships' bridge, and found her there. He instantly apologised to her.

'I'm sorry about losing my temper with you this morning.' His voice was sincere. She lifted her head to look at him, but with the evening shadows, she couldn't see his expression. 'You must be cold sitting there like that, here, put this on.' Patrick pulled his sweater over his head and handed it to her. Tracy took it and slipped it on. She drew in her breath, filling her senses with the aroma of him.

'Thanks.' Her voice was husky. Stars were beginning to show in the evening sky, Tracy concentrated on them and didn't look at him when he spoke again.

'Don't mention it. You're all by yourself, where are the other girls?'

'Jasmine, Mary, Doreen and Joan are staying at a hotel, Jasmine's father arranged it, he's been here, but had to leave earlier today. Tina is with her boyfriend.'

'Where's Charis?

'I haven't seen her.' Tracy's voice was cool, Patrick knew that Charis had nothing to do with the other dancers so he let the subject drop.

'Have you been ashore?' Tracy didn't answer, just shook her head. 'I'm not on the duty rota until the sixth, then I don't get a day off until after we sail. But if you fancy it, I could show you around tomorrow, to let you know that I'm really sorry for how I reacted. And we won't mention records, so there'll be no reason for us to fight any more!' Tracy turned to look at him, but all she could see, was his silhouette against the gathering night. She was grateful for any straw that he handed her and so accepted.

'I'd like that.'

'Great! We'll meet after breakfast in the morning. Wear something comfortable on your feet, we're going to do a lot of walking!' His voice was even, she knew that he was offering her his friendship again and she promptly conceded.

On the fourth, Aaron had set the wheels in motion to find Megan's mother. He took the girl to Coney Island on the fifth. The next day, which was Megan's nineteenth birthday; as a special surprise, Aaron had tickets for a Neil Diamond concert at Madison Square Gardens, then supper at '21' Club. It was the first birthday Megan had ever really celebrated in a grand manner. The rest of her time in New York was spent in sight seeing.

Patrick and Tracy set off after an early breakfast. They visited the Statue of Liberty, the Empire State Building, lunch at the Hard Rock Cafe; the afternoon found them at the Rockefeller Centre on Fifth Avenue, then on to Times Square and a walk down Broadway; Greenwich Village followed, and they ended up in Chinatown for dinner. It was very late when they returned to the ship and Tracy was in a happy dream. She knew that Patrick was on duty for the next two days, so the following day, the sixth, Tracy took off by herself for Fifth Avenue! The liner was sailing at eight o'clock, during the evening of the seventh.

Lee Chung was delighted that his arrangements for Jasmine and the other three with her, had gone according to plan! The five of them sat in the Le Cirque restaurant on the evening of the sixth. The food they had just eaten deserved the excellent reputation that the hotel had. 'When you write to your father, tell him that I'm truly gratefully for this experience.' Doreen smiled and added, 'but if I don't get to bed soon, I'll fall asleep here!'.

'Me too!' Mary and Joan had spoken simultaneously. Jasmine was pleased, at first, when her father had told her what he intended doing, she had been horrified at the amount of money their stay would cost. But Zachery had waved her objections aside, he had wanted to give her a treat, and this had been his wife's idea. So Jasmine had been persuaded to accept the gift. They all stood up to leave the restaurant and retire to their suite.

'I can't help wondering about Tracy, do you think she might want to join us tomorrow, we don't sail until the evening and Coney Island sounds great. Jasmine's remark wasn't made to anyone in particular, but Mary answered her. 'You go on up, I asked this morning if the British edition of the Stage was sold in New York. They seemed to think that getting a copy wouldn't be difficult, so l'll see if its arrived yet. I can phone the ship from reception and see what Tracy is doing tomorrow.' The others agreed and left, Mary walked through the hotel to the reception desk. She enquired about her paper and blinked as the receptionist politely informed her that they had sent a car to the airport and the paper she had asked for would be delivered very shortly. Mary nodded slowly, she hadn't intended that the hotel should go to such lengths to procure it, but then she'd never stayed in such a first class establishment before. She was still wide eyed in amazement, when she realised that Tracy's voice was on the other end of the telephone line.

'Hello.'

'Hi, it's Mary here, tomorrow we're going to Coney Island, then in the early evening we're planning a visit to Radio City, to see what the opposition are doing! Do you want to join us?'

'That sounds great! How's everything going?'

'We'll tell you all about it when we see you. Did Patrick get back okay?'

'Yes.' Tracy's tone was noncommittal. Mary thought it best not to prey over the phone.

'Get a taxi here and have breakfast with us, we're eating at nine in the morning, and don't forget to bring your swimming suit.'

'Okay, see you then, bye.'

'Ciao.' Mary replaced the receiver and wandered aimlessly around, she didn't trust herself to sit down, she was very tired and was afraid of dozing off in one of the convenient and extremely comfortable chairs!

'Hi, why don't I buy you a little drink?' Mary looked at the man in front of her and shook her head. 'The bar here serves the best Manhattan's I've ever tasted, come and try one.' Again Mary shook her head, the man in front of her sounded as if he'd drunk too much already. 'Come on, just one little sip and you'll agree with me!'

'No thank you. I really don't want a drink.'

'Of course you do, everybody needs another one!'

'No I don't.' Mary stepped backwards away from him and bumped into another person. 'I'm so sorry.' Mary stuttered as she apologised.

'Just a couple of drinks in the bar!' With an asinine smile pinned to his face, he continued to annoy her. The female Mary had backed into, looked from her to the man, then lifted her hand and simply caught the attention of the receptionist. And within seconds a uniformed porter arrived on the scene.

'I believe this man has lost his bearings!' The porter bowed slightly and after a slight tussle, escorted the drunk away.

'Thank you, he just wouldn't take no for an answer.'

'You were far too polite.' Mary smiled as she nodded in agreement. The night manager walked up to them.

'Is there anything else I can do for you Lady Bellington?'

'No thank you George.'

'Miss McDonald, your paper is on its way, depending on the traffic, it should arrive here in approximately twenty minutes.' Mary thanked him.

'Oh, if you are waiting, would you like to join me for coffee?'

'Yes, thank you.' Lady Bellington turned and smiled at George. He acknowledged her unspoken request, with an official nod.

'We'll sit over there.' Again the night manager inclined his head, then turned smartly on his heels and left. Mary walked over to the couch where her new companion had pointed, and they both sat down. 'My name is Andrea.' They shook hands. 'Are you here on business?' It was a casual enquiry.

'No, a sort of break, we're part of the cabaret on a cruise liner.' A raised eye brow and Mary found that by the time the coffee had arrived and been poured, that she'd explained the reason she was at the hotel.

'Zachery Chinnock, I know him slightly, my father has some business contracts with him.'

'A small world!'

'Banking can be.' While Mary drank her coffee, she found herself studying her companion. Fine facial features, what looked like naturally blonde hair, cut short, styled to brush back from the forehead. High cheek bones with a classical straight nose. Andrea's full lipped mouth was large and tended to droop at the corners, but at the moment she was smiling and her pale gold eyes glowed with animation. The hands that held the cup and saucer, had long tapering fingers and Mary noticed that the nails were clipped short, with no glimmer of polish. The only jewellery was a plain gold signet ring, worn on the index finger of her right hand. The suit that Andrea was wearing, was elegant, but more in a male fashion than female. But the style, although slightly severe, looked really smart on Andrea.

'Your paper.' A porter presented Mary with a folded copy of the Stage.

'Thank you.' She didn't open it, and as Andrea had stood up, so did Mary.

'It was very pleasant meeting you, I hope you continue to enjoy your work on the cruise liner.' Andrea's voice was friendly and Mary felt a warmth for her, and impulsively asked if she would like to join their expedition to Coney Island. Andrea hesitated, then declined, explaining that she had prearranged meetings to complete the documentation that was required to ship the stallion she'd bought in Kentucky, back to England. Adding that she bred hunters on her father's estate in Leicestershire. They parted.

Maurice returned to the ship at lunch time on the seventh; he was exhausted, but would not have missed the past three days for anything! Ginger was also very pleased with himself. Not only had he successfully sold the heroin he'd bought in Hong Kong, but he'd also been told of a suppler in Ciudad Bolivar, the port in Eastern Venezuela, accessible to ocean going liners, and this ship just happened to be calling there on a later cruise. Ted had enjoyed New York, he'd fallen in with a white collar worker at the docks and spent his time eating and drinking in the bars and cafes which Greenwich Village abounds. He'd put his ambition on hold, telling himself that there was still plenty of time. He met a bubbly red head, and he acknowledged to himself, that if she'd had any money, or had a better job than waiting on tables, then he wouldn't have had to think twice about marrying her. They had spent three days laughing and enjoying each other physically. When Ted went back to the ship, he shrugged off the feeling that he was losing something special, muttering to himself, that he couldn't ever contemplate living in a one bed roomed apartment, she even had to go out to do her laundry!

Passengers for the first Caribbean cruise started to arrive soon after lunch on the seventh of June. Patrick was on duty, he'd seen Tracy as she'd left the ship early that morning. They hadn't spoken, he'd been standing on the open bridge deck. His impulse had been to call out to her and ask her where she was going, but at the time, the Captain had been speaking to him, so he'd had to stand there and wonder. He found he was mulling over the places she could have been going to at frequent periods, during the rest of the day.

The tugs pulled the liner away from the dock, then nudged the vessel into midstream, before the slack of the thick ropes, snapped out of the water with the tension of being towed. A buffet supper was being served in the dinning room from eight until ten that evening. Charis was the only member of the cabaret show to have a meal, all the rest of them, were already in their cabins. Once clear of the Hudson river mouth, the liner headed north to pick up more passengers in Boston. The next day at sea, had no special entertainment organised. The Captains' welcoming cocktail party, would be held on the tenth, after the ship had left Boston.

Sailing between New York and Boston a group of the cast were standing on an outside deck. Tina was the only member of the show that had any knowledge of Boston, and had happily given them the benefit of it. Of course, once the news of her engagement to Bill Ryder became public, it had spread around the crew and Patrick, wanting an excuse to join them on deck, walked up and offered his congratulations to Tina.

'Thank you.' Tina was still starry eyed from spending time with Bill. Patrick hadn't been able to speak to Tracy since their day out together in New York. Tracy smiled as he spoke to her now.

'Are you planning to go ashore in Boston?' Tracy shrugged her shoulders. 'You should, it would be a shame to miss it, although we do call again, but not until the New England Cruise.'

'I'm looking forward to that, although I've visited New York and Boston before, I've never been to Main, or Newfoundland.' Tina was jubilant, she looked so radiant, that Patrick found himself grinning at her and lost the opportunity to continue speaking to Tracy. 'And I'm insisting that Tracy comes ashore with us in Boston, we're going to walk the Freedom Trail, if you're not on duty, do come with us.' Patrick had tried to swap his shift, but hadn't been able to.

'Sorry, I can't make it this time.' Tracy let her head drop then quickly turned to face the sea, she didn't want the disappointment she was feeling to show in her expression.

The Freedom Trail took all day. When the girls returned to the ship at eleven that evening, just an hour before they sailed, Tracy complained that she knew more of American history than British. But admitted that if the food served in the Locke Ober was really traditional, it was no wonder that the British had been thrown out! She had been going to add a quip about fish and chips, but the outrageous response she'd just received, couldn't be topped, so she'd bowed out on a hit! While Tracy had been walking around Boston, she'd made up her mind not to give up on Patrick, he might just want friendship, but she didn't and for the first time in her life, she started to think of ways to change his mind. Her conclusion was that she and Patrick had to make love, she was certain that would kick into touch, his crazy idea of anything platonic! They had to be lovers, nothing else would satisfy her.

Tracy smiled to herself, in her past, she couldn't think of one man, who she had wanted this badly, but then, she couldn't recall any man that she'd fancied that hadn't been as eager to jump into bed, as she was herself!

On leaving the port of Boston, the liner headed south, its destination was the island of Bermuda. There were three days at sea before the ship reached Hamilton, and besides the Captains' cocktail party, shows one and two were performed. Once there, as well as visiting Hamilton, the girls also managed to reach St. George, the original capital of Bermuda. The spell on the beach during the afternoon, topped up their tans, and the briefness of their bikinis passed almost unnoticed. But as Maurice strolled by, he did mention the dire consequences if they returned to the ship with suntan lines that would spoil the look of their costumes. Joan told Maurice to leave the girls alone, stating that as they hadn't so far produced white patches, that their costumes didn't cover, that they were unlikely to do so now! He did ask where Charis was, but only received noncommittal answers.

The two days at sea between Bermuda and the next port of call passed quickly, there was a different show each night. Everyone agreed that San Juan was very Spanish. Tracy had found out that Patrick wasn't on duty on her birthday, the nineteenth; it was the day that the ship visited St. Thomas. She'd asked Patrick, very casually, if he'd been there, and when he'd said yes, she'd enquired if he knew of a picnic place, not too well known. He'd taken a couple of minutes, then nodded, she'd smiled. Patrick had offered to show the girls where it was, and had added that they should take swimming costumes and towels, explaining that the pool below the waterfall was deep, so that they could bathe if they wanted to. Tracy had agreed, then headed straight to the kitchens. By telling the chef that it was her birthday on the day the ship docked at St. Thomas, she persuaded him to agree to provide her with a small packed lunch for two! Then made all haste to inform the girls that Patrick had asked her to spend her birthday with him, adding that she'd celebrate with them later at the fancy dress ball! Megan had raised an eyebrow, Tina had wished her luck. Jasmine and Mary just smiled!

Tracy woke up early, then showered and washed her hair. She put on a scanty pair of panties, a simple sun dress, and sandals, leaving her hair loose. When she met Patrick, she offered an evasive excuse for being by herself. But he didn't prolong that conversation and happily took the basket from her. He ushered her to one of the waiting taxis, gave the driver the directions and held the door open for Tracy to get in. He waited until the car had left the docks, then handed Tracy a small box.

'Happy birthday.' She smiled at him then opened it.

'Patrick, it's beautiful.' She looped the gold chain bracelet over her finger. He grinned as he took it from her and fastened it around her wrist. 'Thank you, I'll keep it forever!' Half an hour later, Patrick was making arrangements with the driver to pick than up at four o'clock that afternoon. It was about a ten minute walk from the road, inland to the waterfall. And Tracy was momentarily mesmerised by the beauty of her surroundings. The vegetation was luscious and the sound of the running water, added magic to the scene.

Tracy had chosen to bring a bikini that covered very little of her body, she was pinning her hopes on the fact that he wouldn't be able to resist her. In her mind, it had to be today. Patrick had taken such a hold over her, that she felt incomplete without him. The need to know that he could love her eclipsed everything else in her life. She would not accept the idea that friendship was all there could be between them. Not Patrick, how could she ever think of him as just a mate? When all her being wanted to be joined in a physical love. As well as adoring the man, she needed him as desperately as any woman had ever hungered over the man she's in love with.

Chapter 25

In fact, Tracy didn't need her plans, she and Patrick had been exploring their paradise when she'd tripped on an exposed root! Instinctively he'd caught her in a strong steadying grip and so stopped her from falling. The rest, as one could say, was inevitable! Naturally he lost himself in her! Tracy's heart began to hammer as she realised that he was going to kiss her.

Patrick's senses exploded and whatever ideas he'd devised on not becoming physically involved with Tracy, instantly evaporated. He brought her supple body against his and the hunger he had tried vainly to ignore, swamped his being. He'd never kissed any other woman with such compelling passion or desire, that was now issuing from him.

She eagerly responded to him, arching her back, to press herself more against his forming erection. She knew that they would finally make love. Then Tracy felt a flutter of panic, would she be disappointed? She usually found sex satisfying. Would making love be so different? The blood in her veins was now pounding with an ever increasing velocity. His kisses inflamed, not quenched, that burning fervour growing incessantly with every second.

Their clothes disappeared, only the gold of the bracelet Patrick had given her, glinted in the sunlight. The sensual touch of bare skin, sent shock waves reverberating through each soul. Within their embrace, they sank fluently to the ground. Patrick felt ten feet tall as he heard her voice echoing her body's response to him. He spread his fingers, enveloping her breasts, then kissed her on her mouth once more.

She lay under him, the fire that coursed within her very centre, took her breath away. With every fibre of her being she gave of herself, never before in her life had she felt like this. She desperately wanted to feel him in her. She could hear her voice, as well as her body, making love to him, and it felt so right. She arched herself under him, by spreading her legs.

He knew that he could not wait, she was driving him insane with her sexuality. Patrick unconsciously filled his lungs with air, then drove deeply into the hot wetness of her inner sanctum.
Soon his thrusts pummelled with relentless potency, until they reached the zenith of their desires.

They lay together, time meant nothing, no other thought had the power to enter into their world. For them, it was as if there had been no other knowledge of love, at that moment, their pasts receded into oblivion. Only the present and each other breathed.

Tracy clung to him, although her breathing had almost regained its normal rate, she didn't want to break this intimate contact between their bodies. Slowly she let her hands trail caressingly over his lithe body, traversing down his back until she could spread her fingers on his firm buttocks, then began to kneed his flesh. She smiled as she felt him begin to throb again in her, and knew this was the onset of another erection. She found his lips and once more, began to kiss him passionately, panting as he sucked her tongue further into his mouth. Their kisses seared with intensity.

Patrick lifted his head, he needed to slow his rampant craving to climax again. He swung his legs out and reluctantly withdrew his member from the heaven of her body, then knelt back on his knees. He looked at her lying beneath him and admitted to himself that he was obsessed with her, but was that love? Then his desire for her eclipsed all other thoughts and he fondled her heaving breasts. He was dominated by her. He moved his right hand down her body, skimming over her flat stomach, until he found her moist slit. As Patrick's fingers tantalisingly probed the wet hotness of her femininity, he lowered his head, this time his mouth covered a hard nipple, sucking hungrily at the flesh of her breast; while his finger peregrinated her inner velvet softness, his thumb, finding her most sensitive place, quickened its erotic meter.

Tracy moved her legs further apart, opening herself to Patrick. The magic of his movements impelled her blood more swiftly through her veins. She arched her back, panting uncontrollably, she could not stop herself from climaxing again, her juices flowed over his hand. Her body quivered and tingled as she floated back from her summit. His mouth released her breast, and she watched adoringly as he lifted his hand and put his fingers into his mouth, tasting her. Tracy raised her shoulders off the ground and sat up. Tenderly she moved her hands to his swollen member. Spreading her fingers along his length, she caressed him, delighted that she could please him with her artistry. His groans of sexual relish, echoed within their enclosed domain. Tracy then gently pushed Patrick backwards, until he was lying flat on the ground. With the tip of her tongue, she began to weave seductive circles on the sensitive skin near the tip of his rigid member, erotically perpetuating his desires for her. As her name ripped through his throat, vibrating passionately through the still hot air, she planted kisses along the throbbing length of his swollen and hard masculinity.

When Tracy's mouth finally crowned his member, Patrick had to trap the breath in his lungs to stop himself exploding. While her lips claimed him, he felt her tongue traversing his tip. When she began to suck, he stretched his arms over his head and tensed every muscle in his body to hold onto his control. With passion burning in his soul, he starred at the blue heavens above and knew that he would soon reach there. Patrick could hold on no more, with shaking hands he raised Tracy's head, their glances momentarily locked before he transferred his hands to the top of Tracy's arms, then drew her nubile body along his. The feel of her naked skin, electrified his already mercurial awareness of her. When their lips met, their kiss reached an intensity unknown to them before. Patrick rolled with her, so that once again Tracy was lying under him. This time, there was no waiting, as she arched her body towards him, he entered her. Pushing deep into the hot wetness that was driving him crazy with a desire that he had not known could exist for him.

Each movement they made, the other answered with love and joy. They scaled with one another to the heights of rapture, thrilling at their shared sensuality, as they celebrated their union of love.

They did swim, their naked bodies skimming through the clear water. And as they drew near each other, their physical magnetism resurged again and again. When they remembered their picnic, they spread out their towels and sat feeding each other, never thinking about dressing. Patrick dismissed his nagging thoughts about her past, he was unable to concentrate of anything but her naked beauty. The day passed. The enjoyment they had shared, left them so happy, the warmth permeated from their feelings and surrounded them with a web of happiness.

Tracy didn't came back into the reality of time, until her shower. The fancy dress ball being held that evening, was a major event for the passengers. Nearly everyone on board joined in the fun. Most holiday makers actually brought their costumes with them, but some of the younger members, did make outfits from whatever they could lay their hands on!

Megan and Tina had taken one look at Tracy's face when she'd returned from her picnic with Patrick and nodded at each other. It was written in very large capitals, for anyone to read, that Tracy had had a blissful day. But they did ask, and received the dreamy answer they had expected. Megan hadn't yet cut into the sari length that she'd bought, so she put it on in the Indian fashion, threaded some jewellery through her hair, and wore lots of rings and bracelets borrowed from the others and declared herself ready. Tina had asked Maurice if she could wear the fairy outfit, she'd used at Christmas, and as he was still in a heady mood from his jaunt in New York, he'd agreed! During Tracy's trip to Fifth Avenue, she'd spotted a black silk, full length dress, in one of the smaller boutiques. It looked stunning, but designed from such a simple idea. The robe was cut from one piece of material to form an oval outline, then folded in half to make the actual dress. It had a diamond shaped neck line, and four small slits at the waist, positioned six inches each side of the centre, and a gold tasselled tie belt had been threaded through them, leaving the material from the wrist to the waist hang loose from the arms. The long sleeves fastened at the wrist and the skirt of the dress draped from the arms as well as the shoulders, the original idea could have been taken from the eastern caftan. Tracy had tried it on and then bought it, as well as a black silk tasselled tie belt; the assistant told Tracy, that she could change the colour of it whenever the mood took her! So tonight the belt was black, Tracy was going as a witch to the fancy dress ball! She had fastened narrow strips of black ribbons in her hair, to add some flavour! She looked sensational, the dress draped from her shoulders, the soft material clung to her uptilted breasts and exquisitely showed off her sculptured figure.

All officers attending the fancy dress ball, did so in full dress uniform! That was one of the first rules Captain Beamish had posted! Patrick wasn't on duty and he'd told Tracy that he'd be at the party. Tracy hadn't been into the dining room, so the first time he saw her, was as she walked into the ballroom with Megan and Tina. All three of them look beautiful, but Patrick's eyes were glued to Tracy. His blood was boiling, not only from her appearance, but also from some lewd comments he'd just overheard.

'I shouldn't let ignorance spoil anything for you.' Patrick dragged his eyes from Tracy to stare at Joan. She just shrugged her shoulders then continued speaking. 'One of the things that will always be a constant surprise to me, it is a fact, that one will always meet with vulgarity. You don't have to bother about other men's jealousy's where a beautiful woman is concerned, it is inevitable that you will always have it in tow! The balance is with the female!' Patrick breathed in, and then let the air slowly out through his nostrils. He looked back at Tracy, their eyes met and she smiled at him, then started to walk gracefully towards him. The group of young male passengers that had annoyed him, moved into her line of vision, but she didn't even glance in their direction. She arrived at his side, her smile proclaiming her feelings for him. Patrick swallowed hard, even after spending the day making love with her, her presence still had the physical affect on him of making him want her. He shifted his feet and was glad that the jacket of his dress uniform was styled long enough to hide his eagerness!

'Hi, tonight I'm a witch!' Her eyes had taken on a darker shade of grey, accentuated by her make up and the reflection from the black dress.

'You certainly have cast a spell.' She smiled, the outline of her crimson lips showed vividly.

'Are you bewitched?' He watched as her breasts moved slightly as she breathed. His answer was simple.

'Yes.' The Chief Engineer walked up and manoeuvred a strategic withdrawal! If Captain Beamish noticed any of his officers not circulating, he always read them the riot act! Tracy found herself talking to a rather fat Cleopatra and smothered a yawn. But every time her eyes found Patrick's, a warmth of contentment filled her anew.

The next day's show was Space Odyssey, it was one of Tracy's favourites. Last night she and Patrick had said good night to each other, under the strict eye of his boss and today, duty had called! After the show, she'd gone straight to the Neptune Bar and waited.

Patrick finished his watch at ten that evening, then dived into a shower; fifteen minutes later, he practically ran to the bar. He found Tracy sitting by herself at a table in the far corner. He ordered himself a Budweiser and a glass of white wine for her, then walked over to join her.

'I want to talk to you.' She smiled as he sat down besides her.

'Thanks.' She raised her glass and sipped it, then asked; 'what about?'

'Us.' She opened her eyes at that, as far as she was concerned there wasn't anything to say. 'About our relationship?' He watched as she leaned forward in her chair and put her hand on his arm as she said.

'I love you.' He swallowed some of his beer then nodded. 'So?' She questioned. Patrick didn't know how to put his doubts into the right words, but he did know, that unless he did sort out his fears, then they could escalate into monsters and destroy what they had. 'Don't you love me?' Her voice had trembled slightly as she'd spoken.

'Yes I do. But that is the problem.' Tracy spilled a little of her wine as she flinched at his words.

'What?' Patrick looked at her and all he wanted to do was to kiss away the scared look from her face, but he forced himself to continue, trying to explain.

'I wasn't looking for you, well what I mean is, falling in love. I just hadn't considered that happening to me for a while.' Tracy just sat there and stared at him. 'I mean, marriage is a big step.' She let her breath go and shook her head.

'You crazy fool, don't scare the hell out of me like that.' It was now Patrick's turn to look flummoxed.

'But don't you want to marry me?'

'To tell you the truth, marriage hadn't entered my head.' Now she grinned and raised her shoulders. He smiled at her and tried to remain calm, but the dress she had on, clung to her figure, showing off every curve, and that movement had only served to accentuate the tempting shape of her breasts.

'Oh God! How the hell are we supposed to talk about our future, if all I can think of is your body and how I want to bury myself in you.' His voice was low and vibrated with emotion.

'I think that's the best idea you've had all night.'

'But it isn't.' He drained his glass, got up and went to the bar. Tracy watched him, her eyes fastening onto him, for the first time in her life, she had no interest for any other man. Tracy had found it so easy to cast off her previous attitudes and concentrate all her energies on Patrick. But she realised that Patrick had a more serious perception of life running through him then she had, and she would have to settle his qualms before they poisoned his love. She lent back in her chair and studied his back. He looked so good, his trousers fitted tightly across his hips, and his upper body, even from the back view, was sculptured into a gorgeous muscled physique. She bent her head as he turned towards her.

She had some quick thinking to do and it had to be done now. She smiled as he placed a wine glass in front of her.

'Thanks. About us, why don't we take it one day at a time?' He looked at her, he just wanted to give in and not care about tomorrow, but could he do that, was he capable of just living for today. Tracy could see the troubled expression flitting across his face. He was too serious. But if tomorrow was going to be a stumbling block, because he needed to think about it, and she didn't even want too, then she'd compromise, in fact, she acknowledged to herself that she'd most probably do anything to keep him. 'Do you want to get married?' Patrick looked at her for some seconds before he actually spoke.

'I always thought that if I ever did fall in love, then yes, I would want to marry her.'

'And you don't want to marry me?' Suddenly her voice sounded very young and vulnerable.

'I honestly don't know.' He cringed at the hurt he saw he'd inflicted on her. 'But I do love you Tracy, like I've never loved any other woman.' She blinked back the rush of tears that had sprung to her eyes, and to steady her panic, she sipped at her wine before she spoke.

'Does the question of marriage have to be answered right now? What I mean is, couldn't we get to know each other better and then later, maybe we could talk about it again.' As he watched her, he knew that she was hurting inside.

'You were right when you told me when we first met, that sex would get in the way.' Tracy shook her head and set her glass down with a snap.

'We didn't have sex, we made love, and if you don't know the difference, you're a bigger fool than I thought!' Patrick lent forward and took her shaking hands into his firm grip.

'Tracy I'm sorry, you must know that I didn't mean that how it came out, it's just that even now, I want you.' She heard the tension and frustration in his voice and nodded.

'Me too.'

'But will we always be able to solve our differences by making love? She wanted to blurt out that they could even settle the world's problems that way, but didn't. 'What do you think?' His question brought her head up.

'All I know Patrick, is that I've never felt this way before and I don't ever want to lose you.' He pulled her to her feet and they left the bar. They ran up stairs and out onto the deck, it was a brilliant starry night and there were no other people in the vicinity. He took her in his arms and kissed her. He didn't know what their future would be, but for now, he could not stop loving and wanting her.

Tracy melted into his embrace and clung to him. His kiss ignited the smouldering fire that had continuously burnt within her since they had first made love. When he raised his head, they were both panting. 'Now you have to go to your cabin, before I lay you down on this deck!' She heard the raw emotion in his voice, and forced herself to agree with him.

'I suppose it would be against regulations if I didn't go!' He nodded.

'And as we both share cabins.' He let his voice trail off, but she understood, that he didn't want to demean their relationship with a quick grope on the deck.

'It's a good job that you have enough self control for both of us.' She'd tried to make her tone light, but frustration had edged in. His head swooped down and his lips found hers again. Fire and heat passed between them, their pluses raced. 'But remember Patrick.' She was almost breathless and her voice was very husky with emotion. 'We can only make love, it wouldn't matter where or when, or even how! It would be love, nothing else!' With that, she forced herself to turn away from him and walk along the deck to the stair well, where, she lifted her hand, blew him a kiss, then disappeared through the doors.

Chapter 26

Tracy and Patrick spent the rest of that cruise talking, well, most of the time! When they met, they would sit together chatting about themselves and their families, school days and careers. Patrick never asked her about previous boyfriends, he still shied away from her past sexual relationships. Being on the ship they had no privacy, so talking was their main occupation, rather than physical. When they kissed good night, they always parted not wanting to! But the confines of being crew members imposed this restriction on them. When they arrived back in New York on the first of July, Patrick was lucky enough to be off duty and they went ashore to The Derby restaurant in Greenwich Village, their meal was delicious. Patrick's plan had been to keep the night on a friendly basis and return to the ship later. He wanted to have a serious talk with Tracy about his worries concerning their future together, but after the meal, he knew that the first hotel they came across would be where they stayed the night! He wasn't just falling in love with her, he acknowledged that he was never going to recover; when he was drowning in her, then her past had no power to invade his mind. But during the sane hours, when his brain was occupied with his normal duties, then his doubts started and the awkward questions loomed large! 'Do I love her enough to trust her? Is she capable of being faithful to me?' The answers to these were definitive to his future happiness with her. Tracy was in her own private heaven, she loved Patrick with every fibre in her being. The reason she never asked about his past affairs was because she wasn't curious about them; what was ineluctable to her was that she was and going to be, the only woman in his life today and for each new dawn.

The next cruise sailed at six o'clock on the evening of the second of July. Mary first saw Lady Andrea Bellington in the ship's dining room; in response to a lifted hand, she walked over and spoke to her.

'I didn't realise that you intended to travel with us!' Andrea smiled and raised a quizzical eyebrow as she answered.

'I had no definite plans, but when I discovered that I had a couple of weeks spare before they can fly the stallion to England, I couldn't resist playing truant! If you've got nothing else planned, why not join me for a drink later.'

'I'd love to.'

'Which bar do you recommend?'

'Oh, the Neptune is where we usually go.'

'Sounds fine, I'll see you there later.' Mary nodded then went to her own table. A show was never scheduled for the evening that the ship left port and on the first full day at sea, the official function was generally the Captain's cocktail party. After the meal, Mary invited Jasmine and the other girls to meet Andrea and have a drink with them. Lee Chung excused himself as they left the dinning room. He recognised the name immediately and intended to let his boss know as well. Jasmine was unaware of the close communication between Lee Chung and her father, a daily occurrence was not unusual. Mary had already told the girls how she'd met Lady Bellington at the Mayfair Regent. They all went to the Neptune bar and found Andrea waiting at a table with a bottle of white wine and two glasses. She smiled as the party walked in and in her accustomed manner, signalled the waiter. By the time everyone had sat down, more wine and glasses had appeared on the table. Mary sat in the chair next to Andrea and introduced everyone. Conversation was light hearted and when Lee Chung joined them twenty minutes later, Jasmine presented him to Lady Bellington, he bowed formally before sitting down. They all enjoyed the evening and Andrea found herself included in their proposed trip when the ship docked at Nassau on the sixth.

The cocktail party on the first full day at sea was as usual, a success. Andrea wore an oyster coloured long satin straight skirt and fitted jacket. The pearl choker around her neck, gave off the lustre of reality. The Captain made a lengthy task of introducing her to his senior officers, but when she eventually managed to escape from him, she made a fourth with Jasmine, Lee Chung and Mary. Ted prowled around but found nothing of interest until he spotted Lady Bellington! He couldn't believe his luck. She was in her mid thirty's, single and rich! He attached himself like a limpet to her. After the party, Andrea asked the others to join her in the Neptune bar. Jasmine declined, she had letters to write, Lee Chung left with her. Mary and Ted accepted. Andrea asked if they had any preference and as neither had, she ordered chartreuse liqueurs.

Ted made himself more comfortable in his chair and sipped curiously at his drink. The green liquid in his glass darkened its shade as his hand hid the light. He was relieved that it tasted okay, but it wasn't what he would have chosen. He wasn't a fan of liqueurs and very rarely drank them. He preferred his booze in a large glass, something he could swallow in generous quantities! He'd decided that it shouldn't be any problem to get Lady Bellington into bed to impress her with his aptitude for sex and from then on, life would be rosy! From the snippets of conversation that he'd paid attention too, he already gathered that she was unattached at the moment and still living with her parents. He let his imagination gallop, picturing himself lording it very gallantly over her domain. Ted was trying to think of a way to get rid of Mary when his wandering thoughts were caught by Andrea's voice.

'Shall we take a stroll around the promenade deck?'

'Yes.' His prompt reply made Mary blink, but Andrea merely shrugged. Mary nodded her head, then stood up. The three of them left the bar and leisurely sauntered to the outside deck. The night was warm, the breeze billowing in from the darkness was refreshing. They walked abreast until they reached the stern, then lent against the rail looking at the wake left by the liner's progress, as it cut through the halcyon sway of the water. Ted moved very close to Andrea's side and made contact with his thigh against her. She stayed still. Pleased with this, he draped his arm on her shoulders. At that, she turned her head and gave him a slightly frosty look. Ted's conceit took that as shyness on her part and produced one of his practised smiles, but was a little perplexed when he did not receive the welcoming response he'd expected from her. Instead he saw a questioning look. He thought that maybe she needed a little more encouragement, so he grinned and winked at her. Now Andrea's eyebrows rose and to underline her statement, she also gave a slight shake of her head. Ted was puzzled, but didn't alter his position, instead he gently closed his fingers on her shoulder, kneading her flesh. Andrea straightened up, this time her look was hard. Ted was still wondering why she wasn't snuggling against him.

After waiting for him to remove his arm, which he hadn't done so, Andrea flicked his hand off as she moved away from him. She stopped about two feet from Ted and let her disdainful eyes travel from his face, down his torso to his highly polished shoes, then flashed quickly back to catch and hold his gaze. Ted suddenly felt garishly uncomfortable. He wasn't stupid and knew that she had given him a definite brush off. He swallowed and nodded his head, shoved his hands in his pockets then left. Mary, whose concentration had been solely on the stars until Andrea had moved, had watched the interchange with fascination. Her astonished gaze followed Ted's retreating back along the deck.

'Don't you like him?' Mary's naive statement produced a sudden laugh from Andrea.

'In what way?' Her counter question puzzled Mary, she just shrugged her shoulders, so Andrea continued. 'If you mean as a friend, he doesn't impress me, that kind of person is always very self absorbed. But if you're referring to him as a sexual partner for me, the answer is no, I am a lesbian.' At Mary's staggered look, Andrea carried on, keeping her tone even. 'I'm sorry if I've shocked you, but I assumed you would have known.' Mary just stared open mouthed at her. Andrea stood there calmly, her voice when she spoke again was still very composed. 'Do you want me to leave?'

'No.' Mary had also shaken her head as she'd replied. Andrea walked back to the rail besides her. Neither spoke for perhaps ten minutes until Mary asked. 'Does it bother you?' Andrea turned to face Mary.

'Do you mean, am I concerned that my sexual preference is for a female and not a male?' Mary jerked her head, nodding quickly. 'No, why should it?' Mary continued to gape at her, she couldn't believe that this woman wasn't embarrassed. Her own family had so openly denounced anything that they considered unnatural, that she'd felt guilty. Mary had been so distressed when she'd realised her own sexuality, that she had never examined the possibility that any female could openly admit to being a lesbian. Yet here was a woman who was well balanced and even seemed happy. Mary felt a sudden surge of jealousy for the other's composure.

Andrea watched Mary keenly, then asked her if she would like another drink? She smiled gratefully and agreed, they returned to the Neptune bar where Andrea ordered two brandy's. The room wasn't crowded and they sat at an unoccupied table. Andrea didn't speak, she knew that Mary had a lot to think about and so they just sat there sipping their drinks. When they'd finished, Andrea suggested that they call it a night.

'Are you tired?' Mary's question surprised Andrea, but she answered straight away.

'No. But I thought you needed to think, that's all. Tomorrow is another day.' Andrea smiled at Mary, then added, 'we could meet for breakfast?' That was agreed and they parted.

Mary walked back to her cabin and found Jasmine was still awake.

'Is anything wrong?' She looked at Jasmine sitting there comfortably in her bunk, it was plain to see how happy she was now that she had found her father and been accepted by him, even Jasmine's shyness seemed to be ebbing. A wishful yearn threaded through Mary as she longed for her parents to find it in their hearts to still love her, if she told them the truth about herself. But she knew that was a hopeless dream, she'd tried, but even at the mention of lesbianism, their disgust and anger had frightened her. 'Well?' Mary still didn't say anything. 'Don't you like Andrea?' That was a question Mary could answer.

'Of course I do.'

'That's great! She likes you.' That simple statement unexpectedly filled Mary with hope, and excitement echoed in her voice when she spoke.

'I think she'd be a good friend, you know, kind, dependable and trustworthy.'

'Yes, I'm sure she would. My mother once told me, that if anyone was fortunate to fall in love with a true friend, then the relationship should last because it would not be based purely on passion. Are you seeing her again?' It wasn't so much the words the intonation Jasmine had used which surprised Mary.

'What do you mean?'

'I'm sorry, I wasn't being nosey in a spiteful way, I'm a friend and I care for you, but not in the way I think that Andrea does.' It was a night for shocks for Mary, this was another one.

'You know that I don't like men as a sexual partner?'

'Yes.'

'It doesn't bother you?'

'Why should it?' Now Jasmine sounded surprised. Mary shrugged, then said.

'You're not and well, I suppose I thought that you might feel strange sharing a cabin with me.' Jasmine giggled.

'One of my mother's good friends is a lesbian and I get along with her.' Jasmine seemed to think that she'd explained her feelings adequately. Mary just stood there smiling, relief at being accepted for herself felt so good.

Mary and Andrea spent the following day talking to each other. Mary explained about her family's revulsion against any group of people that differed from them, so much so that it had caused her to feel guilty and ashamed. With patience and tact Andrea helped Mary to gain some self respect for herself. Neither of them bothered about joining in the quiz night, and after dinner, spent their time with a bottle of wine by the swimming pool. There was only one other couple there and they were in a world of their own as well!

Maurice reversed the dates of shows one and two, so that 'Hollywood' would take place on the fourth of July! It was a hit! The next day the liner docked at Nassau. Everyone planned to meet in the dinning room for breakfast, but Tracy was late getting ready and told the other two that she'd catch them up later. When Tina explained the situation to Patrick, who wasn't on duty and was going ashore with them; he went off to hurry her up. He arrived at her cabin and rapped on the door. It opened just enough for Tracy's head to pop into view.

'What kept you?' Her hand shot out and dragged him through the door, then shut and locked it behind him.

'You're naked.'

'This is my bunk.'

'But the others are waiting for us.'

'At the moment they're eating breakfast! Now me, I'm only hungry for you.' She smiled at him, her fingers already busily undoing his jeans.

'Tracy you're crazy.'

'For you, I'll admit to that. I want you to make love to me Patrick, is that so bad?'

'No. But what will the others say when we don't turn up?' She giggled then answered.

'We will, just not in time to eat breakfast!' Tracy pushed his jeans and shorts down over his thighs.

Patrick felt Tracy's hands caress his masculinity, he looked at her, she was smiling, he kissed her. Patrick's sanity swamped in a tide of desire. He cupped her breasts, rubbing his thumbs erotically on the firm peaks of her succulent nipples as he felt her stroking his developing erection. Their lips joined again, each thrusting a tongue into the others welcoming mouth. Their breathing quickened considerably. Now Tracy triumphantly curled her hands possessively around Patrick's fully extended member. 'I love you so much Patrick.' He pulled her hands to his lips and kissed her palms, then swept her into his arms and lay her on her bunk. She pulled him on top of her and he entered her straight away. He drove repeatedly into the hot wetness of her.

Tracy crossed her ankles over his back and met his thrusts with loving eagerness. They built within them, the ultimate sexual force that can be generated by two people in love with each other. Then definitely rode on their passion until their wave peaked and cascaded, enfolding them both with happiness and satisfaction. Twenty minutes later, they met the others coming out of the dinning room.

Everyone spent a happy day exploring the old town of Nassau. Tracy entertained them all with her haggling over prices in the outdoor bazaar. Nobody left the straw market without a new hat! And that evening they dressed for the occasion when they visited one of the casinos. By the time they finally returned to the ship, they were all exhausted.

On the two days at sea between Nassau and Jamaica, shows one and three were performed, Paris Night Out and a South Pacific Fantasy. Andrea spent most of her time with the dancers. They liked her, her open and frank manner made it easy for them all to get along. Charis was impressed with her title, but would not allow herself to be drawn into the group. Andrea was again included as they planned their next port of call, Montego Bay! Jasmine wanted to see Greenwood, Elizabeth Barrett Browning's ancestral home; Tina wanted to walk through a tropical rain forest; Tracy wanted to see Dunn's River Falls, water falls had a special meaning for her now; Megan had heard that you could raft on the waters of the Martha Brae, this time, it would be a gentle ride; the others fell in with the proposed plans and most were satisfied!

July the tenth found the ship at sea again, heading for San Juan, Puerto Rico. Nobody got up for breakfast, but Mary did meet Andrea after lunch. They sat besides the pool and sipped their chilled drinks and occasionally took a refreshing dip in the cool water. Most of the younger cast members spent their afternoons on the smaller aft deck, only going to the pool to swim. The passengers always congregated on the open deck around the swimming pool, crowding it and the water! The crew members customarily gave the passengers all the space they needed to thoroughly enjoy their holiday! That night's show was Bow Bells, the following evening, China Town was performed. When the liner docked at San Juan, everyone found the Spanish flavour of the old town fascinating and even Tracy was impressed with the Fort of San Cristobal!

The ship sailed from the old world charm of San Juan and the next show was the Space Odyssey. By the time the liner reached

Saint John on the fourteenth, everyone was ready for a relaxing day spent on a perfect white sandy beach. Mary spent most of her time with Andrea, they were becoming very close. Between Saint John and their next port of Tortola, Megan's favourite show, Rio Carnival was performed, she found the music and choreography exciting. The botanical gardens on Tortola were a myriad of colour and heady fragrances. Maurice wanted to buy some of the more exotic blooms to decorate the cabaret floor for the following night's show, which was the Arabian Tales, but Joan managed to dissuade him by telling him that she doubted that the flowers would survive! Saint Maarten was next on their itinerary and divided the group, half thought that the Dutch influenced town of Philipsburg more interesting, the others voted for Marigot, with its French cafes, of course Tracy plumped for Mullet Bay! From the Dutch Antillies, there were three full days at sea and the entertainment was first, the Broadway show, then the passengers amateur night, and finally the cabaret show was staged, before the ship arrived in Bermuda on the twenty second of July. Hamilton was a home from home for the British members of the crew, only hotter!

Chapter 27

The ship was heading north again and the final show for this cruise was a major success. Maurice had just finished with his upbeat version of 'Swing Low, Sweet Charity', and behind him stood the full cast of the show. Ted didn't like that particular tempo for the song, but the applause was good. Maurice stood in the centre of the cabaret floor bowing and smiling, he loved the sound of an appreciative audience. The next day was the twenty fourth of July and the Captain's Farewell Cocktail party. On the following afternoon the liner would dock in New York.

That last morning Andrea didn't go to the dining room for her breakfast; so after Mary had finished her meal, she went to look for her.

'Come in, I'm packing.' As Mary walked into the cabin, she saw three open cases, two on the bed, the other on the floor.

'Can I help?'

'Thanks, the clothes in the wardrobe should fit into that.' Andrea pointed to the case on the floor. Mary nodded and started to take the things out of the cabinet, methodically folded the garments, then neatly packed them. But she was finding it difficult to concentrate on what she was doing, her gaze automatically kept veering towards Andrea, whose large drooping mouth was softly relaxed into a dreamy smile. Mary longed to see those pale gold eyes glow with passion and found that her own breathing was accelerated and shallow, even her hands trembled. She had never experienced this intensity of feelings for any other person, but if she told Andrea how she felt, what would happen, she was so afraid of rejection. As Mary bent to lay another jacket into the case, her eyes flitted to where Andrea was stood, the slate grey silk dressing gown she was wearing, draped softly, and as she lent forward the diaphanous material showed the slender outline of her body. Mary had to drag her gaze back to the task she was doing.

After half an hour the packing was finished, Andrea was the first to speak.

'Well that's certainly cut that job in half.' As she'd spoken, she'd moved across to the chest of draws, where she'd taken a small box from the top, then turned back to Mary and said. 'This is for you.' Mary was so surprised, she just stood there. Andrea walked up to her and placed a present in her shaking hands. 'Go on, open it.' Mary's fingers quivered as she carefully lifted off the top of the box. Inside on a bed of velvet, was an intricately engraved gold ring. 'I hope that I've gauged the size accurately and it fits!' Andrea took the ring out and slipped it onto the middle finger of Mary's right hand. 'Great! Do you like it?' Mary was speechless but she managed to smile as she nodded her head. They were stood very close to each other and Mary desperately wanted to thank Andrea, not as a friend, but as her lover. Yet all she could do was to stare hopelessly at the person whom she most wanted. She didn't even have the strength to speak.

Andrea watched her closely, smiled then snapped the lid back on the box before she flicked it onto the bed. 'I hope that you don't think that I'm rushing things, but when you are back in England, I'd like you to visit my home. I could even teach you to ride, I've got a couple of good hacks we could use, that's if you fancied it?' Mary found that she was shivering with trepidation at the thought of being separated from someone so special to her. 'Is there anything wrong?' There was deep concern in Andrea's voice. Mary knew that she had to speak.

'No! Except that I want to tell you that I do really care for you and I just don't know how to tell you. It's stupid, but I'm so afraid of saying the wrong thing and losing you.'

'You couldn't!' Andrea beamed as she took both Mary's shaking hands in her steady clasp. 'My only wish for the future, is that you will always be with me; I'm hoping that is what you want as well?' Mary quickly nodded her head. Andrea hugged her. Mary laughed and cried at the same time, then she became aware of the physical contact of Andrea's body against her's. Mary raised her head and they both looked sincerely into each other's eyes. They stayed motionless, drinking in the other, until their lips slowly moved together and they kissed. Softly at first, poignantly exploring each other, then as their feelings deepened, passion swept in and their kiss inflamed their latent desires.

Mary felt Andrea's hands move and unzip her dress. She let Andrea pull it over her head and was unconcerned where it landed. Then her bra disappeared and when Andrea's fingers went to her breasts, she arched her back to facilitate more caresses. Andrea's fingers gently cupped her throbbing flesh and Mary let out a sigh of intimate anticipation. She'd wanted to touch Andrea for some time and now had the courage to push her robe from the other's shoulders. It slipped down Andrea's arms and Mary gazed hungrily at her, then she untied the belt and the silk whispered as it fell to the floor.

Andrea stood in front of Mary with no embarrassment about her nudity. She knew that this was a new experience for Mary and she wanted her to enjoy it to its fullest. They had become friends over the passed two weeks and now the natural progression to physical love was happening for them both. Mary stood before her unsure of expressing her feelings, so Andrea gently moved the dancer's finely shaped hands to her breasts and then kissed her again. Slowly Mary's hands began to traverse over her skin and gradually became more demanding.

Mary had never experienced anything so wonderful before, she found Andrea's body beautiful and exciting to touch. She tentatively spread her fingers, caressing Andrea's slender shape, hoping that she was giving as much pleasure and happiness as she was receiving. The burning thrills running through Mary accelerated as she realised that her movements were creating sexual enjoyment for her lover.

Andrea held onto her control, she held back the urge to devour Mary's body. To kiss and touch her so passionately until, finally Mary would reach an orgasm; but that was for later, for now, she would let Mary discover the thrills of intimacy to be shared with a loving partner.

Andrea's breath was now coming in short sharp pants, she was finding it untenable to hold back any longer. When Mary's fingers finally parted the hair of her moist slit and started to stroke her. Andrea's breath raked through her and she kissed Mary again, this time she held nothing back. Her tongue thrusted its way into the other's mouth. Their kiss portrayed all their desires for each other and built an ever increasing fire between them. Then with deft swiftness, Andrea knelt in front of Mary and hastily pulled her panties down. Mary stepped out of them, opening her legs as she felt Andrea's fingers parting the wet triangle of her pubic hair. A groan of elation vibrated in Mary's throat as Andrea claimed her womanhood with her mouth. Very soon, Mary reached her first orgasm. When Andrea sat back on her heels, she was still panting.

Slowly Mary bent down in front of her, then hugged her. She felt so wonderful that she wanted to give Andrea the same feeling.

Slowly Mary pushed Andrea's knees apart, then inched herself forward. Mary had enough sexual knowledge to know how to give Andrea satisfaction with her fingers. They looked at each other with eyes of love. Mary's hands were shaking as she spoke.

'I want to bring you now.' Andrea swallowed hard and nodded. Gently Mary placed her fingers in position and started a slow rhythm. Mary watched Andrea's expression of gratification grow and was thrilled. She didn't need any encouragement to quicken her movements to bring on Andrea's climax.

They were now lying on the floor holding each other. Their bodies pressed intimately together. Each conscious of the other's beauty. Andrea stroked Mary's hair and smiled as she felt the other's fingers caress her breasts. Time seemed irrelevant, they were wrapped in a cocoon of discovery. When they kissed again, Andrea gently pushed Mary flat. Then left a trail of erotic kisses down Mary's neck until she reached her breasts. Now Andrea's mouth claimed the rosy peak of a tempting nipple in her mouth, her tongue sending electric shock waves through the other's body. When Andrea knelt up, she curled her legs under her before she lent forward, then lowered her head to trace a seductive path from Mary's breasts down to her saturated femininity.

Blood pounded through her body as she embraced Andrea's love making. In her wildest dreams, Mary had never thought that she could ever unite with another person in this intimate way, yet here she was, being caressed in such a way that she was racing forward to perfect rapture. And the desire to touch her lover in this way multiplied as Mary was transported even higher.

The happiness she was giving to the other woman was in its self stimulating for Andrea, but she became even more aroused when she felt Mary's hand push its way into her own hot wetness, creating even more incredible emotions within her. She was panting hard, as again she brought Mary to the heights of an orgasm.

When Andrea sat up, so did Mary. Her inexperience forgotten, she claimed a succulent breast with an eager mouth and sucked hard on the nipple, while her fingers still moved erotically arousing her new lover to another sexually satisfying climax.

Mary gave a last tender kiss to a throbbing nipple before she sat up. Their happiness was so real that it filled the room. Inextricably, their lips came together, the kiss they shared held tenderness as well as passion. At last Mary felt complete. There was no guilt or disgust with herself, she was happy, she'd finally met a person who she could truly love and was in love with her.

Life had taken on a new and fulfilling meaning for her. Now the future seemed to offer something very momentous and she was no longer afraid. When their kiss ended, Andrea lay back under the gentle pressure from the other's hands. Fleetingly Mary sat still to cherish the memory, before she bent forward, her lips nuzzling Andrea's ear and neck, then with feathery kisses, tantalisingly roamed over her body until she reached her goal. Mary felt erotic pleasure as her lips and tongue explored intimately. She felt Andrea's hands on her legs and let herself be gently pulled flat, but did not break the carnal bond which was exciting her so much.

Andrea lifted Mary on top of her and parted the wet hair, to once again claim the sweet wetness with her mouth. Together their desires built to the pinnacle of rapture, once there, triumphantly soared, then drifted with ethereal fulfilment. When Mary slid onto her side, Andrea rolled and kept their bodies together. Their passion still torrid. Then each explored with their fingers, arousing the other, before passionately kissing the hot wetness which they had again created. And simultaneously scaling the heights, once more they descended slowly through the veils of repletion.

Andrea was the first to move, she stood up, then pulled Mary to her feet. They went into the adjoining bathroom, filled the tub with warm water, then liberally poured in some aromatic salts. While they bathed together, they made plans for their future. When the ship arrived back in Southampton, Andrea would be there waiting for Mary, they would live together in Leicestershire. The water was getting cold, so they reluctantly got out. Then dried and dressed. The ship had docked half an hour ago and the passengers were now disembarking. Andrea had persuaded Mary to spend the night ashore with her, at a hotel. There was a car waiting on the dock, they got into it without a backward glance. Mary would return to the ship before it sailed. Once Andrea was back home, they planned to write to each other, also Andrea suggested that they could go on holiday once Mary left the ship. When asked if she had any preference for a destination, Mary had shaken her head. Andrea said she would surprise her!

Megan had gone ashore to meet Aaron and have dinner with him, he still had no news for her on her mother's whereabouts. Patrick was on duty and Tracy had lost any interest in going anywhere without him. Tina phoned Bill, she was now counting the days until October, when she would be with him again. Maurice broke one of his self imposed rules of not mixing business with pleasure and succumb to the lures of Alexander, the young officer spent several hours in his cabin. Joan and Doreen went ashore and enjoyed strolling along Fifth Avenue, then afterwards splashed out on an expensive meal at The Four Seasons, both agreeing it was the highlight of their year! Charis was also shopping, but when she saw them during the afternoon, she deliberately kept out of their view. Ted went on the prowl, but came back in a bad mood. Ginger went by himself to the cinema.

Patrick was walking aft on the upper deck when he spotted Ted leaning on the hand rail, about four feet from the main passenger entrance on the port side studying the dock and his own glance flicked in that direction. As he looked he saw that it was busy with cabs and private limousines circumspectly shuffling for the nearest position to the gang way. Hundreds of cases of all types and sizes were stacked ready to be brought aboard. When Ted straightened up, the movement caught the corner of Patrick's eye. What had attracted his attention? Patrick studied the commotion and found the main players. It was staged around a stretched limousine, with Mississippi number plates. The prominent player, in a simple plain dark dress, was directing the scene by ordering the chauffeur to help carry a sea trunk, a porter had already been commandeered to carry another large piece of luggage and she herself, clutched a square vanity case. Following this possession from the car to the ship, waddled a rather fat middle aged female dressed in flowing chiffon, in a style that had been in fashion thirty years ago. The breeze wafting in from the east, could only flap the wide brim of her straw hat, it was anchored firmly in place by a very large hatpin. Patrick grinned! The retinue proceeded to board the liner.

Ted wasn't in a good mood. He'd studied the passenger manifesto for over an hour and still the only name to fit his requirements was that of Miss. Libby Jane Putts. And as he'd already watched her come aboard, he wasn't impressed with her looks at all. He told himself not to panic as there were still three more cruises before they set sail to return to Southampton. He was enjoying this life, the weather was favourable, the food good and the service on board was excellent. He would find it very difficult to go back to his old life style of trailing around the cabaret circuit and living out of a suit case. He squashed a flutter of rising panic. He had to marry a rich woman, there was no other way. He'd consumed his usual large dinner; he frequently congratulated himself on never putting on too much weight! Of course he acknowledged that he'd thickened out a little over the past ten years, but with his height, he could afford this minimal spread without worrying over his looks. He decided to go to the Neptune bar for a drink.

Patrick had come off duty at eight o'clock that evening, he'd showered, changed, then eaten before strolling down to the bar to find Tracy. The more he saw of her the deeper his feelings became, but he still had nagging doubts over her past affairs and if he could now really trust her. She was sitting with Tina and Megan. He asked what they were drinking.

'White wine.' Both Tracy and Megan had chorused together.

'Rye and soda water for me, thanks.' Tina smiled brightly at Patrick, but she was thinking of Bill.

Ted walked in about ten minutes later and bought himself a drink, then sat at their table. The conversation was general until Margaret, from the Purser's office joined them. Then Ted directed their topic around to future passengers!

'Actually, we're fully booked for the short cruise at the beginning of September.' Margaret giggled, then added. 'So many Jones and Smiths on the list!'

'Those 'at sea' breaks are always the same!' Patrick's voice had been very bland.

'The trip I'm looking forward to is the one after that which goes to South America.' Tracy turned to Patrick. 'Ever been there?' He nodded then answered her.

'But not with this company, I believe this is the first cruise they have taken so far down.'

'Yes,' Margaret answered him, 'and it's a big success, all the state rooms are booked, in fact when we left New York, only three of the four bedded cabins on D deck were still empty.' Ted stared hard at her, then abruptly smiled, he had to see that passenger list, then he could find out if there were any candidates coming aboard.

'I'm looking forward to the northern cruise, that scenery at the end of August and beginning of September should be beautiful.' Everyone agreed with Tina, except Ted. In his opinion, millionaires liked the sun! He spent the rest of the evening being very pleasant to Margaret. He wanted a quick look at the future passenger lists. When the party broke up, Ted walked casually back with the Purser's clerk. As they passed the office, he asked if he could check if a mate of his from England was booked for a cruise! They both knew he was lying, but as she didn't see any harm in his request, she unlocked the door and let him in. While Ted scoured the names, she tidied her desk. This shipping company was renowned for their personal touch in the care of their passengers and to make sure that everything was done for their comfort, the passengers who booked the staterooms and de luxe cabins, nearly always had a short bibliography on tastes, likes etcetera, noted as a reference for the staff. Ted had found this so useful in the past. And now it held nothing for his future. There were of course the odd rich female coming aboard. A retired headmistress, but she was seventy; a widow, semi crippled with arthritis, accompanied by her nurses, she'd be to busy popping pills for his use; then there was a typist, Ted shrugged and wondered were she'd got the money from for such an expensive stateroom, and as she was booked on the northern cruise, he dismissed her as a none starter! The were maybe half a dozen more names, but none that Ted thought had any likelihood of fitting his personal requirements. As he walked back to his cabin, he made up his mind it would have to be Libby Jane Putts. There was no mystery about her, she was single and came from a very well known wealthy family. So she was fat, what did that matter? It didn't look as if she was beating men off! Maybe she'd be so grateful to him for his attentions, that she'd most probably bite his hand off, when he asked her to marry him.

Chapter 28

At breakfast on the morning of the Captain's Welcome Aboard Cocktail Party, Miss Libby Jane Putts didn't put in an appearance. But that didn't worry Ted, he wasn't planning to start his assault until later. He was going to be very courteous and polite for the first few days at sea, making his first direct move on the day the ship called at the Bahamas. He was in earnest and did not intend to make any mistakes in the way he handled the forthcoming proceedings.

Rose folded her arms across her chest and shook her head several times.

'But I want too.' The high childish voice seemed alien to the fat middle aged body it belonged to.

'Well Miss Libby, it just isn't appropriate!' Libby flounced over to her bed and dramatically threw herself across it. 'Now that's no way for a Southern Lady to behave!' Rose sounded unimpressed, she'd witnessed these tantrums all of her life, but there was still patience in her tone! 'Come on Miss Libby and sit up. You have a lunch appointment with the Captain and the time is passing! If you don't let me get you dressed you're going to be late, and that isn't polite now, is it?' Libby pulled herself up, her flabby mouth scowled.

'But I like the pink dress best.'

'And you shall wear it tonight for the party, but not for lunch.'

'I could keep it on all day.' Libby's high pitched voice maintained its whine. 'I will.'

'Certainly not! No one from home would wear the same frock all day, and so you know, now do come over here and let me help you with this nice cream outfit. You know it's what your brother would want you to choose.' At the mention of Robert's name, Libby sniffed, but did as she was told.

Libby ate an enormous amount of food at lunch, then went back to her stateroom, let Rose undress her, decided to lay on her

228

bed, then went to sleep. When she woke up she insisted on getting dressed for the cocktail party. It was too early, but Rose let her and when she was ready, she spent the rest of her time parading in front of the mirror, rather in the manner of a small child, who was very pleased with herself!

Ted always took care choosing what to wear and this evening was no exception. He went to the party early and wandered around as the room filled with passengers. All the clothes were expensive and most people were very fashionably attired. But there were always the oddballs who had no dress sense whatsoever, and no matter how much they spent on their wardrobe, they never managed to look the part. Libby Jane Putts fell starkly into this category. Nature hadn't given her a metabolism to cope with her sweet tooth and greed for food, or the mental strength to control them. So she was fat! Her heavy breasts sagged onto her bulging stomach. She was only five feet, two inches in height and plain. Nothing about her stood out, except her size. From birth, she'd been hemmed in. Reared by her father, who's views on life were unduly old fashioned, she hadn't really had a chance to become anything but a drudge! His health had started to deteriorate thirty years ago and she had been kept at home to be at his beck and call. The nurses employed to care for him, had drifted in and out of Libby's orbit, but none of them had ever made any impression on her. But her father had died over a year ago and her brother and his wife wanted her out of their house! So she had been sent of this cruise with the hope that the family's money would lure some grasping male into a marriage. Robert wasn't worried about losing any of the family assets he guarded so jealousy, Libby had no personal ownership to any property and with her demise, her annuity ceased. And Rose was under strict instructions not to tell Libby or her proposed husband any monetary or health details appertaining to Libby. Once married, Libby could move from the family estate into a house they owned in Putts Landing. It was in an excellent position and large enough to be classed as one of the best houses that the small town could boast of! It had, among its other attributes, six bedrooms and a very elegant drawing room, with French glassed doors that led out onto a veranda running the full length of the house which faced the river. Also it had it's own private landing stage. It had always been Libby's dearest wish to be a married lady and be mistress of that house. It was an old tradition in her family that one of the married daughters occupied that house. But one had to be married, the unwed daughters never left the estate!

And Robert wanted Libby out of his immediate vicinity in the future because he was planning that his young wife should become pregnant. He had given her enough time to settle down and as their second anniversary was coming up, it was now time that she produced an heir! So of course, Robert had told Libby if she got married she could move into her own home. Also that she could take Rose with her and as many servants as she needed. He had pleased her with that statement, and her simple mind had not questioned the reasons behind his generosity, they were in there own way very basic, his pride could not allow the locals to gossip about the family! Anyway Robert did not expect that situation to go on for too many years. Libby had the same defective heart condition that their mother had died of! He comforted himself with the thought that her doctor didn't think she would reach the age of sixty!

Ted tipped the content of his glass drown his throat and put it on a tray, that a passing steward was carrying. Then he walked slowly across the room. Libby stood within the Captain's group as Ted passed very close to her, making eye contact, he smiled courteously. As he arrived beside Megan, Tina and Tracy, he glanced back and his eyes again encountered Libby's, she blushed. Ted was pleased, but he turned and joined in the conversation the girls were having. As a group they looked stunning; Tina's little black dress, made so fashionable by Jean Muir, accentuated her classical beauty, she wore her long blonde hair loose; Tracy had chosen her fringed silk mini dress, the white of the material contrasted with her tanned skin; and Megan was wearing the emerald green sequinned creation she had made from one of the pieces of material Maurice had given her, with her hair secured into a tight stylish knot on top of her head, the intensity of her eyes had a mesmerising effect on most on lookers.

'Have you been to New Orleans Tina?'

'Yes, it's only just over three hundred miles from my home town and the road is good. Its more or less, the Louisiana coastal route through Lake Charles and Baton Rouge.'

'More American history!' Megan ignored Tracy's quip and asked.

'As we're docked there overnight, are you going to see your parents?'

'I was, they were going to have a short break holiday and drive to New Orleans the day before we dock. But Dad broke his leg two weeks ago, he fell off his horse!' Tina laughed, but deep affection was plainly evident in her voice and Megan wondered fleetingly about her own father, a sudden burst of loneliness overrun her, then the image of Aaron rose, and with it a feeling of tenderness wrapped protectively around her. Tina continued, 'and so when I phoned them from New York, I told Mom not to bother, in the circumstances it would have been a difficult journey.'

'That's a shame.' Tracy put her arm around Tina's shoulder and gave her a quick hug of sympathy.

'I was going to hire a car and go and see them, but they both think that a round trip of over six hundred miles in twenty two hours, is just too much. But never mind, Bill and I are planning to fly back to the States in November and stay with my family.'

'Meeting the in laws!' Tracy's sense of humour made her twist her face to illustrate pure agony!

'Idiot, they'll love him.' The conversation carried on, Ted smiled, adding his mite, but most of his attention was concentrated on Libby.

It was about half way through the party and the group around the Captain had drifted apart. Now Libby was marooned by herself in the middle of the room and looking very mulish. Ted wondered why on earth she had chosen a style of dress that showed up her lack of shapeliness. The taut material over the expanse of her chest looked as if she had a tyre on as an undergarment, and the tight waist only accentuated her tubbish stomach. His eyes travelled up and he was surprised when he realised that she was staring at him. He could not now look away without insulting her. Although Ted hadn't planned on talking to Libby today, he now felt obligated to stroll over and speak to her.

'How do you do.' He had never felt so gauche in his life, but she beamed at him as she answered.

'I'm very well thank you, but I don't believe that we have been formerly introduced.' Ted had to smother a laugh at the picture she made as she fluttered her eyelashes at him. An acid comment flashed into his mind, only to be immediately dismissed, instead he told himself to just think of her money!

'My name is Ted Hunter, I'm English and delighted to make your acquaintance.' The slight bow Ted made with his head and shoulders impressed Libby so much so, that she simpered as she told him her name.

'Miss Libby Jane Putts of Putts Landing, in the State of Mississippi.'

'I'm charmed Miss Putts.' Ted grinned, he felt as if he was acting in a remake of 'Gone With The Wind!'

His courtship of Libby developed equably over the next few days, she had even dispensed with Rose when he'd taken her out for tea during the afternoon that the ship had docked at Nassau. Now as they walked together around the decks, she put her arm through his. Ted was aware that bets were being placed, by the irreligious, on him staying the course! He even had Ginger to place a considerable amount on himself doing just that! It amused him that he could win money in such a way. After careful scrutiny of Ted's face, Ginger had also laid money on him succeeding! During the shows, Libby would sit at the front and stare with adoring eyes when Ted sang. He was always polite to Libby and did not take up the offer from a bored wife accompanied by her indifferent husband. Ted looked, but was not tempted, he was not stupid enough to put his future in jeopardy by flaunting another women in front of Libby!

The next port of call was Tampa; Ted asked Libby to go ashore and dine with him. She agreed. He chose a moderately priced and quiet restaurant. Libby ate her usual large amount of food and also surprised Ted on the quantity of wine she drank, but it had little effect on her, he guessed that she must be used to alcohol. On the way back to the ship, Ted stopped to admire the stars. Libby gazed up like a child and when Ted kissed her, she blushed a rosy pink! It had only been a light touch, but it had flustered her. It was then that Ted grasped that Libby had no sexual experience. It was on the tip of his tongue to exclaim about her virginity, when he realised that she would have taken that as an insult. Of course she hadn't been with a man, she might be in her mid fifties, but from what she'd told him of her life, the free love of the swinging sixties hadn't amounted to much in the face of her father's will! Ted looked down at her and knew that she hoped he would kiss her again. He lowered his head and made contact with his mouth against her flabby lips. When he heard her sigh, he slowly moved his hands to the expanse of her bottom and with a little pressure, brought the lower half of her body to a juxtaposition against his. After this, Libby's eyes were wide and expectant. Ted gave her an encouraging smile and then he nuzzled her ear before kissing her neck.

Libby's eyes were glued on Ted when he raised his head. Her hands shook as she felt his move from her bottom. She felt a flutter of apprehension as Ted's hands slowly ventured across her ponderous breasts; but she was excited, that at last a handsome man was courting her. Libby felt triumphant, no longer would her sister in law be able to make cruel jokes about her. As Ted had kissed her and was now touching her like a married couple acted, he would be bound to ask her to marry him. But just to make sure that he would be quite sure that she'd be a willing bride, Libby thought that she should give him some more encouragement. So with his hands still gently moulding the taut material stretched across her massive bosom, she rushed into speech.

'When I get married, my brother is going to give me the house at Putts Landing for my very own. It's big, lots of room and the entrance hall is tiled, so it's real cool in the summer.' She felt his fingers squeeze her flesh and stuttered as she sustained her narrative. 'Rose is going to be in charge of the other servants, and her daughter will come as well, she's been to cookery school; you should taste her fried chicken, I can eat a whole one all to myself!' Ted wasn't surprised at the size of her appetite! But he was more enthusiastic over congratulating himself on landing in clover! To advance his position with her, he planted a swift kiss on her unsuspecting mouth. But being curious, he'd wait, he wouldn't propose until he'd checked a few details with Rose. Libby was slightly breathless as she placed her last ace on the table. 'I have my own bank account, and every month more money is put into it.' Ted released the pressure he'd maintained on her bust and hugged her to him. As he was a lot taller than her, she couldn't see the unholy grin on his face as he realised his hands couldn't meet at her back. But he did kiss her again before he strolled jauntily back to the ship. Libby tottered excitedly beside him.

The next day Ted bumped into his quarry on the deck, Libby was also there, but as she was lying full stretch in a lounger and was snoring, he ignored her and started a conversation with Rose.

'Hello.' Rose looked up from her book. She recognised him immediately and after a quick look in Libby's direction, indicated the empty chair on her vacant side. 'Is this your first cruise?' Rose's ancestors had survived slavery and she'd inherited the capability to accurately sum up character. She put Ted unerringly into the white trash fraternity. She didn't need to be told that he was after Libby's money. But she also knew that Libby would be happier living in a different house than that of her overbearing brother for her remaining years, so she smiled kindly at him and replied.

'Yes.' Rose wanted to laugh at the ludicrous expression that had sprung to Ted's face, even if he'd wiped it off instantly; he'd wanted her to give all the information that she had and now she sensed he didn't know how to lead with a further question. Rose took pity on him, after all she would be at the house to look after Miss Libby, so as long as he was going to be kind, then she would help! It was a shame that Mr. Robert wouldn't hear of letting Miss Libby live at Putts Landing without being married, but in some ways he was just as pig headed as his father had been! She cast another quick glance at Ted, confirmed to herself that she could handle him, then spoke again. 'Miss Libby likes you a lot.' Ted smiled, Rose nodded. 'Talks about you all the time. Animated, that's what she is. Like a child in a sweet shop with money to spend, and Miss Libby has always had lots of cash to spend on whatever she wanted.' Rose stopped and wondered if she'd said enough, or would he want to know anything more. Ted caught himself nodding and broke into speech.

'I understand that Libby lives with her brother and his wife.'

'Well she does now, but if she got married, she'd move into the big house at Putts Landing, that's even got an orchard in the grounds, and stables, not that Miss Libby rides, she never took to horses.' Ted had all the data he required. He couldn't believe his luck, not only did she have a substantial private income, but also a large house! He got up and couldn't help the grin which had spread across his face as he strolled off to make his plans on when he should propose marriage to Libby.

Ted went back to his cabin and pulled out a large case from under his bunk. Five minutes later, the case was back where it lived and Ted had a diamond ring between his fingers. He'd won it playing poker fifteen years ago. He'd had it valued and been pleased that it wasn't a fake. He was going to tell Libby that it had belonged to his mother. He put it into the inside pocket of his wallet and zipped the compartment shut. He'd take Libby ashore for dinner when the liner reached New Orleans the next day and pop the question on the way back to the ship after he'd had the chance to kiss her several times! That way he was sure he'd get the answer he wanted.

The fifth of August had dawned and nobody, who wasn't confined by duty, missed the spectacle of the ship entering the mouth of the Mississippi river. The city that the liner was heading for was that of New Orleans, which lay about a hundred and seven miles inland. The scenery, now bathed in the brilliant morning sunshine, was admired by all. Charis had refused an offer from Joan and Doreen to join them for the day. She had turned the other five girls down so many times in the past, that now they didn't bother to include her in their plans. Most passengers stood on the promenade deck, hoping that would give them the best view of the approaching city. Tracy had taken the other four girls and Lee Chung to the narrow forward deck, just under the bridge, the aspect from that vantage point was remarkable! It was just on noon when the gangway was open for the passengers to disembark. They left the forward deck and joined the end of the queue to go ashore themselves. Patrick was on duty until eight o'clock that night, so Tracy was spending the afternoon with the others before returning to the ship to meet him.

The shriek from Tina startled everyone. She was excitedly jumping up and down, waving both her hands in the air!

'What's the matter with you kid?' Anxiety had broadened Tracy's accent. Tina didn't answer, just pointed widely at the dock. All eyes looked, but Megan was the first one to spot him.

'It's Bill!' Now impatient to get ashore, Tina was hurriedly making her way through the throng of people between her and the exit off the ship.

'We won't see her again until we sail!' Was Tracy's cryptic remark! Mary, Jasmine, Megan and Lee Chung all nodded their heads.

Chapter 29

The visit to the city of New Orleans turned out to have momentous consequences for a number of the cast. Tina flew from the gangway straight into Bill's arms, then into the waiting cab, which took them to the Maison Dupuy, on Toulouse Street, situated in the French Quarter. Not the most expensive hotel in the city, but in Bill's opinion, it had the essence of the old town in its bricks and mortar! He explained during the taxi drive, that he'd had a dose of the flu and his doctor had given him a week off from the show, to rest his voice. Of course, after three days of high temperature and feeling sorry for himself, the idea of seeing her again had miraculously aided his recovery and here he was for thirty eight hours! His flight in from London had landed three hours ago, which had given him enough time to drop his bag off, (he'd booked into the hotel when he bought his flight tickets!) More than satisfied with the room, Bill had then got a cab to the dock to pick Tina up. He now grinned and told her that he'd catch up on his sleep on the plane tomorrow evening!

'By the way, what do you want to do tonight?' She laughed as she answered him.

'All I want is to be with you.'

'Entertainment wise?' Tina lent forward and kissed Bill full on the mouth. By the time, the cab reached their hotel, both of them were breathing fast. They practically raced to their room and tore their clothes off as they started to make love. They managed to fall asleep for about forty minutes during the early hours of the morning!

Megan, Tracy, Mary, Jasmine and Lee Chung, spent the first part of the afternoon on a walking tour of the French Quarter of New Orleans, finishing at the bronze statue of General Andrew Jackson, the focal point of the park named after him in eighteen hundred and fifty one. Then Tracy bowed out from the remainder of their arrangements, as she was heading back to the ship to meet

Patrick. The rest of them strolled on to Decatur Street and the Tujagues restaurant. The excellent mix of French and Creole food on the menu, plus the laid back ambience, was just the perfect ending to their day that they had hoped for!

Being an ex boy scout, Patrick had telephoned from New York and booked a room at the Lamothe House for tonight. His idea of not making love to Tracy at every opportunity that arose had somehow slipped from prominence in his mind. The Chief Engineer had highly recommended the hotel on the Esplanade Avenue. Just after the ship had docked in New Orleans, Patrick had been given ten minutes to dash off from the engine room, to the nearest public phone booth and had been lucky enough to reserve a table for two at the Court of the Two Sisters for dinner that evening; and at Brennan's for breakfast tomorrow morning, he figured they'd be hungry! Both these restaurants were on Royal Street, which ran from east to west, crossing the Esplanade Avenue, which went from north to south. He wanted this to be a special time for him and Tracy, so had made his plans carefully!

Ted had thought hard about where to take Libby for dinner, he'd finally decided on Le Ruth's, it was expensive, and he hoped she'd be suitable impressed! The stream boat trip organised for the afternoon was enjoyable; they had sat together in the shade and sipped iced bourbon! He'd dutifully admired the country houses she'd pointed out on the river banks. He was glad that there was only two weeks left of this cruise, it was costing him a fortune to escort Libby around! But he had been saving his wages and had made a couple of lucky bets. Ted wasn't a heavy gambler, but liked the odd bet if he thought he stood a good chance of winning.

Libby had put on her favourite pink dress and naturally the ring was too small, but her euphoric joy on receiving it pleased Ted, also he was relieved that she kept it and told him, she'd have it altered! In thc cab returning to the ship after their dinner, Ted had pressed his mouth against her lips, then moved his left hand under the full skirt of her dress and found his way to the flabby white flesh of her thighs. There he felt stocking tops, suspenders and finally, the satin material of her loose fitting voluminous knickers. He ignored her distracted fluttering and squeezed his hand between the flesh at the top of her legs to push his finger tips against her virginal femininity. His mouth was still in hard contact with her's, which muffled her agitated protests.

By the time they had reached the ship, Libby was more flustered and ruffled than she had ever been in her past life. When she realised that Ted had taken her to his cabin and not her own, the door was locked behind her and she stood in the middle of his small cabin, as hopeless as a beached whale.

Ted had no intention of letting Libby go until he'd taken her. He was desperate to secure his future and he had found out enough about her and her family to know that once he'd had intercourse with her, marriage would be a forgone conclusion! There was after all still a couple of months before the end of his contract, and he wanted some insurance that Libby would not change her mind. He smiled at her, all he saw was that she was shaking. But in case she was going to prove awkward, he gave her no time to consider what was going to happen. He wrapped her bulk in his arms and really kissed Libby, a floating image of the sexy little charmer he'd met when the ship first docked in New York, helped his erection gain impetus.

Libby gasped in fright, then felt quivers inside. She hoped that whatever was going to come next, wouldn't be any worse, than the scorn that was sure to be heaped on her by her sister in law, if she went back to live permanently with them at the big house! Libby desperately wanted to be engaged on this cruise, she would do anything to be able to move into the house at Putts landing. There she'd be able to eat what she wanted and invite the members of the Ladies Guild to her own house for tea! It would be wonderful to be a married lady! She was hardly aware when her pink dress was undone and discarded. Then she felt her knickers pushed down around her thighs and went scarlet! She just stood still while Ted moved behind her and unhooked her brassier and suspender belt, then peeled her remaining underclothes down to her ankles. Libby stepped out of them like a bemused child and made no fuss, when he led her to the bed. Rose had told her, that engaged gentleman expected more than a good night kiss, but she hadn't been any more specific!

Ted didn't undress himself, he didn't want his fiancée to panic at the sight of a naked man. He told her to lie down and she did. He stared at her, in the given circumstances, he'd never seen such a mass of etiolated flesh before! He realised that he was losing his erection, gave himself a mental shake, and slipped off his jacket and shoes, then got on top of her. He balanced himself with his hands flat on the bed each side of her head and kissed her, telling himself that she was an inexperienced virgin and had no one to compare him with! It could be as fast as he wanted it to be! The thought of penetrating where no man had been, began to excite the primeval drive in him and he felt his member twitch again. Ted closed his eyes and pushed his tongue into her unresisting mouth. He moved immediately from her lips straight to her bosom, shifting his weight further down her body as he went. His hands squeezed her breasts together, pushing her nipples close. He was surprised when he found a prominently raised peak in his mouth and sucked hard, first at that one, then the other. He was concentrating solely on his objective and never gave a thought to the feelings of the woman under him. Ted would never admit that having sexual foreplay with Libby could excite him, he just told himself that his sexual performance was so good, that he could perform at any time! When he lifted his head up, his eyes were closed, he didn't even glance at Libby, just moved his hands between her thighs and pushed her legs apart, then slipped a finger into her slit. He was relieved to find she was already wet. By now his erection was fully extended, so he undid his trousers with his other hand. The idea to get undressed flashed into his mind, but he dismissed it just as quickly. He thought it better to get it over with before she changed her mind and proved difficult. Ted manoeuvred himself into the correct position between her open legs, shoved his pants out of his way, then used both hands to guide himself into her. Once in, he instantly leant forward to grip her shoulders, so that he had her pinned to the bed. Ted ignored Libby's squeals as he repeatedly drove hard, once he'd started the penetration of intercourse, he would have found it impossible to stop until his erection had deflated. Within a couple of minutes he had climaxed and then flopped on her and it didn't take long for him to regain his breath, then he lifted his head up to look at her. He was shocked to see that her cheeks were tears stained, in fact she was still whimpering. Hurt and fear very evident in her eyes. That wasn't in his game plan, she should have been all smiles by now. He had to think fast! His automatic gear engaged, he uncoupled himself, reached over her and made demanding contact with his mouth on her's, working her lips with his before his tongue snaked inwards. Unerringly his right hand travelled swiftly down her body and began gently stroke her pubic hair. When he lifted his head, he moved off the top of her and lent sideways, propping himself up with his left arm. Libby was still laying flat on her back with her legs sprawled open. He grinned triumphantly as he saw the trickle of blood that had stained the cover under her. His finger now invaded her slit and found the exact spot he wanted, then his mouth fastened onto a nipple. His assault on her senses resulted in her first orgasm.

Now Libby smiled hazily, happily accepting the future. She hadn't liked the first part, when Ted had laid on top of her, that had been dolorous! But then when he'd moved his body off hers and his mouth had suckled at her breast, while his fingers had created the magic for her; she'd trade in the unpleasant couple of minutes which preceded that wondrous ending, any day of the week! Now she knew why those girls looked so exhilarated and giggled so much in the kitchen after they'd been out courting with their boyfriends! She couldn't wait until they were married and wondered how often he'd do it!

When the liner left New Orleans, it headed south for three days to the port of Cozumel, situated on the east coast of Mexico. But the village of Playa Del Carmen was the eventual destination of those interested in the relics of the past. The archaeological finds in this area were so well known, that people were curious to visit the place. Once in the main port, transfer to a local ferry was necessary to reach the smaller Mexican village. There the ancient Mayan ruins of Tulum were perched high on a ridge; and then to visit the Xelha, a group of volcanic lagoons, now filled with crystal clear waters, could transport an open mind to an ancient and mystic world. But, of course, if determined to stay in the twentieth century, the shops of Cozumel would do that!

From there, the liner headed south-east wards to Colombia. During the stop over at Cartagena, Ted was escorting Libby around the shops, when he actually caught sight of Diana. He stopped dead in his tacks. Libby just stared at him, wondering what he'd seen to make him look so angry. She gazed around her, but saw nothing. Ted recovered himself, denied that anything was wrong, shrugged off his reaction as a figment of her imagination. That night, after Libby had retired to her cabin, Ted carried on drinking and Ginger had reluctantly helped Patrick put him to bed!

Tina lost her appetite, then a couple of days later, started eating fruit for every meal! She thought that maybe she'd eaten something unusual that had made her feel sort of funny, but not ill! When the ship docked at Ocho Rios, Jamaica, Tina settled for a restful day relaxing at the beach with Tracy; Patrick, alas, was on duty! Megan had shopping she wanted to do, but Mary and Jasmine, revisited Elizabeth Barrett Browning's house. On the seventeenth of August, the ship was once again docked at Fort Lauderdale, Florida. Tina phoned Bill, but didn't tell him about her funny tummy! She didn't want him to worry about her health! Anyway she felt that she'd soon be fine!

Since his engagement, Ted had been invited into Libby's stateroom to share her afternoon tea. It was the day before they arrived back in New York. It had been finally settled that their marriage was to take place on twenty third of October, that was the date of Libby's fifty sixth birthday. At first Ted had refused, stating that his contract with Maurice wouldn't end until they arrived back in Southampton on the twenty seventh. Libby had sulked, she wanted to get married on her birthday, that would make it very special for her. For a number of years now, it had been only because of Rose that there had even been a cake. Her bother and his wife had no interest in Libby's welfare, and didn't care that it upset her that she only received cards and presents from the staff of the house, with nothing from her relations. Libby and Ted were alone in her cabin, now they were officially engaged, Rose often left them alone! Ted stood over Libby, there was an angry edge to his voice.

'Maurice would screw me if I left the ship in New York.'

'So what! I would send the car for you, and you need not even say that you are not returning. Anyway, Maurice could not really stop you from leaving, could he!' This statement had been made in her petulant high pitched voice. But the belligerent look on Ted's face was making her regret her hasty words. He wanted to shake some sense into her, then began to think about her idea. The cost to himself, swung the matter in Libby's favour. If he didn't return to England, he wouldn't have to pay his air fare back to the States! He'd ride in luxury from New York, all the way to Putts Landing in Mississippi! And arrive there as someone of consequence! He smiled and felt big. He'd enjoy dropping Maurice in the shit with his bosses. He wasn't worried that they'd sue him, his contract was with Maurice and not with the shipping company and that old queen wouldn't waste money on lawyers. Ted straightened his shoulders and nodded his head.

'Okay, have it your own way Libby and send the car for me on the eighteenth of October.' He stressed his next words, 'and make sure it's there.'

Libby was so surprised to get her own way that she clapped her hands and laughed. She was sat in a large arm chair dressed in a lime green dress, which was very similar in style to her pink one! Tight bodice and full skirt, except that this neckline was cut much lower!

Ted sniggered as he thought about how mad Maurice would be when he realised that his singer was no longer aboard the ship when it sailed from New York to Southampton. He wished he could be the proverbial fly on the wall to witness that scene. He brought his mind back from the future to the present. Libby was bouncing in her chair with jubilation! The flesh of her bosom wobbled freely with her movements. Ted felt confident of obtaining Libby's assets, now with the added bonus of getting the better of Maurice, his ego had been immensely inflated, he felt great, and he wasn't the sort of man to ignore the start of an erection. He lent over her and roughly pulled the shoulders of her dress, and her brassiere straps, down her arms to her elbows. Once released from the restrictions of her bodice and underwear, Libby's breasts had flopped out. Ted knelt down in front of her and as his fingers squeezed her bare flesh, his mouth devoured each nipple in turn. It didn't take long for his erection to become fully extended. When he let go of her breasts, his hands disappeared under her skirt; he flicked it up out of his way and it landed across her face! Ted hauled her bottom towards the edge of the seat as he dragged her knickers down to her ankles, then hurriedly pushed her knees apart. She was left sprawled in the chair in her stockings, still attached to her suspenders. Then he quickly undid his fly and directed his hard member straight into her.

Libby waited, her breath coming in short little gasps. His continuous pummelling was lasting longer than before. Then she realised that the sensation he'd given her with his fingers on the night of their engagement, was happening again now. Rose had told her that part of it would get better the more they did it, and it was! His movements had been drilling her for perhaps five or six minutes. Still buried under her skirt, Libby grinned as her orgasm topped.

Ted finally climaxed and then sagged against her. When he lifted himself off her, he just knelt in front of her and his focus was on the wet moist triangle of pubic hair; her body, or who she was, even her name, wasn't important; he liked the taste of a woman and at that moment, he was controlled by his appetite.

Libby was surprised as she felt his mouth sucking at her, but was thrilled by the movements of his lips and tongue. She squirmed in joy as she came again.

When Ted stood up, he stared at the fat stomach and legs splayed out in front of him, net petticoats covered the top half of her body. He tidied himself up before he pulled the skirt of Libby's dress down over her knees, then immediately left.

Libby had stayed slumped in the chair with her breasts exposed and her knickers still around her ankles. Rose found her smiling like a cat who had just finished the cream, but knew where the store was kept! Rose prepared a bath, she didn't begrudge Libby her little thrills and pleasures in what was left of her life.

Rose finally managed to shepherd Libby off the ship, but they were the last passengers to disembark. The entourage that had brought them, was on the dock ready for the return journey. Ted couldn't help smirking as he admired the limousine, he could already see himself relaxing in the back during his own trip to Putts Landing; not trusting Libby with the details, Ted had previously confirmed them with Rose. He now stood on the deck, with a smile pinned to his face until the car drew away. Then he strolled around well pleased with himself. Passengers for the next cruise were not boarding until the following day. But the arrival of a large saloon car, caught his attention just as he was about to go to his cabin. A woman in her thirties got out and walked up the gangway. She was a looker and knew it! Ted walked quickly back to the main deck and managed to casually bump into her. She dropped her briefcase, but it didn't open. His smile of apology was also a sexual invitation. They chatted to each other, thoroughly enjoying the other's flirting manner. She was a holiday representative just confirming a booking. Ted had no hesitation in accepting her offer of dinner that night at her flat and he'd have taken a bet that sex would be the main dish! It was satisfying for his ego that he could still pull a good looking woman. He returned to the ship the following afternoon. He had no intention of being faithful to Libby, if any opportunities were offered, he'd take them up! He assumed that it wouldn't prove difficult to keep Libby purring, as long as he didn't flaunt his mistresses in her face! The next day as Ted wandered back along the docks, he spotted Megan getting out of a limousine, that elusive memory flashed into his mind again, and as usual, he couldn't remember who she reminded him of!

Chapter 30

Captain Beamish almost grinned as his honoured guest entered the ship's lounge where the Welcome Aboard Cocktail party was being held. His chest swelled with pride as he shook her hand and he considered that this was the epitome of his career so for!

Charis, who considered that dress sense was next to Godliness, gazed with unashamed worship, and she wasn't by herself; Lavinia Vaughan's entrance was a practised piece of professionalism. She had spent all her adult life acting, and this was just another occasion, that it wasn't on a stage or film set, was immaterial to Lavinia, her whole life had and always would be, a performance! No one could ever remember her losing her control in public. The tone of her voice certainly altered with her moods, she could purr or freeze her opponents at will. And Lavinia regarded every human being she met as a challenger! She didn't class the people she knew well as friends, but did pride herself on her carefully chosen list of acquaintances!

Ted recognised the famous actress immediately, he stood behind a potted palm, seething! He'd checked the list for this cruise and her name hadn't been on it. As he covertly watched Lavinia, the fact that he was engaged to be married to Libby, never entered his head. If given the chance he would have no hesitation in ditching Putts Landing for Hollywood! Out of the corner of his eye Ted spotted Margaret near the door and made a bee line for her, more or less dragging, rather than guiding the Purser's assistant through into the corridor.

'When did Lavinia Vaughan book for this cruise?' His manner was excited and edgy. 'Ages ago, it seems that she's the secretary who is occupying the stateroom on A deck. Her private aide has announced that Miss Vaughan does not want any publicity, just a relaxing holiday.' Margaret gave him a cheeky grin as she returned to the party. Ted marched off, he needed time to think out a plan of campaign; Lavinia Vaughan was much more to his taste than Libby Jane Putts!

'That gown must have cost a small fortune!' Tracy's voice was low, but Tina and Megan had no trouble in hearing her, they both nodded. 'It looks as if it's moulded to her figure, and yet it's not really tight!'

'Just expensive!' Tina's chuckle was soft enough not to travel beyond their intimate circle.

'To be able to create that perfection from a piece of material!' Megan nodded as she was speaking. 'Well, that's what I call a gift!'

'Yes! But,' Tina answered without taking her eyes off Lavinia, 'everyone of us has a talent.'

'Of course.' Tracy's accent was exaggerated, just as her facial expression was! Tina giggled, but added.

'I'm not just talking about us as dancers, I mean the rest of the human race. I think that we are all gifted, but in lots of different ways, and the sooner people respect themselves for what they are and not crave for the moon, then maybe everyone would be happier.'

'I think you've lost me! Coming from Liverpool, sometimes we have to have things spelt out!'

'What I mean is that you don't have to be a brain surgeon to have pride in your work; no matter what you do, as long as you put your best into it, then there can be happiness!' The other two looked unimpressed, so she added. 'I don't mean that people shouldn't try, or have no ambition, I don't mean that, it's just that there has to be balance.'

'That's a fabulous way to think.' Megan looked at Tina as she was speaking, 'but I'm afraid that I have to admit that with most people I find it very difficult to even like them, let alone trust them.'

'But you're okay with us!' Tracy jerked her head in Tina's direction. Megan smiled, but actually she was thinking of her past. Tina nodded her understanding. Megan had not really explained her childhood in any detail, just stated that she'd been brought up in an orphanage until the age of twelve, when her maternal aunt had shown up with her husband in tow! Megan had been reticent about filling in any further details, it was more what she'd left out, than had put in, which had given them the feeling that things had drastically deteriorated. Tina and Tracy hadn't pushed for additional information, just accepting that which had been given.

From the cocktail party, Captain Beamish had proudly escorted Lavinia to his table for dinner. He left his other guests to his senior officers, his sole attention was on her. Charis couldn't help staring! She was surprised to see how little food Lavinia ate, and drank even less; her wine glass had not been refilled and it was still half full when she left the table. The dark draped chiffon glided across the floor, definitely enveloped in her expensive perfume. Lavinia moved exquisitely, she seemed to be able to bestow upon her fawning audience the idea that they were special to her and she sincerely appreciated every single one of them! That she neither knew or cared about them, didn't register in their consciousness at all.

Ted couldn't believe his luck when he spotted Lavinia strolling on the upper deck, he practically ran and met her at the forward corner.

'How do you do, I must tell you that I'm your most ardent fan. My name is Ted Hunter.' He'd ended with a triumphant smile. Lavinia, whose pose was so anchored that even being suddenly interrupted in this way, couldn't throw it, graciously inclined her head. Her eyes might be half veiled by her lashes, but she was shrewd enough to sum him up and came to the conclusion that as he was moderately dressed, with reasonable manners, but his name had not been on the passenger list, he must be a crew member and as he wasn't in uniform, that only left the cabaret! He confirmed her suspicions by his next words. 'I'm the male vocalist on board this luxury liner.' Lavinia smiled, he wasn't bad looking and had enough physical attraction for her, that a shipboard flirtation, might not be objectionable, but would he want more than she was willing to give? That was the question she had to ask herself. She'd think about it. Lavinia hadn't done anything without prior thought for the past thirty years, and she wasn't about to spoil her record now, he wasn't that tempting!

'Maybe we could have a drink at some other time, unfortunately I have a prearranged meeting for tonight.' Ted beamed at her, he nodded and agreed, side stepping from in front of her and licked his lips as he watched her walk along the deck.

Charis stayed perfectly still, neither Lavinia or Ted had been aware of her presence, but she'd been close enough to see and hear what had just taken place. When she was satisfied that they had both gone, she stepped out of the enclosure that had sheltered her from their view. Charis was very well aware of Ted's specific reason for his engagement to Libby and considered that she knew enough of him to accurately interpret his move for the famous actress. But what Charis didn't know and couldn't hazard a guess, were the intentions of Lavinia towards him! Charis didn't like Ted. But then, she very rarely liked or disliked anyone. Wrapped in her own insular world, the rest of the human population just wandered around her outside perimeter. If she let a person in, it was by careful discrimination. Of course, she occasionally had a boyfriend, but it had to be someone of importance. A boss, or someone who had private money. She'd broken that rule with Kevin, because she'd been drunk, and it had landed her in trouble, it was a mistake she wouldn't make again. She walked slowly to her cabin, still pondering whether or not to tell Lavinia Vaughan that Ted was already engaged.

Lavinia didn't go ashore when the ship docked at Newport, she'd visited the place before and having the liner almost empty, pleased her. That is when Charis found herself as the only other person in the dining room that lunch time. She smiled and Lavinia returned the unspoken greeting. At the end of their meal, it was Lavinia who initiated their conversation.

'Newport cannot tempt you?' Charis smiled and shook her head. 'Then why don't you join me for an iced tea?'

'Thank you, I would like to.' Charis stood up and they left the dinning room.

'We'll use the balcony adjoining my stateroom. I'm eluding the attentions of the Captain.'

'Bores do tend to be pompous!'

'And in general, fat!' Both females were enjoying their verbal destruction of the man. After their first drink, silence settled calmly in. Lavinia had asked Charis to join her for the sole purpose of finding out if she knew anything about Ted and not being the retiring type, led with a direct question. 'Do you find Ted Hunter attractive?'

'No.' The suddenness of the answer had slightly surprised Lavinia.

'Might I ask, why not?' Charis didn't hesitate.

'On the last cruise there was a middle aged female version of Captain Beamish, but without his brain, and Ted went after her, he ended up becoming engaged to her. She has money, otherwise, he wouldn't have given her the time of day.'

'You sound very annoyed? Is there a personal reason?' Charis shook her head before she answered.

'No, I am more aggravated by her stupidity in being conned by him.'

'So he's after money?'

'I overheard Maurice and Joan talking about him, he took this job to find a rich wife.' Lavinia nodded and shrugged her shoulders, if Ted was after a permanent relationship, then she would not bother with him, she neither wanted or needed a husband.

The liner left Newport that night and docked the next morning at Boston. Charis had been delighted to accept an invitation from Lavinia to have lunch ashore. They left by limousine and dined at the Ritz Carlton Hotel Restaurant. Charis was impressed, not only by the meal, but also by the reverential way everyone treated Lavinia, who was never condescending, but always gracious, in a manner that Royalty had, it was as if it was her rightful due.

Ted had been disappointed that he hadn't been able to find Lavinia before she went ashore, he'd planned to put the next step of his campaign into action. He prowled around the ship to save spending money ashore, he was now regretting the amount he'd spent on entertaining Libby. Still, that was water under the bridge, and he couldn't do anything about it. He was also puzzling on how to still collect on his bet, he hated the thought that he'd lose anything by dropping Libby, although that wouldn't actually stop him. When he saw Lavinia and Charis come back aboard, it was evident that they had spent an agreeable time together. He momentarily wondered why Lavinia had chosen a stuck up female to have lunch with instead of him, but decided that it wasn't worth his effort to fathom the female psyche and grinned as he figured he could use Charis to get closer to Lavinia.

The following night the Paris show was performed, usually Ted was one of the first to leave the dressing room, but tonight, he took his time. Charis was of course, always last! As soon as Joan and Maurice had left, Ted spoke.

'I hear that you and Lavinia Vaughan were very pally over lunch yesterday.' Charis looked surprised that he was addressing her; as she considered that his statement didn't need answering, she turned her shoulder on him and carried on putting her things tidy. 'I'll come straight to the point.' Ted wasn't going to mince his words, or there meaning. 'You either convince Lavinia that I'm the best thing since sliced bread, or I'll tell everyone on this tub of metal, that you were the reason that Kevin killed himself.' Charis still had her back to him; the look of shock that flashed across her face hovered starkly, before she masked it into polite indifference. That her pulse hammered fast enough to make her feel sick, wasn't now apparent on the surface. It seemed that Ted didn't expect her to answer, as he swaggered out of the room.

Charis didn't know how long she had stood there, her mind was frozen. She could neither think or move.

'Oh, it's you! I thought perhaps the light had been left on by mistake.' Joan's words seemed to act as a switch for Charis, she gave a perfunctory smile and walked out. She went straight to Lavinia's stateroom and knocked the door. It was opened immediately.

'I'm sorry to disturb you but I have to speak to you.' Lavinia indicated to Charis to enter.

'Sit down.' Charis chose a chair opposite to the one that looked as if it was being used. Charis felt as if she was giving evidence at her own trail, and the only sentence she could see in her future was that of failure.

'Last December I had intercourse with an officer on this ship, which resulted in a pregnancy. I knew that it would be a mistake to go through with that, so I had a termination. The man concerned felt differently, and when he found out, he got so drunk that he collapsed, inhaled his own vomit and died. I thought that no one knew of my connection with him, but it seems that Ted Hunter knows of it.' Here she paused, but only for breath. 'He has just told me that if I don't persuade you that you should go out with him, he'll spread the story around the ship.' Charis stopped. She had been looking straight in front of her while she'd been talking and was still doing so. Lavinia stood up and walked around the room, straightening, already perfectly placed ornaments.

'He wants to swap me for the woman he's already engaged to?' Charis nodded, then added.

'She's fat and I should imagine he finds her boring.' Here Charis swiftly looked at Lavinia. 'Whereas you would be a considerable boost to his ego.' A slight smug expression flitted across Lavinia's face before she spoke.

'Tell me about her.' Charis rose her expressive eyebrows in surprise and couldn't help herself asking.

'Why?'

'I've out manoeuvred better men than Ted Hunter before breakfast and still eaten a hearty meal!'

'There really isn't much that I know; she was on the previous cruise with her maid, but if you ask me, Rose was more of her keeper than her servant.'

'Anything more?'

'Nothing, expect that her name is Libby Jane Putts, her bother's name is Robert and they come from Putts Landing in Mississippi.'

'That will do!' Lavinia smiled. 'Now all I have to do is find out what Ted knows about her!'

'Ginger Morris might have that answer.'

'No, I think I'll find out from the source. This cruise might not be so flat after all!'

Ten hours after Charis had visited Lavinia's stateroom, the liner was docked at Bar Harbour, Maine, and Miss Vaughan had delighted Ted with an invitation for lunch. A car was waiting for them; she had organised everything and when she paid the bill, Ted settled back and enjoyed another brandy. This was the kind of woman he preferred, one who knew who she was and where she was going! The ship left port at six o'clock that evening, and Lavinia decided that she would state that she had a migraine and dine in her cabin. She wanted to miss the Fancy Dress Ball that night, she didn't think the party would be worth the effort of getting dressed! With a little subterfuge, she would keep her fans happy.

Charis wandered around for perhaps half an hour and heard on the grape vine of Miss Vaughan's headache. She returned to her own cabin. She didn't know how Lavinia was going to shut Ted up, and the desperate thought that it couldn't be done, nagged incessantly at Charis. Tina had had to wait at the main post office for Miss Vaughan's aide to finish his phone call before she could telephone Bill; she had been in a chirpy mood, but now felt very deflated, so she decided to give this evening's entertainment a miss. Maurice was still in a benevolent mood, so Megan and Tracy had gone as elves! Mary and Jasmine had put on short black dress, with small white apron's tied jauntily around their waists, at first they had been amused, but after a while, being constantly asked to fetch fresh drinks, took the edge off their prank, so they both bowed out and returned to their cabin to write letters.

Another day at sea, saw the Hollywood show being performed. Lavinia had a drink with Ted afterwards. She sat and sipped her iced tea, while he downed half a dozen whiskeys. When he attempted to escort her to her stateroom, he found himself politely rejected, but in a way that he felt that next time he asked, the answer would be different. She really was a very talented actress!

When the ship docked at Halifax, Nova Scotia, everyone was charmed with the Victorian atmosphere that still prevailed in the town. The various trips ashore were relaxing. As well as admiring the beautiful scenery that part of Canada had to offer, the local restaurants were found to be excellent. During the next three days, the ship hooked around the Isle of Breton and into the mouth of the Saint Lawrence River. On September the first, they were docked at Gaspe, in Quebec Province, and again Ted had lunch with Lavinia. She purred like a contented cat and he was sure everything was going to plan!

On the way back southwards, the liner called in at Saint John's, in Newfoundland and on the seventh of September, docked again in Maine, this time at Portland. It was here that Miss Vaughan's aide had a visitor. That afternoon Lavinia pored over the dossier on the Putts family, that had arrived earlier. By now, she knew all that Ted had thought fit to find out about Libby, the only information he hadn't imparted, was the fact that he was engaged! Lavinia now knew how to deal with him. That evening, she had set the stage to play her little game on Ted.

'As the amateur show is the only public entertainment for tonight, would you prefer to join me in my stateroom?' Her voice purred sexually and Ted's grin split his face.

'Certainly.'

'After dinner, shall we say, nine thirty?'

'Yes!' He was sure that Lavinia's smile was offering him utopia. Promptly at the requested time, Ted knocked on her door. He was let in by her aide, who asked what he wanted to drink. Ted had already indulged his forthcoming success with a few drinks at the bar, but he still asked for another whiskey on the rocks.

' Please sit down.' Lavinia indicated an armchair, she herself was reclining on the sofa. Ted had wanted to sit beside her, but thought it best to play it cool until the help left! 'It is really remiss of me not to have congratulated you on your engagement to Libby.' Ted choked as he swallowed. His startled eyes bulged out from their sockets! Lavinia smiled, she knew this was going to be easy. 'I know the family. Did you realise that Libby's brother doesn't have any children, therefore she is the only heir to the fortune. And the family has so much influence, even in Hollywood, nobody but a fool would think of crossing Robert Putts, even if he's a man on the brink of eternity!' Ted gulped the rest of his drink, and his glass was immediately replenished. Lavinia deemed that she had said enough, she had seen far too many people's schemes flounder with over indulgence of conceit from the conspirator. Ted's thoughts had a hallucinating effect on him as the vision of his horizons rapidly broadened beyond his expectations! He saw no problems for him to take everything that was Libby's.

'Really, Ted's too stupid to see though the fairy tale I've told him. He's so busy patting himself on the back to even consider that I exaggerated about Robert's health, age or their family's influence!'

'But later?' Lavinia shrugged her elegant shoulders as she answered.

'What does that matter. It would be your word against his. But once he is off this ship, he will have to make the best of it and marry Libby Putts.' Charis was looking hard at Lavinia, then she let herself relax and her smile held genuine warmth. 'Do you know something Charis, I've come to realise what a good actress you are, when you've finished this cruise, why not fly out to Hollywood and stay with me. Dancing is alright as a short term career, but what are you going to do next?' Charis had always secretly hoped that by the time she was too old to dance, that she'd be married to a wealthy man. She looked hard at the older woman in front of her; she didn't look like the generous type, willing to offer help to a stray hound that passed her door.

'Won't you be too busy with your own career to bother with mine?'

'No!' Lavinia shrugged her shoulders. 'The rubbish that I'm being offered lately isn't worth the effort. But to launch a young starlet onto the scene, now that would be something I could put my energies into!' Charis breathed in, smiled, and slowly nodded her head. 'Good, give me the date that you arrive back in Southampton and my aide will arrange your flight out.'

Chapter 31

The liner had docked back in New York on the tenth and as the next cruise was four days at sea, one could have expected the cast of the cabaret, now being seasoned travellers, to feel blasé about it; yet there were acute diverse feelings of excitement running through them. So much so, that Maurice asked Joan if anything had happened that, he was unaware of. After a moments hesitation she shook her head negatively. She didn't know what Ted and Ginger were up to, but did know that Maurice would create a non-existent mountain out of Tina's good news, so the later he heard about it, the better it would be.

Tracy, Megan and Tina were in their cabin just before breakfast on the morning that the ship had docked in New York.

'I think I'm pregnant, so today I'm going to make an appointment with a gynaecologist for when we are next in port.' The other two just stared at Tina, surprised, but not really shocked. Megan was the first to speak.

'When do you think it happened?'

'New Orleans.' An infectious giggle erupted from Tina, 'I'm only just over one month!'

'But are you sure?' Tracy had shrieked her question. Tina nodded, then answered.

'I think so! Actually, it was something Joan mentioned that put the idea into my head! I'm going to get one of those home pregnancy tests, just to make certain.'

'I thought you said that you were going to make an appointment to see a doctor on the day we get back from this four day jaunt?' Megan could always be relied upon to keep her feet firmly on the ground.

'I am, but I can't wait until then to find out, I want to know today.' Tina beamed at the other two as she sat on her bed, hugging her knees. 'As soon as I've eaten breakfast, I'm going ashore.'

'Patrick's on duty, so I'll come with you.'
'Okay.'
'I'll see you both later, I'm having lunch with Aaron.' Tina felt a swift pang of compassion for her friend and prayed that soon she'd have some good news herself.

On reaching port, the first thing Mary always did was to check the mail for anything from Andrea. As there usually was something, she would then go off by herself to open it. It was normally a letter, but Mary had also received little presents. This morning's mail had a very special surprise in it. Andrea had written to say that she had arranged their holiday! It was for the Saturday after the liner docked back in Southampton, they were flying out to Cairo, the excursion included a boat trip down the river Nile and a tour of the pyramids. Mary was thrilled, not only at the prospect of seeing these ancient monuments, but being with Andrea again, she really missed her. Mary had found a contentment that she thought she would never experience in her life.

On the morning of the first day at sea, of the four day trip, Tina did her own pregnancy test and it proved positive. By the end of the day, Maurice had found out. He exploded! It took Joan over a hour to calm him down. And he wasn't convinced until after the show that evening. It had been the Paris Night Out and the thought of his lead dancer being unwilling to perform the can can had been giving him nightmares. But his fears were groundless. Tina danced well, and he admitted that she was glowing and looked even more beautiful. At the end of this four days at sea, once the ship had docked, Tina was one of the first off! Tracy and Megan had offered to go with her, but she declined. She wanted to do this by herself. That tea time, the jubilant telephone conversation she had with Bill, gave her more happiness than she thought possible and she returned to the ship in a happy daze!

Megan was surprised when Aaron arrived at the harbour with his suit cases. He explained that he was sailing with them for the next cruise and asked her to join him for a drink in his stateroom. Megan knew, without Aaron saying anything more, that he had bad news for her. She walked silently with him and didn't ask any of the million questions barging through her mind. Aaron closed the door and asked her to sit down. He then poured out two brandies and placed one on a small table at Megan's elbow.

'There is no easy way to tell you this my dear and to be evasive would be cruel.' Aaron paused slightly, but Megan didn't say anything, so he continued. 'I am so very sorry to have to tell you this, but I'm afraid that your mother is dead.' Megan wanted to cry out denying that fact, but no noise came from her, only a tremor ran through her and she started to shiver. Aaron put down his own glass and went to her, he lifted her out of her chair and hugged her shaking frame to him. Aaron knew that he had a lot more to tell her, but that could wait, she'd taken enough for now. He'd wait until later in the cruise to give her the rest of the information he had.

The ship reached Fort Lauderdale on the nineteenth of September, but Megan didn't want to go ashore, Aaron stayed with her. She had asked Aaron to inform the girls, also stating that she did not want to talk about her mother. Megan spent all of her free time with Aaron, she arrived at the dressing room for each show, after which she'd leave. It wasn't until the twenty eighth and they had reached Bequia, one of the Grenadines isles, that Megan felt able to accompany Tina and Tracy when they went ashore. They spent the afternoon laying on a sandy beach, most of the time just listening to the soft sound of the gently lapping sea. But it had done Megan good. That night she sat on the floor at Aaron's feet and she was able to cry.

The liner arrived at Grenada two days later, and Aaron decided that he would tell Megan how her mother's death had been discovered.

'The local council were improving the sewerage system and had to dig up the back yard of your Aunt's house.'

'New drains?' His nod was abrupt.

'When the remains were unearthed, the police were called in and started an investigation. At first, your Aunt denied any knowledge, but the remains were identified as your mother. The post-mortem results also revealed that she was murdered, your Aunt stated that your Grandmother must have killed her, then put you into an orphanage. But as she was living in the house at the time, it seems improbable that she would not have known all the facts; she has even said that she was unaware that her sister was pregnant! Which in its self is hard to believe, but impossible to disprove!'

'Will the police be able to do anything?'

'It's unlikely, and I'm afraid you have to consider the conceivability that both your Aunt and your Grandmother were jointly implicated in your mother's death. But after this amount of time, unless there is substantial forensic evidence, it would only be wishful thinking that there will be any case to prosecute.'

Megan just sat there, first she had to accept the fact that her mother was dead, and now she had to face the knowledge that her own relations had killed her.

The news of Megan's mother seeped its way through the cabaret members and a dank atmosphere settled over most of them. But not Ted, he was too busy savouring his future prosperity to bother about anyone else. And Ginger Morris had a pressing purchase deal in Ciudad Guayana to occupy his mind, to the exclusion of everything else.

The entrance to the Orinoco river is more like an inland sea, than estuary. Once in, the liner made its sedate progress westwards to the port of Ciudad Guayana. Aaron insisted that Megan join the trip to the Angel Falls, and for a little while the splendour of the sight elevated her depression. But during the trip back along the river to the sea, her frame of mind floundered. Aaron thought that he had better tell Megan who her father was, it would make her angry and even hostile, but that he judged, would be better that this fatal hebetude state that she was now in.

'Ted Hunter?' Megan's cry had been a stupefying screech.

'The statement that your mother's old school friend has made and the photograph that she gave to my investigator prove it.' Megan violently shook her head, then crumpled to the floor sobbing. Aaron crouched besides her and wrapped his arms around her. He comforted her until she had stopped weeping.

'I'm not crying for him. I hate him. It's his fault that my mother died. God I wish that he was dead and not her.' Aaron just held her close and let her rant and rave until her temper was exhausted.

Ashore, on the island of Tobago, Megan saw Ted swaggering towards them, she turned and ran. Tracy went after her, Tina stayed with Aaron to confront Ted.

'Are you going to tell him?' Her voice had been very low, but Aaron had understood her perfectly, she continued. 'I think you should. Well, what I mean is that he has to stay out of Megan's way.' Ted arrived with a smile on his face.

'Where did Megan and Tracy hare off too?' Aaron ignored his question, but took an envelope out of his inside jacket pocket. He took out an old photograph and handed it to Ted. It was a faded black and white snap shot, but the likeness between Megan and her mother, was unmistakable. It might have been taken twenty years ago, but Ted could not help but recognise himself. He looked up, he was still smiling when he made his statement.

'I knew Megan reminded me of somebody I'd met before.' Tina bit her lips and turned away from him. When Aaron spoke, his tone was icy.

'There is indisputable proof that you are Megan's father; her mother is dead, she was murdered just after giving birth. Your daughter was first dumped in an orphanage, and then later abused by her relations.' For about a minute there was silence, then Ted blustered.

'Don't look at me like that. It's nothing to do with me. The girl shouldn't have got pregnant. You can't sit in judgement on me, I didn't deliberately bang her up and I'll tell Megan that.' Ted seemed to think that he should be abolished of all blame and there was even some indignation as he bragged. 'Females throw themselves at you. What's a man supposed to do, say no!' Aaron was in his sixties and not an overly physical man, but he couldn't help himself, he clenched his right fist and swung wildly at Ted's head. The receiver staggered, but did not fall over. Tina went pale and instantly pulled Aaron away from Ted, who at the moment was feeling his jaw bone.

'Please let's get out of here.' Her voice recalled Aaron to his senses and he nodded at her. They walked hurriedly away.

After a great deal of discussion, without Megan, it had been decided between Aaron and the other four girls, that Patrick would be the best person to tell Ted that he must keep out of Megan's way and not try to speak to her about her mother. The callous details of the story had shocked Patrick, but he'd promptly accepted his role. Ted was left feeling battered. Patrick's verbal censure had left him wounded! But he still tried to place the blame firmly onto the female shoulders. The beginning of October brought the next port of call, Barbados.

Within the next week, the ship visited Saint Vincent, Gauadeloupe and Antigua, and under less sordid details, Ted's attitude towards Megan would have been very funny, he treated her as if she had the plague. As the liner continued on its way north, on the surface for the cabaret members, the general routines of shipboard life seemed to regulate themselves again. But underneath the currents still had barbed teeth and the Captain's Farewell soiree, was more like a stand off at a political function than an end of cruise party.

The sharp knock on their cabin door made all three girls look surprised; when Tracy opened it and Bill walked straight in, Tina jumped off her bunk and threw herself into his arms.

'My contract with the show in London has finished a month early so pack, we've got a plane to catch.'

'What?'

'You told me on the phone that you wanted to tell your parents in person about our baby; so here I am, I've booked seats on an internal flight to Beaumont and we have to be at the airport by noon.' Tina uttered a squeak of delight as she nodded her head several times, then flew around the cabin with an opened weekend bag in one hand, stuffing it with what ever her other hand came into contact with. 'We fly back early on the twenty first and I'm sailing back with you.' Tina gave Megan and Tracy a quick hug before she left. On the way to the airport, Tina explained to Bill about Megan's parentage.

A limousine with Mississippi number plates was parked discretely at the far end of the harbour, but after most of the passengers had disembarked it was driven to a more prominent position nearer the gangway. Ted had already packed his things, but his luggage was still in his cabin. He was having a heated conversation with a member of the crew. Ginger Morris was an interested bystander

'Look mate, her own car is here to pick me up, why else would I be going now?' The sailor shoved his hands deeper into his pockets. It looked like him and his mates were going to lose their money after all. This bloke sure was determined to get hitched to that fat old woman he'd got himself engaged to. 'I want my winnings now, or I'll ram both my fists down your scrawny throat.'

'Alright, hold your horses will you.' Slowly he drew one oily hand out and in it was a rolled bundle of notes. Ted grabbed them and quickly counted the amount. Then he peeled off ten, which he handed over to Ginger. 'Now that's the way I like to do business.' Ted shoved his own winnings into his trouser pocket and laughed out loud as he walked away. Within the next ten minutes, he'd retrieved his cases from his cabin and left the ship. Ginger knew that Ted was not going to make the return trip to Southampton on the liner, but as he had made a few quid on the deal, he now had no more interest in that situation. As he was dealing in heroin, a ton was only chicken feed in the cash stakes, still it had been easy money and he wasn't the type to ever sneeze at an opportunity to make more for himself.

Aaron took Megan back to his apartment for the three days the ship was docked in New York. But as he still felt that he should continue to support her, he'd decided that he would make the next trip as well. He had to change cabins as the stateroom he'd occupied for the cruise was already booked for the voyage to Southampton, as were the other staterooms, but he did manage to find a de luxe cabin on the next deck, and had his luggage moved straight there.

It was the eighteenth of October and the weather in New York was wet, cold and thoroughly miserable! After Patrick changed from his uniform, he showered and got dressed, then went to meet Tracy, they had planned to go ashore and have supper. She greeted him with the statement.

'I don't know what to wear.'

'You look fine to me.'

'Ha ha! Where are we going to eat?' Patrick hunched up his shoulders. He lent against the closed cabin door and as his hands were pushed deep into the pockets of his trousers, that made them very taut across his hips. His jacket was open and he had a casual sweater underneath it. 'We said just a snack sort of meal, nothing fancy.' He nodded. 'Then I think I'll just change my top, but keep this skirt on.' The latter item of clothing she'd just referred too was mini length and made of a fine woollen fabric which wrapped around to fasten at the waist band.

Patrick started to whistle the opening bars of a favourite tune, but got no more than the first half dozen notes out, when he drew his breath in too quickly as Tracy peeled her top off. Now his eyes followed her as she padded around the cabin looking for the pair of shoes that she wanted. Patrick gulped, then swallowed! She had her back to him and was now bent over rummaging in her wardrobe. Her knees were straight and the dark opacity of her tights, outlined her long legs. The hem of her short skirt had disappeared and left her bottom and thighs silhouetted. He straighten his shoulders and grinned as he strode over to her. Patrick bent, moulding his body against her's and his hands went to her breasts. His fingers eased successfully inside the material of her bra, then erotically teased her nipples.

'Patrick?' When he answered her, his mouth was very near to her right ear.

'Yes?' His breath sent a sensual shiver tingling down her spin.

'Let's move before we fall into the wardrobe!'

'Fine by me.' During this conversation they hadn't changed their stance, she was still in the same position as when she'd first bent over. Tracy felt his chest lift off her back, and she was able to slip her hands to her bra fastening and undo it. As they straightened up, she dropped it at her feet. Patrick nuzzled her neck, then said. 'I'm not moving my hands, can you get rid of the rest by yourself?' Tracy gave a sexy chuckle as she answered him.

'I think so!' It was easy to unbutton and let go of her skirt, then wriggled erotically against him as she divested herself of her remaining clothing. She pressed back against him as she said. 'You'll have to let go while I undress you.'

'No other way?' Tracy smiled as she shook her head. Patrick reluctantly released her breasts, grinning at her as she turned to face him. Tracy took his jacket off and flung it on Megan's bunk, then pulled his sweater off. She was tempted to kiss him, but refrained, she wanted to strip him first, so she knelt down, then jettisoned his shoes and socks. Next his trousers went and the only item left was his underpants. She hooked her fingers onto the waist band and very slowly dragged them lower, once she'd uncovered his manhood, her mouth claimed his forming erection and quickly enhanced the hardening.

When he finally stepped out of his underpants, Patrick's chest was heaving. He swooped, pulling Tracy into his arms and his lips locked onto her's. Their kiss was passionate, the blood in their veins pumped expeditiously, their pulses raced. Now their tongues intertwined, tasting each other. He had his feet firmly planted apart and used his fingers to squeeze her bottom and push her more firmly against him.

Tracy's arms were tightly linked around Patrick's neck when she lifted her feet off the floor and wrapped her legs around his body. They were still kissing each other as she worked her hips down until she could feel the tip of his erection touch the triangle of soft hair covering her femininity. She gasped in her throat with her need to feel him penetrate her.

Patrick moved his right hand to guide his member into the waiting, hot wetness of Tracy. He groaned in delight as he felt her contract her internal muscles to grip his swollen manhood. His breath became even more shallow when he felt her start to slowly gyrate her hips. Patrick stepped slowly, but steadily forward, until his was able to grip the support of one of the upper bunks with his left hand to keep their balance.

Tracy dropped her head back and concentrated on her rhythm. She knew that her movements would galvanise both their sexual appetites. When she did raise her head, she was panting so fitfully, that her breasts jerked with each breath she took. Her voice murmured sexily in her throat.

'I'm coming!' He didn't answer her as he couldn't, but he did blink his eyelids, as a muttered moan of agreement shot through his consciousness.

Chapter 32

Tina and Bill had flown back to New York and returned to the ship by cab. As the tugs pulled the liner away from the dock, they were locked in each other's arms. Her parents had been delighted to meet him and as they already knew that their daughter was planning to get married after her contract with Maurice had ended, setting a date for early November, didn't throw them at all. Neither did the knowledge that they would be Grandparents in the spring; that filled them with pride.

The liner had left New York at noon the previous day. This morning the steward on D deck carried news of Ted's empty cabin to the Chief Steward, who had promptly passed the information on to the Captain. But as in all close knit communities, the grape vine simultaneously circulated it. Considering his volatile nature, the eruption bubbling from Maurice, lacked direction. If he was tempted to throttle anyone, it was the Captain! Beamish strutted pompously around his office, demanding that Maurice continue to fulfil his contract with the shipping company. How he expected Maurice to materialise a singer to replace Ted, was left unsaid! Maurice found his only recourse was to snarl an incoherent reply and storm out of the office.

'Joan that bastard has screwed me up! I've always known that I shouldn't have given him a contract in the first place.' This outburst was just as much to do with his personal dislike of Ted, as well as rage at being let down. 'It was your idea to give him the damn job, so what are you going to do now?' The sarcasm in Maurice's voice, underlined his anger! For the first time in her life, Joan wanted to leave him to stew for a while, but old habits die hard.

'It's already sorted.' Maurice was caught in mid bluster and his astonishment was easily discernible. 'When I learnt that Ted had done a bunk, I went and asked Bill Ryder if he'd mind stepping into the breach!' She grinned as she continued, 'he will be delighted to sing Ted's numbers in the shows.' She had never seen Maurice's expression change so swiftly from anger to triumph; it happened so quickly that it was staggering! 'He's just asked for a rehearsal with the band!'

'Of course, I'll arrange that right away.'

'I've already given him the words and sheet music, Bill doesn't think that there will be any problems. The songs are 'standards' and he, more or less, knows them.' Maurice beamed, and the fleeting thought, that again Joan had saved his bacon, he automatically dismissed, instead, congratulated himself on his charmed life!

Megan and Tracy were alone in their cabin, Tina had vacated to Bill's stateroom for the duration of this trip. It might have been against company policy for a crew member to fraternise, (openly by sharing a bed) with a passenger, but technically, now that Bill was singing in the cabaret, he had a foot in both camps and the Captain didn't pursue any action!

'It is definitely Nick Panzarella and Liam Millar! I nearly fell off my perch yesterday at the cocktail party. And you should hear Nick's voice, it's so sexy!' Megan glanced up, she was getting ready for dinner. She had secured her hair on top of her head, then pinned its length into intricate coils.

'Have Patrick's charms disintegrated overnight?'

'No.' Tracy shook her head indignantly. 'But because I'm in love with the guy, doesn't mean that I can't appreciate what's out there, I just don't need to touch any more!' A faint smile flitted across Megan's face as she took the dress she was going to wear out of her wardrobe. 'That's gorgeous! You must have splashed out a fortune!'

'No, Aaron gave it to me for my birthday, I just haven't worn it before.' Megan stepped into a velvet evening dress, the colour of her eyes. Tracy zipped it up. 'What do you think? Is it too plain?' Tracy stood back and gave her frank opinion that she had never seen Megan look better.

'Honestly kid, that dress emphasises what it should!' Megan smiled again as she smoothed her hands down the soft fabric. The high neck had a mandarin collar, the sleeves were long and buttoned at her wrists; the bodice and skirt were panelled and cut from single lengths of material, so that there was no seam at the waist; it fitted perfectly over her slender hips, then gradually flared, so that the width at the hem, meandered gracefully as she walked. Tracy stood up and shook out the folds of her evening gown. She was wearing the dress she'd brought in New York, the one she'd worn when she went to the fancy dress party as a witch. At the moment her hair was tied up into a top knot, she intended to brush it loose after the show. 'Are you ready?' At a nod from Megan, Tracy laughed, then added, 'let's knock them dead!'

Patrick stood at the bar, he was surprised that the two famous men were so casual. Not in their attire, that was as expressive as it was smart! But they were talking about football, as if it was a Saturday night back home! If it had been, then these two very famous stars, one from films, the younger a pop singer, would have been mobbed. Patrick was lent with his back against the bar, feeling good! He had been included in their conversation and had joined in without any self consciousness.

'I didn't think that Americans followed the European game?'

'Not all do.' Here Nick grinned as he added, 'but then, not every American comes from an Italian family who are still crazy enough to support A. C. Milan!'

'I'm a Manchester United fan myself!' Liam picked up his drink, but out of the corner of his eye, he caught sight of Megan and Tracy as they walked into the bar with Aaron. His head swivelled in their direction. A soundless but appreciative whistle vibrated through his lips and he set his glass back on the bar. 'I'll toss you', this remark was made to Nick. 'Heads for the redhead, tails for the brunette! I just love it when I can't loose!'

Patrick pressed his back hard against the edge of the bar counter and tried to calm his twisted blades of anger, but only managed to clamp his mouth shut.

Nick eyed both females with the knowledge of a connoisseur, his smile portrayed his experience, even if his tone slightly mocked.

'What is that phrase one should use in this situation, ah yes I remember, 'a better man than I Gunga Din!' I was charming to both of them at the bash yesterday and was politely turned down, twice! Now, I am getting too old?' Nobody could have stated honestly the Nick Panzarella had lost his sex appeal, if anything, the forty year old star had matured magnificently, his body was as supple and strong as ever it had been. All of the female population who worshipped at his feet, felt that he was just, if not more sensual now, than in his youth! Nick's smile crinkled the skin around his dark eyes.

Aaron led the girls to Patrick. The young singer introduced himself.

'I'm Liam, this is Nick and I suppose you might know Patrick!' Tracy laughed, the headiness of the situation, easy to hear in her voice.

'Hello Liam and Hi Nick.' Then she turned to Patrick, her eyes sparkled and as she moved to his side, her lips caressed his.

'So you do know each other! Sorry mate, I didn't realise that I was trying to poach!' Liam gave a cheeky grin and added, 'I didn't know the score!' Suddenly Patrick realised that he could trust Tracy. What more proof did he need. Here were two men, who could make a hell of a lot of females throw their boyfriends, or even husbands out of the window, holding out invitations to Tracy and she wasn't batting, even one eyelid! At last he could now accept that she wasn't interested in another man and he'd learnt to keep her past were it belonged! Patrick laughed out loud as his arm circled Tracy's waist. He knew that he loved her and she was in love with him, so now he was certain that she'd always be there; he could hear wedding bells ringing! He inclined his head to whisper in her ear.

'Stop that, or I'll have to drag you out of here and carry you off!'

Tracy giggled, but relaxed her fingers and released the teasing hold she'd had on his bottom. She was glad that he had his back to the bar and no one could see what she was doing with her hand!

By now all the introductions had been performed and not only had Tina and Bill joined the group, but also Mary, Jasmine and Lee Chung. Towards midnight, Patrick had been persuaded to get his guitar and sing a few songs. It was past two o'clock in the morning when the party finally broke up.

Megan was gradually coming to terms with all the events that had turned her life inside out! But she still sometimes woke after only a couple of hours sleep and found it impossible to drift off again; then she was in the habit of getting dressed and walking around the empty decks. And tonight was no exception. It was cold, the sea was choppy and the wind buffeted her as she rounded the corner. Megan was just about to retrace her steps when she saw a figure coming towards her. She had no reason to wait, but did.

'Why can't you sleep? I have the excuse that my metabolism doesn't know what time zone I'm in.' Liam grinned at her. Megan found herself smiling back at him. 'Making this film with Nick has been a hell of an experience for me, in more ways than you would think. We seem to have been jetting to so many different places in the past two months, that when I do get to sleep, I sometimes wake up and wonder which city I'm in!'

'Poor thing!' Her sarcasm was belied by the laugh in Megan's voice.

'You should have a coat on, want mine?'

'No thanks, if I do, you'll be the one to freeze!'

'Then let's move inside and both survive.'

'Okay.' They hurried along the deck and Liam tried to protect her from the wind; as soon as they reached the door to the lobby, he opened it and ushered her in. As she was still shivering, Liam didn't hesitate, he took his jacket off and wrapped her in it. They smiled and as they were so close together, their lips met fleetingly in a whispering kiss. They both apologised to each at the same time, then broke into laughter.

'This voyage is kind of short to get to know you!' Megan nodded her head in agreement. 'But shall I try and raid the kitchen, fancy a hot drink or something?' Megan wanted to stay with him, then suddenly felt very self conscious.

'No, I think I'll try and get some sleep.'

'Are you okay?' She knew that his question related to their brief kiss and smiled happily as she nodded. Liam accepted her answer and escorted her back to her cabin. 'Maybe life will throw us together again?' She glanced at him as she answered. 'I think I'd like that.'

'I'm certain I would!' Megan wondered if he'd kiss her again. She opened her cabin door, then turned to say good night. His lips claimed hers swiftly once more, then with a charming smile he left her.

The South Pacific Fantasy show seemed to be totally out of step with the cold and ruff weather going on outside! But everyone enjoyed it and the tans that the dancers still had, looked stunning with the costumes! Most gathered in the Neptune bar after the cabaret. Nick congratulated Maurice on the professionalism of the show, and the older man's chest swelled at least two inches. Joan felt it wisest to turn the conversation before Maurice's ego took flight!

'What is the film you're making about?'

'Liam and I are both playing undercover cops investigating a syndicate, whose speciality is the theft of gold bullion on an international scale! So there is a lot of travelling and of course every other scene is a hand to hand fight.' Liam butted in.

'We also have to use guns, I had to have lessons on how to carry the thing, let alone fire it!' Nick grinned, nodded and then said.

'Our next shoot is in London, then we go on to Paris.'

'Is that where the film ends?'

'No, that's New York, but we've already shot that and it's in the can!' Joan knew what he was talking about and nodded her understanding.

That night, not only Patrick sang, but Liam with Cindy and Crystal joined in. Eventually everyone in the bar was singing along to the Beatles hits. When the party broke up, Patrick and Tracy disappeared into the night. Liam walked Megan back to her cabin. Once again, they stood in front of her door. Liam played with a lock of her hair while she fitted the key into it. Then he kissed her. This time they both indulged their senses a little further. But when Megan lent back again the door, she stopped Liam from kissing her again, she wanted him too, but as she didn't really know what he was like, she was afraid of being used. Megan had put all that behind her.

'Good night.' Megan left Liam outside, but his smile had been of understanding, not disappointment. Although on the surface Megan looked as if she was coping, it was the thought that she no longer had a goal in her life that frightened her; and now she had the added complication of Liam, she knew it would be all too easy to care for him. She had previously spoken to Aaron about reopening Miss William's dancing school in Cardiff. But when he'd said the time wasn't right and reminded her about the investigation going on there, Megan had agreed with him. That left her with the prospect of another audition, which meant losing the security of the close friends she made on this trip. That thought depressed her. Aaron had asked Megan to return to New York with him for an extended holiday, but she knew that she needed to keep busy and the best way to do that would be to get another contract. She undressed and tried to get some sleep.

It was the third day at sea crossing the Atlantic and Aaron was worried that although Megan was putting on a brave face for his benefit and that of Tina and Tracy, that really she was afraid that her life was going to become empty of friendship again. She might have stated that as Ted Hunter had never been in her life as her father, she didn't think of him as such, but that he showed no interest in that fact, had to affect her, and Aaron was very anxious for her. He was sat in the reading room staring out at the grey water, lashing itself about, when unconsciously he began eavesdropping in on a conversation.

'Yes, you don't have to tell me that he's good, I've got eyes and ears! But where is the money going to come from? Can you tell me that?'

'Mortgage the house!'

'No. We've never done that and now isn't a time to start with any new strategies.'

'Then get a partner.'

'You know I don't like any interference with my shows, I always back them myself.'

'Yes, agent, producer and backer, but costs are rising.'

'I shouldn't have let Henderson persuade me to invest on the Stock Exchange.' There wasn't any bitterness in his voice, it was just stating a fact!

'What's done is done.' The female had agreed with the same sang froid. 'But it is a shame that we can't afford to give Patrick a contract for Liam's tour, it really is.'

'I know, but what do you think of using the profits from the first half, to offer him a spot for the last ten venues of the British tour!'

'That's something to think of, and we still haven't got the dancers!'

Usually Aaron was not a person to make any rash or sudden decisions, but today was different. If this couple were putting on a show staring Liam Millar, and lack of money was the only thing stopping them from offering Patrick a contract, then Aaron would step in with the extra cash as long as they hired Megan and Tracy as two of the dancers. That way, Aaron felt sure that Megan would be able to look forward with some confidence, to her immediate future. Half an hour later, Fred and his wife were shaking hands with Aaron. Two hours later, Patrick was in Aaron's cabin, facing Fred Stein.

'Look son, what I am offering you is the opportunity to make a record and join a tour that starts in the middle of next January.'

'I know, it's just that I saw what a mess my father made of his life chasing dreams of stardom, and I've always been determined not to make the same mistake!' Fred laughed and shook his head.

'I'm not promising you the moon. What I am saying is cut the record and join the tour. I pay you monthly during the contract, and you also have your share of the royalties from the record if it sells! And if the show gets off to a good start and the seats go, then I hope to extend the tour into Europe and then hopefully, the

States will beckon. But what happens after this particular party is anybody's guess.' Mrs. Stein now added her piece.

'Firstly, it would be three months work, just like a contract you sign when you go to sea. The major differences would be singing in theatres and living out of a suit case. If the seats sell, the tour will go on. The life can be good, especially with friends. We're hoping that Tracy and Megan will join us, we need two dancers.' Patrick dismissed his negative thoughts, that final statement had made up his mind. He wasn't looking forward to being separated from Tracy and this way, they would be working in the same show. Patrick nodded his head.

'Okay.'

Fred rubbed his hands together, it had been a very busy, but satisfying day. He might have a partner, but the man wasn't going to be breathing down his neck, he wasn't even going to try and put any spokes in the arrangements. His wife broke into his thoughts.

'Will it change much having two female dancers?' Fred shook his head, his thin eyebrows made a straight line under the many that were already etched into his forehead. 'Didn't the girls in South West Three want male dancers.'

'Yes and they can still have them, with the money Aaron is putting into the show, we can have a dozen tip pee toes if we fancy!' They smiled at each other. 'We'll use the two girls to back a couple of Liam's and Patrick's songs and the band's instrumental number during Liam's break.'

Tracy and Megan were both thrilled at the offer from Fred Stein. Megan was looking forward to getting to know Liam better and had agreed to spend the time between the end of this trip and the rehearsals for the tour, in New York with Aaron, she was going to be in the States for Tina and Bill's wedding anyway. Tracy and Patrick were was also invited to the wedding in Beaumont. Mary had to say no because of her holiday with Andrea, and Jasmine had to as well, she was already late starting her first term at university. Out of politeness, Tina had asked Charis to the ceremony, and then felt guilty at her own relief, when it was declined!

Captain Beamish surveyed his guests at his final Farewell Cocktail Party with immense personal pride. Although the sea condition was more than a little rough, his guests of honour had shown up. Not that he considered Liam as anything special, but Nick Panzarella was a different matter. Beamish had seen everyone of his films and was very impressed. He intended to have a photograph taken with the star, that would compliment the one he'd had framed of him and Lavinia Vaughan. Over the years, he had collected ship board portraits of quite a number of well known personalities.

Maurice looked steadily around the room, it had been an interesting year, even if it had turned out somewhat more eventful than he'd anticipated. Now he was back to square one, he had no dancers and only two of the acts would take up the option. He was glad that Doreen wanted to sail again with the next show, but Ginger Morris was another kettle of fish, Maurice wasn't sure he wanted the comedian around. If what Alex had let slip, then Ginger was playing a dicey game and could end up in shit! But the twelve months option was there, and if he wanted it, what excuse was there not to accept it. Joan was wondering what on earth Maurice was thinking about, his expressions, always very mobile, were now changing so rapidly, that she found herself blinking in astonishment.

'What's the matter with you?' There was a lot of curiosity in her voice. Maurice's own thoughts forced his defensive reply.

'Don't look at me like that, after all what did I do except, take six girls!'